WITHIN RANGE

THE BLADE KINGS

BOOK 5

RUTH STILLING

ISBN 978-1-0686000-8-1(PAPERBACK)

Cover art by Sam & Mel|Ink & Velvet Designs

Interior design and formatting by Alyssa Garcia

Editing by Jovana Shirley, Unforeseen Editing, www.unforeseenediting.com

Proofreading by Virginia Tesi Carey

Within Range

To the girls who dream of a daddy in the streets—and screaming his name between the sheets.

TRIGGER/CONTENT WARNINGS

Dear Reader,

Thank you so much for choosing to read *Within Range*, the fifth and final book in The Blade Kings series.

While this book is a contemporary fictional romance and, of course, has a happily ever after, I want to bring to your attention certain themes featured within this story so that you can make an informed decision about whether or not to continue reading. Please be aware that the following information does contain spoilers; however, I want to offer all my readers the opportunity to be fully versed in all potentially triggering scenarios prior to reading.

Within Range contains sexually explicit content and strong language throughout the entire story. It is also a forbidden, not-his-baby love story with a fourteen-year age gap between the main characters.

In addition, you will find on-page physical abuse (a slap across the cheek), including manipulation and gaslighting from an ex-spouse. There is discussion of cheating within a marriage (not between the main characters). Billie's ex-boyfriend is also psychologically manipulative, as are his parents.

There is on-page pregnancy and discussion of birthing. The

book does not contain pregnancy loss, but there is reference to a complicated birth, which is off-page.

Finally, there are multiple on-page altercations and discussion of bruising and blood loss.

Emmett and Billie's love story is, without a doubt, one of my absolute favorites I've written to date. With a large helping of angst, male yearning, and a love that runs deep, these two will take you through so many emotions as you will them to be together and find their happily ever after.

Oh, and Emmett? He is the book boyfriend of dreams, living rent-free in my head since he first hit the pages.

I hope, after digesting these warnings, that you feel comfortable to continue reading, and I'm so excited to bring you the final installment of a series that is so close to my heart.

Enjoy Emmett and Billie!

Lots of love, always,

Ruth

PLAYLIST

"Bleeding Love" by Leona Lewis
"Heroes" by David Bowie
"Invisible String" by Taylor Swift
"Tears Dry on Their Own" by Amy Winehouse
"You Should Probably Leave" by Chris Stapleton
"You to Me Are Everything" by The Real Thing
"We Have All the Time in the World" by Louis Armstrong
"Hands to Myself" by Selena Gomez
"Treat You Better" by Shawn Mendes
"I Think We're Alone Now" by Tiffany

CHAPTER ONE

February

EMMETT

Do you know what I hate? Surprises.

So, I guess I should be grateful that my first day as a divorcé is playing out exactly as I predicted.

With a cold beer in one hand and my long-term friend, Scott Quinn, sitting opposite me in a run-down bar a couple of blocks from his place, we've barely uttered a word to each other since we took a seat in this sticky booth.

The decree landed in my mailbox this morning, a rubber-stamped document confirming the end of my thirteen year-long marriage and the start of a new life.

"Aren't we supposed to be celebrating and drinking to my newfound freedom?" I muse, pointing at Scott's bourbon.

He slowly turns his glass around on the coaster, eyeing me carefully.

I've known Scott for almost as long as I was married to my ex-wife, Maria. You could say that fate had a hand in our friendship when we both showed up to a classic car event in downtown Brooklyn, driving almost-identical racing green Jaguar E-Types.

He took one look at the tan leather seats I'd recently had restored, and it was love at first sight. We've been inseparable ever since, a connection I didn't think would last, not with the reluctance Maria showed when it came to socializing.

To some extent, I could understand her hesitancy. As a commercial airline pilot, she spent most of her time at thirty-five thousand feet, and when she wasn't responsible for the safety of hundreds of people, she wanted to kick back and chill.

Trouble was, the more time rolled on, the more isolated she became. To the point where she hated me heading out with my teammates after a hockey game. At first, I thought it was because she wanted to keep me all to herself—we were young and in love and couldn't get enough of each other. That was, until she started retreating from me too.

I guess that our marriage died from a thousand cuts—arguments that lasted for days, sleeping in separate beds night after night. Then came the jealousy and paranoia—Maria was convinced that I was playing around with other women, and that only got worse when I insisted that I needed to at least show my face at our postgame hideout, Lloyd's. She'd call me from wherever in the world she was on a layover, demanding that I switch the call to video so she could be sure that I was alone.

The longer we were married, the more control she demanded over every element of my life. It was exhausting, and ultimately, it drove a wedge between us. Now, at thirty-five years old, we aren't the same people that we were when we met in college. She assured me that she could handle the NHL lifestyle when we started dating in our sophomore year and I told her that I was drafted to the Blades. Back then, we loved each other, and I would stop at nothing to make our relationship work. In the end, it was me who filed for the divorce, and that's a bitter pill to swallow when you dedicated your life to someone, only to wind up with a bachelor pad and a few fancy cars, but no one special to head home to each night.

"I'd say that raising a glass to the dissolution of your marriage is dependent." Scott sits back in the booth and shakes out his floppy brown hair.

"On what?" I drawl.

He lifts a shoulder and takes a sip of his neat bourbon, setting the glass back down on the table. "If you feel like celebrating. Freya tells me that Maria isn't exactly overjoyed right now."

It's both a blessing and a curse that the one friend Maria did make—and keep—during our marriage just happens to be Scott's wife. Freya is a good person and the type of friend you'd want during a divorce, but Maria and I need a clean break, and I don't see how that can happen when there's a chance that our paths will keep crossing.

"She wanted the divorce as much as I did," I reply, running a palm across my unshaven jawline.

Scott looks at me, deadpan. "You know what I mean, man. This whole situation is shit." He blows into his cheeks. "When was the last time you even saw each other?"

I shrug. "A couple of weeks back. I was coming up your driveway, and Maria was leaving the house. She waved briefly and got into her car."

He shakes his head, almost like he's in disbelief over everything. "These past six months you've been separated; Freya and I have been waiting for you to work things out. How many times have you 'split,' only to reconcile a few weeks later?"

I lean forward, bracing my elbows on the table. "Exactly, Scott. The marriage was over way before I moved out. Maria knew it; I knew it." I motion to my friend. "And if you're really honest, you and Freya knew it too. All we were doing each time we got back together was kicking the can a little farther down an inevitable road."

I don't receive a response as Scott downs the rest of his bourbon. He looks way more troubled than I thought he would over this.

"Nothing has to change about our friendship," I reassure him. "And when I'm done with hockey after next season, we can head out in our cars a bit more." I manage a smile. "Maybe even hit the golf course on the regular, like a couple of pensioners."

Scott's brown eyes lower to the table in front of us, heavy shoulders slumped. "Actually, quite a bit is going to change."

I remain quiet, waiting on him to elaborate.

"Billie," is all he says.

"What about Billie?" I reply, feeling worried over the way he just said his daughter's name. "Is everything okay?"

The last update I got from Scott—which was only two weeks ago—there was no sign of any issue with her or the pregnancy. Or maybe that's just how I interpreted things. My head has been firmly up my ass lately, and I'm acutely aware that I've been a subpar friend at best.

When Scott eventually looks at me again, my heart falls in my chest. Billie might be his only daughter, but she's also been like a niece to me. I've known her since she was nine, and even though I haven't seen her in years since she left for college in Austin, I still think of her as family.

"She's coming home. To live."

Confused, I massage the bridge of my nose. "Wait. I thought she was going to stay out in Texas, move in with her boyfriend, and finish up college while his family helped out with child care?"

Scott throws me a look, revealing that my assumptions are way off the mark.

So, what the fuck has changed?

Picking up a spare coaster, my friend begins ripping it apart, shredded pieces falling to the table.

"Not exactly," he drawls. "I held off telling you because I figured you had enough drama on your plate with the divorce, but … let's just say that the baby's dad isn't making good on the promises he made to Billie and us. Next week, they were due to move into their new place in the same neighborhood as his parents, but Tucker backed out, saying that he thought the rental was too expensive." He tears a chunk off the coaster. "He's been ghosting Billie ever since. Not that he was particularly present from the day he found out about the pregnancy."

I scratch the back of my neck, my own issues suddenly feeling insignificant.

"In a last-minute decision, Billie has made the call to fly home before she's thirty-six weeks along so she can have the baby here. Freya and I already hated the idea of her staying in Austin with people we barely knew." He clears his throat, likely to get rid of rising emotions. "Our girl has barely been home since she left for college, and each time we visited her, Tucker's family were conveniently busy." He shakes his head. "She might be almost twenty-one and thinks she has life covered, but she's doing the right thing to come home where we can support her." What's left of the coaster falls from his hands. "That fucker got her knocked up and is refusing to accept his responsibilities. She's still my baby, for Christ's sake." His voice wobbles on the final few words.

I can feel the burn of rage deep in the pit of my gut. Maria and I never had kids, but that doesn't mean I can't sense a fraction of the desperation Scott is experiencing right now.

"You should've said something sooner," I tell him.

Scott just shakes his head at me. "It's not like you could've done anything." His voice adopts a darker edge. "Not unless you want to fly your six-foot-four frame south and beat the living shit out of Tucker. If I get within a hundred yards of him, I swear I'll break his fucking neck."

For a second, I consider offering to do just that.

Instead, I try to remain calm for the sake of my closest friend. "I'm not making any excuses here," I begin, quickly raising a hand at the bartender to bring Scott another bourbon. "But perhaps Tucker is freaking out. You told me that he's only a year older than Billie, right?"

He nods his head once.

"Maybe it's a case of him needing to pull himself the fuck together and step up to be a man."

Another bourbon is set in front of Scott, and he tosses the shot down in one, swiping the back of his hand across his mouth.

"Billie thinks he's messing around with someone else."

That information hits me like a bullet between the eyes.

"The fuck?" I grind out.

"Yep," is all he says, clearly incapable of forming further—appropriate—words.

"She can't be sure he's cheated, but when she found a questionable message on his cell from an unknown number, it was the final straw, and she made a devastated phone call to Freya. Her flight leaves tomorrow, and we'll work the rest out when she gets here."

I scramble for something I can say to make this shit situation any better.

"Is his family still going to help out with finances? Given that Billie and Tucker are in college."

Scott doesn't need to say anything. From his expression alone, I can tell that it's doubtful.

"I think they all want to wash their hands of the pregnancy and pretend like it never happened. Billie agreed to remain in Texas, trusting that they would support her beyond the minimum child support payments ..." He practically spits his next statement. "It's not like they can't afford to."

"I don't even know what to say."

He scoffs. "What the fuck can you say? We're literally left holding the baby. I'm going to sell Shelby to help her out."

I pull back, shocked.

Other than Billie and his wife, Shelby is the most important girl in Scott's life. A 1960s Jaguar E-Type, inherited from his late father. If sold privately, he could expect to raise a hundred thousand dollars, but I know it would break his heart. Scott is a blue-collar worker from a family who worked tirelessly for every dime they had, so to raise that kind of cash would likely mean remortgaging his and Freya's home if they didn't sell Shelby.

Billie's home too.

My voice is low when I say, "You can't do that, buddy."

He lifts a defeated shoulder. "Every dollar we have is tied up in the house, so that just leaves Shelby. I'm struggling to afford the rental on the garage anyway, so I guess selling her and downsizing will solve two issues. Billie and the baby need the money."

My beer is almost room temperature when I take another pull. "How much does she need?"

Scott's head darts to me, a warning in his gaze. I've never offered him money because I always knew he would tell me to shove it up my ass. He's proud, and so is Freya. But this is about his daughter, and when it comes to Billie, Scott will do anything for his child.

"Don't even go there." He sits back in the booth. "And anyway, you just got a divorce and lost fifty percent of your wealth."

I sit forward. "And? I'm one of the highest-paid defensemen in the league. How much does Billie need?" I repeat.

The conflict inside my friend is clear as he falls silent, and I request another bourbon on his behalf.

"We can't take your money, Emmett."

"Hypothetically speaking ... how much would be enough?"

He shakes his head, dismissing my question.

"How much?" I press.

I should probably drop this, but a desire to feel useful drives my determination to at least get a number from him. Maria might've taken fifty percent in an uncontested settlement, but it's the twilight of my hockey career, and I have more money than I can spend.

Scott swallows thickly as I slide a fresh glass of bourbon toward him, his eyes down and not on me.

"With the sale of Shelby and a loan we were looking to set against the house, we thought maybe a hundred and fifty thousand dollars. It would pay off the remainder of Billie's student finances and give her a head start with wherever she wanted to live when she and the baby eventually move out—whether she chooses to stay in Brooklyn, go back to Austin or find somewhere totally different."

"Done," I confirm without a second of hesitation.

"No," he counters.

"Yes," I volley back.

"We can owe you it. I'll set up a repayment—"

"Not happening," I interject, blowing out a long breath. If the table wasn't between us, I'd clamp my hand on his shoulder or pull him into an embrace. "I want to do this, Scott. For you, for Freya, and for Billie and the baby. How many times have you been there for me? Shitstorm after shitstorm. From my divorce to a knee injury that almost ended my career prematurely." I pin him with a sincere stare. "Let me do this one thing for you guys. I haven't got kids of my own, and at thirty-five, hell knows I don't think I ever will. My money will die with me, and all I have to spend it on is cars, golfing vacations, and boring investments."

I don't miss the glaze as it forms across his eyes. He's still uncomfortable with this, but he knows it's the right decision to let me help out.

"Freya and Billie can never know."

I raise a brow at him. "I don't think keeping stuff from them is a good idea. And anyway, where will you say you got the money from?"

Scott rolls his lips together in thought. "I have shares in the company I used to work for. In total, they amount to nothing like the kind of money we need, but I'll tell Freya they appreciated quickly, and I'm taking advantage by cashing them in. They were originally earmarked for our retirement, but she'll want to use them for Billie and the baby." He clears his throat, guilt twisting his features. "I guess if the shares technically exist, then it's not a total lie."

"Scott, I—"

"I don't want to hear any more, Emmett," Scott cuts me off. "This is the deal: you help out my family, and I get to call the shots on what I tell them."

I don't like it, not one fucking bit. But Freya isn't my wife, and Billie isn't my daughter, and there's no way I'm leaving my friend in the lurch.

I finish the rest of my beer and set the empty down in front of me. "All right. I can have the money in your account by the end of the week."

CHAPTER TWO

BILLIE

In a matter of days, Tucker and I were supposed to be unloading boxes into our new place, debating what color to paint the nursery since we decided not to find out our baby's gender in advance of the birth.

We were supposed to be making a new home and life together as we waited out the final few weeks before we became a threesome and our lives changed for good.

Instead, I'm standing in my childhood bedroom, its four pink walls covered with adolescent posters, serving as a harsh reminder that my life has descended into a complete fucking disaster.

Austin was going to be the start of everything for me—a chance to pursue my dream career as a lawyer. A chance to prove to Mom and Dad that I wasn't their shy little girl who needed to be sheltered. I could've stayed and studied in New York and lived at home, but that wasn't enough for me. I wanted to move states, change time zones.

Instead, I'm right back where I was. And this time around, I need my parents more than ever.

Arms around my huge bump, I move toward my bedroom

window and stare out into the yard of our brownstone house, the place Mom and Dad brought me home to when I was a newborn.

Being back in Brooklyn wasn't what I wanted for our child, and not because my parents aren't amazing people or I didn't have the best childhood—because I did. I just wanted to show my baby the world and give it to them as well. That's what Tucker told me when I broke the news that we were pregnant as we lay sprawled out on the couch one lazy night I stayed over at his place.

Maybe I was foolish to believe him when he promised that he'd stand by me and that the surprise pregnancy was as much his responsibility as it was my own. He talked about marriage and spending the rest of our lives together and how this baby was only the start of our family that we'd expand when we were both ready.

"Total bullshit," I whisper to myself as the cold February air whips through the trees lining the bottom of the yard, the wooden swing Dad hung from an old oak tree crashing against its trunk.

When I met Tucker eighteen months ago, he was just entering into his junior year and me into my sophomore. For him, it was love at first sight—or so he told me the day he finally asked for my number at a house party he and his friends were hosting.

I should've known back then that he didn't truly mean a word that left his mouth, and I guess I could be forgiven for falling under his spell. He was a year older than me, insanely hot with dark hair and big brown eyes, and the guy every girl on campus wanted to bag or bed, depending on who you asked.

I didn't care that he came from money or that his parents owned a high-flying law practice, and I certainly didn't see his family as a meal ticket to the career in criminal law I always wanted.

Regardless, that's how they eventually treated me—like a freaking criminal. Convinced I was looking to ride on the coattails of their youngest son.

Fuck off.

I'd left Brooklyn with five-hundred dollars in my checking

account and student loan agreements that would likely take over a decade to repay, and do you know what? I was good with that. I was comfortable forging my own path in life because that was exactly what I dreamed of when my dad loaded the final box into the U-Haul van and we drove the twenty-six-hour drive to Austin.

Am I scared to have a baby with a guy that I've been dating for less than a year? Yes. Hell, I think I'd still be freaking out if I was in my mid-thirties and we had been married for ten years. But I trusted Tucker, I trusted his family and their promises, and I had no intention of going back on my own to him—that I would stick around in Texas and not return to New York, consequently taking his child with me.

Honestly? I can't be sure where it all went wrong, but somewhere along the road—about the time when I started to show—Tucker's attitude changed. He started going out more and more, claiming that he wanted to make the most of his freedom while he still had it. We got into fights over the craziest things, and eventually, we stopped having sex too. Or at least, I stopped having sex. Conversely, Tucker was getting it on with every girl who looked his way. Or that was what the rumors suggested.

At first, I brushed off the whispers around campus, chalking them up to mean girls who had tried and failed to bed one of the hottest boys in school. I was used to their gibes from the very beginning of our relationship. But then came the pictures and the videos of him dancing and grinding up against other girls. They were harder to deny or even ignore.

And finally, when I plucked up the courage to confront him right before I turned thirty-three weeks pregnant, my boyfriend proved just how bad of a liar he actually was.

I can still feel the humiliation as his pathetic denial ripped through me. I should've walked out on him there and then, and I would have done it if it hadn't been for the baby. Instead, I stuck around for two weeks, trying to convince myself each night I climbed into his bed alone that he wasn't out screwing other girls into the early hours.

If it wasn't for Clara—the one friend I'd actually made in college—I think I'd still be lying in Tucker's bed right now, blaming myself for his infidelity.

"You need to call your mom and dad and tell them everything, Billie. And then you need to leave Tucker Price and move back to Brooklyn. It's time you started putting you and the baby first because God only knows your boyfriend and his family aren't going to."

Clara's words stung like I'd landed face-first into a beehive. But despite the way my heart protested, I knew that she was right. I couldn't deny it. The final straw though came when I reached out to his mom, Allanah, in one last-ditch attempt to salvage whatever I had left with her son.

"You know what I think, Billie?" Her words were cutting and judgmental as they came down the phone. "I think you got yourself pregnant to entrap our youngest son. Tucker has done nothing but support and love you, but the second he spends some time on himself, you don't like it. My boy is as faithful as it gets, and you're lucky he hasn't tossed you onto a trash heap like countless other men would've done. If you want my advice, be grateful for what you have."

That was the last time I heard from his family, other than an email from Tucker's dad, confirming that they would be stepping back from providing additional support due to the "smear campaign" I'd spread throughout campus. If sharing with family and friends that you think your boyfriend and father of your unborn baby is cheating amounts to dragging someone's name, then I should be suing left and right for the bullshit that's been spread about me over the years.

Crying isn't the answer, and I know that. Repeatedly, I've told myself that I'm not alone in having and raising a child and that I didn't make the biggest mistake of my life when I decided to keep the pregnancy, trusting that I had the right people in my life to survive even the toughest days of motherhood.

Society tells women that we can have it all—the career, the

family, the social life. But what about when the man who got you pregnant chooses himself above you and his child? What then?

A treacherous tear hits my cheek, and I swipe at it in disgust.

How many more times will I cry over him?

"Billie, baby?"

Mom's whispered voice has me spinning around to face her as she cautiously enters the room and takes a seat on my bed. I can tell she's noticed the unshed tears in my eyes, although she doesn't say anything, simply palming my duvet and inviting me to take a seat.

The house is almost silent, which is unusual. Mom always has something playing on the radio, dancing around the living space while Rufus, our Jack Russell terrier, side-eyes her from his basket.

Today, there isn't any music playing or a judgmental look from my dog because Rufus passed away over Christmas. I should've returned home for the holidays, but instead, I spent it with Tucker and his family, sitting at a grand table in an even grander dining room, pretending to be someone I wasn't.

I never fit into his life—a Brooklyn girl from a working-class family. No matter how many times I tried to prove that I was with Tucker for him and not his money or connections, that message fell onto deaf ears.

"Seeing you upset breaks my heart." Mom tucks a piece of wavy red hair behind my ear before taking one of my hands in hers. "But witnessing your silence is tearing me apart," she admits. "Talk to me, Billie. I want to support you through this, but I can't help if you don't let me in. Have you and Tucker officially broken up?"

I shake my head. It isn't an answer to her question, more a sign of confusion. "I don't know what we are. After I told him that I was taking a leave of absence from college and coming back home, he told me it was for the best and pretty much ended the call."

Mom intertwines our fingers, shifting on the bed beside me. "Do you want it to be the end with him?"

I shrug, still conflicted over my feelings despite everything that's happened. "I don't know."

"If ..." Mom's voice fades out when Dad enters my room and sets the final suitcase down by my feet.

"The truck's fully unloaded, Bill. How about I fix you something to eat?" He's trying to be upbeat and show that this isn't affecting him in the same way it is Mom. Or that he doesn't want to tear Tucker limb from limb and feed him to a pride of lions.

I guess that's what decent fathers would do—protect and defend their own. Fight for their offspring in any way that they can.

Unless your name is Tucker Price.

"I'm not hungry," I reply, gaze dropping to the dark green suitcase Dad just set down.

It has all of my textbooks inside, ones that I'll likely never need again. I might've taken a leave of absence, and college might be promising me all the help and support when I return, but we all know I'm fighting a losing battle. I can barely go five minutes without needing to pee, and I'll have even less time when the baby arrives. I'll be surviving each day, and studying will be a thing of the past.

At least for the next eighteen years.

My stomach protests, growling into the quiet room.

"When was the last time you ate?" Mom asks.

"A packet of Cheez-Its on the flight."

Mom makes the kind of noise only mothers can make—one crossed between concern and annoyance. "You're eight months pregnant, Billie. You have to keep up your strength."

"I'm fine," I counter, releasing her hand and twisting mine around in my lap. "I'm not hungry," I repeat.

My cell vibrates once on the nightstand, and Dad picks it up, brows knitting together when he takes in the message across the screen.

Deep down, I know I should walk away from Tucker and his toxic family. Still, I can't help but cling to a lasting hope that he will stay true to all his promises. If not for me, then for the sake of the baby.

My eyes are still locked on my phone when Dad eventually hands it to me.

CLARA

Your flight landed over three hours ago. Are you home? Have you heard from Tucker? I overheard a couple of girls in the library talking about him. Apparently, he was seen at another house party last night. I could wring his goddamn neck!

"You need to eat something, Bill," Dad persists.

"And I said that I'm not hungry," I snap, dropping my phone into my lap, hands covering my face.

The sob that breaks free from my throat is automatic, but not unexpected, and I feel the warmth and scent of Mom as she wraps her arms around my shoulders.

"What if I took us to Miguel's for lunch?" Dad suggests, knowing that Miguel's is my favorite Mexican restaurant.

It has been since I was five years old. We'd go every year for my birthday and sometimes with Mom and Dad's best friends, Emmett and Maria. Although that's likely to change, too, since they just finalized their divorce.

"Can we afford that?" Mom's voice is soft and low.

Another wave of nausea washes through my stomach. Of course they can't afford random meals out. My parents now have to support me and a whole new person in a matter of weeks. Along with converting their spare room into a nursery which won't be a cheap expense if I decide to live at home once the baby outgrows their bassinet.

"I have it covered," Dad quietly replies.

It's like they think I'm not listening or I can't hear their exchange.

“I’m right here, you know? You can’t talk around me like I’m still a child and I won’t figure out that the conversation is really about me.”

I look between them both. They don’t deserve my anger and frustration to be pointed at them. Still, it flows from me in waves.

Dad runs a hand through his brown hair and glances at Mom as she plucks one of her dark strands from my green sweater dress.

“Do you want to go to Miguel’s?” she asks.

When my phone vibrates in my lap, I flip it over to see another worried message from Clara.

“I don’t want to go anywhere. I just want to sleep,” is all I say, standing from the bed and massaging my lower back.

Mom rises and pulls back the duvet, exchanging another look with Dad that, once again, they don’t think I notice.

“Okay, Bill,” she says, helping me out of my dress when I try to pull it overhead and struggle.

I hear the soft click of my door as Dad leaves the room, and I turn back to Mom, swallowing down another onslaught of upset.

“He’s gone, isn’t he?” I ask her, confident that she’ll know I’m referring to Tucker.

She helps me out of my tights and sets my clothes on a chair in the corner of the room. I can’t remember the last time Mom tucked me into bed, but I accept the comfort and safety it brings.

“I don’t want you to give any more energy to Tucker or what he may or may not do next. It’s pointless, trying to control what men—and especially guys like him—do.”

I note the way she said *him*. She’s as mad as Dad is.

I let my head sink into the soft pillow, the familiar and rare scent of home filling my senses. “I wish it were that simple.”

With a single kiss to my forehead, she looks down at me through her beautiful blue eyes, nothing but love and sincerity in them.

“Unfortunately, it really is that simple, Billie. Because if you don’t focus on you and this baby, then you’ll have way more problems than just an asshole who can't get his priorities straightened out."

CHAPTER THREE

EMMETT

"Did the money reach you all right?" I ask Scott before I'll be forced to switch my cell to Airplane mode.

Flying by private jet has its benefits, including being permitted to make calls right until takeoff. Still, that doesn't prevent the side-eye I receive from my captain and center, Jack Morgan, as he takes a seat next to me.

"Yeah, it landed in my account late last night."

Scott sounds less sure of me sending the money than when we spoke a few days ago in the bar.

"It's yours, no questions asked," I reassure him, trying to sound as vague as possible.

While I trust my teammates fully, I'm certain that Scott and Freya wouldn't want their business shared with anyone—well, if Freya knew the full truth.

Scott clears his throat. I know he's at work today, likely sitting in his van outside the school where he's a full-time janitor. "I want to at least pay some of it back."

"Not happening." My retort is fast and sharper than I intended, garnering another look from Jack.

I switch my phone to the hand nearest the window. Ordinarily, we would be in single seats, but almost the entire team is flying out to Lake Garda this bye week to celebrate the wedding between key Blades defenseman Tommy Williams and his fiancée and New York Storm goalie, Jenna Miller.

It's a crazy-long flight to Italy, but that's where Tommy wanted to wed his girl, and who were we to say no to New York's latest power couple? The entire city is obsessed with them both, and being honest, flying ten hours is the only way to fully eliminate attention from the paparazzi.

I work to soften my voice. I want Scott to accept the money willingly, not ram it down his throat. "How's Billie doing?"

Over the plane's engine noise, I still hear his sigh.

"That good, huh?"

"She's not eating much, and she thinks all this is her fault when really ..." He breaks off, and I can visualize his knuckles turning white as they wrap around his steering wheel. A little like mine would if I ever got my hands on Tucker.

"When I get back from Italy, I'll stop by. It must be at least three years since I last saw Billie."

"Over three years," Scott clarifies. "You haven't seen her since she was seventeen. That's the last time she was home for the holidays."

Memories of Billie sitting opposite me at the table push forward from the depths of my brain, along with the turkey Maria tossed on our kitchen floor during an argument. I wince at the way we imposed ourselves on the Quinns that year, thanks to my ex-wife's childish behavior.

"That's right," I say, difficult memories morphing to a smile when I recall the way she annihilated me at Monopoly and then shoved her win and the bet we'd made in my competitive face later that night when we were doing the dishes and everyone else was watching TV.

Billie Quinn has always been a spitfire with top banter that made me belly laugh, even before she delivered the punch line. I hate to think of her hurting at the hands of an asshole and his family. I'd reach out and text her to let her know that she had people around her if that wouldn't be weird as fuck. We've barely spoken since she left for college.

I shift in my seat as Jack takes a cup of hot water from the flight attendant and snags a tea bag from the front pocket of his hoodie, adding it to his mug. I stare at him for a long moment as he stirs the bag around carefully.

The British are fucking weird sometimes.

"Why the fuck were you flirting with our friends' teenage daughter?!"

More memories from that Christmas race back. The accusation Maria slung at me before we even pulled out of Scott and Freya's driveway was fucking ridiculous, and she knew it too. I remember almost crashing the car when I threw my hands up and turned it back around on her, hypothesizing that she was being unfaithful, given that was all she could fucking think about or throw at me every time I spoke to any female who wasn't her.

"You're going crazy, Maria," I snapped back, turning into our driveway and hitting the brakes way too hard, throwing us both forward in the process. "Next, you'll suggest that I'm screwing Freya behind your back." I scoffed and stared out of the windshield. "I've never given you any reason to doubt me, yet you repeatedly hurt me with ludicrous allegations."

"It's Billie's birthday next week." Scott's voice penetrates unwanted memories of my ex-wife, cutting them short before I spiral into the abyss that is my divorce. "Why don't you stop by and say hi? She'd likely welcome a friendly face."

"The big two-one, right?" I ask, knowing exactly how old Billie is and that her birthday is right around the corner.

She always said that she was born on Valentine's Day because she was the most lovable human being on the planet.

"You're too damn cocky for your own good, Bill." The gibe I made as she flicked soapy water in my face that Christmas heats

my body for an uncomfortable second. Along with the look on Maria's face when we came back to sit in the living room.

We were messing around, just like we always had. Billie was a fun girl, and I was in love with my wife. End of story.

"And before you ask, no. She doesn't want or need anything for her birthday." Scott's tone is deadly serious, as is the attendant's when she announces that we're about to depart and to switch all devices to in-flight mode.

I choose to ignore my friend's warning. There's no way I'm showing up empty-handed on arguably the biggest birthday anyone can have. And if Scott won't give me any pointers on what kind of gift to get his daughter, then I'll just have to go rogue with my choice. Maria always sorted that kind of shit out.

"I gotta go," I tell him. "We're about to take off, and my captain is slurping his tea, to the point where I can barely focus on anything else."

Jack's head darts to me, eyes narrowed with annoyance when he brings his cup to his mouth and slurps even louder.

When he chokes on his mouthful, I offer a sarcastic smile.

Scott just chuckles, and it's nice to hear him laugh. He's under a lot of pressure, but honestly, I can't recall a time when he and Freya haven't been struggling to make ends meet financially. I know he's been tempted to sell Shelby more than just once, especially when Freya's late parents were taken into a care home and fees spiraled way beyond the scope of what their insurance would cover.

"Put me on speaker," Scott instructs, and I do as he asked.

"Jack," Scott continues after a couple of seconds, "I want to see the Blades lift the Cup again this year. Oh, and for you to beat your goal-scoring record."

Jack's all cocky bravado as he takes another unnecessarily loud sip of tea. "It's already in the bag, Scott."

I roll my eyes at my teammate and disconnect the call. "No one likes a show-off, Jack."

Scott has met some of the guys on postgame nights out. Each

time, he's hit it off with Jack. That said, everyone gets on with our captain. He's the golden retriever and glue that sticks the team together. Aside from my former teammate, Sawyer Bryce, he's the best captain I've ever played under.

Jack releases a heavy exhale, reclining his seat once we're in the air and the seat belt signs are turned off.

"What's eating at you?" I ask, surprised over his change in mood.

He closes his eyes, folding his hands over his chest. "Nothing."

"Oh, well, that's definitely convincing."

Jack cracks an eyelid and looks at me. "I'm not happy about being away from Esme for four nights, and neither is Kendra."

Esme is Jack's seven-month-old daughter, and Kendra, his wife, is Jenna's best friend and teammate. All the bridal party flew out to Lake Garda two nights ago.

"You could've brought her along," I say, having zero clue how hard it is to travel across the world with a baby.

Jack shakes his head, his British accent more obvious than normal as he replies, "Nah. The jet lag we're all about to have will be hard enough to overcome, never mind having to do it with a baby. I'm surprised our general manager signed off on this trip, to be honest."

"As long as we bring our best game next Saturday, the GM will only see it as good for team building."

Jack nods his head once, brown hair flopping over his forehead. "Did you ever think that we'd be going to Tommy's wedding?" He snorts a laugh. "This time last year, I wouldn't have attended his funeral, and now he has us all wrapped around his finger and Sawyer as his best man."

He isn't wrong. Tommy Williams, formerly Tommy Schneider, was the guy on the team everyone hated, and he loved it. It felt like every game he played in, we lost because he couldn't keep his gloves on or his fists out of opposing players' faces. But then he met Jenna, and once they sorted out their differences, sparks flew for all the right reasons. He's a good guy and precisely why so many of the team are on a flight to go celebrate the rest of his life with the woman he loves.

As the attendant hands me a beer, I push away memories of my own wedding day in a Vegas chapel. I genuinely thought that I was in love with my college sweetheart, and neither I nor Maria could wait to get hitched and call it forever.

I hope Tommy and Jenna's marriage doesn't go the way ours did.

"How are you doing?" Jack asks, likely sensing my discomfort over our conversation. He's always been intuitive like that.

I shrug and take a pull from my beer. "What can I say? My marriage didn't work out. It is what it is."

Bringing his seat back to an upright position, Jack looks unconvinced. I don't want to talk about Maria, but I get a feeling that I won't have a choice.

"Is there anyone else?" he asks me cautiously.

My beer very nearly ends up in the next row of seats as I fight to swallow it. "Are you for real?!" I laugh at the ridiculous notion. "No, there isn't anyone."

He doesn't look surprised at my response, and I can't see a day when I'm not single. Sure, I've slept with a couple of people since Maria, but only because I'm a man with needs and away series can get really fucking lonely at times.

"I think I'd actually pass away if I didn't have Kendra." He looks pained at the thought alone. "We should've been dating when we were in college. Thank fuck fate eventually brought us back together."

A part of me thinks that if I'd met Maria after college, then we wouldn't be dealing with the prospect of rebuilding our lives separately. There's no chance that we would've hit it off in the same way. Even in our mid-twenties, we were different people from what we had been in school. I'm ready to argue and tell my captain that it was a good thing he and Kendra got together when they were a few years older when I'm interrupted by my phone vibrating on the tray table. A message coming through via Wi-Fi.

BILLIE

This is probably the most random and out-of-the-blue message I've ever sent, but Dad just told me you're planning to stop by for my birthday. Seriously, you don't have to do that. I'm a mess, and no one wants to see me right now.

Hi, BTW. It's been a while.

Billie's right. This is the most random and out-of-the-blue message, but it pulls a smile from my miserable fucking brain nonetheless.

"Who's that?" Jack asks, dropping his eyes to my screen, lips curling into a grin.

"My niece," I tell him.

He looks horrified at his own inappropriate thoughts. "Shit, sorry." His expression turns to confusion. "Wait. You've never mentioned having a niece before?"

"She's Scott's daughter," I clarify. "I'm one of those unofficial uncles we all have."

Jack's face is devilish-looking, and I want to cover it with my palm and tell him to take his messed-up ideas elsewhere.

"So, she *isn't really* family then?"

I'm typing out a response to Billie when I throw Jack a warning glare. "Take your mind out of the gutter and concentrate on drinking that weird-ass pond water." I nod my head at his tea.

He sputters out a laugh, which I ignore, attention back on Billie's message.

ME

Who said I was coming over solely to see you?

BILLIE

Over three years since we last saw each other, and you're still giving me shit.

I scroll up on our message history and see the last time we spoke was almost a year ago—me sending a quick text to wish Billie a happy birthday and her telling me that she was at a house party before hitting the library for an all-night study session.

Jesus, life can change in the blink of an eye.

ME

It's who I am. Plus, I figured you could use the laugh. Along with unnecessary bath salts or something equally predictable for your birthday. I know that you hate surprises just as much as I do.

My fingers hover over the keyboard, desperate to type out a message to ask how she is. They grip my phone tighter when I see her responding.

BILLIE

For what it's worth, I'm sorry about everything with Maria.

I hold my phone tighter.

ME

Me too.

BILLIE

I'll be home for a long while now, so I guess we'll catch up at some point. Especially since all my high-school friends have left town these days. You really don't need to make a special effort on my part.

ME

It's Valentine's Day, and I'm newly single. I have nothing better to do.

BILLIE

Umm … thanks?

ME

You're welcome.

BILLIE

I guess by that logic, we're both in the same boat.

I know she's referring to Tucker, and I sort of want to ask her more about it. But it doesn't feel appropriate or like it's my place after so much time has passed since we last spoke.

ME

I'll be over soon with lavender bath salts and a pair of fluffy socks.

BILLIE

Where are you for the bye week?

One thing about Billie? She's arguably a bigger sports fan than her dad. At least, she was when she left for college, and it seems that nothing has changed since she knows our playing schedule. She even came to a couple of games with Scott back in the day and before Jack started playing for the Blades. She also loves soccer just as much as I do, even if her theory over who's the best player in the world is way off track.

I smile at memories of sports-related debates and how she always had a smart answer for everything.

ME

Italy for a wedding. I'm on a flight now.

BILLIE

What I wouldn't give for an Italian Pinot Grigio.

ME

Well, as of Valentine's Day, you'll be LEGAL to drink it. After the baby's born. Obviously.

BILLIE

Oh, please. You and I both know I drank before I was pregnant. Or have you forgotten your days in college, when they still had wooden money?

ME

I'm old. Not dead. And, yes, I remember college. Thank you very fucking much.

BILLIE

Wine can be my birthday gift since you insist on buying me something.

ME

I'm not buying you wine, Billie.

BILLIE

Dry Italian Pinot Grigio. Nice and light with citrus notes.

ME

No.

BILLIE

Yes.

ME

Drop it, or I'll spill to Scott about underage drinking.

BILLIE

Emmett, I'm unexpectedly pregnant and about to drop out of college. Do your worst.

"Nice little chat you have going on there ..." Jack's breath fans the collar on my shirt as he leans over to read my exchange with Billie.

I know he's only trying to fuck with me since that's all we ever do on this team. I ignore him—again—and type out a final response.

ME

I'm about to land, so I gotta go.

It's a lie; we have at least another nine hours to go. Regardless, my teammate's prying eyes, combined with conversations about underage drinking with my best friend's only daughter, drive me to wrap things up.

BILLIE

Sure. Me too. I just landed in the Caribbean for an all-expenses-paid vacation. Catch you —and a crisp glass of Pinot—later!

CHAPTER FOUR

EMMETT

I've been a pro hockey player for well over a decade now.

During that time, I've witnessed my fair share of craziness—from insane hits to PR scandals and the absolute mayhem that ensues when your team finally lifts the Cup.

Having your coach plan his own defenseman's wedding though? That's a new one and every bit as wild now as when Tommy told us that Coach Morgan—aka Jon Morgan, NHL Hall of Famer and all-round nice guy—was going to arrange everything, bar actually being the officiant.

Up until now, I've only ever seen the stoic side of Coach Morgan, the face of reason and professionalism. But as he glides along the courtyard with a five-tier cake stand in one hand and a white bird cage in the other, I find myself questioning everything I once thought I knew about this guy. Or—and maybe more accurately—if I accidentally ingested magic mushrooms during breakfast.

"I'm ... actually lost for words right now," I say to Jack as he comes to stand next to me, all of us dressed in dark blue suits with white dress shirts open at the collar.

Jack doesn't look at all surprised by what he's witnessing. "Come to think of it, I think that's why the GM signed off on the whole team traveling to Italy—he didn't dare say no to Jon. He's living out his dream right now."

I look at my captain. "He just coached us to Cup victory. Surely, that was his dream."

Jack makes a face that isn't totally agreeable.

"Listen ..." Jensen Jones—our goalie coach and Jon's former teammate when they played for the Seattle Scorpions—joins us, standing on the opposite side of me to Jack. He crosses his arms over his chest and shakes his head in Coach's direction when he slides a headset on and begins pointing at staff members. "Let him have his moment in the sun. He's been banging on about wedding planning since I can remember. He's attempted to plan pretty much everyone's wedding other than Archer's. And that was only because he eloped."

Like our goalie can hear the conversation from across the courtyard, he offers us a salute and then lifts a pint of beer in our direction. He married his wife, Darcy, who just happens to be Jack's sister, a couple of years back, before anyone found out that he'd gotten her pregnant. To say that the shit hit the fan when Jack found out about their secret relationship and pregnancy would be the understatement of the century.

"Are the girls nearly ready?" I ask, checking my watch.

The ceremony is in less than twenty minutes, and Coach looks like he might burst a blood vessel.

Jack worries his lip. "Kendra messaged me a couple of minutes ago. Jenna's hair needs to be refixed, so they're running behind."

"The last time I checked the inventory, I hadn't ordered three extra statues for the courtyard." Coach power-walks toward us, now holding half a dozen peacock feathers and ... a fucking porcelain swan.

Jesus. I'm putting in for a trade before the March deadline.

"We didn't want to get in the way of your finest hour."

Jensen's voice drips with sarcasm, earning a low chuckle from Jack.

Coach narrows his eyes at his center. "You were supposed to be folding napkins in the Naples suite ten minutes ago."

Jack's eyes flare wide, and he turns on his heel, striding off without another word.

Coach turns to Jensen then, dropping the porcelain swan into his arms. "I need you to set this up on the far end of the buffet table. I told management three times where it needed to go, but somehow, it still found its way into the lobby."

When Jensen takes off with his instructions, a sense of dread settles inside me. I'd rather run sprint drills than deal with the way my coach is staring me down right now.

"You get a free pass, Emmett."

Hearing him use my first name feels foreign. He always addresses me by my last name.

"Why do I get off lightly?" I ask him.

Without a doubt, Jon Morgan is the best coach I've ever played under. My respect for him as a player and now leader is huge. He's turned the Blades around from the mess we were in when he took over the job. I've played my best games and recovered from the worst injury of my career under him, and I can't think of another guy I'd rather see out my pro days playing for.

He drops a hand onto my shoulder, and my throat instantly turns thick. I'm not an emotional guy, and I wasn't expecting this interaction to go how it is. I anticipated him shoving those feathers up my ass for being unhelpful.

"Thanks for showing up. Tommy, Jenna, and the rest of the guys can only imagine how tough this is for you, so soon after ..." He trails off. "Well, after Maria."

Warmth from his palm radiates through my suit, and I swallow down my emotions. It's true; I'm not particularly stoked to be here, but I'm not about to miss my teammate's big day or a chance to spend some time with the guys. Realistically, I'd have been riding out the next few days in the gym or lying on my couch if I hadn't flown out here. I need to keep my head busy and away from spiraling thoughts.

"It is what it is, Coach," I confirm.

That phrase seems to be my go-to these days. It says nothing and everything all at once and is a great way to sidestep difficult feelings. Because getting a divorce from the woman I once thought I was in love with fucking sucks.

Coach considers me for a moment, the ridiculous feathers blowing in his face. It's February and not exactly warm in Lake Garda, but mercifully, the weather has taken pity on Jenna and Tommy with blue skies promised all day.

"If it's any comfort to you, I was single and looking at the end of my pro career when I met Felicity."

Felicity is Coach's British wife and mom to Jack and Darcy. From what I heard about their love story, they were like fated mates, and he pursued her relentlessly before she finally gave in and agreed to date him.

"I'm not looking for anyone," I reply, meaning every word. "Aside from a few hookups here and there, I can't see me ever wanting to get involved with the opposite sex again."

Coach lifts a doubtful brow. "That's what they all say right before they meet the one."

I chuckle at that. It's low and dark and absolutely filled with cynicism. "I already had my chance, and it didn't work out." I look around the dressed courtyard. I might think that he's fucking crazy, but Coach has nailed the venue. "I guess that's why I'm here—to celebrate and remind myself that some people do fall and stay in love. And I hope that goes for Jenna and Tommy."

I can't deny how uncomfortable it is, having a heart-to-heart with Coach Morgan. On the contrary, he looks like he has conversations like this on the daily. A part of me envies that he can open up so easily. I see a lot of the same in his stepson, Jack, and I internally thank myself for never bringing kids into my former marriage—they'd have been closed off if they'd followed in my footsteps or an insane level of paranoid if they'd taken after Maria.

I reach up and adjust my glasses even though they were perfectly fine in the beginning.

"I'm here if you need to shoot the shit or talk anything out—you know that, right?"

With a nod, I clear my throat and then reach out to take the peacock feathers from him.

"Where were you headed with these?"

That's another thing about Coach. He's perceptive, just like Jack, annoyingly so at times.

Sensing that I'm done with talking about weddings and marriages, he waves an exasperated hand at the feathers. "Anywhere but the dining hall. They're killing the modern vibe in there."

"I PROMISE to cook and clean for you since you hate it so much." Tommy draws a laugh from the guests with a line from his vows.

Jenna swats him in the chest, kicking up the laughter a couple of octaves. In a stunning yet simple white gown that hugs her athletic figure, she looks up at the man she's about to make her husband.

Other than my interaction with Jon, I haven't struggled to keep my emotions in check. But the second the officiant asks Sawyer for the rings and he only produces one for Jenna, my heart jumps into my throat.

Tommy has kept pretty tight-lipped about today, leaving mostly everything to Coach. We all assumed he'd get a band similar to Jenna's, but that's obviously not the plan when he pulls off a piece of tape from around his ring finger to reveal Jenna's name inked into his skin.

Her hands instantly cover her mouth, and I pull off my glasses, quickly swiping underneath my eyes before anyone notices. Tommy is covered in tattoos, and pretty much all of them are from before he met his girl, although something tells me that while her name is the smallest tattoo he's ever gotten, it's definitely the most meaningful.

"Apparently, you don't have to exchange rings to legally seal a marriage."

He hooks his pointer finger under her chin, and tears tumble down her cheeks when he takes a step toward her. You could hear a pin drop in the courtyard, the swirling wind only adding to the romantic atmosphere.

Did Maria ever look at me like Jenna's looking at my teammate?

"And I don't need a ring. A band of metal is too temporary since it can be separated from my body. I *never* want to be apart from you. I once told you that while I've changed so much since I got my tattoos, they will always have meaning—a reminder of the man I left behind and the one I want to be for you. Only ever for you. I asked the artist when I got it done to go as deep as he could because I never want our love to fade. This is my most significant tattoo." He closes his eyes, resting his forehead against Jenna's. "And when we become a threesome"—he palms her stomach, and the entire thirty-something party of guests collectively gasps—"I'm going to add their name to my body as well. Right where the scissors cut through the thread over my heart. You put me back together, Hellion. This reformed bad boy is so in love with you."

I look over at Jenna's friends, who are all scrambling for tissues. Kendra, her maid of honor, tips her head up to the blue sky and blows out a steadying breath.

This is a marriage for the ages. Even my bruised and disbelieving heart can't deny the sincerity in Tommy's words. He's found his girl, but more than that, he's found his family.

CHAPTER FIVE

Valentine's Day

BILLIE

The swing at the bottom of the yard creaks as I shove my pregnant ass into the small space between the ropes and gently move back and forth.

Today was not how I envisioned celebrating my birthday. I think I'd be slightly less pissed if my favorite beef tacos from Miguel's hadn't set off a bout of acid reflux before I even finished the first shell.

"Do you want me to fix you some soup, honey?" Mom appears at the patio doorway, a tentative smile tracing her lips as she takes me in.

She used to push me all the time on this swing when I was a child, and while I just turned twenty-one, not much has really changed.

An acid burp rises up my throat as I push out, "Just a glass of water, please."

Rubbing my sternum, I shift on the uncomfortable wooden seat, darkness quickly drawing across the sky.

"Okay." She looks mildly irritated by my refusal to eat anything more. "Why don't you come inside? It's getting cold, and Emmett just pulled into the driveway. You should come and say hi." Mom furrows her brow in thought. "He's not exactly going through a great time either."

In a twenty-four-hour period, where I've been nothing but grumpy and irritable, I feel my damp mood give way to lighter feelings, and I internally smile at the messages I recently exchanged with Emmett. We haven't seen each other in years, but you wouldn't know it from the way we slipped back into banter with ease.

When I slide off the swing and head back into the kitchen, pulling the patio door closed behind me, I can already hear Emmett's deep voice filtering from the living area, along with a chuckle that sounds forced.

"Bill," Dad immediately says as Emmett finishes typing something on his phone before he locks the screen and centers his attention on me.

It's not the first time someone has done a double take in my presence, especially over the past couple of months. My body has changed a lot since I was eighteen—and not just because of the pregnancy. My hair is fuller and longer and has naturally turned a deeper red that I love. In my teens, I struggled with recurring acne on my cheeks and chin, but the Texan sun helped to cure my skin complaints and gave me a healthy glow I'd never managed to achieve living in Brooklyn. All that said, I know the main reason behind people's surprised reaction is how freaking huge this pregnancy has made me. I have stretch marks where I never thought skin could stretch, and trying to carry a baby—who I'm told will be well over nine pounds when born—inside my five-foot-four frame is a challenge, to say the least.

I quirk a brow at Emmett just as my dad receives a call, no doubt from the recently appointed overbearing principal at the school where he works.

He begins speaking and slips into the kitchen, closing the door behind him and leaving me and Emmett alone. Hades, my mom's black cat, sits next to Emmett on the couch.

My gaze tracks from Emmett to the large, glittery purple gift bag set down by his feet.

His cheeks flush a light pink when I point at the bag, lips twisting into an amused smile.

"Is the oversize bag to hide the bottle of wine you brought back from your fancy trip to Italy?"

Emmett sits back on the couch, crossing his left leg over the opposite knee.

Listen, I might be heavily pregnant, and this guy might be more like family, but we all have that one hot uncle who you can't help snatching a sneaky glance at every once in a while. Especially when you turned sixteen and boys became more interesting with their shirts off. Emmett Richards is exactly that "uncle" for me. The girls in high school would incessantly ramble on about how I should invite him to give a talk during physical education or how I should find a way to palm his tight hockey butt and pass it off as a slip of the hand.

And I have thought about how firm his ass really is, right around the time we went away as a group on a vacation to Miami and he removed his shirt in one easy motion when we spent a day at the beach.

I wet my lips and quickly roll them together, attempting to suppress thoughts I shouldn't be having.

Ever.

I'm pregnant, and I don't even know if I'm single.

Not that, if I were single, it would ever be appropriate to think about my dad's best friend—who just happened to be fourteen years older than me—getting naked.

Let's not even talk about his square-framed glasses or the way the black frames contrast perfectly with one of the finest male complexions I've ever seen.

Emmett Richards is nice to look at, and I'd either need to be blind or not yet born to miss his good looks.

I'm still waiting for his reply when my mind retrieves itself from the gutter, and I pray that he isn't as good at reading minds as he is at playing hockey.

"I didn't get you any wine, Bill." His eyes flick momentarily to the gift bag still set on the floor beside him. "They only had Chardonnay."

I deadpan and lean forward to catch a glimpse of what's inside. Matching purple tissue paper blocks my view, and I huff out a frustrated breath.

Why am I acting like a fucking teenager right now?

"You didn't need to buy me anything." I meant what I said in my initial message the other day that he didn't need to stop by, let alone with a gift.

He's had several birthdays since I last saw him, and I didn't even send him a card. Although Mom probably scrawled my name on one from them.

"Oh, I didn't. This?" He motions to the bag. "This is for someone else. I dropped in on your parents on my way over to see her."

I smirk, my previously bad mood feeling even lighter. Just because I said that he didn't have to make an effort doesn't mean I don't appreciate the fact that he has.

"Well, she's a very lucky girl then," I retort. "Especially if she likes purple ... and lavender bath crystals."

Emmett smirks at me, and it's hot as hell.

"How are you doing, Billie?"

His change in tone and subject catches me off guard, and I automatically wrap my arms around my swollen stomach.

Most people can't tear their eyes away from my huge bump, almost like pregnancy is the sum of who I am. The looks and stares around campus were difficult to ignore, making it even harder to dismiss the notion that, in the eyes of others, Billie the person ceased to exist the second she became an expectant mom.

Emmett, on the other hand, doesn't take his eyes from my face as he patiently waits on a response.

"I'm doing fine," I lie.

Physically, I'm good. The pregnancy is perfectly normal, and I'm still planning to go ahead with a vaginal birth in the local hospital. Mentally? Well, that's a completely different story and something I'm not ready to talk about. With anyone.

"How are you doing?" I ask the question before he can call me out on my bullshit.

I know Mom and Dad told him all about Tucker because they have always shared everything going on in their lives with Emmett and Maria. Hell, when I got accepted into Austin University, Maria was dropping off a card before I even messaged my school friends.

"I'm doing fine," he replies, flat tone matching mine.

Walking across to the window seat, where I used to devour my favorite romance novels, I flop into the plump cushions, embracing the comforting feeling as softness wraps around my aching spine.

I need this baby out, stat.

The silence between us feels awkward and heavy, and I question if my recollections of our banter and dynamic were viewed through a rose-tinted lens.

This guy is over a decade older than you, Billie. Of course you were never friends. He's a good person, simply concerned for his best friend and his irresponsible daughter, who got herself pregnant and screwed up her chances in life, along with her parents' financial future.

"Sorry about that." Dad bursts into the room, pocketing his phone. "Another leaking pipe at school for me to fix on Monday morning." He rolls his eyes. "For now, a bucket will have to do, and let's just pray we don't have another rainstorm between now and then."

Dad looks at me and then at Emmett, just as his friend's steely-gray eyes leave my face and focus back on Dad.

"Freya is making clam chowder for supper if you want to stay?"

Emmett clears his throat like his mind wasn't really in the

room, briefly fidgeting with his glasses. "Yeah, why not? I was going to grab a bite when I got home, but Freya's chowder can't be beat."

Unable to stop myself, I tip my chin at the purple bag. "I thought you had a gift to deliver?"

Emmett's eyes narrow just a fraction at me, not enough for it to be obvious to the onlooker, but I see it, and a bubble of laughter pops out of me.

Not saying a word, he stands from the couch and follows Dad toward the kitchen.

Curiosity gets the better of me, and I waddle across to the bag, pushing the tissue paper to one side. A jar of salts, fluffy pink socks, and yep ... a bottle of expensive-looking Pinot Grigio all sit inside.

I startle when I look up to see Emmett standing in the doorway, one hand braced on the doorjamb above his head. His fitted black T-shirt rides up to reveal a sliver of toned skin, and I fight to keep my eyes on his face.

Pack it in, Billie.

He's staring straight at me, but not in a heated way. More with a fascination that flushes warmth to my cheeks. Especially when he breaks into a smile, which crinkles around his eyes.

Releasing the doorjamb, he pushes a hand through his light-brown hair and shoots me a serious look. "Happy birthday, Bill. I'll share a glass with you when, you know ... it's appropriate."

CHAPTER SIX

EMMETT

When I pull into my private parking lot set beneath my apartment building, I angle the rearview mirror and examine the roof of my mouth.

I have never scarfed down chowder so damn fast in my life. Sure, I was hungry, having neglected lunch, but it wasn't the hunger pains that drove me to eat way faster than the food was cooling.

Have I stepped into a parallel fucking universe?

Because Billie Freya Quinn went and got hot over the last three years, and regardless of the pregnancy, she turned all fucking woman.

It's not that I've never seen or appreciated a stunning woman before. Of course I have. It's just that I've never been attracted to someone who is wildly off-limits, her taunting beauty daring me to steal another glance as we ate in my best friend's kitchen.

Mercifully, Billie didn't stay downstairs for long, choosing a nap over torturing me for an extended period. Not that she needed to be sitting opposite me for my brain to meander to places it should never venture. Like conjuring up an image of her flushed cheeks when she first saw me or the perfect curve of her full lips when they tipped into a sweet smile.

"You shouldn't have bought her the wine or checked out her ass when she bent down to look inside the gift bag," I quietly berate myself, dropping my head to the steering wheel on my Jaguar.

"You used to play in water fights and blow up her inflatables for the pool," I hiss to myself, hoping to embed the message deep inside my subconscious.

"This single life is driving you fucking crazy." I keep going.

Things were way simpler when it was just fights with Maria and I spent countless nights sleeping in the spare bed, stroking my dick to thoughts of when we were happily married.

"Are you all right?"

Sawyer's wide grin stares back at me when I startle and glance to the left, certain that I'm now hearing things to go with my sordid fantasies.

With the engine still running, I lower the driver's window.

"What are you doing here?" I ask, voice flat, my head still resting against the steering wheel.

When Sawyer doesn't immediately answer, my treacherous mind takes advantage of the pause, wandering back to Billie, deep red hair framing a perfect heart-shaped face.

I throw the driver's door open, and Sawyer jumps out of the way.

"Whoa," he gasps at my sudden movements. "It's Valentine's Day, and I came to check that you're doing okay." He pauses, looking concerned. "Jesus, buddy. What's going on?"

I don't answer, slamming the door and hitting Lock on my key fob. The engine powers down, and my window automatically closes as I stride toward the private elevator that leads directly to my penthouse.

Sawyer follows behind, and we both ride in silence. Thankfully, I don't have to put up a front in my former teammate's presence; he's the kind of guy who would never repeat what he witnesses. He's a vault, and I miss playing with him on the defensive line after he retired last season from the Blades. We'd played together for nearly a decade, and he's, without a doubt, one of the best defensemen the NHL has ever seen.

"Your place is looking better," Sawyer voices as we both step into my apartment, and I instantly head for the kitchen, tossing my keys onto the white marble counter.

"Better how?" My reply is a touch irritable, but I'm confident that he won't take my mood personally.

He knows I'm a miserable fucker at the best of times, especially after Maria.

His eyes rove the open-plan living space, landing on a single rubber plant, set in the corner of a stark white room. I moved in over six months ago and haven't hung a single thing on the walls other than an eighty-inch flat screen above the fireplace.

"Homier," he confirms, lips pressed together to stifle his amusement.

I snag a couple of Gatorades from the fridge and hand one to Sawyer.

He twists the cap off and downs half the bottle before moving over to the black leather couch that was already here when I moved in. When we separated, I let Maria keep all the decor, opting for a clean break away from everything. Truthfully, I haven't hung a single picture because I don't have any, other than a frame of my parents on their wedding day. When Dad passed away and my brother, Beau, and I emptied their house in Rochester, that was the only item I wanted to keep.

Like Sawyer, I'm not especially close to my brother, and following my parents' deaths, Beau has only gotten more distant, having moved to Florida with his family, while I stayed in New York, where we had been born and bred. Maybe our similarities are why my former teammate and I get along so well—we're both grumpy as fuck defensemen with difficult families. Although Sawyer's now happily married to Collins after the death of his late wife, Sophie.

“So, are you going to tell me what’s eating at you?” he asks from the couch as he grabs the TV remote from my coffee table and flicks to a random channel.

“Just make yourself at home.” I wave a hand in front of me and push off the counter, taking a seat next to him on the couch.

Of all the fucking programs to land on, it has to be the movie *Pretty Woman*.

Jesus, Billie could be a more petite, younger version of Julia Roberts.

“Collins’s favorite movie.” He points the remote at the screen.

That doesn’t surprise me; his pink-haired biker-chick wife is obsessed with the ’80s.

Sawyer briefly glances at me, pulling a deep breath into his lungs and releasing it slowly. “It will get easier—you know that, don’t you? Right now, all you know is a life with Maria as your wife. You will build a new one.”

Elbows braced on my knees, I lean forward and eye him carefully. Sawyer knows what he’s talking about; the guy has dealt with more grief than most. And that’s exactly what a divorce causes—grief.

“Will it though?” I drop my head between my shoulders, knowing he’s right but struggling to let his reassurance sink in.

“Yeah,” he simply replies. “It will. Having the divorce finalized is the closure you need. Up until that point, you were concentrating on legal paperwork and getting yourself set up in a new place. Now that it’s all sorted, your mind has the time to wander, and that’s when shit gets really difficult. It was the same for me when Sophie died. Once her funeral was done and people started going back to their everyday lives, that’s when reality really hit.”

I remember it well. Sawyer was a fucking wreck, curling in on himself and shutting everyone and everything out. While I know that Maria hasn’t died, I’m still determined not to isolate myself. That shit doesn’t do anyone any good.

“I feel like I’m losing my mind.” I speak after maybe thirty seconds, thumbs pressing into the bridge of my nose. I hesitate for a second before the words explode from me like a shaken-up soda bottle. "I'm even crushing on my best friend's daughter, convinced that she finds me attractive." I tag on a dark laugh because, Jesus, it sounded way more fucked up out loud than it had in my head.

When Sawyer doesn't reply, I finally lift my gaze to look at him, cringe tightening every muscle in my jaw.

I can't believe I just admitted that, even to him.

He pauses the movie, remote falling into his lap.

"Wait. Are you talking about Billie? As in Scott's daughter?"

I just nod my head, speech stolen by firsthand embarrassment. Like many of my older teammates, Sawyer has met Scott and Billie a few times—granted, it was several years ago.

I cringe harder at what he must be thinking.

"Emmett, that's—"

I hold up a hand to cut off whatever Sawyer was about to say. I don't want to hear it.

"She turned twenty-one today, so I stopped by to drop off a gift, and ... yeah." I push a hand through my hair, slapping it against a thigh in frustration. "We hadn't seen each other in years, and things were beyond awkward between us. Billie grew up, and I—"

"Grew in a different way?" Sawyer finishes my sentence, one cocky brow raised.

I point a finger at him. "Not funny."

I can tell that he wants to fall over laughing, and honestly, I'd welcome the break in the tension if the roof of my mouth wasn't still burning like a motherfucker.

"She's my best friend's daughter. The girl Maria and I used to take out for ice cream and went on vacation with." My head is back between my shoulders as I release a maniacal groan. "We used to play ultimate frisbee on the beach."

"Shit." Sawyer winces.

"And she's pregnant."

"Shit," he repeats. "Wait, what?! Is it yours?!"

"No, you idiot!" I announce, jumping to my feet at the horrifying thought. "It's some prick's from college who has basically screwed her over. That's why she's home in Brooklyn. She's almost full-term, and there I was, checking out her ass in the living room."

"Shit."

I roll my eyes. "Can you stop saying that?"

He just shrugs. "I don't know what else to say. Other than you know you can't go there."

I deadpan, almost offended that he could ever think I would. "Of course I fucking can't. And that's what I'm saying. I'm losing my goddamn mind over here."

Sawyer considers my words carefully, tongue poking into his right cheek. "You need to get laid."

"Already did. Didn't work."

His eyes bug out. "With whom?"

I take a seat back on the couch. "Some chick in Colorado and then again in Miami. One-night stands aren't my thing."

Sawyer laughs, and I know what's coming. "Just best friend's daughters."

"Not helping," I sing.

He clears his throat of humor and resets himself to a serious demeanor. "This isn't exactly a huge problem. Just keep your distance from her, which sounds like that'll be easy enough since she'll be busy with baby shit in the next few weeks."

"Have you forgotten my friendship with Scott and Freya?" I ask, sounding like a petulant teenager. I might as well be; I'm already checking out someone fourteen years younger than me.

He winces again. "How often would you typically head over to their place?"

"I don't know. It was way less often when I was still married, but since I turned single ... once, maybe twice a week."

"Shit."

I'm ready to throat-punch him.

"You're just going to have to suck it up and control your eyes.

You find her hot. Big deal. Like I said before, once that baby arrives, I doubt you'll see all that much of her." He snaps his fingers in a light-bulb moment. "And that's your excuse right there."

"What excuse?"

He just smiles like he solved the Enigma code. "You won't want to impose on Billie and the new baby by going over on the regular. Suggest Scott meet you in town or at your place."

Part of me wants to argue over how ridiculous this is. Sure, Billie is hot, and my eyes betrayed me a couple of times today. That doesn't mean I have to shift my whole friendship with her dad because of that. The last person I would ever be tempted to touch is Billie Quinn. I value my life—*and my fucking balls*. That said, this does give me a great excuse to avoid bumping into Maria when she inevitably visits Freya, offering the clean break I really need.

"We're supposed to be meeting up on Tuesday afternoon to watch a Champions League game."

Sawyer motions to my TV. "Watch the game here."

"Nothing would ever happen between us," I say, clearing any niggling doubts Sawyer might have. "Billie is more like a niece than anything else, and I'd set our friendship alight if Scott even knew what ran through my head a couple of hours ago." At this point, I want the ground to swallow me whole. "She's pregnant, for God's sake."

A palm rests on my shoulder. "Like you said, buddy, your mind is everywhere after the split from Maria. You're searching for signs of affection and reassurance that you're not past it. My best guess is, your brain is playing tricks on you, and it wasn't the awkward exchange you think it is. Still, no harm in keeping some distance and getting your shit together."

I nod lightly, convincing myself that he's correct.

"Yeah. You're right, man." I pick up the remote and hit Play on the movie, Julia Roberts springing back to life. "This is all in my goddamn head."

CHAPTER SEVEN

BILLIE

Birthday update: lavender bath salts make a fantastic gift for heavily pregnant women.

Not least because they're soothing my aching body, but they're also helping to calm my racing mind.

Everything had to go to shit the second Mom left for a last-minute girls' trip with Maria to Fort Lauderdale. The baby's movements have been reduced for a longer period than normal, and because she can't get a flight back for the next few hours—even if Maria physically flew Mom home—Dad is going to take me for an urgent scan at the hospital.

All I have to do is wait for him to leave work and drive the twenty-minute commute back home, keep calm, and not stay in this bath for too long even though the warm water and lavender scent are all that's preventing me from spiraling into unhelpful thoughts over what could be wrong.

When my phone buzzes on the shelving unit next to the tub, I reach up and grab it, an influx of mixed emotions hitting me when *Tucker* fills the screen. I knew I needed to reach out and let him know what was happening, but I also correctly predicted that

I'd be met with his voicemail. This is him returning my initial worried call—twelve hours later. I might not be his priority any longer—or ever at all—but his baby should be.

"Hi," I immediately say after hitting Accept.

Other than brief texts about potential baby names—which we still haven't agreed on—this is the first time I've spoken to him since I left Austin.

My hand shakes as I pull the phone away from my ear to check the call is still connected and that he didn't butt-dial me by mistake.

"Hi." Tucker's clipped, almost-dismissive tone flips my stomach.

"I called to tell you that—"

"What is it you need, Billie?"

When he cuts me off with venom, I physically pull back in shock, water splashing over the sides of the bath. In the past, I've witnessed Tucker's annoyance, but this is different. He's never spoken to me like this before.

"Because if it's money, then my parents already made their position clear."

"Excuse me?" My voice is hoarse and not as strong as I'd like. Clearing my throat, I straighten my shoulders. "If you'd given me a chance to speak, then you would have already known the reason for my call."

He mumbles something inaudible. It's not even lunchtime in Austin, but I can tell he's out. Music and laughter in the background clueing me in.

When he doesn't speak again, I take it as my cue to continue.

"I called because over the past twenty-four hours, the baby's movements have been more irregular, and the doctors have asked me to head to the hospital for a scan and monitoring."

"I don't see why that's a problem. They're getting bigger, so moving won't be as easy."

Inhaling a deep, lavender-filled breath into my lungs, I blow out a sigh.

I will not lose my shit.

"Mothers are told to keep an eye on fetal movements and note down any change in pattern. Regardless of whatever you might think, the doctors know best."

Another mumbled noise.

"I don't see why this concerns me, Billie. You decided to move back to Brooklyn, so it's not like I can take you to the hospital."

It's not like you ever would anyway.

I fight back a sarcastic retort, eager not to let this conversation descend into a fight, like so many in the past.

"I'm keeping you in the loop as the father," I tell him, amazed that I have to explain myself.

"Who's taking you to the hospital?" It's the first decent question Tucker's asked me in a while.

My shoulders drop an inch from where they were sitting around my ears. "Dad. He's on his way over to pick me up."

The conversation grows even more stilted when a few beats pass with only the sound of music and more laughter, confirming that Tucker didn't hang up.

"Is that all?" he finally asks.

Anger and frustration give way to upset when I realize that he genuinely couldn't care less.

"Yes." My reply is quick, as I'm determined not to reveal the thickness in my throat. "Wait," I add before he inevitably hangs up.

"Yep?"

I don't need to be a genius to figure out that our relationship is over. Still, that doesn't mean that he gets to avoid an acknowledgment. I'm done with Tucker Price treating me like something he just stepped in when all I've ever done is offer him, and his family, my respect. I have two weeks until the due date, and I need to find closure so I can move on and piece my life back together.

It feels too juvenile to simply ask if we're done, and I struggle to find a way to ask the same question without coming off as desperate or needy. I'm neither of those things despite the picture that's been painted of me around campus, rumors fueled by the guy who I know is growing impatient on this call.

"Listen, I gotta get to class in, like, two minutes, so can we—"

"When were you going to grow a pair of balls and admit that you don't want to be a part of my or the baby's life? Because I don't think this was ever about money, Tucker. I think you freaked out at the prospect of becoming a father before you finished college, and now you're running away from your responsibilities." I prod a finger into the center of my chest. I know he can't see me, but the action only deepens my determination. "I mean, you couldn't even bring yourself to end things with me before you were jumping into bed with other girls." I end my speech on a cynical laugh and wait for Tucker to, for once in his life, speak the truth.

After a second, I feel sure he'll drop the call, although what leaves his mouth next is no surprise.

"I'm not talking about this now, Billie."

Climbing out of the bath, I risk slipping with only one free hand to steady me. "Ah, yes, because I'm in the perfect position to bring this conversation up." My best efforts to remain calm fail as I continue ranting. "How about you look at it this way? The sooner you admit that you cheated and that we're through, the sooner the baby and I will be out of your life for good."

"I fucked someone else."

His immediate response, coupled with the cold way he said it, stops me in my tracks. I knew the truth, but I wasn't fully ready to hear it. Even if I'd convinced myself that I was.

Setting my phone down on the sink, I switch it to speaker and snag a towel from the heated radiator, wrapping it around me for warmth.

"Do you have any intention of being around for or after the birth?" I ask, opting to skip over his confession. I got my answer as his former girlfriend, and now I need to know where I stand as a mother.

"Billie ..." This time, when he says my name, Tucker's voice is a little softer.

Maybe his empathetic tone is born out of guilt for his behavior or what he's about to say next, but honestly, I don't much care. Mom is right; I need to start looking after myself because my ex-boyfriend sure as shit isn't going to.

"I'll take that as a no then, shall I?" I'm incredulous, angry, and—for the very first time during my pregnancy—maternal. Rejecting me is one thing, but hurting my unborn child is quite another.

"I never said that," he argues, background music fading out and replaced with traffic noise. Maybe he is on his way to a class and isn't a twenty-four/seven bullshitter.

A message drops down from Dad, and I tap the notification.

DAD

Billie, can you call me, please?

"It's going to be really hard to visit now that you're in Brooklyn."

"I'm in Brooklyn because I was left without a choice or any support in Texas!" I bite out, quickly typing out a response to Dad and setting my phone down on the shelf. "And physical distance shouldn't really matter when it comes to your newborn baby."

"I have finals this year." Tucker is considerably less self-assured than when he first answered the phone.

Good. He should be downright ashamed of himself right now.

"So, no then?" I press once more, now adamant that he'll own his choices.

"Billie—"

"It's a simple answer, Tucker—yes or no," I cut him off, anticipating his brush-off before he said it.

"No, all right?! No!" he growls, his true colors inevitably

surfacing like a poisonous oil slick spreading across crystal ocean water.

Tucker might like to play the nice guy in college, but I know who he is behind closed doors—a selfish prick who can't see past his college degree or the end of his small dick.

"Thank you."

"Thank you?" he chokes out.

Pulling on my bra, I shrug a single shoulder.

This was exactly the closure I needed from him and everything I'd expected, even if it wasn't what I'd hoped for my child. Because they are my child, not Tucker's. He lost that right around thirty seconds ago.

"Yeah, thank you for showing me exactly who I thought you were. Thank you for confirming that my move to Brooklyn was precisely the right call." I pick up my phone, bringing the microphone to my lips. "And thank you for saving my tears. Because I won't be crying a single fucking one over a guy who failed to keep it in his pants for his pregnant girlfriend."

With trembling fingers, I hit End on the call and immediately navigate to Dad's contact, adrenaline surging through me as I move into my bedroom and begin getting dressed, propping my cell between my ear and shoulder.

"Bill." Dad's voice sounds breathless, and I pause, slowly sinking down on the bed.

"What's the matter?"

He draws in another breath, this one sounding pained.

My adrenaline spikes again.

"I've broken my leg pretty badly."

That's when I tune in to the commotion going on around him, voices asking my dad to stay calm.

"What? How?"

He grunts down the phone. "My van tire had a blowout on the way home and I hit a tree. Thankfully no one else is hurt but my leg is ... yeah, it's not good."

I leap to my feet and tear down the stairs, frantically searching for Mom's car keys. She didn't drive to the airport, and I'm on her insurance.

"Where are you? I'll be right there," I confirm, eyes darting around as I continue searching.

Dad's voice is steady and firm. "No, Bill. You need to get to the hospital. Mom's flight got delayed again due to a thunderstorm, but she'll meet me as soon as she arrives in Brooklyn."

"I can't just leave you," I plead.

"You can, and you will, Billie."

"I can't find Mom's car keys. I'll have to take an Uber."

"Hang on a second." More voices, and another—much louder—groan leaves Dad. "They're putting me in the ambulance now. God, Christ, this fucking hurts."

I'm tempted to crack a joke about how it's nothing compared to childbirth, but think better of it.

In two weeks, I'll be the one screaming in agony.

"Emmett is going to give you a ride to the hospital. He just got done with morning skate and has taken a detour from the gym."

I shoot through to the living area and peer through the blinds just as Emmett's Aston Martin rolls up to the curb.

"Your best friend is going to take me to the hospital?" I ask, trying to ignore the subtle shimmer of butterflies as they bounce around in my stomach.

That man is undeniably hot, and I look like a freaking horror show, hair everywhere and no makeup.

"He's the only person available that I trust."

"Sir, we need you to end the call now, so we can administer pain relief."

I head back upstairs and into my bedroom. "Keep me updated, okay?"

"Will do, Bill. I promise everything's going to be all right."

Dad's soft words of reassurance manifest in tears that run

down my cheeks, and I disconnect the call, snagging my purse from the bed as I close my eyes for a long moment.

"Everything's going to be all right."

CHAPTER EIGHT

EMMETT

In between his gasps of pain down the phone, Scott told me that Billie was ready and waiting to head to the hospital. But as I roll up along the sidewalk, there isn't any sign of movement coming from inside the house.

Concerned, I hit Call on Billie's contact and wait for an answer.

"I'm standing at your passenger window, you goof."

I hit Unlock, and she throws her phone into her bag, pulling the door open as she laughs at the way I jumped out of my skin.

Stupidly, I didn't think through how difficult it would be for her to negotiate the low profile of my Aston Martin, but it's not like I had the time to switch to the Mercedes G-Wagon. I was on my way home from skate when I answered Scott's frantic call.

As Billie attempts to lower herself into the car, panic rips through me. "Wait."

"I can do it," she protests, but I'm already rounding the car, taking her red shoulder bag in one hand and her soft palm into my other.

For a brief second, she pauses and turns to me, big pools of green swallowing me whole. She's feeling vulnerable and likely nervous over the scan, and she doesn't need to voice her emotions for me to guess them.

"Let me help you." My voice barely rises above the sound of traffic and swishing trees.

The weather has been really bad lately with invisible black ice scattered around sidewalks. I slipped on an untreated patch on my way to the rink this morning, and the last thing I need is for Billie to overstretch herself, getting in my car. Or worse, fall.

She's a little like her dad, and the conflict to accept my help wars within her, although she eventually yields, allowing me to take her weight as she slowly slips into my black leather bucket seat. I close the door, heading back to the driver's side.

"It looks good on you." Billie's smile is full and bratty as she drops her eyes to her bag, still looped over my shoulder.

I climb into the car and turn the heating up a couple of degrees. "You think?" I reply, attempting my best Vogue pose. I look like a complete idiot, but at least it pulls a bubble of laughter from her.

As I set the purse in Billie's lap, I get my first real chance to take her in. I know I should be halfway down the street right now, eyes centered firmly on the road ahead. The plan was to keep my distance, but I guess the universe had other ideas, like me taking her to the hospital and sitting within a foot of her while she looks cute as fuck in a fluffy green sweater and blue jeans that have to be sprayed on. And let's not talk about her knitted black beanie or the hot tan leather boots that hug her shapely calves.

Drive, Emmett. Fucking drive.

"How are you feeling?" I ask, pulling into the street and hitting the gas.

From beside me, Billie turns to gaze out of the passenger window. With a light shrug, she says, "Worried about Dad. Feeling like I should be there with him or at least helping with the recovery of his van."

Scott isn't what I was referring to, although it doesn't surprise me that she's more concerned about someone else's well-being above her own. I remember when she was around sixteen, and we were having a barbecue in Scott and Freya's yard; Billie came tearing into the garden, holding a small bird that had broken its wing. Most people—no, nearly all people—would've let the poor thing pass, but not Billie. She basically emptied her modest savings to have the bird treated by a vet. When news broke that the little dude had made it, she insisted that Scott set up a birdhouse in the huge oak tree at the end of their yard, just in case he needed a place to live.

At the time, I thought it was madness, but now, five years later and with a divorce under my belt, I can appreciate how temporary life or things can be.

"Your dad will be fine. His leg will heal and he's damn lucky that his injuries aren't more serious." I attempt to soothe her, taking a left and pulling up to a stoplight.

Billie's delicate fingers twist together in her lap, her red manicure chipped on several fingernails.

"Once he's through surgery and in recovery, the pain will be way better. Then it's all about rehabilitation."

Memories of the pain I endured when I tore my ACL a couple of seasons back resurface, and I quickly push them away. I was convinced that my career was through, sending me into a deep spiral of depression. Part of me thinks that while it wasn't the end of hockey, it was the start of the end for my marriage. Maria was hell-bent on me calling it time in the NHL, frequently giving me long speeches about how "everything happens for a reason" and maybe I "should take this as a hint to call it quits." When I look back, her lack of empathy was palpable, as was her agenda to control another part of my life. Even if I refused to see it at the time, it's as clear as day to me now.

When the light turns green and I pull off, Billie begins chewing on the edge of her right thumb.

"I was actually asking how you were doing," I clarify.

"Just got to get through today and the childbirth, and then

I'll be golden." She reels off major life events like a straightforward grocery list as we pull into the hospital parking lot.

Billie's barely looked at me the entire journey, and when she eventually shows me her eyes, I work out why. Unshed tears form a gloss over them.

Stressed and trying to keep it together, Billie hastily goes to unclip her belt, frantic movements indicating that she's far from okay.

I rest a tentative hand on her upper arm, silently asking her to pause for a moment.

She looks down at our connection and then up at me. One tear clinging to her long lashes. She isn't wearing an inch of makeup; I can tell because her prominent freckles aren't hidden behind concealer.

"Do you want me to wait here?" I ask, respecting the privacy she may need and noting that the pathway up to the maternity building is fully salted.

To my surprise, Billie shakes her head, shocking me further when she adds, "I don't want to be alone for the scan."

"Y-you want me to come in with you?"

"Yeah," she confirms, pressing the button to unclip her belt. "Today has already been crappy, and if the sonographer tells me something bad, I don't want to be alone when I completely lose my shit."

"ALL RIGHT, Miss Quinn, if you can hop up on the bed, then we can check everything over for you."

"I'm not *hopping* anywhere," Billie quietly whispers to me, popping the top button on her jeans.

When the sonographer turns her back and heads to the sink to wash her hands, I drop down into a deep lunge, keeping my hands in my pockets as I do it.

"Baby-free and flexible," I goad.

She just rolls her eyes and expertly hoists herself onto the bed, pulling her sweater up to reveal a naked bump before tucking it under her bra like she's been through this routine a million times over.

This whole thing is deeply personal, and I have zero right to be here. But as I pull up a plastic chair and sit next to my best friend's daughter, I know this is exactly what she needs.

Five minutes with Tucker fucking Price—that's all I'll need.

The sonographer points at me and looks at Billie. "Is this Dad?"

To prevent choking on my tongue, I bite down on it instead. Hard.

"No," she replies with an uncomfortable chuckle. "This is a family friend, Emmett. He gave me a ride here, and I asked him to sit with me while we do this." Her voice drops a couple of octaves, laced with a mixture of sadness and frustration. "The actual dad is in Texas."

I don't miss the sonographer's eyes as they flick to mine before she gets to work, smoothing jelly across Billie's bump and applying the probe.

It's possible she's a hockey fan, and since I'm a veteran these days, my face is well known. That's not the gut feeling I'm getting from her though, more a look of judgment or even uncertainty on Billie's behalf. I guess, to her, this whole setup is kind of weird. Why wouldn't she be here with a friend or her mom?

Reaching up, I take Billie's hand in mine. I don't interlace our fingers, simply wrapping my palm around the back of her hand, resting it beside her on the bed. The sonographer tracks the movement as Billie continues to focus on the screen, totally tuned out to what's happening around her.

My eyes meet the sonographer's, a silent message passing between us.

Judge away because this woman right here needs someone, and in this moment, I'm all she has.

"Oh, there we go!" Like she's hit the reset button on her

professionalism, the sonographer moves the probe half an inch, resting it over the baby's heartbeat.

The sound is clear and strong, and I feel Billie's fingers relax.

"So, everything's okay then?" Billie asks, hope evident in her tone.

The sonographer remains silent, and I'm ready to shove the probe up her ass when she eventually answers Billie. "Everything looks to be completely normal and what we would expect at this point in your pregnancy. However, we would like to monitor fetal movement for the next couple of hours. I'm sure the doctor explained this to you when you called the hospital."

"Yes. They said that it's standard procedure for reduced fetal movements."

I watch the column of Billie's throat work as the sonographer wipes away jelly residue, and Billie sits up, legs dangling over the edge as she lowers her sweater and climbs down from the bed.

"Everything is going to be fine," I quietly whisper.

She just smiles at that. "Do you have time to stick around, or should I get an Uber?"

"I'm not going anywhere," I immediately respond.

Billie winces at me. "I'm sorry I didn't mention the monitoring part. With my dad and this whole morning, I totally forgot to warn you how long we could be in the hospital for." She puffs out a frustrated breath. "You probably have way more import—"

"There's nothing more important than this, Bill," I confirm, shaking my head at her slowly before looking back at the monitor. "Do you want the scan images?"

"Oh, we don't normally offer those for non-routine appointments," the sonographer explains before Billie can answer me.

I've never been gifted at telepathy, but I'm pretty sure the sonographer has no issue reading my mind from the expression I give her.

"Did you want the images?" I repeat my question to the person whom it was originally directed at.

Billie takes her handbag off the back of my chair and hooks it over her shoulder, turning on her heel to look at the sonographer. "How much do they cost?"

She waves a hand at Billie, eyes still fixed on mine. "Nothing at all, Miss Quinn. Let me go and grab them for you now."

I watch the sonographer leave and close the door behind her and then focus my attention on Billie. "How about after we're done in the hospital, I take you somewhere for a late lunch?"

I'm ready to shove my fist straight down my throat.

Stop talking, Emmett. Distance, remember? Put distance between you and your friend's hot-as-fuck daughter.

Billie stays quiet for a second, twisting her full lips in thought.

"Or I can just give you a ride back to your place." I keep talking, secretly hoping that she'll take me up on the lunch offer.

"Well, by the time we're finished up here, I'll probably be able to manage a steak."

I balk at her, equally amused and impressed at the way she isn't afraid to go all in. Especially after the morning she's had.

"I was thinking more like a burger and fries."

She sets a sarcastic palm on my shoulder, pink lips curving into a wicked grin that tightens my chest. "When the millionaire hockey player offers to take the poor student out for a meal, she would be foolish to accept anything less than the whole nine yards."

CHAPTER NINE

BILLIE

When I suggested steak, I figured Emmett would head for a LongHorn or Black Angus Steakhouse.

But after everything came back fine at the hospital, that's not where we ended up.

"Is it cooked well enough for you?" Emmett points his fork at my plate, bringing my attention back to the table and away from our stunning surroundings.

The Skillet is one of the nicest steakhouses in the whole of Manhattan, the place where my parents celebrated their fifteenth wedding anniversary—and Dad still jokes about repaying the loan to cover the bill.

It's only late lunchtime, but the restaurant windows are covered, creating a private and romantic atmosphere.

Emmett's handsome face glows in the light cast from the candle in the center of our table.

"This steak is the best I've ever had," I say around a mouthful, and it truly is. I can't remember the last time I ate this well or even finished a meal.

Emmett sets his fork down and leans forward, bracing his

elbows on the table before folding his hands under his chin. He observes me carefully as I pick up a fry and dip it in steak sauce. He looks more relaxed than he has the past couple of times I've seen him.

"You didn't need to go all out, you know? I was only joking when I said *the whole nine yards.*"

"This is the only place I'll eat steak."

I roll my eyes at him in jest. "You have more money than sense."

He just smirks, picking up his knife and fork and cutting into his steak. "I know the owners. Sometimes, the guys come here after games."

It's easy to forget that Emmett is a huge NHL player whose face is famous across Brooklyn. To me, he's just my dad's best friend and someone I've known most of my life. I might tease him about money and being big time, although his attitude couldn't be further from that. Emmett has always been a humble guy with a big heart, and the way he comforted me today was evidence that not much had changed over the past three years.

"Do you still talk to Maria, or has all contact been cut?"

He stiffens at my question, and I instantly regret asking it. It's not really my place to.

"Sorry." I grimace. "I shouldn't be nosy."

Pulling off his glasses, he sets them on the table and massages the bridge of his nose, closing his eyes as he does it.

"I only mentioned her in case you wanted to talk about it," I offer. "I know she meant a lot to you, and you probably miss her."

Something in Emmett's expression reveals that my assumption might not be completely accurate. I knew very little about their marriage other than my memories of Maria always vying for control over every conversation. But that Christmas before I left for college showed a different side of her. I felt the animosity grow between them. The clipped way she spoke to him when he and I were setting the dinner table. And then they were barely out of our front door before she was waving her arms in his face as they walked down our driveway, in the middle of a fight.

Spying on them through the blinds was probably a bit intrusive, but like I just admitted to Emmett, I'm nosy.

"I don't talk much about Maria to anyone, and I haven't spoken to her in weeks. I guess there isn't much to say."

I nod once and snag a green bean from my plate. It's cooked perfectly.

"I get that," I reply, swallowing down a mouthful. "It's the same way with Tucker. Even though we are going to have a baby together."

Emmett presses his full lips into a thin line, sitting back in his chair as he thinks over my statement. He folds his corded arms across his chest, the sleeves on his gray henley pushed up to the elbows.

I drop my eyes to my plate, eager not to be caught in the act of checking him out.

"Maybe I'm overstepping here, Bill. But surely, new parents—whether they're still together or not—need to be in contact."

He isn't overstepping; he's absolutely right.

I pick up my water glass and bring it to my lips, eyes back on his when I say, "Open communication only works if both parties are willing to cooperate."

Irritation pulls Emmett's brows together. "Tucker won't even speak with you?"

"Barely. I had a delightful phone call with him this morning, where he made it pretty clear that he didn't care about me or the baby. I didn't bother to text him and let him know that everything was normal, only my parents."

He shifts in his chair, not immediately responding. When he picks up his soda and takes a large pull, I watch the tendons in his jaw work. He's mad on my behalf, although he doesn't need to be. I can look after myself just fine.

"I'm sorry, Billie," is all he says as he sets the glass back down on the table and asks a server for another bottle of still water.

Emmett moves and speaks with such confidence. He's all man but gracious in how he carries himself, and I conclude that it only adds to my attraction. No one can ever know that I have the hots for him. Emmett discovering my crush would be enough to bury me alive with embarrassment.

It would also end the most unlikely of friendships. Who knew that a thirty-five-year-old pro hockey player would be one of the best and most valuable people in my life right now?

I opt to change course, redirecting the conversation away from my ex-boyfriend. "Thanks for giving me a ride to the hospital."

When the server sets a fresh bottle of water down, Emmett asks him to hold off pouring and does it himself, twisting the metal cap and refilling my glass before his own.

"He's a fucking prick."

The way he bites out his words catches me off guard. I've never witnessed Emmett lose his temper, although he's right on the edge, and I know it.

"Scott told me that he was cheating on you, and that's why you came home."

I chug a large mouthful of water and swallow it quickly. A huge part of me wants to tell him to leave it.

But my subconscious wills the smaller, more open part of me to speak, and when I do, a cathartic feeling inflates my lungs.

"At first, I gave him the benefit of the doubt. It was all rumors and my suspicions and nothing solid. I didn't want to accuse him of something he hadn't done and believe the bitches on campus over the trust I originally placed in him. That didn't seem fair."

Emmett cocks his head to one side, studying me intently. "How old are you again?"

"Twenty-one. Why?"

He leans forward and steals a fry from my plate, shrugging as he eats it. "That isn't an attitude typical of a twenty-one-year-old. I wouldn't have seen it like that when I was your age."

Seizing the opportunity to be cocky and act exactly my age, I reach across the table and steal a piece of asparagus from his plate, smiling as I bite the end.

"I guess I'm not like most twenty-one-year-olds."

Emmett's steely-gray eyes drop to my mouth, a pink stain creeping across his high cheekbones. Like he's trying to gather himself, he swipes his glasses from the table and sets them back on his face.

A heavy awkwardness falls between us. We've always laughed and joked around, but I've never sensed a shift like the one taking hold in this room.

"I'm just saying that Tucker is a dick, is all," Emmett voices, his tone professional.

I nod and try to keep the conversation light, dropping the asparagus stalk to my plate. "That he is. Trouble is, like my mom said, I can't control his actions or force him to step up and be a dad. All I can do is try and get through these next few months and then figure out finding a job."

Emmett balks at me. "You're not going back to college?"

I want to laugh out loud at the thought. "Tune in to reality, Emmett." I circle my huge stomach and then point at my face. "As if I can finish my political science degree and then move on to law school while single-handedly raising a child. The only way I could do that would be with a nanny. An expensive nanny."

"What about your mom?" he suggests. "You could transfer to a local college, and she could help. I know she'd want to."

"And quit her full-time job as a bank teller?" I retort. "I can just see it now ..." My voice turns sarcastic as I mimic her manager. "*Sure, sure, Freya. You bring the screaming baby into work with you, and we'll turn the place into a day care.*"

Emmett narrows his eyes at me, fighting not to laugh at my wicked sense of humor. "I take back what I said. You make the perfect twenty-one-year-old."

I point at his iPhone set on the table, the model being at least three years out of date. "The same could be said for you. Only older people aren't bothered about the latest technology."

His lips tip into a smile, and as quickly as the atmosphere turned awkward, normal service between us resumes. A rumble of laughter echoes in Emmett's chest as he gazes down at his phone.

"I guess I should update the phone no?"

I shrug. "I was only messing with you. I couldn't give a shit about technology, so long as it works. I'm loving the admission that you're old though."

"Brat."

I point to my face. "Me?"

Emmett's eyes narrow further. "You know you are, Billie."

CHAPTER TEN

EMMETT

"Would it be tempting fate if I declared this season as my best yet?" Jack gazes around our group, eyes finally landing on me as we stand at the edge of the practice rink and drink some fluids.

"With two months left in the season, plus playoffs after that, I'd say that's a brave call to make," Archer replies, trying to catch his breath like the rest of us.

Coach has gone hard with us today after we picked up a loss in Pittsburg. We should've come away with the *W*, but our game was off the pace, other than Jack, who finds top performances from nowhere.

Balancing on one skate, I flex my knee, trying to be as inconspicuous as possible. After two rounds of surgery and the best rehabilitation program available, it still gives me a hard time. Maria was probably right when she said that most players would've hung up their skates and called it quits on their career. What she failed to appreciate is that hockey is more than just a job or a paycheck; it's who I am, and now more than ever, it feels like the only constant in my life.

My perceptive captain drops his eyes to my leg, studying the way I flex the joint. His brows knit together as he returns his eyes to mine.

"Jenna is meeting me at Lloyd's later if you losers want to tag along." Tommy collides with Jack's and Archer's backs as he glides up behind them, wrapping his arms around their necks. "If you're seen out with me, I'll improve your street cred."

Archer rears back, offended at his defenseman. "Did you ever ask yourself why I'm the January model each year for the charity calendar?"

Tommy just smirks, delighted that he's hooked his goalie so easily. "Because the PR team figured that it can only get better from there."

I probably shouldn't encourage our chaotic bad boy, but a laugh leaves me regardless.

"You see, Emmett finds me funny because he knows I'm right." Tommy tips his chin at me.

Banter like this is ordinarily right in our captain's wheelhouse, although I don't need to look at Jack to know why he hasn't engaged with the others; I can already sense his eyes as they bore into me.

"Moore," Jensen interrupts Archer and Tommy's bickering. "Do you plan on finishing up today's session, or are you declaring an early retirement?" Jensen stands at center ice, hands on his hips as he waits for his goalie to quit messing around.

When Tommy and Archer skate away, leaving me alone with Jack, I turn back to the boards and snag my water bottle, keeping myself busy.

My efforts to delay Jack's inevitable inquisition are futile, and I know it.

"Have you spoken to the trainer about that?" Jack's simple nod toward my knee leaves me in no doubt over what he's referring to.

"My knee flares up from time to time, especially after hard

sessions like today. We're deep into the season, and aches and pains are nothing new for me."

Jack clears his throat, and I continue, sounding defensive, "Run the clock on another decade, and you'll know exactly what I mean."

Jack's one of the youngest captains in the league, and even if the accolade is completely deserved, he sometimes lacks the understanding of a veteran captain like Sawyer.

When Adrian Carney, our general manager, was appointed several seasons back, he initially showed an interest in me being Sawyer's successor. He wanted someone with an experienced head who could handle media responsibilities with ease. I was his top pick to take the captaincy, and I wanted it so badly. Aside from winning the Cup, it was the final check on my career bucket list. Then came the injury, which essentially destroyed my chances. Other than me, Jack was the obvious choice, but for very different reasons—at twenty-seven, his captaincy tenure has the potential to be long-term, he's probably the best player on the team, and he's definitely the guy who holds everyone together when shit gets rough.

All that said, I'm not ashamed to admit the kernel of resentment and jealousy I felt toward the guy who had waltzed onto the team and taken the starting center position and then the entire wheel. A lot of the guys felt like he'd only gotten his shot on the team because he was Coach's stepson, and, yeah, I partly bought into that line of thought.

Within the space of a few months, Jack proved all his doubters wrong, including me. Pushing past the resentment wasn't easy. I didn't see the light and drop any hard feelings altogether until last season. But that was on me and my own sense of pride and self-worth. Jack being captain was the reason we lifted the Cup last season, and consequently, I got to at least check off one of my career goals.

"You make me nervous sometimes—you know that?"

I throw Jack a quizzical look. "Why?"

He pulls on his drink and sets the bottle down on top of the boards. "Of all the guys on this team, you're the only one I can't read. I'm Edward Cullen, and you're my Bella. Every time I try to hear your thoughts, I come up empty."

I close my eyes, part amused and part perplexed by this guy. "I haven't read those books."

Jack balks at me in a similar way Archer did to Tommy a few minutes ago. "What about the movies?" He nods to himself like he's recalling his favorite scenes. "Kendra and I had a watch-a-thon during the bye week."

Shaking my head, I clamp a hand on his shoulder. "All right, Edward, I'm your Bella. So long as you promise not to suck my blood or some shit like that."

Grin fading to a more serious expression, he checks over his shoulder, looking to see if Coach needs us yet.

He turns back to me, face now stoic. "I need you to tell me the truth. As your captain, I need to know if you're good for the rest of the season. You and Tommy are our first choice on the defensive line, and you know that. If we need to give you less ice time, then we ca—"

"I don't need a rest," I voice, cutting across his sentence. "I just need to be more thorough with recovery after games and probably step sessions back up with the trainer."

My face is a plea for him to drop the uncertainty and give me the benefit of the doubt.

Just like I did when he was a rookie.

The next few seconds could only be described as a stare-down, although it isn't aggressive, more an analysis of each other's thoughts.

Jack breaks first, and I heave an internal sigh of relief. Maybe he can sense how much I need hockey in the wake of the breakdown in my marriage, or perhaps he recognizes the chance his teammates gave him when he first stepped onto the team.

I don't know. I'm just grateful for the reprieve.

"Do you want to hit Lloyd's tonight?"

"Are you going?" I reply, pleased at the change in subject even though I'm not all that eager to head out.

I was hoping to see Scott after his surgery, but a week later, he still isn't discharged from the hospital, and by the time I get home from practice and change, visiting hours will be over.

Jack scratches at the back of his neck. "I feel like the team needs to bond over the shitshow in Pittsburg. I'll probably show up for a couple of hours."

My low mood tempts me to decline and spend the night slumped on my couch with a meal for one.

"You should come out." Jack's encouraging voice has me wondering if he is, in fact, Edward Cullen.

Going out with the guys is an option I didn't have when I was married to Maria, and I know I should take advantage of my newfound freedom. Still, the only time I've felt remotely motivated to socialize is when I've been around Billie.

"Listen," Jack continues, "if I'm coming out and choosing you guys above my beautiful baby girl and wife, then you can pry yourself away from a date night with yourself and whatever trash fiction you do like to read."

"Thrillers. I like to read thrillers," I clarify.

Jack turns his nose up. "To each their own, I guess. There's something about a romance that just gets me going." He leans into me like he's sharing the secret to happiness—maybe he is. "Kendra has a small collection of sports romance books, and let me tell you ..." His eyebrows rise into his hairline. "You can learn some stuff from those pages, buddy. I've made her scr—"

My hand shoots up in surrender. "Yeah, yeah, great. Whatever you say, Cap."

With his arms folded across his chest, challenge blooms in Jack's eyes. "If I promise to stop talking about romance books, do you promise to join us tonight at Lloyd's?"

"You speak like I have a choice in the matter," I huff out and take another drink.

He smacks me on the chest, interpreting my response as a yes.

"Good man. You never know; you might even find a girl to have a little fun with. I think it's high time you hooked up."

I'm tempted to reveal that I already tried that and it didn't work. The words don't leave my mouth though as unsolicited thoughts of Billie come flooding back.

What should've been a quick lunch after the hospital turned into three hours of us talking about anything and everything. From her courses in college to the "friends" she made and lost when everything went down with the pregnancy and Tucker.

When I'd first set eyes on Billie a couple of weeks ago, I had been shocked at how much she'd changed and even more freaked out by her beauty. Last week, as we ate steak, she surprised me again, only this time it was at her maturity and levelheadedness. I meant it when I told her that not many twenty-one-year-olds would have approached the cheating rumors like she did. Hell, my ex-wife couldn't stop shooting baseless accusations at me, no matter how many ways I tried to prove my loyalty to her.

Tucker Price is a fucking idiot. I don't need all thirty-five years of my experience to conclude that.

"I'm not interested in getting with anyone." I eventually supply Jack with an answer as we slowly glide toward center ice and join the others. "I need to keep my life simple and uncomplicated."

CHAPTER ELEVEN

EMMETT

The way Lloyd's is packed to the rafters is like a baptism of fire for my single status. If we weren't holed up in the private section, we definitely wouldn't have seats.

Don't get me wrong; I've been out before with the guys, but never without a "curfew" in place or one hand on my pocket, feeling for the familiar vibration of Maria's call.

"It's like a freaking cattle market in here," Jensen Jones's wife, Kate, yells across the booth.

We're only sitting a few feet apart, and even then it's hard to hold a conversation.

Christ, I'm fucking old.

While most of the twenty-somethings in this bar are approaching the resident DJ—that none of us had any idea would be playing tonight—requesting songs, I'm tempted to head over and ask him to turn whatever shit he has spinning down so I can at least keep my hearing.

I nod over at Kate. Other than her being in her early forties with blonde hair and blue eyes, I don't know all that much about Jensen's wife.

"If this is what I can expect on the rare nights out we get, I'm calling a hard pass, right here, right now," she huffs out to Felicity.

Literally everyone is out tonight, reaffirming that I was right to make the effort and put on a white button-down and black jeans. It would've looked bad if I hadn't shown, even if I'm already counting down the minutes until I can leave.

Jack sets a beer down in front of me and Sawyer before sliding two more across to Archer and Tommy. "These are on the house. Apparently, an anonymous Blades fan picked up the round."

"Can't be much of a fan if they're plying my team with booze," Coach puffs out, earning an eye roll from Jensen.

He picks up his own beer and takes a large pull, setting it down on a satisfied exhale. "I personally think the beer tastes better in Brooklyn. Or maybe I just got tired of the same bars in Seattle."

"Loud music and beers aside ..." Felicity wraps an arm around Kate's shoulders, pulling her into her side. They couldn't look any more different since Felicity has dark brown hair, but you can tell that they've been friends for years. "I'm just happy to have my friend back with me. Killing it in the New York office together while we make plans to take over the world." She winks at Kate as they share an inside joke.

Kate looks mildly placated by her friend, her frown tipping into a smile. "If the twins hate it, I'm heading back to Seattle."

"Umm, and what about me?" Jensen interjects. "I just signed a permanent coaching contract with the Blades."

Picking up her wine, Kate takes a casual sip, eyeing Coach Morgan carefully. She sets the glass back down and casts her eyes around the table. "Listen, there's no such thing as a watertight contract."

She fixes her eyes on her husband, and I watch the way he visibly melts.

Damn. He has it bad for her.

"You married a lawyer, JJ." She addresses her husband, using a nickname that makes him beam. "You should know how contracts truly work."

Silence falls across the table, and I take it as my cue to leave. As much as I appreciate a beer bought by a stranger, the anti-inflammatories I'm taking for my knee do not mix well with alcohol.

Approaching the bar, I raise a hand and request a soda from the bartender, pulling out my phone when I feel a vibration in my pocket.

I flip my cell over, knowing it isn't from Maria and I won't need to cancel my drink order.

BILLIE

So, guess what.

A smile tugs at my lips as the bartender slides a soda into my hand.

ME

You tried on the fluffy socks, and they were actually amazing.

BILLIE

No, they made my swollen feet way too hot. The lavender bath salts, on the other hand, were an unexpected triumph. Bravo.

ME

Was that actually why you messaged me?

BILLIE

No. My water just broke.

I fight to keep the sip of soda I just took inside my mouth.

ME

Jesus Christ. Is Freya home?

BILLIE

Yes. I don't need another ride to the hospital, so don't panic. But I thought you'd want to know I'm in an early labor, and it really isn't that bad so far. Although give it a few hours, and you'll probably hear my screams.

ME

Unlikely. I can barely hear anything in this bar.

It's difficult to describe the feeling as I hit Send on my last message. All I know is it feels uneasy, maybe even unnatural, and I don't like it.

BILLIE

Taking advantage of the single life now that Maria isn't keeping tabs on you?

ME

Aren't you in labor?

I let the Maria comment slide. Billie's conclusions are right even if I've no idea how she reached them.

BILLIE

Apparently, I need to distract my mind and relax so the contractions progress.

ME

And you thought that you'd achieve that by messaging me?

BILLIE

Right? What was I thinking?

ME

If you must know, I was dragged out by my teammates, and I'm standing by the bar, drinking a soda.

BILLIE

Party on, old man.

ME

Brat.

BILLIE

But seriously, you're standing on your own in the bar? Surely, you have women surrounding you from every angle now that the world knows that Emmett Richards is officially back on the market.

I should probably pocket my phone and ignore Billie's last text.

That's definitely what I should do.

ME

What are you trying to insinuate, Miss Quinn? I'm old and a little slow on the uptake.

I chug the rest of my soda, gripping my phone tightly in my palm as I watch Billie type and then stop, and then begin typing again. My heart hammers in my chest, excitement sparking through me for the first time since I can remember.

Technically, I'm doing nothing wrong. Realistically, I'm walking a tightrope.

BILLIE

Don't play dumb, Emmett. You know precisely what I'm saying. Or have you not caught sight of your reflection before?

I decide to take Billie's message as the compliment it is.

ME

Don't make me blush in public, please. I'm trying to come off as cool in a sea of twenty-something adults.

BILLIE

Well, take it from a twenty-something woman —you're cool. And you should definitely have a good time tonight. Switch up your soda for a beer to start.

Speaking to Jack about my injury was like pulling teeth, but my fingers move across the keyboard with ease. As easy as it would be to glide them through Billie's soft waves.

ME

Truthfully, I'm not drinking alcohol because I can't. My knee isn't the best, and I'm self-medicating.

Billie knows all about what I went through. While we didn't speak much when she was in college, I do remember her making one frantic phone call to me when news broke of the injury, along with images of me in a knee brace. Over and over, she repeated that my career wasn't through and that I'd come back stronger.

My smile grows broader at the memory.

BILLIE

I don't like any part of your last message. What do you mean "self-medicating"? Are you seeing the trainer?

ME

Has anyone ever told you that you're bossy as shit?

BILLIE

Shut up and answer my questions.

I throw my head back, laughter bursting out of me.

"Who's got you all worked up?"

A familiar female voice I haven't heard in weeks pulls me back into the room, blaring music filling my eardrums once more.

I slip my cell into my pocket before Maria gets a chance to read Billie's name.

"What are you doing here?" I automatically ask, turning to take in my ex-wife.

She looks nice in a long-sleeved black dress that hits just above her knee, along with knee-high black leather boots. But despite the way she looks or how beautiful she is, nothing about her presence changes the regular beat of my heart. I remember a time when I could barely breathe when she walked into a room. And now? Now it feels like I'm scrambling for words because there's nothing more left to say.

We just ... died.

"Here with some work friends," she replies, tossing her long, dark hair over one shoulder.

A waft of familiar perfume hits me, but again, I feel nothing.

I'm tempted to point out that she rarely did that when we were married, let alone show up at a place where she knew my teammates and their partners hung out. But what's the point? All it would do was create tension and draw out a conversation that I already want to bring to an end.

Maria hesitates for a beat, brown eyes searching mine.

"Are you dating, Emmett?"

If the bar wasn't directly behind me, I'd take a step back to create some space between us.

"I don't see how that has anything to do with you, Maria," I volley back.

She steels her shoulders, ready to double down. I can predict her next move from a mile away.

"I'd just like to know what's going on"—she tips her chin at the pocket holding my phone—"so I can be prepared for whatever supermodel you're pictured with next week."

Closing my eyes, I remind myself that nothing good can come from arguing with her. We're divorced and belong in each other's past.

"I'm not seeing anyone, Maria."

She scoffs lightly and lifts a champagne glass to her lips, taking a small sip. Her eyes dart briefly to my group of friends. They could've been her friends, too, if she'd given them a chance.

"But you will be soon."

"Are you seeing anyone?"

I couldn't care less, but I'll do anything to remove the spotlight. It's hard to believe that I'm talking to a woman in her mid-thirties who flies planes for a living. Confidence should ooze from her.

"I've been on a few dates," she says, swirling the bubbles around in her glass.

If she's trying to make me jealous, then she isn't succeeding, only underlining a level of hypocrisy I didn't think she was capable of.

Done with this conversation, I point at my teammates, noticing Jack is keeping a watchful eye on us. I'm sure he's thinking the same thing as me: *What the fuck is she doing here?*

"Well, it was great to see you and everything, but I've got a group of friends waiting for me," I confirm.

Her stony face softens a fraction. I know she's been hurt by the divorce as much as I have. The difference is, I know the only way to move on and heal is to do exactly that.

"Billie just went into labor."

Her words stop me in my tracks, and I spin on my heel to face her.

Maybe it's just my imagination or my mind playing tricks on me, but I swear I catch a smile as it momentarily pulls at her lips.

"I know," I tell her. "Scott got in touch."

I turn over my shoulder to look at my friends again, and Jack is still fixated on us both.

"Is that all, or did you need something else?"

She just shrugs, taking another sip of champagne. I don't like the way she's acting, but, hey, that's nothing new.

“No, that’s all I need to know. Have a great night, Emmett, and enjoy your free drinks. I’ll likely catch you sometime after the baby arrives.”

CHAPTER TWELVE

BILLIE

Big blue eyes framed by thick, dark lashes stare back at me from the bassinet set in the corner of my bedroom.

I'm pretty sure this is the first time Blake has been simultaneously awake and not screaming until her little lungs couldn't scream anymore.

Sitting on the bed next to her, I heave a sigh of relief. It's been a week since we returned from the hospital, and in the ten days Blake has been on this earth, a minute hasn't passed without my mom by my side, helping me navigate breastfeeding, changing diapers, and generally offering me respite where she can.

With Dad completely out of action and unable to work until his leg is healed, the original plan she had—to take extended unpaid leave, as agreed with her boss—has gone up in flames.

We need the money, and the only one capable of earning right now is Mom.

As Blake drifts into a peaceful sleep, the faint noise of our front door opening causes her to stir, but mercifully, it isn't enough to wake her entirely.

"Hey." I hear Emmett's muted voice as it filters from the bottom of the stairs. "Sorry I'm a bit late. Practice overran, and the traffic was fucking terrible."

My dad responds with something, although it isn't loud enough for me to make it out, and I kick my feet up onto the bed, lying down and closing my eyes. Seeing Emmett would be great, but keeping Blake asleep and grabbing some myself is what I need, regardless of the shitty timing.

I've got no idea what time it is or how long has passed when I snap my eyes open and stare straight at the bedroom door.

"Hey." Emmett's hand is all I can see as it wraps around the doorjamb. "Is it okay if I come in?"

I quickly sit up and attempt to fix my hair as I sleepily reply, "Yeah, sure."

His gray eyes land on me first before tracking to the bassinet, reminding me of the first time we set eyes on each other following my return from college. Every time I'm with Emmett, I'm Billie Quinn and not Billie the mom, and I like the way that makes me feel.

Slipping a hand into the pocket of his black jeans, he crouches down beside Blake as she happily sleeps away, hands raised above her head and sucking on a pacifier.

Her mass of dark hair reminds me of Tucker, but she has my freckles and nose.

One thing I've noticed about guys, especially ones who aren't fathers themselves: they're often clueless as to how to act around young kids and babies. They stand awkwardly or freeze completely on the spot.

Emmett does neither as he very gently rocks Blake's bassinet the second she begins to stir again, soothing her back into a peaceful rest.

I look on, still dressed in last night's pajamas, but not much caring either.

He pulls a silent breath into his lungs. "She's beautiful, Bill. You did really good."

Emmett knows the birth wasn't completely straightforward. Every single part of my birthing plan went out the window, replaced with a forceps delivery that I guess I should've expected, given Blake's size. I needed stitches, and the doctors kept me under close monitoring for an extra day before finally discharging us back home.

Adjusting the pillows behind me, I reach over and grab my water glass, taking a couple of sips before setting it back down on the nightstand. "Yeah, she's a stunner."

Emmett's eyes are back on mine. "How much sleep have you been getting?"

I shrug like it's no big deal when I'd actually murder for an unbroken three hours. "Not much. Blake has colic, and it's been really bad."

I know I look like shit. This past week, I feel like I've aged at least a decade. Even if I had the time for my skin care routine, there isn't an illuminating eye mask or brand of concealer powerful enough to hide the dark circles around my eyes.

"I knew you were having a girl," he says, briefly turning back to look at my daughter. He rises to his full stature, towering over me as he pushes his second hand into the other pocket of his jeans. "And Blake is a really pretty name."

I suppress a yawn, attempting to hide it with a hand. "It was my first choice and Tucker's last, so it seemed like the best option."

His expression immediately morphs from relaxed to uptight, lines creasing into his forehead. "Have you heard from him?"

I thought I'd be more disappointed to get nothing more than an acknowledging text back from my ex-boyfriend, shortly followed by a second message, confirming that he will "meet the financial obligations as the father."

In reality, I'm not. In time, I'm sure I'll feel sad on Blake's behalf and maybe even sorry that I picked a heartless prick for a father, but right now, the cycle of survival I'm in won't allow me to think past the next five minutes or when I might be able to grab my next nap.

I shake my head, but don't say anything.

Emmett's exhale is audible and laced with frustration as he takes a seat at the foot of my bed.

"How long have you been here?" I ask.

Emmett pulls his hand from his jeans, pushing back the sleeve on his Blades hoodie to check his watch.

"Whoa!" I quietly announce, rearing back in jest. "I'm blinded by the diamonds on your Rolex."

He looks at me, deadpan. "About an hour. I left your gift downstairs."

This time, when I pull back, it's from shock. "Gift?"

He rolls his lips together, and I swear to God I notice the pink flush that stains his cheekbones.

"I figured Blake would be getting spoiled enough. It's always the moms who get forgotten." He pulls off his black baseball cap, runs a hand through his thick brown hair, and replaces it backward. "At least, that's what they say on the forums."

He blushes further, almost like he's revealed too much.

"More lavender bath salts?" I ask, deciding not to double down on his embarrassment.

"Actually, yes." He chuckles. "Plus something else ... but you'll have to open that one to find out."

I narrow my eyes at him, tipping my head to the side, which causes my messy bun to fall lopsided. "You can be a real mystery, Mr. Richards."

Of all the responses I anticipated, a wink was not on the list. Goose bumps break out over every inch of my body, and I wrap my arms around my middle, which is almost back to normal already.

"What are you doing this afternoon?" It's small talk, and I hate it, but I'll say anything if it shifts my focus away from the memory of his wink.

"Taking you and Blake out wherever you want to go," he replies without a beat of hesitation.

I stare back at him, wondering where I zoned out and missed a part of the conversation. "Taking us out?"

He rises to his feet, gently rocking Blake's bassinet. "Yeah. If you want to, that is. Scott said that you've been pretty much stuck inside, and the weather is a little warmer today."

My eyes drift out of my bedroom window. Bright blue skies and the tiniest buds on the trees promise the first signs of spring.

"Don't you have other stuff you need to do?"

"Like what?" he counters.

I bite down on my bottom lip. I'd love nothing more than to head to Prospect Park—one of my favorite places in Brooklyn. Still, I already feel like Emmett has gone way beyond helping me out.

"I don't know. Gym time, practice, chilling out at—"

"My afternoon is free," he cuts me off, voice soft but sure.

I'm about to accept his offer and then shake my head at the final second. "It's too much to ask. Besides, we couldn't fit Blake's stroller in your Aston Martin."

"I'm in the G-Wagon."

Emmett steps toward me and leans down until our faces are level. A waft of his woodsy cologne reaches me, and I subtly inhale it into my lungs. Mixed with eucalyptus, it's the perfect post-shower scent.

"What other shit excuses have you got for me, Miss Quinn?"

I'd laugh if it wouldn't risk waking Blake.

"I need to take a shower and get dressed," I say.

His eyes drop down my body. Despite my wearing pink sleep shorts and a matching long-sleeved top, Emmett hasn't looked below my neck once.

Well, not until this moment anyway.

He snaps his eyes back to mine, prominent jawline tightening a fraction. "I can wait."

"You don't have to." I try again, more for the benefit of my growing guilt.

Emmett completely ignores my weak protest just as Blake begins to wake. "Where do you want to go?"

It's my turn to flush. "Prospect Park." I haven't been there since I got back from Austin. "I think Blake would like to see the ducks."

When my daughter releases a soft sob, I climb to my feet and lift her out of the bassinet, holding her against my chest.

She smells amazing—a baby scent Mom says to make the most of since it will fade as she grows older.

Emmett moves to the other side of my room, picking up Blake's diaper bag and setting it on the bed next to us. "Does she have everything she needs in here?"

When our eyes connect, I know he can see the emotion as it coats my vision.

"Is everything okay?" His voice is layered with concern.

The temptation to admit the truth—that his kindness is the reason behind the lump forming in my throat—is strong. Tucker should be the one sorting Blake's bag even if he's the last person I'd want to take her to the park for the first time.

I swallow past the lump, feeling a sense of relief that it's Emmett instead of my ex.

"Hormones," is all I say in the end. It's an easy lie and a more than believable one too. When new mothers claim that having a baby fucks with your emotions, they aren't freaking kidding.

He looks like he wants to say something, although he doesn't. Instead, he reaches a hand out to Blake, smoothing a huge palm down her back.

Her sobs ebb in response, although I chalk it up to a coincidence. This man might be comfortable around children, but there's no way he can be a full-on baby whisperer.

"All right." Emmett's voice is a touch gravelly. "Do you want me to watch her while you take a shower? I'd ask Scott, but it might be dark by the time he's climbed the stairs." He snorts a laugh, which pulls one from me.

"Yes, thanks," I reply, setting a calmer Blake back down in her bassinet. "Her diaper bag has everything she needs in it." Our eyes connect again, spreading a warm, safe feeling throughout me. "I'll be right back."

CHAPTER THIRTEEN

EMMETT

Jack renamed the group chat: Blade Boys for Life.

SAWYER

I'm retired. How am I still a member of this group chat?

TOMMY

Let's be real. It's not like this group chat is ever about hockey.

ARCHER

And even when it is, the conversation quickly descends into chaos.

JACK

Oh, just fuck off.

ARCHER

I rest my case.

JACK

And here I was, about to invite you all over to our place for dinner and drinks next Saturday. I'm now reconsidering my generosity.

ME

What the fuck did I do?

JACK

Only Emmett is invited.

TOMMY

You actually are your stepdad.

JACK

Take that back, Tommy.

TOMMY

Nope. I don't tell lies.

SAWYER

I'm confused. Are we being invited to dinner and drinks or not?

JACK

If you all say sorry, then yes.

ARCHER

Can't make it Saturday night. I'm busy banging your sister.

JACK

I'm going to rise above your comment, Archer.

ARCHER

That's very mature of you. Well done.

SAWYER

If this dinner invite does in fact exist, then I'll bring Collins and Ezra.

TOMMY

I just checked with Jenna, and we are a go for next Saturday.

ARCHER

Emmett is very quiet ...

JACK

Like out-on-a-date quiet.

ME

I'm out, but it's not a date.

JACK

leans forward in chair Who are you out with?

ME

I'm alone.

ARCHER

I'm calling bullshit. His reply was too quick and defensive.

TOMMY

He literally had to type two words. How long did you want him to take?

JACK

Shut up, Tommy.

SAWYER

What time is the dinner next Saturday?

JACK

7 p.m.

JACK

Talk to us, Emmett.

Pulling down on the bill of my cap, I check over my shoulder for signs of Billie returning from the restroom with Blake.

Jesus. Diaper changes take forever.

ME

I'm not on a date.

ARCHER

Where are you?

ME

Prospect Park.

JACK

Oh, that's five minutes away from our place. I'll come see you.

ME

No.

Every single member of the group chat begins typing at once.

JACK

Called it.

ARCHER

My boy took a girl to the park.

SAWYER

I once took Collins to a park. It was a date.

TOMMY

Emmett, just say the word, and I'll knock them all out for you.

ME

I'm with a friend. She just had a baby and needed to get out of the house. She didn't have anyone to give her a ride, so I offered.

As Jack starts typing, a direct message separate to the group chat flashes on my phone screen.

SAWYER

Billie?

ME

Yeah.

SAWYER

I see the plan to stay away is going well then ... good work.

ME

Things have gotten complicated since we last spoke.

SAWYER

Complicated, as in you put your dick in her?

ME

NO! Complicated, as in Scott broke his leg in an accident, and other than her mom, she doesn't have a whole lot of people around her. So, I'm helping out.

SAWYER

Sure you are.

ME

Are you going to actually say anything constructive or just continue to goad me?

SAWYER

You need to tread REALLY fucking carefully. I remember telling Archer something similar when he started up a fuck-buddy arrangement with Darcy. However, this is a whole new level of danger. You know that, right?

The icy sensation chasing down my spine has nothing to do with the chill in the air.

ME

Just because I find her hot doesn't mean that I'd make a move.

"Who's hot?"

My in-game reflexes have nothing on the speed in which I lock my phone and shove it into my pocket.

Billie's petite shadow looms over me as I remain seated on the park bench facing the duck pond and slowly close my eyes.

Shit. Shit. *Shit.*

"Who's hot?" She repeats her question. Her voice sounds unsure, but not freaked out.

Maybe she didn't see the rest of the message thread?

When I still don't answer, she rounds the bench and comes to sit next to me, placing Blake back into her stroller and covering her with blankets so only her face is exposed.

Billie might not have planned to become a mother at this point in her life, but she sure as shit is a natural. So much of her reminds me of my parents before they passed, especially the caring look in her eyes—like she'd find a way to part the oceans if that's what it took to keep her child safe and happy.

"It's okay if you don't want to tell me," Billie clarifies, offering Blake her pacifier. "I shouldn't have read the text, letting curiosity get the better of me."

I reach up, adjusting my glasses, and Billie tracks the movement, pulling her bottom lip between her teeth as she does.

"It's no one you know. Just someone I met on an away series."

The lie sounds believable, and I hate that I'm being dishonest with her. The last person I want to deceive is Billie. However, in this situation, I don't have much choice.

It's like she's looking through me as I finish up my sentence, her mind wandering to another place.

"I can only imagine how hard it is to move on from a marriage." She sits back on the bench, diverting her attention to the duck pond. "It must feel like a bomb has gone off in your life."

"Yes, and no." My response is automatic and brutally honest, almost like my subconscious is trying to make up for the lie I just told.

Billie's eyes dart to mine, big green irises holding me captive. "What do you mean?"

A seed of doubt blooms in the pit of my stomach. I'm unsure

of how much to divulge. Maria is still a huge part of Freya and Scott's life, and the last thing I want to do is throw shade on my ex-wife. At some point, it's inevitable that we'll cross paths, and ultimately, what goes down in a marriage should almost always die with it too. That thought isn't enough to stop me from sharing with Billie though, the words tumbling from me with relative ease.

"Maria's paranoia and constant accusations over me being unfaithful drove a huge wedge into an already-failing marriage."

Elbows braced on my knees, I clasp my hands underneath my chin and look at her.

Nothing in Billie's expression indicates surprise. Maria was the master at masking her insecurities, carrying off a barrage of passive-aggressive comments with an easy smile, just like she did that night in Lloyd's bar.

"Emmett."

When Billie says my name but nothing more, I hold my breath, equal parts anxious and intrigued over what she'll say next.

"Billie," I counter, playfully nudging my knee against her thigh.

She chews on her thumb, the tension in her body language making me realize that there's nothing playful about this moment.

Above the sounds of wildlife and the whistling breeze, I hear myself swallow.

Billie does the same before quietly asking, "Did … Maria ever accuse you of having a thing with me?"

Fuck.

A dismissive laugh tries to rise up my throat, but fails under the weight of reality or maybe even the truth.

"Having a thing with you?" I repeat. "No. Flirting with you the last Christmas before you left for Austin? Yes."

Wide eyes grow even wider as she stares back at me, jaw agape. "Really?"

I nod because that's all I'm capable of.

Billie chews on her thumb again, and like a freaking idiot, I reach up and wrap my palm around her fingers, pulling her hand away from her mouth.

I should let go, but I don't, maintaining our connection way longer than necessary.

Her soft palm fits perfectly in my hand, reminding me of the real truth in the last message I sent to Sawyer—there's no way I could ever make a move on Billie Quinn. It would be safer to pull the pin from a hand grenade and hold it to my chest until it detonated.

But despite all the danger signs, images of the girl I'm still holding the hand of scroll through my mind—fantasies centered around how beautiful she would look beneath me, the way I wouldn't stop until the smile I know so well and love became a permanent feature on her face, erasing a legacy of pain inflicted by her shitty ex.

Billie's eyes drop to where we're still holding hands, resting on the wooden bench between us.

"Was any of what Maria said true?"

"In what sense?"

Her long, wavy hair floats in the air as a gust of wind blows through the park, a scent of nutmeg filling my senses.

"Well, I know you never cheated because that isn't who you are." Her words are punctuated, underlining the confidence in her statement. "If Maria thought you were unfaithful, then she really didn't know you well at all."

I remain quiet because I know Billie hasn't finished speaking.

She looks up at me through dark lashes. "I'm asking if Maria was right about us flirting?"

Common sense gets the better of me, forcing me to release her hand, and I clasp mine together before messing with my fucking glasses. Again.

None of this conversation is right.

What the fuck am I doing?

"What answer do you want me to give, Billie?"

She flushes pink, tearing her eyes away from me and focusing straight ahead. "The truthful one."

I clear my throat, determined to get a handle on the building tension between us. "Maria interpreted our friendship as more, and she had a habit of doing that with any woman I spoke to or even looked at. You and I"—I motion between us—"we've always had this affinity, joking around and bouncing off each other. My ex-wife let her paranoia see something that wasn't there."

At least not until now for me.

I can't tell if she looks disappointed or if she's in agreement, as Billie's face turns expressionless. So much of me wants to take her hand back in mine and embrace the comfort her touch brings. It feels like words aren't needed when I can feel the warmth of her soft skin.

A couple more beats of nothing pass, and then she resets herself, shaking her head to rid thoughts she obviously doesn't welcome.

"Can you drive Blake and me home now?"

CHAPTER FOURTEEN

BILLIE

"You don't need to rush into making a decision, sweetheart. You could be back in college within a few months. Paying rent and caring for Blake while trying to study might prove to be too much."

Mom eyes me over her mug, taking a sip while she awaits a response. We've been apartment-hunting all morning and stopped by a cute café in the local area for coffee and the best cakes in downtown Brooklyn.

I've been living with my parents for over a month, and I already need my own space. Sure, living at home is cheaper and saves money, but Tucker's financial contribution would help toward some of the rent on my own place, and Dad has offered to cash in shares to pay off my student finances and cover living costs until Blake is old enough and I'm ready to find a job. Ordinarily, I'd turn down Dad's offer and tell him to keep the investment, but desperate times call for desperate measures, and I need to start rebuilding my life—something I can't do while I'm cooped up in my childhood bedroom.

Mom and I both know I'm not heading back to college

anytime soon, regardless of whether I study in Austin or Brooklyn. It's time to acknowledge my reality.

"Just because I won't be living at home doesn't mean I won't come by all the time with Blake. You can still care for her whenever you want. I just ..." I drop my eyes to the wooden table in front of me, breaking off a piece of brownie.

Mom studies me for a beat, exhaling a long breath. "It's only been a matter of weeks, Billie. You've barely found your feet, and I'm concerned that you'll be lonely, living by yourself in the center of town."

Earlier today, we found the perfect one-bedroom apartment with exposed brickwork and beams. It's not set in the fanciest part of Brooklyn, but it has character and charm, and it's perfect for Blake. The landlord explained that a single woman had lived in the apartment for over a year without any trouble or safety issues. The rental was reasonable for the area, and it just felt like home when we walked in. I want to go for it and move straight in. Dad's all for it; the only skeptic is sitting in front of me, staring down into her coffee mug.

I reach out and take Mom's hand in mine, glancing briefly at Blake as she continues sleeping in her stroller. Her colic attacks have thankfully eased over the past week, making my decision to move out an easier one to reach.

"I'm not going back to college, Mom. At least not yet anyway. My life has changed, and so have I." I squeeze her hand tighter, silently asking her to look at me. "And I think I'm okay with that. Blake has to come first, and right now, I can't give her everything she needs because I spend too much of my time locked away in the house, too far from civilization and places like this." My eyes rove the cute café. "I know I have you and Dad, but I'm already lonely, confined to a small bedroom in the suburbs. I need to get out and make new friends and then start searching for jobs as soon as I can."

Mom analyzes our joined hands. "I'm worried about you living in a strange place."

I shrug. "If I don't make a change, my mental health will go downhill. A chance to stand on my own two feet was one of the reasons why I chose Austin."

She nods like she gets it.

Mom is an only child, like Dad, and both are fiercely independent. I think that's why they accepted it when I chose not to travel home much when I was at college. Instead, they'd fly to visit me when they could afford it.

"What will you do for work?"

I twist my lips, no clue what the future holds. "I don't know. Maybe I'll be a server in a place like this." I smirk at her. "Or become a bank teller."

She looks horrified. "No way. The hours suck, and the pay is even worse. You have the whole world at your feet, Billie. And you know Dad and I will help care for Blake whenever you need."

Emotion stings my eyes, and I release Mom's hand to take a bite of brownie, the salty-chocolate goodness helping to fix a smile on my face. "I know, and thank you. When Blake is old enough, I'm going to research nurseries, and Tucker will have to contribute his share." I clench my jaw, determined to believe what I'm saying. "I'll figure everything out."

Mom still looks unsure before she finally asks, "When are you going to reach out to the landlord and pay the deposit on the apartment?"

"Right away," I tell her. "Dad says the money is ready when I need it, and I don't want to miss out."

She shifts in her seat. "I'm mad at your father."

Mom may be the kindest, sweetest woman I know, but she can also be the scariest.

I lift a brow. I know she's already annoyed that he neglected to change the tires on his van, and the insurance is refusing to pay out on the accident which is only adding to their financial woes. That said, a part of me feels indirectly responsible for what happened. If Dad hadn't been so distracted by the bullshit going on in my life, he might've paid more attention to servicing his van. "What's he done now?"

She clears her throat and tears at the untouched croissant in front of her. "I had no clue what he'd done with the shares or how many he actually owned, until he suddenly told me the value of what he'd cashed in. Apparently, they'd shot up in value, and he saw it as the perfect opportunity to help you and Blake out. He'd told me years ago that he stopped paying into the share scheme when he left his previous job." Her face contorts. "I would've preferred to have been kept in the loop and not had a bomb dropped on me while casually making dinner."

"A pretty nice bomb," I reply, although I understand why she'd be irked at the secret. They've always had an open and honest marriage, so it was a shock for me too.

"He said that he wanted to surprise me with the additional shares he'd bought when we both eventually retired. His plan was to take me on the trip of a lifetime with some of the money." Her eyes flick to mine. "I'm pleased we're using the cash on something more important."

More guilt swims through my veins, forcing me to look away for a moment. No one deserves all the things life has to offer more than my hardworking parents.

"I promise that I'll make the most of your money," I tell her.

When she retakes my hand, I know it's a plea for my attention. "So long as you're happy, Billie, then that's payment enough for us. Anyway"—she chuckles—"when you're a high-flying lawyer, dominating the world, you'll be able to afford whatever you like. Including a two-week break in Mauritius for us both."

The sudden chime of a bell ringing above the café door grips my gaze, but it's not the sound that steals my attention. That award goes to the pink-haired beauty dressed in motorcycle leathers.

Tucking a black helmet underneath one arm, she casually strolls toward the counter, waving hi to who I assume is the owner. Every customer—male and female—in the place has their eyes on her as Mom swivels one-eighty in her chair.

"She's ... quite something," she comments, turning back to look at me, eyes wide with awe. "Freaking stunning in fact."

As the biker chick places her order at the counter, a sense of familiarity settles over me, almost like I've seen her somewhere before.

"She's absolute goals," I agree with Mom. "A true queen."

Mom pushes her chair back, flicking her eyes to her granddaughter. "Well, while everyone's busy staring at the runway model at the front, I'm heading to the bathroom."

In my mom's absence, I take another sip of coffee, pulling out my phone to check for messages.

CLARA

I don't know if you already found out, but I didn't want you to hear this via anyone else.

Tucker is dating Rachael Fowler. They made it official last night on socials.

Like Blake can sense my distress, she releases a small whimper, and I set my phone on the table before lifting her, along with her pink cashmere blanket, out of the stroller and resting her against my chest.

After a couple of beats, she settles, and I pick up my phone, navigating back to the text thread with Clara.

ME

I hadn't heard, and she's welcome to him.

I hit Send and swipe underneath my left eye.

"He doesn't deserve your tears."

Taking a seat next to Mom's empty chair, the pink-haired girl sets her helmet down on the table and proceeds to spread a thick cream on what I think is a scone before smearing strawberry jelly on top.

I remain transfixed until I finally croak out, "Excuse me?"

She lifts her deep brown eyes to mine, her winged black eyeliner applied to perfection.

"I said that he isn't worth your tears. Crying over an asshole feeds his audacity. The only emotion a man is entitled to pull from a woman is joy." She winks suggestively. "If you catch my drift."

Despite myself, a bubble of laughter bursts from my chest, garnering a smile from her in turn.

"That's better ..." She pauses, waiting on me to supply a name.

"Billie," I say and then point to Blake as my daughter peacefully stares up at me with inquisitive eyes. "And this is Blake."

She sets her knife down and wipes her hands together, offering one out to me. "Collins."

"That's your first name?" I ask, liking that we both have uncommon names.

She just smiles. "It is."

Supporting Blake with one arm, I pick up my coffee and take a sip.

"So, am I right?" she asks, getting straight to the point. "Are your tears being wasted on a douchebag?"

"Exactly right." My confident response catches me off guard, almost like this girl's directness is contagious.

Collins nods once, taking a first bite of scone and closing her eyes as she swallows. "Thought so." She tips her head in the direction of the restrooms. "Is that your mom?"

Collins must've clocked who I was sitting with when she first entered the café.

I feel my cheeks heat before confirming, "Yeah."

She tips her head to one side, eyes narrowing a fraction. "What's wrong about being seen out with your parents?"

I set a kiss in the center of Blake's head; her soft hair is always a soothing sensation. "Nothing's wrong with it," I reply. "I'm just not supposed to be here." I motion with my chin toward Blake.

"In Brooklyn, with a baby. I should be thinking about my senior year in college, basking in the Texas sun."

For a second, I worry that my statement sounds ungrateful for what I have when, truthfully, I couldn't be more thankful to have Blake in my life.

I set my eyes back on Collins, hoping she will understand what I'm trying to say.

Her knowing smile unravels the knot of tension forming between my shoulder blades.

"But isn't that what's great about life?" Her voice is full of wonder as she casts her eyes around the café, packed to the brim with customers. "I personally love it when life throws you lemons or a curveball."

"Why is that?"

She leans forward, lowering her voice. "Because that's when you find out who your real people are." When she sits back in her chair, a slow smile creeps across her face. "When the going gets rough, those around you—old and new in your life—show themselves for who they really are. Including yourself. You discover the depths of your determination and strength." She tips her chin at Blake. "Her father is the one responsible for your tears, right?"

I roll my eyes at thoughts of Tucker and Rachael linking hands around campus. She was always after him, and she was one of the main girls who started up the cheating rumors. She was likely telling the truth and sleeping with him long before we broke up.

"How did you guess?"

Collins takes another bite of scone and waves her hand like she's dismissing the mere thought of my ex-boyfriend.

I snort a laugh at her disdain.

"Call it female intuition." She clicks her tongue. "My best advice? Focus on those around you who are showing up right now. *They* are the people who count."

It doesn't take much for images of Emmett to appear, along with a sensation of his rough palm against mine. We've barely spoken since that day at Prospect Park, the whole trip coming to an awkward end when I made the biggest fool of myself—pretty much asking him if there had ever been something between us.

What the fuck was I thinking?

I grimace at the memory and look over at Collins as she stirs sweetener into her coffee. "I think I already screwed up my friendship with one of those good people."

She lifts a single unaffected shoulder. "Well, if you have, then they likely weren't your person in the first place."

I quickly glance over at the restrooms to see Mom stepping out, on the phone, lifting her finger in the air at me.

With at least a couple more minutes of privacy, I decide to take advantage and divulge my fuckup to a complete stranger who, to be honest, I trust more than most people I've known for years.

"What if I told you that the person I screwed up with is fourteen years older than me, happens to be my dad's best friend, and his ex-wife is tight with my mom?" I decide to leave out the part where he's a famous NHL player.

Collins's eyes grow to the size of the saucers set on the back wall of the café. "You slept with him?"

I shake my head quickly. "No. No, I didn't sleep with him." I cringe at her. "But I did ask him if there was something between us." I cringe. Again. "And then things got a little awkward and I wanted to vanish into thin air right there and then."

She just chuckles and sips her coffee. "So, he's the hot older-uncle type, huh?"

My nod says it all.

She quirks an interested brow. "And you say his ex-wife is tight with your mom?"

I nod again.

She makes an excited sound, and I blow out a laugh.

"Girl, you have got to fuck him."

My eyes drop to Blake, who is now thankfully sleeping.

Collins mouths an apology at me before continuing her

ramble. “Forbidden naughtiness is the best kind. If things got awkward between you both the other day, it’s probably because there’s truth in what you asked.” She points to her stomach. “Gut feelings never lie, and I’m telling you that he’s one thousand percent digging that hot bod of yours.” She winks, and I flush. “If he’s single and so are you, have some fun. You can’t help who you find attractive.”

Her advice is either the best or worst I’ve ever received. There is no middle ground when it comes to what she’s said.

I roll my lips together, just as Mom ends her call and makes her way back to us.

My eyes connect with Collins, a rare shot of excitement pulsing through me. “I’ll give you one thing, Collins.”

Her smile turns devilish. “Oh, yeah? And what’s that?”

I respond with my own filthy grin. “You sure know how to play with fire.”

CHAPTER FIFTEEN

EMMETT

Setting the final box down in the center of Billie's double bed, I cast my eyes around her new place. It's clear this building is an old warehouse or factory that has been converted into apartments, which are larger than the average you would find in Brooklyn.

Now that I've seen the place firsthand, I understand why Billie secured a low rental. It needs a ton of work—kitchen cabinets barely hanging on to their hinges, walls that look like they haven't seen paint in years, and hardwood flooring that has definitely seen better days. I'm not even sure the refrigerator and couch will last beyond the six months lease she signed.

But as I close the door on her new bedroom and step straight into the kitchen and dining space that leads down into the living area, I realize that none of the rough edges in this apartment bother Billie because she's simply happy to have her independence back.

Whether she's noticed me watching her dance around the kitchen with Blake strapped to her chest or not doesn't stop me from leaning against an exposed brick wall and taking in one of the best sights I've ever witnessed.

With Scott out of the question and Freya picking up extra hours, my volunteering to help Billie and Blake move didn't carry the same guilt I usually feel when I think of excuses to spend more time with my best friend's daughter. Like offering to take her out for lunch and choosing the best steakhouse in town because I knew the owners took their time over service and that would mean an extra half hour in her presence.

Secretly watching Billie whenever I get the chance though? I'm pretty sure that's not fundamental to a successful house move, even if it's impossible to tear my eyes from her.

Amy Winehouse's "Tears Dry on Their Own" plays through the blue retro radio on the kitchen counter, and as Billie spins around to adjust the volume, her eyes connect with mine, bringing their dance session to an abrupt halt.

She turns down the music, and I push off the wall, making my way over to both of them.

"Don't stop on my account," I tell her, the broad smile I'm wearing reflected in my voice.

Billie moves some hair away from her forehead, a rosy tinge staining her cheeks. I can't be sure if she's embarrassed or flushed from an afternoon of moving boxes, but I know that I like that look on her, especially the sheen of perspiration making her flawless complexion glow.

Coming to stand a few feet in front of her, I push away inappropriate thoughts and shove my hands into the pockets of my gray sweatpants, restricting any urge I might have to suddenly reach up and swipe my thumb above her brow.

Billie Quinn is off-limits.

"I didn't know you were into Amy Winehouse." I bite down on my bottom lip when she flushes a little pinker, color traveling down the column of her throat. "Didn't she die before you were even out of diapers?"

Billie deadpans in a way only she can, causing me to burst out laughing.

"Not true. And even if I wasn't out of diapers, that doesn't stop me from listening to every song of hers."

She strokes a dainty hand through the soft, dark hairs atop Blake's head.

"Is this one your favorite?" I tip my chin at the radio, still playing the same song.

She shakes her head, eyes following my arms when I fold them across my chest. Moving is hard work, and I removed my sweatshirt earlier, leaving me in a Dri-FIT shirt that hugs my toned abs. I probably should put my sweatshirt back on now that I'm starting to cool down, but I'm having too much fun watching Billie's eyes.

Jesus, Emmett.

"'Back to Black' is my favorite, but this song feels more fitting to my life right now."

Billie's response pulls me from my thoughts, and our eyes snap to each other.

"Fitting how?"

When Billie spins on her heel and heads for her bedroom, I figure it's time for Blake's nap.

I don't move from the spot I'm standing in, patiently waiting for her to return so we can continue our conversation. I want to know what's got her so twisted up.

"What did you mean when you said fitting?" I repeat my question as she emerges from the bedroom with a baby monitor.

Billie sets it down on the kitchen counter and then comes to stand in front of me, at least a few inches closer than we were before.

Pulling a black hairband from around her wrist, she throws her long, wavy hair into an effortless bun, hands slapping against her thighs when she's done.

I should probably keep my eyes fixed on her face, but I've

learned over the past few weeks that they like to betray me, along with my moral compass.

So, I check out the way her tight black leggings cling to her perfectly shaped legs.

"It's just a female power ballad, one that makes me feel less shitty about Tucker and his new girlfriend."

I almost swallow my tongue, quickly bursting out a, "What?"

Billie nods like this news is neither surprising nor a big deal, but I know it is. I can see it in the lines as they crease around her big green eyes. I know because she needs to hide her feelings and hurt over it in the first place.

That feeling is familiar for me, too, as is the need to disguise it.

What I haven't established—and it's something I'm growing more desperate to discover each time we're together—is, does her hurt stem from the way she feels about Tucker, or is the pain on Billie's face more to do with rejection and loss?

For me, it initially began as the former. Even while we were still together, I could feel myself losing Maria as the relationship and love we'd built slipped through my fingers. Now, it's more to do with circumstance and fear that I'll never find that again, and if I do, it's possible that Maria will get there before me.

I take a step toward Billie, the fragrance from her nutmeg shampoo surrounding me as I enter her space.

I'm closer to her than I should be, than I need to be, and I wonder if she'll retreat and take a step back.

She doesn't, and I inch forward until I can see the flutter of her pulse point.

"It doesn't matter if it's his words or actions that make you cry, Billie. The mere presence of your tears tells me that he isn't man enough and he *definitely* isn't the one for you."

Billie's chest stops mid-rise, and I hold my own breath, waiting for her to respond.

"You think Tucker is a dickhead?"

The sound of her voice washes relief through me. My last

statement was designed to offer her reassurance, but it came off as way more than that. Suggestive almost.

I smirk, fingers twitching in my pockets, desperate to brush the few remaining strands of hair from her face.

Anything that obstructs my view of Billie's eyes annoys the shit out of me.

"Does that question even warrant an answer?" I say with a smile.

Billie's tongue peeks out, sliding a wet trail across her bottom lip. "I guess not, no."

We stand, eyes fixed on each other for the longest moment before she breaks the connection, gazing around her new apartment.

"It's going to take me forever to unpack everything. Mom promised she'd stop by tomorrow after her shift to help out, but I hate being surrounded by boxes. It feels like I've been living like this for an eternity—all my things inaccessible and stored away." She releases a heavy sigh, breath fanning against my face. "After a while, it gets to you."

I should probably—definitely—leave and let her spend her first night in peace. I have an early morning skate and a gym session I need to get through, including a rehab workout for my knee.

"What if I pulled out my phone and ordered a pizza, and then we got to work on making this place feel more like a home for you and Blake?"

Her full lips slowly curve into a smile, and the guilt I was feeling a second after I suggested sticking around to help out ebbs, replaced with satisfaction that I turned Billie's mood into a happier one.

"What kind of pizza are we talking about?"

The way she asks a trivial question in such a serious tone has me chuckling as I finally pull my hands from my pockets, phone secured in my left palm.

"Because if you choose anything with anchovies, then I'd rather live out of boxes and suitcases for the rest of time."

I pause on searching for local pizza joints that deliver. "What about with pineapple?"

She rises to her tiptoes, peering over my phone to check what I'm adding to the cart. "If I said that pineapple was my favorite topping, would our friendship be over?"

When our eyes meet, we're even closer, lips inches apart, breaths mixing.

She tastes so good.

Back away, Emmett.

I've known Billie for over a decade, and during any of those years, if I'd been asked if we were friends, my answer would've been an unequivocal yes.

Today, that word feels inadequate. Maybe even inaccurate.

"Not many people like pineapple on their pizza." She continues talking. "Clara, my friend back in Austin, thinks it's the grossest thing she's ever tasted."

I scroll to a large pineapple pizza with everything, hitting Add to Cart just below the image.

"It's a good thing I'm not Clara then, isn't it?" I barely recognize my own voice. It's gravelly and intense when all we're doing is ordering takeout.

She heaves a faux sigh of relief, rocking back on her heels and swiping a hand across her forehead.

"Okay, phew. For a minute there, I thought that I was another friend lighter."

I drop my phone into my pocket, one hand coming under Billie's chin.

I want her attention.

I don't want this moment to end.

My eyes bore deep into hers, holding Billie a prisoner to my unspoken thoughts.

"I want you to know something."

"What's that?" Her response is a whisper, tongue peeking out an inch.

"That there aren't any contingencies on us and our friendship. Whether it's pizza, hospital appointments, or staying late to help unpack some boxes, I'm always going to be here for you. When you get let down by people, it's easy to fall into the cynical trap of mistrust, and I don't want that to happen to you. You're too much of a good human, and I won't let you retract into a shell. Moving here was a brave fucking thing to do, and I'm actually in awe. So, even if it takes us until two a.m. to get you all set up and moved in, then that's how long I'll stay."

I drop the hand from under her chin, shoving it back into my pocket.

Fuck, fuck. *Fuck.*

"Emmett ..." Billie begins speaking, but trails off, unsure of what to say next.

My throat runs dry.

I went too far, my hands powered solely by protective instinct and insane levels of attraction toward this girl.

A girl who is also the daughter of my best friend.

A girl who is fourteen years younger than me.

The last girl I should be thinking about getting naked and laying on the empty kitchen counter to our right.

Her lips part, more words ready to tumble from them.

Frustratingly, it isn't her thoughts that fill my ears next.

"That's the intercom." Billie's eyes fix on her front door, and I turn over my shoulder, pissed at whoever is standing on the other side.

I *need* to know what she was going to say.

I look back at Billie. "Either you have a visitor or that's the fastest fucking pizza delivery in history."

CHAPTER SIXTEEN

BILLIE

My eyes lock with Emmett's, and I point toward the intercom. "I should find out whoever it is at the door."

I expect him to step aside so I can get past him.

He doesn't, and the ringing continues. His gaze holding me in place as my pulse thumps in my ears.

After another few seconds, Emmett takes a step back, granting me access to move toward the door.

I take a couple of steps down to the living area, my body on autopilot while my mind reenacts everything that just went down between us.

Holy shit. Did I just witness a darker side to Emmett Richards?

I pick up the receiver and absentmindedly speak into the phone. "Hello?"

"Oh, great. I was about to give up." A female voice huffs into my ear.

"Is this the pizza delivery?" I ask, eyes flicking to Emmett.

He's still standing in the same place, back to me, hands stuffed into the pockets of his gray sweatpants. The bill on his backward cap is tipped up, like he has his head bowed.

"Girl, I'm down for trying my hand at most jobs. But delivering pizzas is not one that appeals to me."

The way the girl speaks is familiar, but I brush away that thought, centering my attention back on Emmett, who still hasn't moved.

"How can I help you then?"

"I promise I'm not a weirdo or anything, but it's cold as shit out here, so can you just let me up, and I'll explain everything when I'm out of the rain?"

I chew on my bottom lip, more inclined to say yes to a stranger with Emmett here. "Sure."

Replacing the receiver, I hit the door release button and wait for the random guest to reach my second-floor apartment.

"Can you check on Blake for me, please?" I ask Emmett.

He spins on his heel, gaze telling me that he's still thinking about our last conversation.

Same.

With a nod, he stalks off toward my bedroom, and I slide the safety chain and bolt when there's a knock on my door.

My jaw almost hits the floor.

"Collins?"

"Billie?" She looks as shocked as I feel.

"What are you doing here?"

She pulls down the hood on her black raincoat and points inside my apartment. "It's still no warmer in this freaking hallway."

Standing to one side, I let her in.

She spins on her heel, apologizing several times for dripping all over my floor.

"This has to be the craziest coincidence ever." She starts talking as I close the door and lock it. "I'm guessing you're the new tenant who put a deposit down on this place a week ago?"

Collins looks almost proud as I turn around to face her, gaze traveling toward my bedroom for signs of Emmett.

I offer Collins a confused but warm smile. "I am. Although that still doesn't explain why you're here."

She shrugs in the same way she did in the café. "Well, this is why it's crazy. I'm the previous tenant. I moved out quite a while ago when I met my now husband." She waves a hand in front of her. "Anyway, they struggled to fill the place because it needed so much maintenance and the cheap-ass landlord refused to address it." She screws up her face at a thought, rainwater dripping from the ends of her pink waves. "Speaking of incompetent, it doesn't matter how many times I call my motorcycle insurance and tell them that I've moved, no one seems to freaking listen." She scoffs. "I don't even own that particular bike anymore!"

I'm pretty sure my jaw is hanging open.

"You used to live here?"

Collins nods. "Yep, and I've been coming by every few weeks to check for mail since I refuse to pay for extended mail forwarding and the landlord usually just leaves any packages or letters with my old neighbor."

That's the kind of stubborn behavior I'd exhibit. I like this girl even more.

"Well, I only moved in today, but I'll be sure to keep an eye out for you."

Collins is no longer looking at me, head turned and eyes fixed on my kitchen area.

"E-Emmett?" is all that leaves her mouth.

She focuses back on me, motioning between me and the man standing in my apartment, a guy I'm guessing she knows.

Emmett's steely-gray eyes don't blink, bewilderment written right across his face.

"Wait." He points to me and then Collins. "Do you guys know each other?"

My mind races, initial thoughts of Collins being the girl Emmett was referring to as "hot" that time I caught sight of his text chat. I clear that thought immediately. The huge diamond ring she's wearing is a reminder that she's very much taken.

When her shocked expression turns scheming, I realize that she's connecting the dots.

"Hang on a minute." She holds up a hand and gives me a knowing glance, coupled with a wink. "Is Emmett the good person who you ... you know?"

My cheeks burn under the weight of her words. Sure, she didn't give away any details about our conversation the other week, but she also doesn't need to. It doesn't take a genius to decipher her facial expression and my flaming cheeks to figure out that I have a crush on the New York Blades defenseman and my dad's best friend.

"How do you know each other?" My question is designed to take the heat off me.

Clearing his throat, Emmett takes a couple of steps down to our level, walking toward us until we're in a kind of triangle.

"Collins is married to one of my closest friends and former teammate, Sawyer Bryce." He holds his hand out, motioning to Collins. "Billie Quinn, meet Collins Bryce."

The only one who doesn't look like they want the ground to swallow them whole is Collins. And that doesn't surprise me since I get a hunch that very little knocks this girl off-balance.

"Billie and I already met at Rise Up a week or so ago," Collins clarifies for Emmett.

She doesn't look away from me, making it very hard for me to hide the truth behind my attempts to play this cool.

Emmett is exactly the person I was talking to her about, and she knows it.

She clicks her tongue, setting her eyes on my front door. "Okay, well, I'm going to head back home now." She pulls up the hood on the raincoat and makes to leave, stopping just before she slides the dead bolt across the door. "I don't know what's going on, and to be honest, it's none of my business." She turns to look at us both, her previous playful demeanor now more serious. "But I'm guessing by the looks on your faces that I'm the last person who was supposed to show up, or maybe it's more that I interrupted something."

Emmett pulls at the back of his neck. "Billie and I are friends, and I was helping her move in."

There isn't any judgment in Collins's voice as she pulls the door open and holds her gaze on me. "Like I've said to many of my friends on a number of occasions, a man's eyes never lie, even if their mouth does."

After the click of my apartment door, there's nothing but silence between us both.

The tension is palpable, unbearable, a thousand words passing between our lingering glances.

But here's the deal: just because Collins believes that Emmett has a thing for me, that doesn't necessarily make it true. And it for sure doesn't make it any less awkward as I bite on the inside of my cheek, trying—and failing—to find words to breach the impasse between us.

Right before Collins showed up, he had his hand under my chin, our light banter having morphed into something new and more serious.

I don't want to lose my friendship with Emmett, and I'm determined not to run away with the idea that he's here, in my apartment, for any other reason than he's a friend trying to help me believe everything he said in the kitchen.

"Billie, I think we need to talk." When Emmett finally speaks, his voice sounds deflated, flat, and frustrated.

Everything I feared about this situation is playing out right before me. He's figured out that I have the hots for him, and like a fucking schoolgirl crushing on her PE teacher, I brace for his inevitable exit from my life.

A line has been crossed, and I'm the one who fucked up.

On a deep swallow, I force myself to look at him. "Go ahead."

One hand is back in the pocket of his sweatpants, and as he moves closer to me, every inch of my skin feels like it's been shocked with a zap of electricity.

Blowing out a long breath, I ready myself for rejection. The rejection he assured me would never come.

With his free hand, Emmett pulls off his glasses, pinching the frames between his thumb and forefinger.

I remember when he used to wear contact lenses more, although I prefer him in glasses. They suit his chiseled face so well.

"I've never been a guy who tells lies. In fact, I've always prided myself on giving the truth."

I roll my tongue along the roof of my mouth, the sensitive feeling offering a momentary break from anxiety over what he's going to say.

"And because you are the absolute last person I would ever want to lie to, I'll be honest and address the elephant in the room."

He breaks off, chest moving rapidly beneath the thin fabric of his black shirt.

"In the park last week, I told you that we've always had an affinity. Our jokes, banter, the way you'd kick my ass at Monopoly each year and never let me forget it."

Those memories don't make me smile like they've always done. This time, they tighten my chest.

"I let you believe that nothing had changed for me now that you're back in Brooklyn. Truthfully, when I showed up with your twenty-first birthday gift, I expected to find an older version of the young woman I'd always gotten along with."

My throat is thick, voice croaky when I ask, "And what is it you found instead?"

He runs a rough palm across his mouth, gaze dropping down the length of my body for the briefest second.

"I found a woman who took my goddamn breath away. When she walked into my best friend's living room, I had to fight to keep my jaw closed and eyes where they belonged." He shakes his head, dropping it between his shoulders.

I take a step closer, his compliments spurring me on. I want to hear more of them.

Specifically from him.

"You're stunning, Billie. Like, really fucking stunning." He blows out a humorless laugh, probably in response to his admission.

I feel the same way. This whole conversation is madness. Dangerous. Stupid.

"If circumstances were different, I'd ..." He trails off, and I want to scream into my couch cushions.

"You'd what?" I press.

He replaces his glasses and reaches up, resting both palms on top of his baseball cap, one over the other. The motion showcases the strong muscles in his biceps and prominent veins in his forearms.

I fight to keep my eyes on his face, just like the battle he previously described.

"Tell me what you'd do. You said that you would never lie to me."

He shakes his head, and my heart drops an inch.

"Keeping some thoughts to myself doesn't mean I'm lying to you, Billie. It means I'm using my fucking brain for once and not digging myself into an early grave when it comes to your dad."

I don't respond because what can I say? My dad would absolutely murder him if he touched me. Especially after everything that went down with Tucker.

He squeezes his eyes shut. "My ex-wife is your mom's best friend. I'm fourteen years older than you, and all I can think about is ..."

"What?"

His eyes snap open, gray irises way darker than I've seen them before.

"I can't allow myself to go there with you. Not even in my own mind."

I know it's a bad idea to reach up and place a palm on his chest. Still, that doesn't stop me.

His body is as hard as stone, the strong, fast beat of his heart unmistakable as I whisper, "Anything we say to each other will never go any further. I promise you that."

He debates telling me for a moment; I can see the war in his eyes.

"No." He wraps his hand around mine, dropping our joined hands down between us. "This is the one and only time I'll ever speak to you about how I feel." His eyes rove my apartment. "I'll stay tonight, share a pizza with you, and help you unpack, and then I'll leave, and we'll never talk about any of this again. You got that?"

"But?"

"No buts, Billie." He interlaces our fingers, jaw ticcing and under strain. "This is the way it has to be, and I'm not going to change my mind. I'm freshly divorced, and you have your whole life to live in a new place with Blake."

Against my own will, I breathe a soft, "Okay."

When he releases our hands, I feel the loss, like I'm standing outside in the pouring rain, the heat previously coursing through my body immediately doused in cold.

Like he's retreating, Emmett takes a step back from me, hands sliding straight into his pockets.

"Okay, cool." He turns on his heel, ripping a large brown box open in one easy motion. "Show me where you want to store your skillet."

CHAPTER SEVENTEEN

EMMETT

SCOTT

Hey, buddy. Are you still good for tomorrow night? Freya wants to finalize numbers.

Sitting on my bench in the white towel I wrapped around me at least ten minutes ago, I continue to stare down at the message from Scott. It's Freya's birthday tomorrow night, and each year, she hosts a full dinner party to celebrate.

Friends and neighbors will be there, including Maria.

Although it's not the prospect of seeing my ex-wife that has my ass glued to the bench and head spinning out.

It's been a week since I walked out of Billie's apartment at one a.m., and we haven't spoken since. By the time I left, all her major boxes and cases were unpacked, even if the same couldn't be said for the true depths of my feelings.

Just admitting my attraction to her was a mistake. The second the confession left my mouth, I wanted to take it back. Not because I didn't mean every word. Jesus, I wanted to go a lot further than simply pointing out how stunning she was. Regardless, telling her with my words or showing her with my body would have moved us into dangerous territory, and there's no hiding away now that the cat's out of the bag.

And if I'd ever questioned whether or not she felt the same way, then her reaction laid any of those doubts to rest.

We're into each other, and there's no denying it. The difference is, I know that my feelings for this girl run deeper than surface level, and that's a scary fucking thought. Not least of which because I shouldn't even find Billie attractive, never mind have her laugh and smile on repeat in my brain as I stare up at my bedroom ceiling in the dead of night.

Scott's text arrived over three hours ago, and I've typed out multiple responses since, all without hitting Send. The first was a direct question, asking if Billie would be there; another where I tried to surreptitiously find out the guest list; and a final text, where I admitted everything to him. That draft got deleted in record time.

I've lost count of the number of occasions I've stood in the shower, braced my palm against the cold tiles, and gazed down at my hard dick, desperate to jerk off to thoughts of how well Billie would swallow me, how good it would be to bury my face between her sweet thighs. The flush of pink that so often painted her cheeks would turn crimson as she unraveled beneath me, right after I punished her for giving me back talk.

"I'm assuming you don't have press duties tonight." Archer takes his usual seat next to me on the bench, wet hair dripping onto my phone screen.

I side-eye him, and he swipes a quick hand over it, snapping away droplets of water.

"You played well tonight," he says, bracing both elbows on his knees.

I don't respond because it's bullshit. We kept a shutout against Boston, but it wasn't the performance I needed. Every other length, it felt like my knee was going to give out.

"Want to talk about it?" Archer's usually playful voice is way more serious when he tips his chin at my phone.

I continue to stare down at Scott's message right before I give up on a reply and toss my cell into my bag.

"It's not really something I can talk about," I confirm, mimicking his stance. "The last thing I needed in life was more complications, but somehow, I've managed to find them."

"Or they've found you ..."

Archer's unexpected reply pulls my attention to his face.

"Don't you agree that the best things in life come to you when you least expect them?" he continues. "Take Darcy, for example. I was the NHL's biggest playboy, and I was good with it too. Did I plan to fall in love with my teammate's little sister?" He shakes his head, a smile creasing around his blue eyes. "Nope. It just happened. And now I have a stunning daughter and wife to show for it."

I appreciate the sentiment, even if his situation is entirely different from mine. Jack was always going to be pissed at Archer for banging his sister in secret, but his life—and maybe even the structure of his face—was never at risk.

"If you and Maria made a mistake splitting, then it's never too late to go back and fix things."

My laughter punctuates an otherwise silent locker room as Archer watches on, confusion knitted between his brows.

"Yeah, you couldn't be any further from the mark if you tried," I tell him.

My goalie maintains his silence. He wants me to elaborate, and I have no clue what words to use next. I've known and played with Archer for a number of seasons, and with each year that's passed, I've seen him grow into someone I know I can trust with my private business. Even if he might not always understand it. He knows Maria and I had an on-off marriage for a while, and at one point, I remember announcing that we'd split, my declaration fueled by too much booze and heartache. He was there for me then, and he'll be there for me now.

"Maria and I are finished; there's no going back for either of us. Not this time around and never again."

Archer runs a hand through his wet hair. "Is there someone else? Because you're giving me vibes like there might be."

I blow out a quick breath. "Yes—no—maybe." Our eyes connect. "How did you guess all that just from my vibes?"

He looks at me like it's obvious, circling his own face for effect. "You remind me of me when I was pining after Darcy, but knew I couldn't have her."

I jump up from the bench, his observations hitting way too close for comfort.

He follows me, golden-retriever enthusiasm overtaking his expression when he bumps his shoulder against mine. "I'm right, aren't I?"

"Just leave it, okay?"

His eyes land on the open training bag, my cell sitting on top of folded clothes. "It's someone you can't—or shouldn't—want, isn't it?"

Archer's serious tone pulls a, "Yes," from me, along with a deep rumble from my chest. "Although her life is possibly more screwed up than mine right now."

He pauses with his T-shirt halfway over his head, speaking through the material. "Screwed up how?"

I roll my eyes even though he can't see me.

"She just had a baby, and her shitty ex bailed on her."

"Prick."

I nod once. "She had to drop out of college as a result."

Pulling his T-shirt down, Archer's eyes practically bug out. "Whoa! Back up a step, man. Did you just say *college*?"

This is right about the point where I should stop speaking. But, hey, Sawyer and Collins are in the know. Might as well let Archer in on it too. Hell, maybe we could announce it on the Jumbotron next game.

"She's twenty-one before you go and lose your mind."

He points at my chest, hand hovering over the only tattoo I

have. "And you're, what ... thirty-five?" He takes a second, counting on his fingers before moving to his toes. "Jesus, that's fourteen years!"

"Very astute, Moore. Would you like a gold star?"

He rolls his eyes at me this time. "No. But seriously, next, you'll tell me that she's your niece or something."

My grimace says it all.

"Holy fuck!"

I clap a palm over his mouth, wincing as I check to make sure that we're still alone. Mercifully, we are. "Obviously, she isn't my actual niece," I grit out. "But she is the daughter of my and my ex-wife's best friends."

Archer's beam is enough to power Brooklyn, and I'm tempted to slap my hand back over his grin.

"Has anything happened between you two?"

The faintest hint of nutmeg wraps around me. It would've been so easy to seal my mouth over Billie's that first night in her apartment, just to see if she'd kiss me right back. Whenever I'm around her, the urge to be reckless with my heart and body grows stronger. I'm desperate for this girl in every way possible, my willpower dangling by a thread.

Shoving away temptation, I shake my head at Archer. "Of course not, and it never will either. What started out as a good friendship has turned confusing since she returned from college in February. I should've kept my distance, but circumstances keep bringing us back together, and ..." I massage my temples, attempting to alleviate the stress headache building behind them.

"And you went and caught feelings."

"I haven't got feelings for her." My answer is immediate and a lie, even if I'm standing here, trying my hardest to deny it.

Archer looks doubtful. "Okay, Emmett. Whatever you say. Because if it was a case of banging her, then you'd definitely be staring at your phone, and you'd *definitely* be this relaxed about it all."

"I just got a divorce," I grind out.

"And I just told you that the best things in life come at you when you least expect them."

I grab my wash bag, throwing my arms out to the sides. "Nothing about this situation is good."

Guilt slams into me. Everything about Billie is good. Whenever I'm around her, I feel good, happy, at peace. I feel like I'm in my early twenties, not taking life too seriously. Even after our awkward exchange, we still ate pineapple pizza together and laughed over the loose cupboard doors and the flickering light in the fridge.

She's freaking perfect.

My eyes drop to the floor, and I close them slowly.

"Everything about her is flawless. What's not ideal is our circumstances."

Archer's hand lands on my shoulder. Even though he's several years younger than me, it feels like he's the experienced one in life.

"Then you have your answer ..."

He pauses just long enough for acid to rise up my throat.

"Despite your attraction, it isn't worth the collateral damage it would do to your life if her family ever found out that you were sleeping together."

A protest is right on the tip of my tongue, begging to be voiced.

It would be worth the damage. She's already dismantling me. Piece by piece.

"You're an NHL star and almost as good-looking as me." He grins. "If it's sex you're after or even the feeling of being close to someone, then go on a few dates. There are plenty of other ways to scratch an itch without risking long-term friendships and ..." Archer presses his lips together, hand squeezing around my shoulder. "Imagine Maria's reaction if she found out that you were sleeping with her best friend's daughter. I don't know Maria that well, but from what I've worked out over the years, she isn't the type of woman who would go away quietly."

He's right about Maria, but wrong over Billie being an itch to scratch. I could never get enough of her, and that right there is going to be the death of me.

I swallow down more obsessive thoughts about the redhead I can never have. "Sawyer advised me to keep my distance a few weeks back, and that's exactly what I told her. I made it clear that we could never go there."

Archer nods. "Listen to Sawyer, and you won't take a wrong turn."

Reaching over to my bag and pulling out my phone, I reopen the text thread with Scott, pausing to look up at Archer. "If I decline the invitation to this dinner, it'll be obvious that something is off."

Archer just shrugs. "Then don't. Reply, confirming that you'll be there, and then play the greatest game of poker you've ever played. If this girl ..." He trails off, realizing that I never gave him her name.

Go big or go home, I guess.

"Billie," I confirm.

He gives me a single nod. He met her once at a game before she went to college, but in typical Archer fashion, he probably can't recall who she was, likely too busy with the girls in his lap.

"And if this girl tries to tempt and get all sexy with you, then you need to shut that shit down. I'm telling you, Emmett, if this truly isn't about feelings and it's more about your dick and its lack of action lately, then no girl—runway-model hot or not—is worth losing your mind over."

Keeping my head down so my goalie can't see how much Billie means to me, I quickly type out an acceptance text to Scott before tossing the phone back into my bag.

"Thanks, man."

Archer takes a seat at the bench, sliding one foot and then the other into his sneakers. "Anytime. And remember"—he circles his stoic expression—"practice that poker face."

Of all the potential troubles I'm facing, an ability to hide my true feelings is not something my teammate should be concerned about. I just proved that during this conversation.

It's how the fuck I'm going to deal with my growing obsession and not sacrifice my sanity in the process.

CHAPTER EIGHTEEN

BILLIE

Every year for her birthday, Mom organizes a full dinner party and invites her close colleagues and friends.

When I was younger, I used to chalk up these massive, elaborate dinners to her love of food—she'd spend hours in the kitchen, trying out new recipes.

Tonight, I've concluded that while she loves to cook, she also loves to plan; every detail has been considered—from matching napkins to place cards written in calligraphy.

It's the perfect night, for sure.

The only thing that could make it better? If Emmett would look at me. We've been sitting directly opposite each other all dinner, and for the entire three-course meal, he's concentrated on talking with our neighbor, Terry, and Dad about hockey and classic cars.

It feels like I don't exist to him anymore, and I know it's because he's trying to avoid me.

It would be a lie to claim that I haven't missed our check-in chats via text, but I also get why he's backing away and putting distance between us.

Things have shifted since I returned from Austin. The air feels thick whenever we're in the same room. And while there's a delicious kind of tension simmering between us, one that reached an all-time high in my apartment a few days ago, that atmosphere also doubled as a warning. We're treading a fine line through very murky waters. One false move, and we could easily tumble right over the edge—or even into bed together.

When Emmett confessed his attraction, I battled to inflate my lungs, let alone admit to feeling the same way. The young-girl crush I had on my dad's best friend has morphed into something much more. Something I never felt for Tucker or any other guy before him. Emmett commands a room, but doesn't demand its attention because he already has it—every pair of female eyes, to be exact. And as I gaze around the table with at least seven other women, that fact has never been as obvious as it is tonight.

My eyes land on Maria. With long, sleek black hair that falls just past her shoulders, she's undoubtedly one of the most glamorous women I've ever seen. Tonight, she's wearing a fitted red velvet dress with a sweetheart neckline that cuts just above her bust. On her wedding finger, she wears a different ring from the engagement rock Emmett gifted her just after they graduated from college—something Mom would frequently talk about and fawn over.

Like she can sense my eyes on her, she tears her attention away from Emmett and sets her focus on me. I offer her a warm smile, which she tries—and fails—to return. If I didn't know better, I'd interpret her stoicism as hostile, convinced she has my apartment rigged with surveillance equipment.

Maria holds my gaze, forcing me to be the one to look away.

I stare into my half-finished glass of red wine, the first alcoholic drink I've had since giving birth to Blake.

"Has everyone finished with their dessert?" My question is automatic and definitely an excuse for me to stand and grab Blake's baby monitor. "I can clear the dishes if you are."

"No, no, sweetheart." Mom flaps her hand at me, her voice slurred, actions clumsy. "We can deal with those later."

"It's fine. I got it," I say, rounding the table and beginning to collect dishes.

When I reach Maria's bowl, she holds up a finger, asking me to wait. "I'm not done with mine just yet."

"Do you plan on licking it clean, Maria?" Mom chuckles.

Reaching into the center of the table, I'm aiming for the small jug of cream but completely misjudge it, knocking what's left all over Mom's pristine black tablecloth.

"Shit! I'm sorry," I groan, grabbing the jug on my second attempt and heading straight for the peace and quiet of the kitchen.

"Is Billie doing okay?" I hear Maria ask under her breath just as I cross the threshold. "She looks really stressed out tonight."

It takes me all of a minute to pack the first load of dishes into the dishwasher, clattering them together as I go.

Determined to keep my brain busy and away from unhelpful thoughts, I move to the silverware next.

"Billie?" Emmett's gruff voice is unmistakable, although it doesn't stop me from working.

Not until I feel the rough edges of his palm as it wraps around my upper arm, asking me to stop what I'm doing.

"What's going on, Billie?"

At the question, I spin around to face him, a fork in one hand and a ladle in the other.

He rolls his lips together, eyes dropping to my hands. "You aren't planning to attack me with those, are you?"

"I'm not sure how much damage can be inflicted with a ladle."

Emmett cocks his head to one side, studying my expression for clues. "I guess that depends on how mad your attacker is. Personally, I know this fiery redhead who very much lives up to her reputation. If she isn't giving me back talk, she's trying to bruise my ego over our age gap."

Despite my shitty mood, I can't help but smile.

He reaches out and takes the ladle and fork from my hands, placing them into the dishwasher. "What's going on, Billie?" He repeats his previous question.

Since the moment our eyes connected, he hasn't taken his off mine, and I feel his weighted gaze all the way into my toes.

"That's not a question I can answer."

There's barely any space between us, but Emmett's tall frame still manages to swallow the remainder. He gazes down at my left wrist; the dainty rose gold bracelet featuring a "B" he gifted me after Blake's birth rests against my skin. I love it so much, and I told him that straight after I opened it.

"And why is that?"

The half glass of wine I had earlier burns into my cheeks, or maybe it's down to his proximity. Either way, I know I'm revealing how much this man affects me.

In a cream silk cami and black faux leather pants that accentuate my curvy figure, I know I look good tonight, and I'm not ashamed to admit that I went the extra mile, aware that Emmett was going to show up. I thought he'd back out after everything that went on, but I should've known better than to assume he'd let his friends down.

And that's what he is—a friend to my parents.

Pulling a breath into my lungs, I let my gaze drop to what he's wearing—a white dress shirt that's open at the collar, revealing a glimpse of chest hair, along with a peek at his toned body, one I had the pleasure of touching not all that long ago. Emmett has this way of carrying off casual so effortlessly—sleeves rolled up to his elbows, a TAG Heuer watch decorating a muscular wrist.

As my mouth waters, I swallow thickly, determined to get ahold of myself.

"Because you already made it clear that we can never speak of us again."

He wets his lips, but it isn't because he wants to kiss me, even if I hope that the temptation has crossed his mind. "I thought we agreed that was the right thing to do?"

He's right; we did. Not that it helps to quell the need.

"Everything just feels awkward, is all." I lean forward and grab a kitchen towel from the counter behind him, ready to dry off the dishes Mom already cleaned.

Frustrated, Emmett practically snatches it from my hands, flipping it over his left shoulder.

"Talk to me, Billie. I don't want to lose you from my life because things got a little weird. That's the last thing I want."

On a sharp breath, I shake my head slowly. "I'd say that horse has already bolted, wouldn't you?"

Emmett moves even closer. If there wasn't a foot's height difference between us, we'd be nose to nose. Instead, he towers over me, head bowed and eyes burning with a need I can't decipher.

I hope it's a need for me, but I suspect he's after answers.

"If you're unhappy, then you need to tell me. I never want you to be unhappy and especially not because of something I've said or done."

I look off to the side, rain beating against the kitchen windows. It's pointless, going over old ground. We've already set the boundaries, and I'm not about to be reckless and test his willpower, even if my body screams to do just that.

"There are a lot of things in my life that aren't ideal at the moment. Some of them I can control, and others I can't. I'm not unhappy, Emmett, but I do need to focus on what's going to serve me."

His eyebrows rise almost to his hairline, but he doesn't speak again.

"I think I made a mistake, moving into that apartment."

"How?"

I pull the towel from his shoulder and turn around to face the drainer. "Everything's falling apart. From the cupboards to the flooring. And the other day, when I tried to run a bath for Blake, the hot water failed."

When Emmett's palm wraps around my waist, a couple of his fingers creep beneath the flimsy material of my cami. Aside from him taking my hand, it's the first real skin-to-skin contact we've shared, and I brace a palm on the counter in front of me, trying to steady myself.

Wow.

"Billie, look at me."

I shake my head, tears welling up in my eyes. I'm determined not to let anyone see how overwhelmed I am. "Just give me a second, okay?"

With the way he's holding me like this, we both know we're taking a risk on being seen.

"Not good enough, I'm afraid. Look at me." His voice is harder, a demand sitting behind his firm tone.

"I've complicated your life enough," I say, scrunching the towel in my left hand. I want to throw it at the goddamn wall in frustration.

Emmett grips the other side of my waist, slowly turning me to face him.

God, Jesus, he looks like a freaking dream. Waves of brown hair falling over his forehead, stopping just shy of the black frames on his glasses.

His eyes drop to my mouth, and he closes them, squeezing them shut like he's in pain. "You made exactly the right call when you moved into that apartment. Sure, it needs some work, but it's yours. A home for you and Blake and a place you can decorate however you want. That day you moved in, I saw it in your eyes, in the way you danced around the kitchen with your baby girl. That was the start of something new for you."

"How long were you watching me for?"

He just grins down at me, hands still planted on my waist. I swear I feel his thumbs circle my skin, but I don't look down to double-check.

"Long enough to establish that you are, in fact, the world's worst dancer."

I balk, the hand gripping the towel now pressed against his chest. "Take that back."

He shakes his head, and I swear when he dips it lower, he considers pressing his forehead to mine. "No, never. Not until you admit that you're a kick-ass mom who just bossed life and got her own place."

I narrow my eyes playfully. "I'm a kick-ass mom who just bossed life and got my own place … even if I'm still a terrible dancer."

His face breaks into a panty-melting smile. "Good girl."

I can't help it; the words tumble from my lips like a waterfall. "Maybe, one day, you can take me dancing and show me how it's done."

I brace for him to pull away or at least drop his hands from my hips. He does neither, holding me in place against the counter, chest rising and falling more rapidly than before.

When he parts his lips to speak, I draw a deep breath into my lungs.

"Ha-ha! Yes. Let me just check if Billie is making the coffee."

The sound of Mom approaching rips our bodies apart, Emmett backing several steps away. He grabs another towel from the side and begins wiping down an already-clean countertop.

Mom appears in the doorway with Maria following up behind her with the rest of the dishes I forgot to collect.

She pauses when her gaze lands on Emmett, clearing his throat as they both step into the kitchen.

"Billie and I were just figuring out how to use your new coffee machine, Freya."

It's a poor alibi, and he knows it.

Not that Mom is any the wiser. She's too high on life—and booze—to notice as she makes her way to the machine and begins filling it with beans.

"That's an interesting comment, Emmett."

My attention snaps back to Maria as she sets the remainder of the dishes down in front of him, lips pursed, eyes suspicious.

"Given, the last time I checked"—she tips her chin at the coffee machine, and Mom fires it up—"that's the exact same model we used to have right before you ended our marriage."

CHAPTER NINETEEN

BILLIE

The following day, my previously bad mood has not improved at all.

How difficult can it be for a landlord to fix broken cupboard doors that won't shut? Three times I called him last night about ongoing issues, every one of my attempts being sent straight to voicemail. In reality, I can deal with a couple of broken shelves and hinges. It's the hot water that's giving me the biggest headache. Blake needs daily baths at the moment, and I need to wash dishes.

With Blake under one arm, I snatch up my cell and try once more to make contact.

"Hi. This is Billie Quinn at number twenty-five." I work to keep my voice professional when, in fact, I would like to shove my landlord's head in a blender. "I just moved in, like, a week ago, and the issues with the apartment continue to stack up. As you know, I have a newborn and—"

The sound of knocking cuts me short.

"Hang on," I continue. "That could be you at my door right now."

Hitting End on the call, I head straight for the front door, convinced that it can only be my landlord since no one else can enter the building without being buzzed up or possessing a key or the code.

"Hey, Bill. Your neighbor was leaving and let me into the building."

Crouching to inspect the seal around the doorjamb, Emmett greets me with a smile that only grows wider when he takes in my daughter, dressed in a unicorn onesie. When he turns his attention back to the door, dissatisfaction crosses his face, and then he rises to his full height in front of me.

As I stand to one side and he enters, I'm acutely aware of my lack of greeting. But when a guy looks the way Emmett does this morning, I think I speak on behalf of most women when I say ...

Hot freaking damn.

In black dress pants that stop just above stylish gray sneakers, he finishes off a mouthwatering look with a casual dark blue button-down, sleeves rolled up to his elbows, revealing my favorite forearms.

Hands in his pockets, he does a three-sixty in the center of my living room, inspecting the apartment in detail.

"Can I help you?" I finally say, a small chuckle rising up my throat.

Even though I was hoping to find my landlord when I opened the door, I'm way more delighted to see Emmett. After last night's awkward exchange with Maria and Mom almost catching us, we haven't breathed another word to each other.

"Has your landlord called you back?" Emmett's eyes finally find mine, a softness in them that doesn't reflect our conversation.

I shake my head, confused. "No. But how do you know I tried to make contact?"

He moves a fraction closer, hands still in his pockets, like they frequently are when he's near me. "I overheard you leaving a voicemail for him last night, right before I left to head home."

Pulling out his cell, he hands it over to me. "Let me take Blake while you key in your landlord's number."

I shake my head. "It's pointless, trying to contact him. I said the same to my dad last night. He isn't even picking up when I call."

Emmett beckons his fingers at Blake, asking me to pass her over. "You just concentrate on giving me his details, and let me worry about getting ahold of your landlord."

I look down at my daughter and then back at Emmett. "Are you sure you can handle her?" I have zero concerns about him holding Blake, especially after the way he was with her before we went to the park that day. Still, a familiar sense of guilt over everything he's doing for us compels me to ask.

He doesn't even hesitate. "I held my captain's baby girl last Christmas, so I know the drill—support their head, but most importantly ..." He trails off and reaches out, taking Blake from my arms before confidently cradling her in his. A big grin pulls at his full lips, and Blake instantly settles into his broad chest. "Most importantly, it's all about smiles and giggles." His face fills with warmth. "Isn't that right, baby girl?"

I should be typing my landlord's number into Emmett's phone, which I've called so many times that I now have it memorized. Instead, I'm gaping at the man standing before me, almost as hard as my daughter is.

Adjusting the fluffy hood over Blake's head, Emmett tips his chin at his cell. "All done?"

"Yeah," is all I manage as I enter the final digit, handing the phone back to Emmett.

I hold my arms out, ready to take Blake back.

He shakes his head and begins pacing the apartment, my daughter's eyelids drooping closed when he puts the phone to his ear.

It must be ten seconds before Emmett speaks in a voice I've never heard before, a clipped edge to a professional tone.

"My name is Emmett Richards, and I'm a close friend of your

new tenant, Billie Quinn." He wraps his arm tighter around Blake, taking a couple of steps into my kitchen and heading straight for one of the broken cupboards. "As I'm sure you are aware, Billie has tried, on numerous occasions, to bring a number of issues with her apartment to your attention." He clears his throat, warm gaze landing on Blake. "Tell me, do you make a habit of ignoring all your tenants' phone calls, or is it just the ones where some effort is required on your part? For example, if Billie were to pull all rental payments until such time that you address the state of disrepair in her property, I'm willing to bet that we would hear from you in a more than timely fashion."

I look on, biting down on my bottom lip.

"I'm not sure if you're a fan of hockey or even care who I am, but let me make one thing clear: Billie Quinn and her newborn baby are your top priority, as is the hot water issue that's currently preventing her from bathing Blake and cleaning dishes and baby equipment." Emmett's eyes flick to mine as he confirms, "Now, it just so happens that you're in luck with the kitchen cabinets since I'm currently visiting and have a toolbox in the trunk of my car. But the flooring by her couch needs immediate attention—by tomorrow at the very latest."

Speaking of the floor, I fully melt into it when Emmett switches the call to speaker so Blake can wrap her tiny palm around his pointer finger, something I thought she only loved to do with me.

"To clarify," he begins, rounding up the message, "I don't need you to call back on this number to make arrangements. I need you to simply start paying attention to two very important people in my life." His eyes find mine again, and I swallow thickly. "The kind of people who would make me take serious action really fast if anyone screwed them over." He leaves his sentence there, satisfied that its meaning cannot be misinterpreted. "Billie looks forward to hearing from you in the very near future."

"My landlord's stopping by tomorrow night when he gets back into town," I confirm to Emmett, setting my phone down on the counter while I watch him tighten the final hinge on a kitchen cupboard.

Blake went down for a nap a half hour ago, and all I've done in that time is drink coffee and observe the show playing out in front of me.

He finishes up and checks the alignment.

I felt sure Emmett would look more pleased at the outcome. It took less than ten minutes for me to receive a call I'd been waiting on for several days.

"What's the matter?" I ask, noticing the pinch between his brows as he rests his forearms on the opposite end of the small island where I'm sitting.

"It just pisses me off," he replies, deeper lines creasing into his forehead. "How long was he going to leave you and Blake in this mess?"

I drop my eyes to the butcher's block countertop. "It's pointless, thinking about that; the important thing is that he's going to make the repairs."

When I cast my eyes up, Emmett's no longer standing in front of me, but right by my side, his familiar cologne causing my thighs to pinch.

A growl emanates from his chest, and he reaches up, tugging at a few strands of his hair. "He knew what he was doing and was testing the limits of how much he could get away with. Assholes like that piss me off. I hate even more that he did it to a woman and her newborn."

I open my mouth to speak, but Emmett gets there first.

"What about tonight? How will you bathe Blake?"

My eyes settle on the empty pan sitting on top of my stove.

"No. Absolutely fucking not," he practically spits. "You can't stay here tonight if that's what you're using to heat water."

I shrug, having done that exact thing for several nights on

repeat. "It's fine. It doesn't take me all that long to heat the water to the correct temperature for Blake."

Like he forgets himself completely, Emmett's hand lands on the arm of my barstool, turning me to face him straight on. "No, Billie. I can't leave you tonight, knowing that's how you plan to spend your evening."

I gaze around at the apartment. "Well, if you have any other bright ideas, then let's hear them. I'm all ears."

There's a hint of challenge in Emmett's eyes. "You could stay over at my place. I have a huge tub and several spare bedrooms."

My eyes grow wider. "Are you being serious?"

He returns my earlier shrug. "Deadly. You can't stay here until your landlord fixes the fundamentals."

"Emmett," I blow out, hands twisting nervously in my lap. "Don't you think that's a little dangerous? What if someone sees me entering your apartment?" I pause, taking a second to choose my next words carefully. "I mean, we both know that there's nothing going on between us, but it could look a little weird to other people."

Silence descends, Emmett's hand gripping the arm on my stool even tighter.

"No one will see us, Billie."

"How can you be so sure?" I counter.

He pushes a quick hand through his hair, eyes drifting away from mine before landing back on me.

Whenever we make eye contact, I feel like I'm learning to breathe for the very first time.

"I have a private elevator directly into my penthouse."

I fight the urge to tease him about being a fancy bastard, choosing to keep the conversation on point.

"The safer option would be to drop me at my parents' place."

Emmett nods a couple of times, acknowledging that I'm right, although I can see he's not paying much thought to the suggestion. We both want to spend time together, even if we aren't admitting it out loud.

"If that's where you'd prefer to stay, then we can gather Blake's bassinet and diaper bag, and I'll give you a ride. No worries."

More silence. More tension. Burning apprehension over how this is going to play out.

Emmett speaks first, his words soft and hushed, reflecting the underlying risk I know he's taking by simply showing up here. "Scott and Freya have no idea that I'm with you right now. I came here straight from morning skate." A grimace pulls at his chiseled features. "If I drive you to their place, then they may ask questions as to why you didn't just call Freya to pick you up."

I chew on my bottom lip. "If they did, I would tell them the truth about us."

Emmett's knuckles turn white. "And what exactly is the truth, Billie?"

I could answer his question silently with my lips. But it's my words that eventually win out, common sense prevailing. "That we're friends and you are stepping up to help out in the wake of Dad's accident."

When Emmett edges closer, a simple swipe of his tongue could reach my bottom lip. His eyes drop to my mouth, revealing that he's having the exact same thought.

"The last time we were alone in this apartment, I made it clear that I would always be honest, especially when it came to you and Blake."

He watches the column of my throat work as I swallow down his words.

"I'm not here today, or any other day, just because Scott is out of action and your mom needs to work. I'm here because I want to be and because I like spending time with you and Blake."

The hand not gripping my stool reaches up to my face, but at the final second, Emmett slides it into his pocket, the slightest show of unease entering his body language.

"I want to spend more time with you both."

I clear my throat, ready to reveal that I feel the same way.

"Is that what you want?" he rushes out, anxiety laced in his voice.

My gaze tracks to the bedroom, Blake's bassinet just visible, her soft snores echoing through the monitor next to me. Truthfully, I have zero idea what will happen if I say yes and we head back to his place. All I know is, other than my baby girl, he's the person that I want to be around the most.

And despite our precarious situation and complicated lives, somehow, everything feels simpler, easier, when I'm in his company.

I wrap a palm around the tense fist he's formed on my stool, fingers relaxing in response to mine. "Yes. Spending more time with you is what I want. Take us to your place."

CHAPTER TWENTY

EMMETT

SCOTT

Hey, buddy. I'm ready when you are.

While Billie is bathing Blake, getting her ready for bed, I get to work on slicing potatoes for the pot roast that I've been slow-cooking for most of the afternoon.

Up until the text I just received from Scott, everything has been going smoothly. Billie and Blake entered my apartment without being noticed.

Slicing the final potato, I pick up my phone and stare down at the message, racking my brain over what he's referring to.

Fuck.

The second Billie strolls into my kitchen, the reason behind Scott's text hits me.

We were supposed to watch a soccer game at Lloyd's tonight, and I offered to pick him up from home, given he's not able to drive at the moment.

When Billie sees my face, she stops in her tracks, Blake's baby monitor suspended in one hand.

Dressed in black leggings and an oversize pink sweater, she looks fucking glorious with her hair piled on top of her head, deep red strands cascading around a heart-shaped face. Women around the world spend hours perfecting their appearance and still come up short compared to Billie in everyday casuals.

Big green eyes drop to the phone in my hand, a silent question in them.

"I was supposed to be heading out with Scott tonight," I explain, scratching at the back of my neck. "And I completely forgot."

She points at the phone. "That's him messaging you about it, isn't it?"

I give her a tight nod.

Coming to sit at my kitchen island, she hops onto one of the stools, splaying her palms out against the marble top.

"It's not too late to go now. I can take over the dinner and leave some for you to reheat when you get home."

I don't think I've ever hated an idea as much as I hate the one she just suggested.

I shake my head, immediately giving her a, "No. I'll tell him that I came down with the flu."

Billie looks unsure, twisting her hands around, as she always does when she's either deep in thought or uncomfortable.

I want to stride across the kitchen and take them in mine, partly for an excuse to touch her and partly so she'll stop freaking out, like I know she is right now.

My body stays rooted to the same spot, fingers moving over my keyboard as I type out a reply to Scott.

"You said that you never lie." Billie's observation stops me before I hit Send on the message, and I look up at her, chest tightening, stomach coiling. "And you shouldn't start by lying to your friend."

She's right; I don't lie. In all the years I was married to Maria, I always told her the truth, especially when she asked me if we were done for the final time. I've also never lied to Scott before, but then I've never been in this kind of situation either.

"I can grab Blake, and you can drop me at Mom and Dad's at the same time you pick him up."

I take my previous thought back. I hate her latest suggestion even more.

When she goes to slide off the stool, I make my decision, hitting Send on a text claiming that I'm sick.

Billie tracks the movement, rounding the counter and coming to stand in front of me.

I set the phone down on the counter, fingers itching to reach out and touch her.

"What are we doing, Emmett?" Her whispered question isn't one I can supply with a straight answer.

"Spending time together because we want to." My urge to touch her wins out, and I reach up, tucking a piece of hair behind her ear. "Aside from tonight, how many more opportunities will we get to do this?"

She pins her bottom lip between her teeth. "You can always come over to my place."

I sigh, "Sure. Because we haven't already had one unexpected visitor. Who's to say the next one won't be Freya?"

"We could tell them that we're friends—because that's what we are, right?"

More impossible questions. Only this time, I know she doesn't need an answer. This is Billie looking for reassurance for what she already knows.

We stepped out of the friend zone a while back. Even if all we've shared are fleeting glances and the occasional tender touch.

I decide to give her what she needs, accepting that the confusing limbo we're in is here to stay. "Do you think that if your dad could see the way we interact in private, he would agree that our relationship is purely platonic?"

A sea of deep green looks up at me, like an ocean with no limit to its depth, an undiscovered underworld I'm willingly being pulled into. I've no clue how far my descent will go, and I guess much of that is down to Billie and if I'm prepared to risk my life, exploring a dangerous unknown.

"No."

Her single-worded response pulls my mouth closer to Billie's. One dip of my chin, and my lips would feel hers for the first time.

There would be no going back, a kiss that would seal my fate. My friendship with her father would be up in smoke. Scott Quinn would never forgive me. *I'd* never forgive me if Billie were my daughter and the man who had insisted on helping out my family by giving money and rides to the hospital made a move.

Even if that couldn't be further from the truth, that's the way he would see things—a richer, older guy bagging his vulnerable daughter after the failure of his own marriage and the demise of her relationship.

Do I want Billie in my bed tonight? Jesus Christ. I've wanted her in my arms since the second I laid eyes on her for the first time in over three years. Back in February, I thought I could control my desire, convincing myself that Sawyer was right when he told me that my attraction to Billie was a fallout from the divorce.

But that was then, and this is now. And the way I'm starting to feel for Billie has nothing to do with my split from Maria. If I wanted to fuck someone, then I'd pick a girl up in Lloyd's and bring her back to my place for some fun.

Except it wouldn't be fun. It would be fucking torturous. All my body craves is Billie Quinn, and all my mind needs is to be around her.

My hand finds her hip, pulling her body into me. It's likely she can feel my growing cock as it strains behind the zipper on my dress pants. I'm risking taking this too far, but the burn in her eyes confirms that she's comfortable with me holding her like this.

I fucking *love* holding her like this.

As she reaches up to my face, I feel sure she's going to cup my cheek in her palm, the bracelet I spent way too fucking long picking out as a gift to celebrate her becoming a mom, shining beneath my kitchen lights. It was risky buying her something so personal and expensive, but Scott and Freya saw it as a thoughtful keepsake, even if all I wanted was for Billie to experience what it's like when a man spoils the girl he can't get out of his head.

When she pulls off my glasses and sets them on the counter behind her, I wonder what she's going to do next.

"Your eyes look just as unsure without lenses."

I press myself into her again, overstepping more moral lines but powerless to prevent the urge. "Do I feel unsure about you, Billie?"

Heat creeps up her throat. "No. But Collins was right when she said that a man's eyes never lie. That's something I should've paid more attention to when I got with Tucker."

The mere mention of that fucker's name douses the fire burning between us. I'm mad as hell about the way he treated Billie and Blake, but his existence also serves as an important reminder as to what this woman has been through. What her body has endured over the past few weeks since she gave birth to her daughter.

She might not be ready for another man, and I should get a fucking grip on myself.

What the fuck am I doing?

I release my hold on her hip, edging back and immediately feeling the loss of her warm body.

Billie gazes at me like she didn't want me to pull away. Even if we both know it was the smart thing to do. The *only* option we should take.

"Is Maria still in love with you?"

My eyes snap to hers. "What?"

Billie hoists herself onto the counter, fixing a few strands of hair that fell across her face, a legacy of pink still staining her prominent cheekbones.

My legs scream at me to move forward and step between her thighs.

"Her comment about the coffee maker at Mom's birthday

meal and the way she looked at you all night ..." She trails off, chewing on the corner of her right thumb. "I think she still has feelings for you."

I can see why Billie would conclude that, and it frustrates the shit out of me.

Reaching forward, I pick up my glasses and set them back on my face, the sharpness of her beauty coming back into focus.

"Maria hasn't loved me in a long time."

She cocks her head to the side, a familiar look of challenge narrowing her eyes. "That's not how it looked to me."

I brace my palms on either side of her thighs and dip my head to capture all of her attention. We might not be able to do the things we want, but I'm sure as shit not letting Billie run away with the thought that a reconciliation with my ex-wife is even remotely in the cards.

"Maria doesn't want me, and I don't want Maria anymore. The difference is, she doesn't want me to be with anyone else. Call it a need to control or an insane level of jealousy. Call it whatever you want."

"But—"

"But nothing, Billie," I cut her off, working to keep my voice firm but kind. "The truth is that Maria and I had been off and on for a long time, even if we kept a lot of our marital troubles out of public view. Crazy arguments led to multiple temporary separations, and by the time we finally called it quits, I had been sleeping in our spare room for months. I wanted out of the marriage because it was toxic, she clung on to what we'd had when we first met and were very different people."

I'm desperate for her to believe me, so I keep talking.

"I don't want Maria anymore." I stop short of what I was going to tag on, finishing my sentence internally and hoping that she can read between our very blurred lines.

I want you. In my bed. Wrapped around me until sunlight creeps through the blinds.

"Do you want to get back with Tucker?"

"No!" She looks almost disgusted at the thought.

Sliding my hand along the counter, I place it over hers.

I can't stop touching this girl.

"And what if he came back into your life? What then?"

As a friend, I'd be asking her that question out of concern, worried that she'd take him back for the benefit of her daughter when plenty of good people co-parent. And while I'm still asking her that question for all of the above reasons, a selfish part of me has to know the truth about her feelings. Because the thought of Billie climbing into anyone's bed other than my own makes me want to pour gasoline on this entire apartment block, light a match, and watch it burn into nothing but ash.

She worries her lip for a moment, eyes moving toward my hallway, no doubt thinking about what's best for Blake.

I give her this moment to process thoughts.

"Tucker returning to try and make amends would never happen." She finally responds with an answer I didn't exactly want to hear. What I wanted was the same hard no I'd received a few minutes earlier.

In so many ways, her reconsideration is a testament to how devoted she is as a mom—putting Blake's needs before her own.

Still, I can't help the next few words as they tumble from my lips.

"He isn't good enough for you."

Billie nods, but I'm not totally convinced she believes it, and that breaks my heart in fucking two. I might not be able to call her my own, but I'll be goddamned if the man she eventually finds isn't absolute perfection for her. He'll have to be to get past Scott, but also to earn my acceptance after I've emptied the contents of my stomach in private.

I don't know how long passes between us, dinner no further along than when I replied to Scott.

"You know what really sucks?" she asks as I head for the fridge, pulling out the same brand of wine I bought for her in Italy.

Her eyes light up. "Gimme!"

Pouring her a glass, I hand it over and resume my previous position at the counter, watching her sip wine like some kind of fucking loser.

"What sucks?"

She swallows another sip and sets the glass down beside her.

"That we can't find more ways to spend time together without it being obvious."

Picking up her glass, I take a sip myself. I don't drink a lot, but I couldn't pass up the opportunity to see how she would react to me drinking from the same glass.

Her mouth pops open, and I swirl the wine in my hand. Male satisfaction rolling through me.

"You could always come to one of my games. You used to with Scott."

She considers my suggestion. "Are we talking me coming to a game alone or with my dad?"

Alone. I always want you alone.

"Either. With your dad would probably be the safest bet. If Freya would take Blake for an evening, you could come to one of our night games and sit in the box with Collins and the rest of the girls."

She looks excited at that, and I'm instantly making plans to ensure it happens.

"With Scott, of course," I add.

Billie just smiles, and I love it.

Handing the glass back to her, I reach for my phone and type out another text to my closest friend, feeling like the worst person on the planet for the shit I've spun him all night.

ME

Sorry again about tonight, buddy. But how about you head to one of the games next week? The family box will be accessible for people on crutches, and if you want, you could bring Billie along. Just like old times, eh?

CHAPTER TWENTY-ONE

BILLIE

Unlike my place, Emmett's floor doesn't creak when I tiptoe down the hallway with Blake at just past five a.m.

To my surprise, Blake slept-in this morning, even if the dark circles under my eyes tell the real story of how I managed less than four hours last night.

I was painfully aware that just across the hallway, Emmett was sleeping only a few feet away. It felt a strange combination of foreign and comforting, staying overnight in his place. With his penthouse set so many floors above street level, everything is eerily quiet, a stark contrast to my apartment that never seems to fall silent.

And speaking of stark, Emmett really needs to start thinking about turning this place into a home. A single small plant in the corner of his living room is really the only color in an otherwise bland box. Everything is neat and tidy, but nothing feels lived in. I remember visiting the place he shared with Maria for the holidays, and I half expected to see some of the same soft furnishings scattered around in here. But I don't recognize a single item from his previous marriage.

He really meant it when he said that the divorce was a clean break for him, the empty walls a reminder that Emmett truly is rebuilding his life.

Adjusting Blake in my arms, I lift my nursing top so she can take her morning feed. The floor-to-ceiling windows provide a breathtaking panoramic view of nighttime Brooklyn, the whole city still smothered in darkness.

I pad across and take in the view, dropping my face to the top of Blake's head so I can inhale her fresh baby scent. She had a ball in Emmett's oversize tub last night, splashing around until her tiny limbs were fresh out of energy.

Maybe that's why she slept so well. Or maybe she simply enjoyed the peace and quiet of Emmett's luxury apartment. Maybe it's neither of those things and everything to do with the man she loves to be held by. The second Blake sits against Emmett's chest, it's like her whole world goes still, eyelids drooping, chest rising and falling a little slower. At first, I thought it was a preference for men, but by the way she squirms in my dad's arms, I think my daughter might follow after her mom when it comes to Emmett Richards.

"We can't catch feelings, Blakey," I whisper into her hair, closing my eyes as she continues to suckle on my breast.

For so much of my pregnancy, I dreaded motherhood. A real fear that I'd fail ate away at me in the dead of night. Being honest, I'm still not sure if I'm pulling it off. Mom is convinced that I'm killing it, although I'd argue that the credit should go to Blake. She's the easiest baby in postnatal classes, drawing envious comments from other new moms about how they wished their babies would learn to chill out.

When I think about it, it's hard to believe that she's Tucker's daughter. That boy wouldn't know the meaning of *relax* if it slapped him right across the face. A tempting thought and definitely an accurate one.

Reaching into the pocket of my robe, I pull out my phone

and take a quick selfie of me and Blake, attaching it to a message for Clara.

Her reply is immediate, but that doesn't shock me. She's likely pulling an all-nighter, the queen of leaving assignments until the final minute.

CLARA

I have a couple of questions. One, why do you not send me more photos of that stunning baby girl? Because ... wow! Two, where the fuck are you? Buckingham fucking Palace?

I blow out a laugh as she returns a photo of her, sitting alone in the library, papers stacked around her, along with three cans of Alani energy drink.

But as my laughter fades and Blake slips into a milk-induced coma, I'm hit with an emotion I wasn't expecting to feel when I first messaged my friend.

Sadness.

My time in that library is over, as is the life I once led around campus. Late-night studying with Clara, followed by early morning sprints to my professor's office to make submission deadlines—that was what my life once centered around. If the campus coffee shop had run out of raisin toast, that was a disaster to me, especially if I had a lecture first thing with Professor Barnett, otherwise known as The Dragon.

Perhaps it makes me a bad mom to grieve the life I once had, and if it does, then I guess I'll have to sit with that reality. Because regardless of the deep way that I love my daughter, the dreams I once had of graduating with honors and studying for the bar exam are all but gone. A promise of support from Tucker and his family has transpired into nothing more than false hope and bitter feelings toward a boy I thought I once loved. And now, as I stand here, looking out over the Brooklyn skyline, I realize that nothing in life is guaranteed, and neither are the people that you think have your back—a hard fucking lesson to learn at only twenty-one-years-old.

ME

If I told you, then I'd have to kill you.

CLARA

Be my guest. If I don't turn in this paper on time, I'm pretty sure my dad will throttle me anyway.

ME

So dramatic.

CLARA

Perhaps. Anyway, back to you and your lavish surroundings.

I look down at a sleeping Blake, thinking about how much I should reveal to my college friend. I'm hesitant to tell her too much, but I also need a girlfriend to talk to about Emmett.

ME

Do you remember me mentioning my dad's best friend being an NHL player?

CLARA

Girl, how could I forget? Although I'm still pissed about the fact that you wouldn't tell me his name.

ME

I'm in his apartment.

CLARA

Cool.

Wait.

At five a.m.?!

Start. Talking.

ME

I'm not sleeping with him, if that's what you're thinking.

CLARA

So, you decided to have a pajama party at his place?

ME

My apartment needs maintenance, and he offered for me to stay here until it's fixed.

CLARA

Sorry, but do you expect me to believe this?

ME

It's the truth.

CLARA

I don't doubt that it is. All I'm saying is, you could've stayed at your parents', no?

I turn on my heel, heading for the bedroom so I can set Blake down in her bassinet. Then I take a seat on the edge of the bed. The only light in the apartment is the one filtering down the hallway from the living room floor lamp. Shrugging off my robe, I take in Emmett's closed bedroom door.

ME

He's my friend, but I can't deny that there's something between us. We've spent a lot of time together since I got back from Austin.

CLARA

Have you guys spoken about it?

ME

Sort of. It's pointless though because nothing could ever happen, even if we wanted it to.

CLARA

Because of his friendship with your dad?

...

ME

That and other complications. Including the fact that he's fourteen years older than me.

CLARA

Shit. Billie, are you asking me for permission to fuck your dad's best friend?

When light suddenly shines beneath Emmett's bedroom door, my heart thumps in my chest.

ME

I don't know what I'm asking for.

CLARA

Well, I'll tell you what you're asking for instead then. Trouble. Your whole world just got turned upside down at the hands of a prick who, by the way, just broke it off with Rachael, saying that he wanted to "make the most of" his final semester. Ugh.

ME

I don't care about Tucker.

CLARA

Good. But let his memory be a lesson in men. You're hot, and this guy is much older. The chances are, he wants to bang you to prove a point to himself.

I shake my head at Clara's last text, and my regret over bringing this up with her grows stronger.

ME

I don't think that's true. Emmett's a good guy.

Shit.

CLARA

Holy. SHIT. You're talking about the Blades defenseman Emmett Richards!

ME

Please, PLEASE don't say anything.

The next thing I know, a voice message lands in our text thread.

Lowering the volume, I hit Play and hold the speaker to my ear.

"Okay, so this is where I take it all back," Clara's giddy voice whispers down the phone. "Bang him. Fuck his goddamn brains out. Emmett freaking *Richards*? Girl, he is quite possibly the hottest thing I have ever seen on skates, and here you are, sitting in his apartment at five in the morning, listening to my voice note when you should be hearing him call you a good girl. Woof."

I snort a laugh and close out the message, setting my cell down beside me on the duvet.

What would Emmett do if I crept into his room, dressed in tiny pajamas?

Maybe his light is an invitation for me to do just that?

With my confidence bolstered and inhibitions at an all-time low, thanks to Clara's voice note, I cross the hallway and stand at Emmett's door, closing my eyes and drawing in a deep breath as I twist the handle.

A large king-size bed sits in the center of another stark white room, one bedside lamp lit and a dark gray duvet thrown back, almost like he climbed out of bed in a hurry.

Turning on my heel, I realize how stupid of an idea this really is when the sound of his shower turning on stops me in my tracks.

With the door to his en suite partially open, the opportunity to take a few more paces and catch a glimpse of the naked body I know I'll never get to touch proves to be too tempting.

My conscience knows that this is wrong on so many levels,

but the increasing thrum of my pulse urges me to keep moving forward.

And when my hand finally reaches the door, pushing it open so I can get a better view, my previously fast heart rate spikes.

This isn't how I expected to find Emmett. I thought he'd be standing under a stream of hot water, massaging soap into his glorious body.

Instead, he's massaging his dick.

Up and down, his fist moves from the base to the tip of a long, thick shaft, the other hand braced above his head, palm splayed out against a white tiled wall.

I should back away and leave, but I know he can't see me, his head bowed between his shoulders, muscles rippling in his back.

Another stroke of his hand pulls a groan from his throat and then ... a breathless cry of my name from his lips. He's close, and I'm wet, thighs pinching as I brace a hand on the doorjamb in front of me.

Move, Billie.

Emmett switches hands, beating a fist against the tiles as his pleasure picks up. He's fantasizing about me, and it's the hottest fucking thing I have ever witnessed.

He's the hottest man I have ever seen.

I toss my gaze toward the ceiling, fighting the urge to reach inside my panties.

"Billie?!"

When Emmett repeats my name, I know it's not a lustful plea.

And when our eyes connect, water cascading down his horrified face, what remains of my soul rapidly leaves my body.

CHAPTER TWENTY-TWO

EMMETT

Curtis Freeman—the Scorpions forward and general asshole—comes barreling toward me on a breakaway, but it'll be a cold day in hell when I let this arrogant prick get the better of me.

The Kronwall I give him is hard enough to send him crashing into the boards, but soft enough to keep him conscious.

"That's for putting our key defenseman in the hospital last season, you fucking piece of shit." I deliver my sentence with a smile as he slowly climbs to his feet, adjusting his helmet.

He squares up to me, knocking his visor against mine. "Schneider had it coming, and he knew it."

"Williams," I bite out. "His name is Tommy Williams now."

"Okay, okay. Either one of you needs to drop your gloves or we restart the play." The ref plants a palm on each of our chests, putting some distance between us.

Freeman's eyes burn with a desire to fight, even if his smaller frame doesn't stand a chance against me. I've been fighting my whole hockey career; he's barely out of diapers.

"Rein it in, Curtis." Scorpions forward, Jessie Callaghan, slides toward us. After tipping his chin at me in acknowledgment, he turns his attention to Freeman, voice dropping low as he tells his center to get a fucking grip on himself. "Are you trying to put yourself in the emergency room? Show a little goddamn respect for what happened last season. Williams nearly died!"

"Come on now, Curtis." Tommy pulls up next to me, chewing on the corner of his mouthguard. "That's no way to make friends when you're already two to one, down in the third. Besides"—he knocks his glove against Freeman's helmet, a patronizing move designed to taunt him—"Richards here would destroy you with his first punch."

"Why are you still here, *Schneider*?" Freeman accentuates Tommy's former last name, hoping to get a rise out of my teammate.

If there's one guy on this team you don't want to piss off, it's one thousand percent Tommy. However, luckily for Freeman, Tommy only fights when he needs to these days, frequently opting to take the moral high ground.

"I save my punches for people who are worth the effort," Tommy retorts.

"Are we going to fight or play?" The ref intervenes again, raising his voice so we can hear it over the crowd.

It's wild in here tonight, and this exchange with Freeman has only fueled the fire. After the incident between Freeman and Tommy last season, there's been a ton of speculation leading up to tonight's game, including whether Tommy would slip back into his former ways and crush Freeman in a fight.

"We're going to play," I reply, eyes tracking to the Jumbotron.

The chances of Billie showing on-screen are slim to almost zero, but I keep my eyes locked on it for a moment longer, letting her know that even when I'm mid-game, she's always on my mind.

"That was some goddamn performance out there tonight!" Coach Morgan moves around the locker room, bumping fists with each of his players in his usual postgame routine, whether we win or lose.

He stops in front of me, pressing his lips together in thought. "Of all the guys I'd want in that position tonight with Freeman, you would've been my first pick. Good work killing the break-away, even better work putting Freeman back in his box."

"Where he fucking belongs," Archer adds right as he bumps fists with Coach and dumps himself down beside me on the bench. "Top of the league, bro. I can feel another Cup coming on."

"Don't fucking jinx it," I jest, pulling my jersey overhead before getting to work on unlacing my skates.

"Are you gracing us with your presence at Lloyd's tonight?" he asks, an unmistakable twinkle in his eye. He knows that Billie and Scott are here tonight since Darcy was the one who met them at the arena entrance. "Or are you entertaining at home instead?"

Pulling off my second skate, I sit down beside him. "Has anyone ever told you that you're the world's most annoying teammate?"

He makes a face akin to pride. "From time to time. But my question was a serious one. Are you coming out to Lloyd's?" He leans closer, dropping his voice to barely a whisper. "And are you bringing Billie?"

My eyes grow wide at the memory of when she not only caught sight of my dick, but witnessed her name tumble from my lips as I brought myself to the edge with thoughts of how she'd suck me so well.

"No one can hear what we're saying," Archer declares, casting his hand around the room, the rest of the team either heading for the showers or deep in their own conversations.

I shake my head at him. It's been nearly a week since I dropped Billie and Blake back home that fateful morning, and not a single word has been exchanged between us since. I'm pretty sure that she wants to die of embarrassment, and I've been thinking about turning Catholic, mainly for the benefit of a confession.

I jerked off to thoughts of my best friend's only daughter.

And I fucking loved every goddamn second of it.

"I'm not even sure she'll stick around for the players' lounge."

Archer frowns at me. "Did something bad happen?"

Clearing my throat, I wait for Coach Morgan to move past us. When I'm confident we have adequate privacy, my head drops into my hands.

"Oh shit a fucking brick. You fucked her, didn't you?!"

"Nope," I mumble. "It's arguably worse than that."

When Archer doesn't reply, I slowly turn my face toward him.

He just sits there, jaw popped open, staring back at me in horror.

"Don't look at me like that," I scold.

"Like what?"

"Like you're judging me. We all know that you did some questionable shit in your time."

His wince is an agreeable one. "True."

"She walked in on me taking a shower."

"Oh."

"And I was jerking off to thoughts of her."

"Fuck."

When Archer doesn't add anything else, I pinch the bridge of my nose, images of her tight body in tiny sleep shorts flashing through my mind.

"Say something," I beg.

"Like what?"

"I don't know ..." I blow out. "Tell me the first thing that entered your head when I told you what happened."

Archer rests his elbows on his knees, brows pinched together in thought. "Does she know that you were jerking to thoughts of her?"

I nod once. "If she was standing there for at least ten seconds, then she heard me speak her name."

"This is bad."

"Thanks for the observation, Captain Obvious."

Archer rolls his eyes at me. "What are you going to do about it?"

I chew on my bottom lip as a wave of sadness washes over me. I've missed Billie and Blake so fucking much this past week, all because I couldn't think of what to say each time I picked up my phone to message her.

"If she shows up tonight, then I'm going to engineer a way to get her alone. We need to talk, and it has to be face-to-face."

A cunning smile grows on Archer's face, and suddenly, it's like I'm talking his language. "I can distract Scott with conversation while you bang his daughter's brains out."

"You're a sick man. You know that, don't you, Moore?"

His shoulders shake with laughter. "No more twisted than you."

I fall silent, unable to argue with that logic.

"But in all seriousness, if you want to spend some time with Billie later, I can double as a decent wingman."

When he holds out his fist for me, I bump it straight back. "Thanks, man. This past week has been a fucking nightmare."

Leaning back against the wall, Archer clicks his tongue. "Last time we spoke, you told me you didn't have any kind of feelings for her. That isn't strictly true, is it?"

The next couple of seconds feel like an eternity as I chew over my response. I can't keep denying how I feel—to myself or to Archer. It's been a long time since I fell for a woman, but I know my heart is heading that way with Billie. The thought of claiming that what we have is purely physical makes me feel sick. I've lost count of the number of times I've tried to avoid catching feelings, yet here I am, sitting on this bench, trying to fight the fact that I'm falling. So, if anything is a testament to how strong I feel or how inevitable we are, then this moment right here is exactly that.

Acceptance should make this whole situation straightforward. Instead, all it does is complicate things further because we can't be together. Not in a relationship or even for a single night. I'm failing at keeping a lid on my emotions, and that's not something I've struggled with before.

"I'm so confused," I sigh. "All I know is, my poker face is cracking, and I'm in so much fucking trouble. Despite all the dangers, I keep wading into deeper waters with her."

Archer already knew what was going on in my mind before I voiced the words, his head nodding along as I speak.

"Are you too far gone to pull back?"

I shrug my shoulders, frustration creeping into my bones. "I don't even know anymore."

He looks at me then, no sign of humor in his features. "You need to act and do something before it's too late and I'm attending my defenseman's funeral rather than lifting this year's Cup with him."

I try to answer, but he carries on, apprehension and understanding laced in his voice.

"If you're too far gone to pull back, then you need to approach Scott and talk to him about where your head's at with his daughter." He slaps his thigh. "But if you can still put a stop to this ... well then, you need to have a serious conversation with Billie and set clear boundaries between you." He knocks his knee against mine. "I'm all for my friends falling in love, but not if it means picking up the pieces of their lives when everything ultimately blows up in their faces. I'm telling you now, Emmett, if you keep going down this road and you two end up falling into bed together, you need to be prepared to kiss your friendship goodbye, possibly along with whatever you have with Billie. This could fuck up her relationship with her parents, too, and you already told me that she's been through a lot."

All I can do is stare ahead at the wall, gut contorting while my head and heart face off with each other—a war sparked by the logic in my goalie's warning.

"I'm falling hard."

From my peripheral vision, I see Archer's subtle nod of acknowledgment. "I know, buddy."

It feels like I'm ingesting razor blades when I breathe my next breath. "You asked me if I'm too far gone, and the answer is yes, but that doesn't mean that I'm too selfish to resist pulling back." On the next swallow, the razor blades rise into my throat. "You were right when you said that the best things happen when you least expect them because Billie and Blake are everything to me." My voice wobbles, no matter how hard I try to keep it steady.

A warm palm rests on my shoulder. "Fuck, Emmett, I'm so sorry that you're going through this."

Closing my eyes, I pray that the darkness will make my next sentence slightly easier to admit. "And the fact that she means so much to me is precisely why I have to let my girl go."

CHAPTER TWENTY-THREE

BILLIE

"You, girl, are one hundred percent starting to show." Kendra rests a palm over Jenna's rounding stomach. "And I'm making the call right now—you're having a boy."

Darcy tuts from beside me, dropping her eyes to Jenna's belly. "I actually think it's twins. Whenever Tommy's involved, a person would be naive to predict anything other than chaos."

The way she delivers her statement in a thick British accent has me chuckling under my breath. Sitting alongside these girls for the game was the most fun I'd had in months, each of them filling me in on stories over the past few seasons. A personal highlight has to be Archer catching Collins and Sawyer going at it in Kendra and Jack's infamous spare bedroom.

"It's not twins." Kate sidles up alongside Jenna, swishing a mass of silky blonde hair over her right shoulder. "When I was three months pregnant with June and Will, I was already picking out maternity clothes." She motions to Jenna's stomach. "This bump right here has all the hallmarks of a baby boy."

Kendra smiles triumphantly. "Ooh ... what will you name him?"

As the girls all continue to talk around the bar, my attention wanders to Dad and Emmett, deep in conversation a few tables away from where we are all standing. My eyes instantly find Emmett's, and a wry smile tugs at his lips.

I want to know what he's thinking, but trying to find a moment with him, where we can slip off and talk, is proving to be impossible.

"We *so* need to meet baby Blake!" Darcy's animated voice pulls me back into the group.

"I'll admit," Collins says next, swirling mint leaves around in her mojito, "as far as babies go, Blake is probably one of the cutest I've seen."

Kate snorts a laugh, her hand reaching out to rest on Collins's forearm. "I remember when Will was born. I was kind of horrified at the state of his face when he popped out. It was all scrunched up. For a second, I contemplated asking the midwife to put him back."

"Mom!"

Kate's eyes flare wide as she registers her son's voice.

Turning on her heel, she taps him on the shoulder. He's taller than the average seven-year-old and he gets his stature from his dad.

"Take that back," he demands, hands propped on his hips, attitude flowing from him—that part of his personality I'm almost certain originates from his mom.

She reaches down, pinching one of his cheeks between her thumb and forefinger. "But look at you now, my love. The best-looking boy in Brooklyn."

He rolls his eyes, a pink flush accentuating his dark hair. "That's what Carly said in class the other day."

I chuckle while Kate scolds her son for kissing girls two years older than him.

"Hey, Bill." Dad's hand lands on my shoulder. "I'm going to head home in a second."

My stomach drops. He'll need me to drive us both, and I haven't had a chance to speak with Emmett.

Balancing himself on one crutch, Dad thumbs over his shoulder toward the Blades goalie, Archer. He's standing by the exit, arms folded across his chest, and randomly, he's looking pretty pleased with himself.

"Archer is going to give me a ride back home so you can stay out with everyone." Warmth creases around the corners of his eyes. "You haven't had a night away from Blake since she was born, and I want you to have a chance at making friends. Mom and I will drop Blake back at your place in the morning."

I shake my head at him, panic swelling in my gut. "She can't be without me for a whole night. How is she going to feed? What if she cries for me and I'm not there?"

Like he anticipated this exact reaction, he just smiles wider. "We still have a ton of your expressed milk in the freezer, and Blake is used to taking a bottle."

My head continues shaking, but he nods his at the same time. "Yes, Billie. You need to start living your life, and Emmett will make sure you get home safely."

When my eyes connect with Emmett's, he's already making his way over to us.

Excitement sparks inside me, the fizz of his presence intensifying with every step he takes toward us.

"I want you to call me the second she cries or even looks like she might need me," I tell him, still really unsure over his plan.

Dad's already backing toward Archer, giving me a thumbs-up and a confident smile as he leaves.

And then I'm face-to-face with Emmett, anxiety swirling inside me for a whole different reason when I take in the way that he's looking at me.

"Have you got a second to talk?"

My mouth runs dry, throat scratchy. "What's the matter?"

When Archer and Dad exit the players' lounge, Emmett

points toward a random door set at the back of the room. "In there, we can talk in private."

With the whole group deep in conversation, no one notices or questions us when we reach the door and enter into a darkened room.

Emmett flicks on a light to reveal a second bar area before closing the door behind him.

It feels cold in here, or maybe that's a feeling of dread as Emmett comes to stand in front of me. I might be young, but I know the look of someone when they're about to tell you something you likely don't want to know. Tucker wore a similar expression when he told me that he was backing out of the rental property we were supposed to be moving into.

"You don't need to say anything." I get there first, determined not to hear what he's about to say.

He links his fingers through mine, and I look away, staring blindly at the empty high stools set around a closed-off bar.

"Look at me, Billie." His voice is steeped in turmoil, reflecting the emotions charging through me.

"I'm not ready to look at you," I volley back, swallowing my upset. "And I don't want to hear whatever it is you're going to tell me."

"Billie."

"Nope," I stubbornly reply.

Emmett takes my other hand, gently squeezing my fingers between his. "I can stand here all night if that's what it takes."

I suck in a sharp breath, eyes still averted. "Good."

Dropping one of my hands, Emmett's callous palm cups my right cheek, swiveling my head to look at him. "Why good?"

While he might be able to control the position of my head, I retain the right to look where I want, which is still directly at the bar.

Finally, my gaze meets his soft gray eyes as they study me intently.

"Because if you stay here all night, then you won't be able to put any distance between us," I whisper.

I watch the way his Adam's apple bobs, and it's all the confirmation I need. That's precisely why Emmett asked me in here.

"Is it because of what I saw last week?" I ask.

Emmett's jaw clenches, tendons working overtime. "No. It's because I never should have been fantasizing about you in the first place."

Despite everything, excitement buzzes through me; the image of Emmett stroking himself and the sound of my name leaving his lips are burned into my memory forever.

"Is my dad onto us?" I fire another question at him, wondering if that's what's pushed him to feel this way.

"No," Emmett repeats. "I'm backing away because it's the right thing to do. For you and for Blake especially." His hand descends to grip my chin, eyes briefly falling to my mouth. "The train we're riding right now is destined for disaster, Billie. The more times I'm around you, the harder it is for me to keep my hands where they should be—by my sides and not running through your hair or holding your chin like this, desperate for all of your attention."

A delicious shiver runs down my spine, butterflies swarming my stomach.

"I wish ..." He squeezes his eyes shut before snapping them open and focusing on the door we just walked through. "I wish I'd met you earlier in my life, and I wish our situation were as simple as it is for so many of my teammates and their partners." He sets his eyes back on me. "But it isn't, and I refuse to make your life any more complicated than it already is."

"You don't have to leave my life," I plead, a sob bursting to break free.

He releases my other hand, both palms now cupping my face. "Oh, Billie. Don't you get it?"

He rests his forehead against mine, and the first tear hits my cheek. I didn't want to cry, but his words contradict his body language. None of this makes any sense—or at least, I don't want to believe that it does.

He heaves a huge breath into his lungs, and then his long exhale fans my face with his addictive scent. "Putting myself first and doing all the things I want with you will inevitably lead to me losing you forever."

"It won't," I protest.

"It will," he counters, wrapping his huge arms around me.

I cling to him like a koala, burying my face in his white dress shirt.

"You're one of the smartest people I've ever met; don't tell me you can't see what will happen because I know you can. If Scott didn't murder me, then he'd definitely never let me near you again."

"He doesn't own me," I force out. "I'm my own person, and so are you."

Emmett hooks his finger under my chin. "There's fourteen years between us. You want to be with someone your age. A guy who can race around the yard with Blake, a man who isn't slowing down when you're just getting going."

He means none of this; it's all bullshit.

"And what if you want more kids? I'm an old man, remember? Born in the days when they still had wooden money."

He chuckles, but I don't return it. I'm too fucking mad at him for spouting crap.

Maybe he can sense my frustration because he wraps his hands underneath my ass before walking us across to the empty bar top. He sets me down on the counter and steps between my legs.

We're perfect kissing height, not that it matters.

I'm twisting my hands around, but Emmett stops my fidget with a firm palm.

"I don't know what this is between us, Bill, but I do know that if we don't get out now, then we're going to end up doing or saying something that we can't undo. You mean so much to me; you light up my goddamn world when we're in the same room. I care for you and Blake, and if stepping back is the only way I can keep you both in my life, then that is what I'll do. Even if it breaks me, I'll hold it together so I can keep you in some form."

"You're already eliminating me from your life." My words sound choked.

He doesn't have an answer for me, and that's because there truly isn't one. The odds are stacked against us, even before we've gotten a chance to explore what this is.

Emmett pulls his glasses off, setting them on my face. My vision turns blurry, but I can still make out the pained smile as it tugs at his lips.

"I wish you could see what I do, Billie. How amazingly beautiful you are. In a few months, this will be something you look back on, and you'll be happy that we took the route we did."

"You don't want to back away from us," I challenge, handing his glasses back to him.

He twiddles them around between his fingers, eyes dropping to the floor as he scuffs the ground lightly with his shoe. "It doesn't matter what I want. This is all about doing the right thing for my girls."

CHAPTER TWENTY-FOUR

EMMETT

If I thought the conversation I had with Billie earlier tonight was torturous, I didn't even scratch the surface.

Watching Billie sink more drinks than I know she can handle, all while I have no control—or right—to stop her, feels like a disaster waiting to happen. And one I can only blame on myself.

Nudging me in the ribs, Sawyer takes an opportunity to speak with me when Billie, Darcy, and Kate all head for the restroom.

"I know I've only met Billie a couple of times, but is she okay? She looks ... I don't know ..." He trails off, following my line of vision as she catches her hip on a nearby table, completely misjudging her spatial awareness.

That's going to bruise.

"Upset?" I finish for him, figuring that's the emotion Sawyer was looking for.

He rolls his lips together, picking up his pint and taking a pull. "Maybe, yeah. It feels like she's drinking to deal with something, and given that she hasn't set her eyes on you once, a part of me can't help but wonder if her demeanor is to do with you."

Guilt swarms my insides. Sawyer joined our group after we all left the players' lounge so he wouldn't have witnessed me and Billie sneaking into the back bar.

"I took some advice from Archer."

He looks horrified on my behalf. "Jesus, really?"

If I didn't feel so shitty, I'd probably laugh at my goalie's expense. Let's just say, he doesn't normally carry the flag for making the best decisions.

I watch the bubbles pop in my soda. "It was the right thing to do and also what you told me needed to happen all those weeks ago."

"You put distance between you both." His statement hits like he punched through my chest cavity.

After I swallow for a second time, successfully forcing rising bile down my throat, all I can manage is a tight nod.

Sawyer folds his arms over his chest, eyes still trained toward the restroom. "How did she take it?"

I release a humorless chuckle. "I think you're witnessing that."

He looks at me then, green eyes full of questions. "And what about you? I mean, you said it was the right action to take, but your face didn't match your words. It still doesn't."

Sometimes, I resent how perceptive my friends can be. When Archer warned me about keeping a good poker face, I was certain that I could pull it off. Tonight, I'm failing miserably, and each time I set eyes on Billie as she attempts to engage in conversation with the rest of the girls, all I want is for her to look at me.

I miss her eyes, even though she's been sitting opposite me for most of the night.

I miss her smile because the one she's been wearing isn't real.

I miss the sound of her laughter, even when she's trying to goad me over being old.

There have been multiple occasions tonight where Billie could've joined in with the boys' banter and revealed some pretty embarrassing truths about my past—like the time I thought LOL in a text was an acronym for *lots of love* and I sent it in the Quinn-

Richards group chat, only to realize that it was not, in fact, an appropriate response to her dog passing away.

"Call me a genius"—Sawyer's deep voice saves me from an emotional spiral—"but I'd hazard a guess that your conversation with Billie isn't quite finished."

I shrug because what the fuck else am I supposed to do? "She's mad at me tonight. The best I can hope for is that she'll let me drive her home, and when she's had some time to cool off, she'll see why I had to do what I did."

"Stop talking bullshit, Emmett." Sawyer is straight out of the blocks with his accusation, and I feel called out. "You know as well as I do that you'll be taking her back to your place tonight."

I flush like a little fucking schoolgirl.

Only Archer knows about her catching me jerking off in the shower, although with the way I'm so transparent these days, I'm almost certain Sawyer doesn't need the backstory.

When Darcy emerges from the restroom alone, making a beeline straight toward me, I know this has something to do with Billie.

We might be celebrating a win against our oldest rivals, the Seattle Scorpions, and while I haven't touched a drop of alcohol all night, my stomach roils like I've sunk ten shots in a row.

Darcy approaches me, hovering her head over my shoulder. "Billie needs to go home. She's only had three glasses of wine, and I thought that was okay, but ..." Darcy's worried eyes tell me all I need to know—she's either reached her capacity with booze or lost control over her emotions. Even worse, both.

I spin in my chair, grabbing my jacket from the back as I stand. Next, I snag Billie's coat and purse from the back of her seat, following Darcy so I can go get my girl and take her back to the safety of my place.

MY INSTINCTS over Billie being mad at me were spot on.

The whole drive home, she barely said a word, gazing out the passenger window of my Jaguar E-Type, hands twisting in her lap. Every time we hit a stoplight, I wanted to reach out and take her hand in mine, interlacing our fingers like I'd done more times than I should.

The elevator pings, and the doors open to my penthouse, yet Billie doesn't move from her position against the back wall.

I hold the doors, head falling between my shoulders. She looks beautiful tonight, hair styled into a braid by Darcy at the game, an oversize blue Blades sweatshirt hanging over the edge of her shoulder.

It doesn't serve me to look at her as often as I do. Regardless, I can't help taking her in one more time.

"Do you want me to take you home?" I ask the same question I repeated twice in the car, each time earning a, "Don't bother," response.

She isn't being petulant, like you'd expect from a person her age when they didn't get their way, and none of Billie's upset is for attention. The dark circles around her tired eyes tell me that she's reached the limit of what she can handle.

And you know what? I don't fucking blame her. A lesser person—like me—would've broken down way before she has, and even now, I can sense she's battling to retain control of her emotions.

For the first time all night, she gives me full eye contact, and I feel that shit in every nerve ending.

"No, it's okay." She wraps her arms around her middle, and I step back into the elevator, bracing a hand on either side of her on the brass railing behind her ass.

She gazes up at me. "You're probably exhausted from the game and then tonight. The last thing you want to do is get back in the car and drive me across town."

Even when she's hurting, her instinct is always about others.

That thought pulls my left hand from the railing, and I plant it on the side of her face.

Closing her eyes, she leans into my touch. Whenever our bodies connect, it's like there's a silent moment, where we both wonder if it'll be for the last time.

"The only thing I want is for you to be happy. Driving you across town so you're where you want to be tonight is the minimum I would do for you."

She sinks her teeth into her bottom lip as her palm finds my hip, and I step forward until there's no more distance between us. Something I vowed to ensure there was plenty of only a few hours earlier.

I'm a fool for this woman, each bad decision I make pulling me straight back into her orbit.

"What would make you happy, Billie?"

She ducks her head, but I bring her eyes back to mine with the softest finger under her chin.

When she finally whispers, "To be near you," I know there isn't anywhere else she's sleeping tonight than in my penthouse—specifically, my bed.

When I wrap my hands underneath her ass, she releases a soft squeal, and I carry her into my bedroom, laying her down on top of the duvet.

She gazes up at me as I take a step back, scrubbing a palm over my mouth to center myself. Every warning and desperate battle to stay away—none of it holds any weight as I observe the way Billie looks sprawled out on my bed, a vision even better than I've pictured a thousand times over.

"I can't touch you tonight." My voice feels foreign and mainly because I hate the words that I'm speaking. Keeping my hands to myself though is exactly what I should be doing, so I'll settle for the warmth of her body next to mine.

I pop the first couple of buttons on my dress shirt, but the tension between us doesn't echo the declaration I just made. It feels like I'm taking Billie to bed so I can slide inside her and stay there all night, and by the way she's looking at me, I know that's exactly what she wants.

"I don't have any pajamas."

Pulling off my shirt and tossing it into the laundry basket next to my dresser, I open a drawer and pull out a white Blades training shirt. This one is too big even for me, so it'll drown Billie's petite frame.

She climbs off the bed and takes it from me, eyes raking over my skin. This isn't the first time she's seen me without a shirt, but it is, without question, the first time she's appreciated my naked chest in this way.

Pausing over my tattoo, dainty fingers trace the ink etched into my left pec; she must not have seen it when I was in the shower. Understandable, given that my hard cock was also on display.

"When did you get the tattoo?"

At the feel of her touch, I want to snatch that training top from her hand and demand that she sleep naked.

"And what does it mean?" she tags on.

I close my eyes, trying to get a grip on myself, along with the raging boner fighting against the zipper on my pants.

"I got it in the offseason. Figured it was time to get some ink, and Tommy recommended an artist."

She twists her lips in thought. "A rising sun normally means a new beginning. Considering when you had this done, I guess that meaning tracks."

When she drops her hand and heads for the bathroom, I wait until the door closes behind her before releasing a long-drawn-out sigh.

"Hands to your-fucking-self, Emmett."

CHAPTER TWENTY-FIVE

EMMETT

When I was a kid, my brother and I used to build pillow forts in our bedroom before we tried to destroy each other's creations.

Last night, I could've built a stone wall between us, and my body would have still found a way to hold Billie's.

Around a half hour ago, I woke up in this exact position—face buried in her hair, right arm looped around her waist, pulling her ass into my hard dick. And as I lie here, berating myself over another line I just crossed, I also know the chances of me pulling away are as remote as the odds of me sticking to my teammates' advice.

I'm an addict, and Billie Quinn is my vice.

Like she can sense my thoughts, Billie turns in my arms.

This morning, I'll be the first person she speaks to, the first person she sees as she opens her eyes and takes the world in.

She isn't the first woman I've done this with, but she is the first to pull those kinds of intimate thoughts from me. There's something magical about that, knowing no matter what the next twenty-four hours hold, at least you got to share your first thoughts with your favorite person.

Reaching up, I run a light hand through her bedhead, fascinated at how someone's hair can resemble silk. "How's your head feeling?"

She winces a little, and the heel of her hand finds her temple. "It's been better. How much did I have to drink?"

"Three glasses of wine." I chuckle. "Don't you remember?"

Her forehead flops against my chest. "I thought it was more than that. Kate bought several bottles of wine and was refilling my glass."

I tip her chin up to look at me. "Did you enjoy getting to know the girls?"

"It was so fun." Billie's smile is automatic, almost like she's recalling memories of her talking and laughing with my extended family. And a little like the way she pulls foreign feelings from me when I first wake, a rare wave of contentment settles in the morning air.

Her smile turns devilish, and I drop my hand to her ribs. I know that look, one that precedes her poking fun at me for something.

"If the next words to leave your mouth concern my age or the wrinkles around my eyes, then I will tickle you until all the air leaves your lungs."

She doubles down, quirking a challenging brow. "That's not what I was going to say actually. But since you mentioned age, I might as well ask the question."

I narrow my eyes at her, fingers hovering over the training top I gave her last night. She can keep it for all I care; it looks damn fine on her and at least she'll have a piece of me wrapped around her when she climbs into bed alone each night. I've no idea if she's wearing panties underneath, even if I'm desperate to find out.

"Go ahead."

Billie places a patronizing palm against my cheek, and I note that she wore her bracelet to bed. I wonder if she ever takes it off. I hope not.

"The last time we spoke, you told me that we had to put distance between us." She looks down at where our bodies are pressed together. "This doesn't look like a lot of distance to me. Or did your geriatric brain forget all about our conversation?"

She's on her back in a millisecond, my fingers teasing her ribs until she can barely breathe, face turning beet red under the strain of glorious giggles.

When Billie tries to pull away, I keep her in place with a hand on her hip, and I hold myself above her by bracing a forearm next to her head on the pillow, marveling at how flawless she looks beneath me. This moment is even better than how it played out in my fantasies.

When she grows weary, I relent, letting her pull oxygen into her lungs.

She's panting, and my chest is heaving for totally different reasons. If we ever had the chance to be together, this is exactly how I'd take her for the first time—me sliding inside her tight pussy, my dick pulling tiny gasps from her swollen lips after I ravished her mouth with mine.

She reaches up, pushing a delicate hand through my disheveled hair. There are so many words we both want to voice, and I wonder what she'll say next when she finally catches her breath.

"You told me you'd always be honest with me, Emmett. And last night, everything you said in that room was a lie."

I don't bother to deny it, too exhausted to fight our reality.

I study her face for a beat, admiring the scattered freckles decorating the bridge of her nose. "What can I do to make it up to you, Mama?"

She pulls back, processing the nickname I just gave her. It feels perfect for Billie. While she's so much more than a mother, this woman has got me wrapped around her little finger, just like she has with her beautiful daughter. I'm waiting on her every word, in awe of her strength.

"Put your hands on me, Emmett."

It's the first time Billie has asked me to go further physically, and, fuck me, do I want to.

I drop my face into the crook of her neck. It would be so easy to lower my shorts and free my cock.

I glide my nose along her sensitive flesh, lips paused over the shell of her ear. "Tell me how you want me to touch you. Where you want my fingers and dick."

When I nudge my knee between her thighs, I swear I can feel heat radiating from her apex.

A breath snags in her throat before she swallows down my question. "I don't care where your hands end up, as long as they're making me scream."

We don't move, a standoff forming between us. Every part of me wants to take this woman; it's what I haven't been able to stop thinking about for weeks.

"If I put my hands on you, then there's no going back. Everything will shift between us."

Behind her lustful eyes, I know she understands the significance of this moment, the reasons why I'm holding back—and not just because of how forbidden she is. Billie's body isn't even seven weeks postpartum, and while I'm no expert in childbirth, I do know that I'm larger than average. Sure, I could tell my brain to take it steady, but that doesn't mean my deprived body would get the memo. My desire to fuck her is bordering feral, and my dick is desperate to destroy her tight pussy the first chance it gets. I'm a man after all, and she is nothing like I've ever seen before. No woman compares to the beauty lying beneath me, waiting for me to make a move.

Sitting back on my heels, I bring her body with me until we're both kneeling in the center of my bed.

"What do you want, Billie?"

Rolling her lips together, she confirms, "I want to have fun with you." She casts her eyes around the bed. "Right here, right now."

My palm caresses the back of her head. "Do you want sex? Because ..." I trail off, struggling to find the right words to convey how badly I want that but how scared I am to take it too far with her. Emotionally and physically.

Billie's eyes reveal that she's finding this just as hard. "I don't know if my body is ready for that, but I do want us to explore each other."

On a long breath, I close my eyes as relief and frustration crash through me. I know sleeping together is too far for the both of us. But, goddamn, I need to touch her, even if my conscience screams at me to keep my hands to myself.

"Are you wearing panties?" I finally ask, thinking over ways I can give Billie exactly what she needs from me.

She shakes her head, and I bring a fist to my mouth, biting down on my knuckles.

"You're fucking killing me here. Have you been bare all night?"

Shaking her head again, she lifts my training top a few inches. "I secretly removed them a few minutes ago; they're somewhere beneath your duvet."

I reach out, circling her wrist with my fingers. "Show me where you caught yourself on the table last night."

When she lifts the top on one side, a black-and-blue bruise, spanning the width of her hip bone, appears. I can't help but trace my fingertips over the mark. It feels like I'm responsible for this.

"Does it hurt?" I ask in a gravelly voice.

"No," she breathes out. "It hurt at the time, but not anymore."

It's only a bruise, but thoughts of anything hurting Billie makes my blood boil, and the same goes for Blake. I've never considered myself to be a primal guy, although I've equally never met a girl who could drive me this crazy.

Need catapults through me.

"Ride my thigh, Billie Quinn. You watched me jerk myself off to thoughts of you; now I want to see how you come apart just by grinding on me."

Slowly, deliciously, she adjusts her body so that we're face-to-face, her knees on either side of one of my own. Even though I haven't set eyes on what I know will be a perfect cunt, there's no denying the heat that radiates from it when I feel her wetness seep through my thin athletic shorts.

"Is all of this for me?" I ask, eyes dropping to her pussy.

She pins her bottom lip between her teeth, head tipping back on the first flex of her hips. "I'm soaking wet for you."

Strands of hair tickle my knee, and I brace my palms on the bed behind me, opening my body up to grant her more freedom to grind against me.

I know that this is a foolish way to justify what we're doing, but I let my conscience run away with a theory that if I don't physically get her off with my own hands, then we're still on the right side of wrong. And if Scott ever asks if I touched his daughter, my response will be the truth based on a technicality.

Jesus, I'm the worst fucking friend in history.

Parted lips, tiny gasps, perfect thighs squeezing around my own—they all push me toward a precipice.

With the way we're going, there's no way that Billie will reach her own climax before I find mine. My girl is too beautiful like this, using my body to chase what she wants.

Her peaked nipples tease me through the training top. They're at the ideal height for me to take them into my mouth, to swirl my tongue around each one. If Billie thinks that I'm as gentlemanly inside the bedroom as I try to be in public, then she's grossly mistaken. My mouth would ruin her flesh in a single night, and my filthy words would repeat in her brain for a lifetime.

I peer up at her, wishing I'd worn my glasses before we got started. "Is that good for you?"

A soft moan is all I need to hear.

"Are you close?"

She doesn't answer me, only rocking a little faster.

"I need you to tell me," I grit out. "Because I'm around ten seconds from blowing straight in my shorts."

Billie pauses, eyes falling to my dick. Her hand reaches out to cup me.

"Wait," I command, redirecting her toward her pussy. "In my world, the woman always gets off before I do."

I don't share the surprised look on her face. Of course Tucker was as selfish in bed as he was out of it.

"Show me how you play with yourself. Let me watch this pussy swallow your fingers."

Heat creeps up her neck. "In this position?" she asks, dropping her hand between her thighs.

I cock my head to one side, unsure if I'm dreaming or if this is really fucking happening. "Why don't you sit back on the bed, hitch my top around your waist, and spread those perfect thighs for me?"

She grows a little coy, and I slide my thumb across her plump bottom lip.

"Are you good with that, Mama?"

When she nods lightly, apprehension fills her pretty eyes.

"Can I ask you something?" I want to ask a question that's been on my mind for a while.

"Sure."

My hands are back on her face. "How many men have you slept with?"

Green eyes track to the bed beneath us, and I hate that she's anything but comfortable.

"Only Tucker."

That's exactly what I suspected, given her age and relatively sheltered life with Scott and Freya. In contrast, I've been with more women than most of the guys on my team. Although I was married for a long-ass time, to say I got around before I met Maria is a huge understatement. I was the biggest fuckboy in my freshman year of college.

"Do you like touching yourself, Billie?"

Her eyes are back on mine, confidence steeling her shoulders. "Yes. Especially when I'm thinking about you."

My balls contract to the point of pain.

This woman is going to annihilate me.

I tip my chin at the headboard. "Go ahead and show me."

She doesn't hesitate, scooting until her back is planted firmly against my headboard, top already bunched around her middle.

All she needs to do is let her knees fall apart, and I'll be privy to the best show of my life.

"Tell me what you want me to do next, Emmett."

Billie proves that inexperience doesn't necessarily translate to incompetence as she takes two fingers and slides them into her mouth.

I'm going to expire.

My voice is gravelly when I attempt to find words. "I want you to part your legs and take them as wide as they'll go. The only view I want this morning is your pretty pink cunt as it weeps for me."

Edging her knees apart, she confirms what I already knew—perfection. Aside from a single strip of short hair, she likes to keep herself bare.

"When you massage your clit like that, what do you think about me doing to you?" I ask, watching the way she works the swollen nub beneath her fingers.

She spreads herself wider. "Eating me out."

Reaching beneath the waistband of my shorts, I glide my palm over my cock, pre-cum leaking down the shaft. With my other hand, I push them to my knees, letting Billie see me without a steamed-up shower door between us.

Although she might try to hide it, I don't miss the flare of her eyes or the way her pupils dilate.

I stroke myself again, tipping my head toward the ceiling. "Do you think my cock would fit inside you?" It's a rhetorical question, but I want to hear her agree that our bodies were made for each other.

"Why don't you come over here?" She pats the mattress with one hand, pushing two fingers inside her tight heat. "I can wrap a palm around it and check."

A maniacal groan rises up my throat.

"Don't fucking tempt me, Billie."

Pulling out her fingers, she pushes them back inside.

"Curl them toward your front wall, like you're beckoning me to fuck you," I command, fist sliding down my shaft. One more pass, and I'll empty all over the bedding.

Like a good fucking girl, Billie does as I asked, mouth popping open in response.

Satisfaction shoots through me. "That's how I'd finger you for the first time. And once I got you off, I'd clean your throbbing pussy with my tongue."

On another curl of her fingers, Billie falls apart right in front of me. Thighs pinching, chest heaving, my name a tortured whisper on her tongue. An echo of the way her name fell from my lips in the shower.

At the final second, I smother the end of my dick with my palm, catching jets of my hot release on a deep growl. My other hand pumps faster, draining my balls of the best orgasm I've ever had.

Billie watches on, gaping jaw mimicking my own expression. That was the greatest sexual experience of my life, all without us setting a single finger on each other.

I should be pleased, relieved even, to have chased my release, pent-up need and desire unraveling into my hand.

But relief couldn't be further from what I feel as I watch Billie circle her dripping pussy, aftershocks of pleasure rippling through her body.

If this is what it's like to watch my best friend's daughter get herself off to thoughts of us, then how the fuck am I supposed to keep my hands off her now?

CHAPTER TWENTY-SIX

BILLIE

Darcy has added Billie into the group chat.

Darcy has renamed the group chat: Babes of Brooklyn.

DARCY

Welcome to the best group chat in North America, Billie! Here, you will find a full complement of strong women with a ferocious love of cocktails, topped off with an appreciation for strong hockey thighs.

COLLINS

All of the above, except for the thighs. I'm more of a butt person myself.

KENDRA

And then there were five. Hands down, the greatest group of girls to exist.

JENNA

Yes to all, replacing cocktails with mocktails for me. And if someone can tell me when morning sickness usually ebbs, then that would be great.

ME

I imagine that joining this group is equivalent to finding out that you're having twins—it's like an instant family! So happy to be here.

JENNA

Also, can we not talk about twins? With every vomit, I grow more certain that Tommy put two babies inside me. Surely, one baby isn't capable of producing this much puke?!

ME

My first trimester with Blake was tough. Things started to settle after that.

JENNA

I'm already in my second trimester, and it feels like I'm getting worse. Last night, Tommy actually slept on the bathroom floor with me. It would've been romantic if I hadn't been cursing him all night for putting me in this position.

KENDRA

Esme didn't give me much trouble at all. But we all knew that Tommy's baby was going to be a handful, even from the womb!

COLLINS

I cannot add anything to this discussion since I refuse to let a man impregnate me. However, I would like to reassure Jenna that I will, in fact, nurture her love of mai tais while she's otherwise indisposed.

ME

Can we not talk about alcohol? I fear I may join Jenna in the puking department.

DARCY

You feel that bad, huh?

ME

When I first woke up, I felt okay, but now my stomach is telling me otherwise.

DARCY

They were large glasses of wine; Kate doesn't understand measurements.

ME

dry-heaves

COLLINS

Did Emmett get you home okay?

Setting Blake down in her bassinet, I can't help the slow smile as it creeps across my face. I know precisely what Collins is implying.

ME

I was safely tucked in bed by ten p.m.

COLLINS

How sweet …

DARCY

Does anyone else here get a feeling that they're a few paces behind?

KENDRA

Spill the tea, Billie.

JENNA

Here, in this group of fine women, we never kiss and tell. Vaults for life.

With Mom and Dad sitting in my living room, having stopped by to drop Blake off, it feels like I'm a preteen in my bedroom, texting a boy I like, feeling too shy to tell my parents about him.

ME

Jokes aside. If any of this gets out, then heads will roll. And I'm not talking about ours; I'm referring to Emmett's.

DARCY

Knew it! The look on his face when I told him that you needed to go home. The way he leaped from his seat to rescue you last night. How he wrapped his arm around your shoulders and led you to the exit. Ugh, that boy is down bad.

KENDRA

Wait. I agree with all of Darcy's observations. But isn't Emmett friends with your dad? They looked pretty close in the players' bar.

ME

They're actually really good friends and have been for years. And that's exactly why heads will roll.

KENDRA

Billie, are you sleeping with my husband's key defenseman?!

ME

I'm not sleeping with him.

KENDRA

Messing around with him then?

JENNA

Can we pause this conversation? I need to find popcorn. My appetite has suddenly returned.

COLLINS

Notice how Billie said that she wasn't sleeping with him, but didn't deny the messing around part?

COLLINS

You stayed at his place last night, didn't you?

Craning my neck to check that my parents are still where I left them on the couch, I type out another text.

ME

He dropped me home just before Mom and Dad came by with Blake.

I slept in his bed. We both did.

Given the circumstances and potential felonies that will be committed if this gets out, I have no right to be this freaking giddy. But that's the effect this man has on me—I lose all ability to see danger. Last night went from miserable to incredible. I slept in his training top, surrounded by his beautiful body. This morning was phenomenal, the memory of his darkened eyes, slackened jaw, and needy remarks taking up permanent residence in my brain.

Last night, when we had finished talking and rejoined the group, my main objective was to drink to forget everything Emmett had told me in the empty bar. Even though I believed none of it, I could sense his determination to go through with what he had preached.

I should've had more faith in the invisible ties that have formed between us. While I might be incapable of picturing my life without Emmett in it, I think it's fair to say that the same goes for him too. Neither of us deliberately set out to end up where we are—or to do the things that we did this morning—and that's just the way it is. The bottom line is that I want to sleep with Emmett, and more than that, I want to explore whatever it is that we have. The fact that I'm his forbidden fruit is inconsequential because he's destined to take a bite, and when he ultimately does, I'm not going to be the one to stop him.

KENDRA

This is A+ content—I'm not going to lie.

COLLINS

I'm disappointed in you, Bill.

ME

Why?

COLLINS

Last night, I told Sawyer that you were definitely going to fuck him. We bet $100.

ME

Wait. Sawyer knows?!

COLLINS

Girl, Emmett told my husband he has been pining after you since the moment he first laid eyes on you in February.

DARCY

If my husband has been holding out on me with this information, I'm going to hold out on him in bed.

KENDRA

I'm confident my motormouth of a husband couldn't keep a secret if his life depended on it.

JENNA

We all know that Tommy has no idea about this. That would involve him actually socializing.

ME

Can we back up for a second? Emmett has been talking to Sawyer about me?!

DARCY

Yep. I just texted Archer, and he already knew. Looks like it's no sex for him for the foreseeable future.

COLLINS

Billie, please don't tell me that you're shocked. Emmett might as well have been carrying a big "I'm pining for a girl I can't have" sign above his head for weeks.

The tingles I felt when Emmett first confessed his attraction to me resurface.

ME

What did he say to Sawyer?

COLLINS

Exactly what you'd expect—that he's slowly losing his mind over you. Oh, and his balls are turning bluer by the day.

DARCY

Archer is a sneaky bastard. Allegedly, he drove your dad home last night to clear the way for you and Emmett to talk.

KENDRA

I'll assume sex is back on the table now then.

DARCY

Oh, yes. I'm going to ride him like Seabiscuit. All freaking night.

I burst out laughing just as Dad pokes his head around the doorjamb, inquisitive eyes falling to my phone.

"Your cupboards, flooring, and hot water got fixed."

Locking the screen so there's no chance of him catching sight of the text thread, I deliberately drop my shoulders in an attempt to appear casual.

"Yeah, my landlord finally came through."

Thanks to your best friend, but let's not talk about that.

He looks a combination of disappointed and pleased. "I was going to fix everything for you now that I'm more mobile. I'm sorry I couldn't get to it sooner, like I'd hoped."

My gaze falls to the crutch he's propping himself up on, one leg still cast in plaster. "You still aren't that mobile. It was my landlord's responsibility."

He worries his bottom lip. I recognize that face now that I'm a parent myself—the one where you internally scold yourself for letting your child down.

"How are you doing for money?" he asks, stepping farther inside the room to catch a glimpse of his sleeping granddaughter. His face turns soft the second he sets his eyes on Blake.

When Dad repaid my student loans and wired me some more for general living costs, I felt sure that would be enough, especially with the child support payments from Tucker.

Turns out, raising a baby is way more expensive than any of us could've foreseen, leaving me with two choices: be truthful with Dad and ask for more money, or find myself a job—and fast.

"I'll interpret the silence as you're running low."

He takes a seat next to me on the bed, resting his crutch against the mattress.

I don't say anything as we admire the gentle rise and fall of Blake's chest.

"If I factor in next month's bills, I have two thousand dollars left in my checking account."

Dad's eyes dart to mine. It's not the answer he wanted to hear, especially given the additional financial strain his accident has put on the household. He hasn't been able to claim on his auto insurance since the accident was deemed preventable if he'd replaced the tires on his van.

"Blake's going through clothes and diapers like crazy, and now that she's starting on formula, that's driven costs up again."

An arm wraps around my shoulders, reminding me of the hugs he used to give when I was a young girl. Sometimes, no matter how old we get, a girl just needs to feel her father's embrace.

"I was selfish to move out so soon."

His arm tightens around me, and he drops his chin atop my

head. "You are the most unselfish person I know, Bill. The most stubborn too."

I poke a soft elbow into his ribs, and he chuckles quietly.

"If Mom can start taking Blake on the weekends, then I can find a job."

A protest rumbles in his chest. "You know we would never have a problem caring for Blake, but you need more unbroken time together as mom and daughter. It's only been seven weeks."

"Yeah, well, most women don't have asshole baby daddies, thankfully."

Dad's body stiffens at the mere mention of Tucker. "How much more do you need to see you through another two months?"

I shrug, determined not to accept a cent from him. "I don't know."

Unwrapping his arm, he picks up his crutch and takes a couple of steps over to Blake's bassinet. It's obvious that he won't accept any form of no from me. Scott Quinn is a proud man who will do and provide anything for his family in any way that he can, even if he has to sell the clothes on his back. I think that's why he fell in love with Mom so easily because she's the exact same. Together, they make the dream team, the kind of modern-day marriage we all aspire to have.

A few beats of nothing pass between us, Dad stroking a gentle hand through Blake's dark hair.

"Leave it to me. I'll have what you need in your checking account by the end of this week."

CHAPTER TWENTY-SEVEN

EMMETT

ME

Morning, Mama.

BILLIE

We need to talk about this nickname …

Morning, BTW.

ME

Is it … a problem?

BILLIE

Only if you stop using it.

ME

I knew you'd like it. It fits you perfectly, given all you ever do these days is boss me around.

BILLIE

Hasn't that always been the case?

ME

True. Although that reminds me ... Messi is still the better soccer player, FYI. Don't think that I've let that debate die.

BILLIE

Ridiculous. Ronaldo proved himself in the Premier League—aka the best soccer league in the world.

ME

Oh, Billie. Twenty-one and legally old enough to drink, yet you still have so much to learn. Maybe you should come over to my place so we can watch a soccer game.

BILLIE

Just like old times. Should we invite my dad too?

ME

That would be a great idea ... if my last text wasn't an excuse to get you alone again.

BILLIE

Really? Wow. I'm slow on the uptake. What kind of alone time do you have in mind?

Sitting up in bed, I reach under the duvet, hand dipping beneath my boxer briefs.

Yep, already as hard as stone.

ME

Would you like a picture?

BILLIE

As much as I would like to say yes, I'm out for an early breakfast with Mom. Might be a bit risky ...

You'll have to describe what you have in mind.

ME

You know, I always had you down as a good girl.

BILLIE

No, you didn't.

Laughter erupts from my chest, and I palm my dick, closing my eyes so I can picture Billie next to me in bed, just as she was a couple of mornings ago.

ME

Well, if we did watch a soccer game, it would likely be an early morning kickoff. I guess it would work out best if you stayed over the night before.

BILLIE

For sure. Trying to get across town first thing would be a nightmare.

ME

To make it even more convenient, we should probably watch it on the flat screen in my bedroom.

BILLIE

Your bed definitely offers the best seats in the house, without a doubt.

ME

Almost. My lap is generally better …

I drag a fist up my dick, and my fingers squeeze around my phone. I'm already close, unmistakable pressure building at the base of my spine.

BILLIE

I can get a bit warm in bed.

ME

Probably best if you're naked then, no?

BILLIE

You also, given that I tend to run hot.

ME

So fucking hot.

When *Scott* fills the screen, I want to toss the phone across the bedroom, my hard-on completely gone, heart racing for an entirely different reason. I'm fucking mortified.

"Hello?" I answer before I'm ready, voice raspy, almost like I was about to engage his daughter in phone sex ...

"Tell me that you aren't still in bed?"

I rest my head against the headboard, blowing out a deep breath.

"Had a late practice and ..." I push back the duvet, my knee just as swollen as it was when I climbed into bed last night. "I needed to get some extra rest."

Street noise filters down the phone.

"Well, I'm sorry to cut your rehabilitation short, but would you mind buzzing me in? I'm about to enter your building."

I bolt up in bed, wondering what arrangements I've forgotten this time.

"I need to talk with you," Scott continues. "Or more like ask you for another favor."

Five minutes later, I've thrown on some clothes, and I have a worried Scott sitting opposite me in the living area.

Reminding me of his daughter, he casts his eyes around my stark penthouse. "My voice actually echoes in here; it's that empty."

Reaching out, he picks up the coffee I made him and takes a couple of sips.

"What's the problem?" I ask, assuming that's why he needs another favor.

His previously concerned expression turns more apprehensive, although it doesn't need to. He should know that I'll always have his back, even though I'm not being fully truthful with him at present.

"It's Billie."

At the mention of her name, full-body trembles set in. I sit forward, bracing my elbows on my knees to try and suppress any signs of anxiety.

Shit. What the fuck does he know?

My voice is hoarse, borderline strained when I respond, "What about her?"

Gaze falling to his hands and with a crutch leaning against the wall next to him, he looks like a broken man. Or at least one carrying the weight of the world on his shoulders.

"You know I wouldn't come to you if I had an alternative." When he brings his eyes back to mine, I can immediately tell what he's going to ask. "The money you loaned to us—"

"Gifted," I clarify. "The money I *gifted* to you."

He clears his throat, an awkward atmosphere settling in the room. "Well, yeah, that money. It's running out faster than I anticipated."

He scrubs a hand over his mouth, struggling to ask me the question.

I decide to step in and make this as easy as I can. "How much more do Billie and Blake need?" By mentioning their names, I know I'm separating Scott and Freya from the equation. This money isn't for them, and that's the only reason why he's sitting in front of me right now. It's the only reason why he brought their financial woes up in the bar that night.

Trouble is, back then, nothing was happening between me and his daughter, and circumstances were very different.

Back then, I wasn't walking a moral tightrope, and therefore giving him money felt like the act of a good friend helping an even better man and his family in a time of need. Now, all that has shifted, and while I'd be still giving the money with all the best intentions, I know if Scott knew the full truth, then he wouldn't accept another dime.

And that's exactly why I can't come clean despite knowing it's the right thing to do.

Billie and Blake trump everything, and I'm not about to see a friend sell his assets—or worse, run up debt to fund the essentials for his family. We both know that Tucker is paying the bare minimum toward Blake's upkeep, and like hell is Billie moving back home to save money. That's if she could break out of the lease.

"Give me a number," I press.

More silence.

"I wouldn't be here if I could get back to work. The sick pay is minimal, and Freya is struggling to pick up more hours—"

"How much does Billie need?" I repeat my earlier question in a soft, almost-coaxing tone.

"She's talking about searching for a job, and I can't have her—"

"No fucking way," I cut him off again, voice filled with emotions any family friend shouldn't really be feeling.

Thankfully, Scott is too caught up in his own emotions to pay any notice to mine or the way the trembles in my hands only increase.

"Forty would probably be enough," is all he says, pain penetrating his words.

I sit back on the couch, studying him carefully. "Are you sure?"

He nods once, and I decide not to press. This is killing us both as it is, and we share the same priority—Billie and Blake.

"I would secretly sell Shelby if I didn't think you would find out and be mad at me."

I arch a brow at him. Scott is absolutely right; I would be mad at him for doing that. Shelby has been in his family for years.

"If you sold her, I'd buy her back, no matter what price the new owner demanded."

Scott just shrugs. "I'm here because I'll do anything for my girls."

Same, buddy. Same.

"When do you need the money?"

"As soon as you have it." He scuffs the floor with his sneaker. "I really appreciate this, Emmett. My family owes you so much."

His gratitude slams into me like a lead weight.

"How about by tomorrow?"

"That would be awesome. And I know Billie and Freya would be really thankful, too, if they knew."

All I can do is subtly nod. There are no appropriate words for this moment, and I refuse to feed him any more bullshit.

I tip my chin at his crutch, knowing the sooner he can be back on his feet, the better. Like his daughter, Scott's happiness relies on his independence. "How much longer until you can get back to work?"

Another shrug. "Two more weeks, and I'll be able to start taking steps without an aid. But it'll be at least eight before I can undertake light duties at work."

I roll my lips together. Things between us feel strange—or maybe that's my guilt showing. We haven't been spending as much time together as usual, and I'm acutely aware of it. That said, he's been housebound, and I've been actively avoiding him where I can.

Like the fantastic friend that I am.

"You really did a number on yourself, huh?"

When his gaze drops to my knee, I know exactly what response is coming.

"Others might not have noticed, but I could see the way you moved on the ice during the Scorpions game. Are you sure that you've got another season in you after this one?"

I fold my arms across my chest, and my reply is defensive. "I'm not ready to say goodbye to the NHL yet."

I can see that he understands, even if I'm not sure he agrees. "And what about after pro hockey? Have you thought much about your life then?" His gaze roves my home. "You need to start building a life for yourself outside of the arena, Emmett."

If I thought that the atmosphere was awkward before, it had nothing on how it feels now.

"Maybe it's time to reconsider dating." He clears his throat. "I'm guessing you already know that Maria's seeing someone."

Three months ago, that kind of news would've sent me into an emotional spiral. Today, all I feel is genuinely pleased for my ex-wife.

"I didn't, but good for her."

Without even thinking about it, I rise to my feet, shoving my hands into my pockets.

Scott follows suit, reaching out for his crutch.

"It was good to see you, man," I tell him, eager to bring this exchange to an end. "And don't worry about the money; I'll get everything transferred to you ASAP."

He reaches out, setting a hand on my shoulder. "You're a good man, Emmett. We're blessed to have you in our lives."

The words *I'm involved with your daughter* are right there, screaming to be released into the open. Every time Scott praises me for being a good friend, the struggle to make eye contact with him increases.

I clamp my mouth shut—for Billie, for Blake, and for the sake of the money I know they desperately need. When Billie and I finally tell Scott and Freya about us, it has to be at the right time, even if I know that the perfect moment likely doesn't exist.

CHAPTER TWENTY-EIGHT

BILLIE

Wrapped in a fluffy white towel, I'm halfway to the bedroom after taking a shower when my intercom buzzes.

I pad past Blake, who's still asleep in her bassinet—she hasn't been sleeping well the past few nights—and I head down the stairs toward the door.

"Hello?" I half yawn into the receiver.

"It's Emmett." His deep voice wraps around me, softer than the towel covering my body.

An automatic smile creeps across my face. It's been a few days since our text conversation got caught short by Dad's visit, and I've missed him.

"What brings you to this side of town?"

His voice grows a touch sultry. "You, mainly. Along with your beautiful baby girl. Can I come up, or do you have another guy keeping you company?"

I snort at the thought. "I think my life is complicated enough as it is, don't you? One second. Let me release the door."

Replacing the receiver, I hit the button and wait for Emmett to climb the stairs, a delicious excitement fluttering low in my belly.

Less than a minute later, he's standing in front of me, eyes fixated on my face.

"Did you just finish morning skate?" I ask, unable to resist exploring his physique.

The last morning we were together, I got to appreciate how perfect he is beneath the training gear that he's wearing today.

Bottom lip pinned between his teeth, Emmett takes a small step toward me. "My schedule says that I should be completing a light session in the gym, but somehow, I ended up driving over here."

I can tell he wants to touch me, both hands sliding into his pockets.

Tipping my head to one side, I feed on the palpable tension growing between us each time we're in the same room. "And what were you hoping to find when you arrived?"

His grin only confirms that he feels the same way over the charged atmosphere. "A beautiful girl, half naked and smiling at me." His eyes drop down my body. "Some might say that I hit the jackpot."

So many times in the past couple of months, I've wondered what it would be like to kiss this man, although none more so than in this moment right now. I think post-practice is how I like him most—his freshly showered scent filling my senses, a backward cap doing something to me I can't explain.

When he closes the space between us, cupping my face in his palms, I feel sure that this is where we'll take another step into the unknown.

"It's a beautiful day outside, bright and sunny with spring flowers lining the roads." He strokes his thumb under my left eye. "Spend the day with me, Mama. You, Blake, and my Aston Martin DB5."

As a teenager, I thought it was the coolest car I'd ever seen, and he looked like a god when he drove it. I thought the same thing when he drove me to the hospital in it too, even though I was having one of the worst days of my life.

"Do you remember losing that bet when we played Monopoly and giving me and my girlfriends a ride to the mall?"

He doesn't hesitate. "I remember. You talked about James Bond the whole way there, and I recall being surprised that you even knew about a movie filmed in the 1960s."

My eyes drop to his lips. "You underestimate me and my taste in music and movies, Mr. Richards."

Emmett pushes out a thoughtful breath as he examines my face. "That's where you're wrong, Miss Quinn. You've always fascinated me. Your quirks, big heart, and love of sports made you one of the coolest people I knew. Someone I wanted to be friends with." He pauses, fingertips massaging behind my ears. "And today, you've turned into an incredible woman that I can't get enough of. Even if I should stop indulging myself in you."

I never want him to stop.

"We won't fit the stroller in the DB5, but I could bring Blake's baby sling," I suggest, eager to spend as much time with him as possible.

"Sounds good." He smiles, mouth hovering over mine.

I stare up into his eyes. "Where do you plan on taking us?"

He rests his forehead against mine, and my heart settles into a steady rhythm, like we have all the time to enjoy each other.

"Somewhere discreet, but equally beautiful and a place where no one can disturb us."

WE'RE fifteen minutes into our drive, and I'm still none the wiser as to where we're headed. All I know is, it's out of town, the roads growing quieter and more rural.

Emmett switched up his regular glasses for prescription sunglasses, his attention fixed solely on the road.

"I think Blake likes the luxurious car lifestyle." I chuckle, eyeing my baby daughter in the rearview mirror.

He rests his forearm over the steering wheel, briefly turning his head to look at me. "I think she likes any life where her mommy is at the center of it."

Warmth fills my chest as we pull up at a stoplight, the road drenched in spring sunlight.

"How many cars do you have now?"

Emmett doesn't immediately answer, lifting the fingers planted on his steering wheel to count. "Six, if you include this one."

I practically choke on my saliva. "So, basically, one for each day of the week?"

His smirk is panty-melting as he shifts into gear. "Almost."

It's another couple of minutes before we speak again. Blake's eyes intermittently droop as she gently falls into a deep sleep.

"If Blake stays asleep in the back, it will be her first decent nap in a while," I say, a yawn threatening to break out. "If you can't already tell by the dark circles under my eyes, this girl right here has had less than three hours of sleep for the past four nights."

We're driving along a quiet road when Emmett pulls into a rest stop, keeping the engine running as he unclips my belt.

With Blake seated directly behind me, there's enough room for him to slide his seat right back.

"Come sit in my lap, Bill."

"I thought we weren't going to touch each other?"

Something in what I just said urges him on, and he reaches across to interlace our fingers and pull me over the center section.

I don't resist, burning anticipation growing strong when I plant my knees on either side of his thighs and feel how crazy our close proximity is driving him.

Pushing away a few strands of hair that have come loose from my bun, Emmett pulls off his cap and sets it on my head, admiring the way it looks on me.

"There isn't a day, hour, or minute that passes where I'm not thinking about you and Blake. When I gear up to hit the ice, I'm wishing you were in the family box. When I'm making my morning protein shake, I'm thinking about what you're having for breakfast and if you managed to get enough sleep that night. You're constantly on my mind, and my obsession is only growing stronger."

My fingers find the toggles on his blue hoodie, and my eyes drop to where I'm fidgeting with it.

"Eyes on me, Mama."

I drop the toggle and do as he commanded.

"I think about you all the time," I confess. "It's like when we aren't physically in the same room, we're still somehow connected."

Emmett lowers his lips to the underside of my jaw, setting a gentle kiss against my skin.

I close my eyes at the sensation, imagining what it would be like to feel his mouth against mine or even between my thighs. I'm not exactly experienced when it comes to guys, but I know that he could—and would—rock my world all night. It's impossible to harbor these kinds of feelings and them not translate into the bedroom.

"I'm so fucking scared," he confesses, voice trembling with genuine fear.

"Of what?" I whisper into his soft hair.

Truthfully, I don't need an answer. The dangers we've been facing have been apparent since the second I walked into my parents' living room that fateful day in February.

He pulls back, eyes full of angst. "When Scott stopped by my apartment the other day, he started talking to me about you and Blake, and I wanted to tell him everything. Holding out on my best friend like this feels like the worst form of betrayal, but knowing that all hell will break loose the moment I confess to my feelings leaves me with no other choice." He pulls a deep breath into his lungs before releasing a warm puff of air against my needy lips. "I'm going out of my mind here, Bill. I'm putting you in danger and being selfish every time I make excuses to see you."

I shake my head at his last few words. "You aren't being selfish; you're being a human."

His hands circle my hips, just like they did in my parents' kitchen. "If circumstances were different, do you know how many times I'd have made you come until you saw stars?" He moves his hand to the waistband of my leggings, skirting his fingertips across the top. "Over and over, just so I could feed my addiction."

Every muscle contracts, pleading for him to go further.

"Touch me, Emmett."

Guiding his hand further, he dips his fingers lower, teasing the thin fabric of my panties.

I drop my face into the crook of his neck, silently wishing for his hand to swipe through me.

"I'm in the battle of my life here." His voice is thick and heavy, heart beating hard enough for the both of us. "I've never wanted something so much in my life." He brushes a finger over my pussy, feeling how damp I am. "You're so fucking perfect for me."

"You're perfect for me too," I breathe out, pulse racing.

His fingers travel to the edge of my panties, sliding gently beneath the seam, but still too far away from my pussy.

I know he can feel my needy heat and hear the low moan as it escapes from my throat.

Blake is still fast asleep, and we have all the time to explore each other without fear of being caught.

"Touch me." I try once more to coax his fingers to where I want them.

He throws his head back, and I know if it wasn't for Blake, he'd allow his frustration to break free.

"Why?" He speaks to no one in particular. "Why couldn't this whole situation be different?"

Wrapping my palm around the nape of his neck, I gently guide his gaze back to mine, tears pricking my eyes.

When we set out on this drive, I expected Emmett to take us

to another secluded park. In reality, I don't think he had any particular destination in mind; his main objective was to steal some more time with me and my daughter.

And while I selfishly want to be around him all the time, I can see the way this is tearing him up inside. If Emmett was going to put his hands on me, then he would've done it already. There's only so many times we can be in this position—torturing each other over a fantasy of what could be. Emmett's the kind of man who takes what he wants, and I'd gladly hand myself over in a heartbeat. Yet despite all of the above, it feels like we're no further forward, as the barriers between us become increasingly insurmountable.

Words I never wanted to whisper rise in my throat, and acid burns a track directly behind them.

"If you need to back away for good, then I want you to know that I get it. Blake and I both get it." My fingers brush through the soft strands of hair at the back of his head.

"I also want you to know that I'm eternally grateful for everything you have done for us these past couple of months. The past decade of my life, to be honest. When I arrived back in Brooklyn, I was a broken girl—lost, scared, and without any friends. I'm where I am right now because of you, fighting another day because of the strength you've given me."

I bite on the inside of my cheek, desperate to finish what I set out to say. "If putting your hands on me means that you'll go on to regret it, then I don't want that to be our legacy. I want the memories of you holding my hand in the scanning room, tickling me until I couldn't breathe, buying me ridiculously overpriced steak and late-night pineapple pizza to be happy and without you feeling guilty because we took things too far and couldn't accept that, no matter how much we wanted it, we could never be more than friends."

CHAPTER TWENTY-NINE

BILLIE

My hand is still in Emmett's and resting on the stick shift when he pulls up along the sidewalk outside my apartment building and puts the car into park.

Other than a conversation about Blake, we haven't talked any more about us.

Letting Emmett know that it was okay for him to choose his own peace of mind and respect for my dad over me was the right thing to do, even if it hurt like hell to say it. The Billie before the heartbreak of Tucker would've clung on to Emmett with everything she had, and at times, that was exactly what I wanted to do. Difficult lessons over the past few months have taught me that no matter how hard you try or how much you crave a person to be in your life, it's ultimately them who has to want you. And while Emmett is nothing like my ex-boyfriend, I need to accept that, in the end, he might not choose me.

The bright afternoon sky has turned overcast, an apt reflection of the mood settling between us.

Clearing his throat, Emmett squeezes my fingers in his palm, and my hopeful brain interprets that as his reluctance to say goodbye.

"You're like no other woman I've ever met." His labored voice sounds like he's underwater, fighting for air.

The urge to invite him upstairs feels strong, but I keep my counsel, waiting to see if he'll add anything more.

Emmett tips his head over his shoulder, face full of awe when he smiles at a wide-eyed Blake as she peacefully observes us both from the back seat.

"I do drive you especially crazy." I force out the words, desperate to bring some relief to the moment.

He chuckles at that, eyes dropping to our joined hands. "Not just crazy, Bill. Fully out of my mind. In more ways than you could possibly imagine."

Silent screams of, *Kiss me*, pinball around in my brain when an ambulance shoots past us. I turn and stare through the windshield, where I see a guy with his back to us hovering at the entrance to my building.

He presses another button on the intercom and waits a few seconds, throwing his arms out to the sides in frustration.

"Let me help you both upstairs," Emmett offers, no doubt having noticed him too.

Throwing the driver's door open, Emmett rounds the car, and I climb out. He pushes my seat forward so he can unclip Blake's car seat before shutting the door behind him.

We're partway to my building when the first hit of dread slams into me, pulling me to an abrupt halt in the center of the road. Since Emmett wouldn't recognize Tucker, he keeps walking, stepping onto the sidewalk with Blake secured in her car seat.

I know I need to keep moving forward and out of the road, but it feels like my feet are glued to the asphalt.

"Bill?"

Emmett's call turns Tucker on his heel, and for the first time since I left Austin, heavily pregnant and with tears in my eyes, I come face-to-face with Blake's father.

"Hey, Billie."

The warmth in his greeting is not what I expected, and neither is the smile that tugs at his lips, revealing cute dimples that once drew me in but now make my stomach roll like I ate spoiled food.

Forcing my legs to move, I join everyone on the sidewalk, eyes flicking to Emmett's face. Contrary to Tucker, his homicidal expression is exactly how I anticipated if he ever laid eyes on my ex-boyfriend.

Jaw ticcing, eyes burning, Emmett takes a protective step toward me.

"Why are you here, Tucker?" I work to keep my voice steady, keying in the code to my building while being sure to hide it from Tucker.

He follows me inside, and Emmett and Blake are close behind as I start hastily climbing the stairs.

When we reach my front door, I pause with the key in the lock, eyes back on Emmett as he stands behind Tucker, wearing the same murderous expression as before.

Tucker nods expectantly at my door, waiting for me to let him in.

While I was always aware that he could show up unannounced since my address was available in the child support documentation we both signed, I honestly never envisioned a time when he would.

"I'm here to talk," Tucker eventually answers, like I haven't already figured that one out. "And who the hell is he?" He motions to Emmett.

I ignore his question and the rude way he asked it and pause with my hand on the door handle, watching Tucker spin around and stroke a soft hand over Blake's head. Truthfully, I'm unsure how to introduce Emmett for fear of putting the wrong label on us. Calling him a friend would be an injustice to how much he means to me, even if I just gave Emmett a route out of my life.

Emmett's knuckles tighten around her car seat as Tucker straightens in front of him, offering out a hand for him to take.

Like I did a second earlier, Emmett completely ignores Tucker, eyes back on mine. He's waiting on my instruction, and I get the feeling that he would do anything I asked of him.

I focus back on my ex. "To talk about what specifically?"

Tucker turns back to me, a confident smile overtaking his face. There's no way he can't pick up on the charged atmosphere or the fact that a towering hockey player is around two seconds from taking him out. That said, sports were never really his thing, so it's likely he doesn't recognize who Emmett is.

Thumbing behind him, he confirms my thoughts when he says, "How about we take this inside and away from the Terminator?"

If this whole situation wasn't so fucked up, I'd be tempted to laugh at the accuracy in Tucker's observations—Emmett's looming stature would intimidate me, too, if I were a first-rate asshole.

Unlocking my apartment door, I push it open and stand to one side, and Tucker enters without a beat of hesitation.

He releases a low whistle as he takes in my home. "Wow, Billie, this place is"—he scratches the back of his neck, cringing on my behalf—"pretty fucking terrible."

When Emmett takes a purposeful step forward, I move back into the doorway, preventing him from doing—or saying—something that I know would do neither him nor his hockey career any good.

Reaching out, I wrap my hand around the handle on Blake's car seat, summoning my best reassuring smile. "I got it. It's okay."

He knows what I'm asking, and even if his leaving is the last thing I truly want, the cold reality is, Tucker is right. None of this has anything to do with Emmett, and he has no place being a part of our conversation.

He presses his lips together, and his thumb brushes along the outside of my hand before he releases his hold on Blake's seat.

"I'm going for a walk, and I won't be any more than a few blocks away. My phone will be on loud, and my car will remain parked outside."

My forced smile is all the confirmation he needs, and he moves to leave, turning over his shoulder to look at me until the door closes behind him.

"I know he isn't your dad." Tucker gets straight into it, taking the steps up to my kitchen.

His eyes are full of mirth as he moves to sit at the small island, waving a friendly hand at my daughter as I set her car seat on the floor by the door and lift her into my arms.

"But he sure as shit looks old enough to be him." He snickers, folding his arms across his chest.

"He's a family friend."

He narrows his eyes at me, suspicion reminiscent of Maria. "Okay, well, if he isn't your boyfriend, then I guess I'm good to press on with what I came here to say."

It's not lost on me that Tucker hasn't once asked to hold his daughter; it's the kind of detached behavior I witnessed repeatedly from his parents toward him.

"Do you want to hold Blake?" I offer, stepping into the kitchen.

He shifts on the stool, clearing his throat as he does. "I've never held a baby before, and I don't want to hurt her."

Neither had I until I gave birth.

For the sake of our daughter, I force a sweet smile, taking a seat on the opposite side of the island.

Blake wriggles in my arms, a hungry whimper leaving her lips.

If the atmosphere wasn't awkward before, it sure as shit is the second I unclip my feeding bra, exposing a breast for Blake to latch on.

Tucker doesn't know where to put his eyes, and I can't deny the way his discomfort bolsters my confidence. Six months ago, he was my senior, yet today, it feels like I've gained the strength of a thousand lifetimes in his absence.

I keep my eyes locked on Blake's, determined to force Tucker to lead the conversation. After all, he's the one who made the trip to be here.

"I've been doing a lot of thinking over the past few weeks."

A softer version of Tucker's voice pulls my attention back to him.

"About what?"

He casts his eyes out the kitchen window, bracing his elbows on the counter in front of him. "About a lot of things that went down, but specifically about you and me."

In the blink of an eye, the confidence I was previously feeling fades, replaced with total uncertainty. Of all the potential reasons he had to show up here, I never expected our former relationship to be one of them. That day I called him about the scan told me everything I needed to know about his feelings and how much Tucker truly cared about us.

Or at least I thought it did.

With his pointer finger, Tucker absentmindedly draws patterns on my kitchen island, lips twisting to the side. "I know that I've been a jerk, so you can spare me the reminder."

My brows shoot to my hairline. "Who's to say that was what I was thinking?"

Beneath hooded eyelids, he flashes me a look I can't decipher. "Why wouldn't you be thinking that? I know I would."

This is Tucker's version of an apology, and while I really didn't need one, my daughter definitely does.

"If you're trying to tell me that you want to be a part of Blake's life, then just know that I would never stop you."

His pointer finger pauses in place, although he still doesn't look at his baby girl. "I want to be a part of both of your lives."

If I wasn't holding Blake, I'd probably fall off my stool. I heard what he said just fine, but disbelief has me asking to repeat his last statement.

This whole situation is clearly killing him, but not in the way I've witnessed in Emmett. Tucker's persona is protective and guarded, whereas Emmett's has always been a battle of will, a pure display of vulnerability. And that realization sends my mind reeling, wondering what the fuck must be going through Emmett's head as he pounds the Brooklyn streets, rain now beating against the sidewalks.

My arms hold Blake a little tighter.

Dropping his head into his hands, Tucker releases an exasperated groan. "Say something, Billie. For fuck's sake, please say something."

I open my mouth to give him something. In the end, only silence materializes.

He pulls at the roots of his dark hair; meanwhile, I'm still fighting to believe that this is all really happening.

"Did you meet someone else?" he asks, cocking his head at my front door.

"Nope," I simply respond. My dating life is really none of Tucker's business.

He puffs out a breath. "Huh, okay."

As Blake finishes up her feed, I refasten my top and climb down from the stool, heading for the bedroom so I can set her down for a nap.

To do that, I need to pass Tucker, and just as I feared, he catches my elbow, stopping me in my tracks.

"Do you want to hold her?" I ask again, perfectly aware that's not why he stopped me.

Heavy heartbeats thump against my rib cage as I let my eyes wander to Tucker's.

The confession as it leaves him is one I longed to hear back in Austin, but I feel absolutely nothing as he admits, "I came here for you, Billie. To make it right between us and to be a father to our child."

Gaze locked ahead on my bedroom door, I stand stock-still. "And I already told you that I would never stand in the way of any healthy relationship you wanted to have with Blake."

His fingers squeeze my elbow tighter. "Why are you ignoring what I said about us?"

Stepping forward, I break from his grasp, quickly entering my bedroom and setting a sleeping Blake in her bassinet.

Tucker's in the doorway to my room when I stand back up, his eyes studying my unmade double bed. He'd be wrong to assume that I've had anyone else in there with me.

Pushing past him, I head straight for the coffee maker. "Do you want a drink?"

He just turns in the doorway, jaw clenched out of frustration. "I want to know why you won't give us a second chance."

My hand trembles as I reach up and snag a mug from a cupboard Emmett fixed, so much of me wishing I hadn't asked him to leave.

"There is no *us*, Tucker. You cheated and destroyed our relationship."

Footsteps sound from behind me as I flick on the machine and spin around to face him, palms cutting into the edge of the counter.

Standing only a few feet away, Tucker hunches his shoulders. "I thought you were a better mom than that, and so did my parents."

Since the second Tucker showed up at my place, anger was yet to feature in the many emotions I felt.

Until now.

"Excuse me?" I question, voice incredulous.

He just shrugs like what he said wasn't the epitome of gaslighting. "If Blake could talk, I'm pretty sure that she'd want her mommy to give her daddy another shot." His eyes rove my home once more. "No kid would want to be brought up in a place like this."

Hurt lances through me. Burning, maddening, searing hurt.

"Who the fuck do you think you are?"

He looks borderline satisfied to get a rise out of me. I can't say

I blame him; I've offered next to zero emotional response since he crossed the threshold.

"Billie," he begins, "you're a college dropout from a poor family, living in a place that looks like it should be condemned."

"That's not true," I volley back, proud of my little apartment even if I can't refute the rest.

He edges closer to me as the coffee machine finishes up its cycle. "It's all true, Billie. But I want to make things right again."

I scoff. "So, you're here to rescue us, right? Like a white knight in shining armor."

He grins, and I hate it. "Something like that, yeah. Plus, there's a bunch of rumors circulating around the country club, and most of them aren't favorable to my family."

I cannot have heard that right. "I-I'm sorry?"

Tucker flushes a color I used to think was cute. "Let's just say that it would be ideal for all of us if you came back to Austin with me. Whatever outstanding rent you have on this place my parents will settle, and the house we originally picked out is ready and waiting for us to move into."

Pressing the heels of my hands into my eyes, I check that I haven't entered an alternate universe. Nothing in real life can be this messed up.

Not even the Price family.

"I need to get this straight," I sigh, hands still digging into my eye sockets. "You want me and Blake to up and leave our lives here in Brooklyn so we can fly back to Texas with you ..." I drop my hands, vision now blurry as I look at him. "All so your parents can save face in their social circles?"

Tucker's lack of response is answer enough.

"Get. Out." I punctuate each word through my teeth.

Like I just pulled a gun and shot him through the chest, he rears back. "You're kicking me out?"

I shake my head at him. "No, Tucker. *I'm* not kicking you out. *We're* kicking you out. Blake and I."

His jaw pops open, and I'm already halfway to the front door.

Yanking on the handle, I motion for him to leave.

Like he did with me earlier, I stop him with a hand to his arm, although he doesn't bother to show me his eyes. "Given that your parents are the ones who call the shots in your life, would you take a personal message on my behalf?"

He remains silent, molars grinding.

"Tell them that if their son ever finds himself ready to step up and be a father to his beautiful daughter, I won't be the one to get in his way. However, that's as far as my patience and generosity are willing to extend. They might see me as a pathetic, poor little girl who got herself knocked up to ensnare their golden son, but they're wrong. They were wrong back when I was in Austin, and they're wrong now that I'm standing on my own two feet here in Brooklyn."

He gives me his eyes, and I lock them with mine, certain that this will be the last time I see them, even if that breaks my heart for Blake.

"If Blake ever asks about her dad, I will always tell her the truth, Tucker. I guess it's down to you as to what kind of parental legacy you choose to leave behind."

CHAPTER THIRTY

EMMETT

Following multiple loops walking around Billie's block, I climbed into my car outside her building and blasted David Bowie on the radio, anything to distract my mind from thoughts of forcing my way into her apartment and pinning that fucker against a wall.

The look on Tucker's face when he clapped eyes on Billie ... I wanted to smack that smirk straight from his mouth.

When my phone buzzes on the passenger seat, I snatch it up and hit Accept on Billie's contact.

"Hey," I rush out, turning the volume down on "Heroes," the rain having thankfully stopped.

If my adrenaline wasn't already at an all-time high, the sound of Billie's soft sobs sends it rocketing.

"He just left, so you're free to come back. If you want to."

How could she think that I'd want to be anywhere else than by her side?

"What happened, Bill?" I try to keep my tone light but fail, burning hatred toward her ex infiltrating my voice.

Another soft sob before she swallows thickly, forcing down a show of vulnerability, like always. "We can talk when you get here."

I'm already out of my car and halfway across the road.

Tucker pushes open the outside door, and I catch it above his head. He isn't a small guy, but I tower above him.

The second he notices me, contempt fills his eyes.

This prick doesn't deserve to inhale the same air as Billie and Blake, never mind have the chance to fuck up the best thing that ever happened to him.

Grabbing the handle, he attempts to shut the door—and consequently me out of the building.

Planted firmly in my palm, the door doesn't even budge, and Tucker huffs out a frustrated breath.

I stare down at him, a smile born from anger tugging at my lips. I scarcely lose my shit, but for him? I'll go nuclear on his ass the first chance I get.

Although I don't know much about him or his background, Tucker Price is everything I hate about certain members of society. Entitlement drips from him, as does a misplaced sense of superiority. I'm sure his rich parents instilled that kind of gross attitude in him, and I'll be only too happy to be the one to bring him crashing down to reality with a few truths of my own.

Billie shouldn't take him back. Ever.

My stomach knots because I know that her choice about who she dates really isn't my call to make. She's her own strong woman, and that's precisely why I'm falling in love with her.

"You can leave the door since I'm headed up to see Billie."

He tries again to slam it shut.

"Who the fuck are you anyway?" he spits, finally relenting and letting go of the door handle.

"Billie's friend," is all I offer, still grinning at him from ear to ear.

He rolls his eyes at that, just as I'd expect him to do whenever he doesn't get his own way. "Don't you think it's a little strange to be 'besties' "—he air-quotes the word with his hands—"with someone half your age?"

I look confused on his behalf. "Don't you think it's a little weird how much you care?"

He stalls for a second. "I am when a creep I barely know is about to visit my daughter."

I blow out a laugh, genuinely entertained by the nerve of this asshole. "I'd say he just left, wouldn't you?"

When Tucker narrows his eyes at me, I let him see a side to my personality that rarely comes out to play. Over my thirty-five years, I've learned that getting mad is never as productive as getting even. But Tucker Price is the type of person who works in simple terms.

When I step forward, the bill of my baseball crap presses into his forehead as I drop my gaze to his.

"What the fuck did you say to Billie up there?"

His satisfied expression corroborates my initial assumptions—he's a cocky prick who thinks way too much of himself.

"I told her to come back to Austin with me so we can make a go of things. Just the three of us."

Panic shoots through me, although I do a good job of hiding it, steely eyes never faltering. "Given that you're leaving alone, I'm assuming that didn't go over too well."

He lifts a shoulder, casually checking out his surroundings. "She's thinking about it for sure. I mean, who would want to live in a hole like this?" He fakes an apologetic wince. "Shit. Sorry, man. I guess you must live around here too."

Just as I suspected earlier, Tucker has no idea who I am.

Scrubbing a hand over my jaw, I know that the best thing to do would be to head upstairs and be with my girl.

And that's exactly what I'll do, right after I annihilate this son of a bitch.

"You're right," I say, nodding my head at the silver DB5 I bought in England last year. I paid over five-hundred thousand pounds for it, and even though I know Tucker's only interest is himself, money comes a close second in the race for his heart. "I live around a twenty-minute drive from here."

Tucker stares open-mouthed at my car.

I hate making any kind of financial flex, but I'll be damned if he thinks Billie and Blake would ever have to worry about money in his absence.

"Are there any more inaccurate observations you'd like to make, or are we done here?" I speak again, pulling his attention back to me.

He shakes his head, eyes wide, like he's seen a ghost. "No. I think we're done here."

Alpha pride fills my chest—an emotion that only seems to surface when Billie and Blake are concerned.

Getting right in his face, I drop my voice to a growl. "Oh, best believe we're fucking done here, Tucker. And you should be grateful about that too ..." I edge even closer until he can feel, as well as hear, every word I'm about to say. "Because if I had my way and you weren't Blake's biological father, then you wouldn't have eyes to appreciate my Aston Martin or the way I'm going to make your incredible ex-girlfriend fall in love with me."

Attempting to intimidate me, Tucker grinds his molars.

Aww, cute.

"I don't know how to break this to you, but Billie just referred to you as a friend when I asked her if you two were dating."

I shrug, unsurprised by her response since, right now, that's the truth. "And? I'm taking it slow with her since she just got out of a toxic relationship with an asshole. Rome wasn't built in a day."

He hates my response, and I love that he does.

"Who the fuck are you?"

Reaching up, I pull on the bill of my Blades cap. "Tell me you don't watch hockey without telling me you don't watch hockey."

He bursts out laughing. "Now the money and flashy car all make sense. Billie must think that all her gold-digger dreams have come true."

My hand wraps around his throat, lifting him from the ground with ease. If anyone catches sight of this, I'll likely be put on waivers by the team. Not that I care.

"The only person who struck gold was you when you bagged a stunning girl who was way out of your league."

Tucker tries to pry my fingers from his throat, but they aren't going anywhere, not until I'm done with him.

"So, let me make this really clear since you obviously struggle with taking a hint."

His eyes are blown wide, and his hands are flailing about like a fish dangling on the end of a line.

"Grow the fuck up, Tucker. Step up and be a father, or back out of Billie and Blake's life altogether. Either way, I'm not going anywhere, and neither is any word about this little interaction between us ... is it?"

He gives me a quick headshake.

"Good."

When I drop him back to his feet, he clutches his throat.

"You're fucking crazy!" he spits.

I smile at thoughts of holding Billie in my arms in the next couple of minutes.

"I'm not crazy, Tucker. Crazy would be walking away from a beautiful daughter. I'm simply a guy who will do anything for the people he cares about ... you should definitely try it, too, sometime."

"Your team would probably have something to say about the way you just assaulted me."

Pulling out my phone, I scroll for Billie's contact, typing out a quick text to let her know that I'm on my way up. I step over the threshold and turn back to him.

"You're a senior in college and hoping to go to law school, right?"

He gives me a tight nod, eyes darting about anxiously.

"Pretty sure getting a girl knocked up and then refusing to

take responsibility wouldn't go over too well in your desired line of work."

He puffs out his chest. "Doesn't matter. I'll inherit my parents' practice."

Of course he fucking will.

Pulling up my social media profile, I show him the screen, just so he can get a clear idea of who I am and the level of influence—or destruction—I can have.

"Let's not start flexing muscles, Tucker."

He clears his throat.

I have zero intention of actually going through with the following offer, but the idea is too funny to pass up. I point across at my car. "Do you need a ride back to the airport, or are you good with the bus?"

Heat spreads across his cheeks. "I'm good."

"Great." I thumb over my shoulder. "So, while it was really great catching up with you, I'm going to go spend some time with Billie and Blake now." I shoot him one last sarcastic grin. "If you catch the next flight to Austin, you might make it back in time for Mommy's curfew."

CHAPTER THIRTY-ONE

BILLIE

The thud of Emmett's footsteps echoes through the stairwell right before he swings my front door open and pauses in the center of the living room.

His chest is heaving, and the sound of my door clicking shut is the only noise between us as he studies my puffy red eyes.

The second Tucker was out of sight, the composure I'd been fighting to maintain while he was in my apartment completely dissipated, allowing the past few months to hit me like a freight train.

Between sobs and a panic attack I never want to experience again, all I could think was to call Emmett. Even if he's already gone way above and beyond what any friend would do, having him near me was all I craved.

He is all I crave.

His hands aren't shoved inside his pockets, like they normally are, when he stalks forward, gray eyes closer to a charcoal color as he comes to stand in front of me.

Reaching up, I set a soft palm over his racing heart.

He drops his gaze to my hand, eyes slowly closing. "I just let

Tucker go without inflicting any long-term damage, but if you tell me that he hurt you, I'll hunt him down and break his fucking neck."

Tangling my fingers into his hoodie, I bite down on my bottom lip, determined not to let more tears emerge. "What he said today would've destroyed me when I was back in Austin." I gaze up at him, shaking my head. "Not anymore."

"Why not anymore, Billie?" he whispers with so much intensity in his words.

I focus on the sunrise tattoo hidden beneath his clothing. "Because now that I know what a real man should look like, there isn't anything about Tucker that I want. He came back here to fix a PR issue for his parents. He doesn't love me or Blake, and I don't think he ever did."

Deep lines crease into his forehead, features overrun with pain. "I was pacing the streets out there, thoughts of you leaving with him when you deserve so much more than he can give you. Both of you." A desperate groan reverberates in his chest. "The way I want to show you how much you mean to me, and how I would treat you like goddamn royalty." He takes my hand and interlaces our fingers. "Both in and out of the bedroom."

"Then why don't you?" I ask, throwing every last bit of caution to the wind.

Today's conversation in the car feels like it never took place after everything that's unfolded since.

When Emmett lifts my chin to look at him, there's a beat of nothing, right before he says two words we've both been longing to hear.

"Fuck it."

Full lips envelop my own, and rough palms wrap around my ass, planting me on the kitchen island. He tastes better than the brief hints I've sampled each time his breath has fanned my face.

He whimpers, and I moan, tongues slowly caressing each other. I've kissed other guys before, but none of those experiences even come close to the way Emmett owns my mouth.

This kiss is commanding yet delicate, frantic yet perfect in every way. Months of pent-up anguish burst free, driving his tongue to take what's been his since the second we set eyes on each other on my twenty-first birthday.

We know there's no going back, that this is the reality we have to sit with when the kiss ultimately ends. I wouldn't want it any different, and by the way Emmett tangles his fingers in my hair, dropping his lips to explore my jawline, it's obvious that he feels the same way.

This moment is long overdue, and the heat pooling between my thighs is a testament to how hard we've tried to resist the inevitable.

Some things are just meant to be, and this kiss was written in the stars.

The man I washed and dried dishes with when I was a teenager, the family friend I harbored an unrequited crush on for years ... is kissing me, cupping my face in his hands, biting down on my bottom lip so he can steal another taste.

How can something so forbidden feel so right?

Breaking from my lips, Emmett's voice trembles, "Remember when I told you that you take my fucking breath away?"

I smile against his mouth. "Yes."

Moving his hands down my body, he rests his fingers on the button of my jeans. He's asking for permission to take things further, and it feels like all my fantasies are finally coming true.

Folding my hands over his, I guide them until my button and zipper are undone.

"Well, it's high time I stole the air from your lungs, Mama."

Blown pupils gaze back at me as he waits on the one answer I was only ever going to give.

"I want you to take me. Right here, right now."

Dragging his right thumb across my bottom lip, he presses his jean-covered cock into my apex. It's hard and long and even bigger than I recall from the morning we got ourselves off in his bed.

Lifting me from the island, he starts for the living room. "I want to take you to bed," he whimpers between kisses. "But with the way I plan to make you scream, there's a high probability that we'll wake Blake, so the couch will have to do."

If I wasn't already leaking through my jeans, I definitely am now.

Laying me on the couch, Emmett kneels in front of me, hooking my legs over his shoulders.

"Have you ever had anyone eat your pussy?"

I pulse between my thighs, certain that if he doesn't get his mouth on me in the next few seconds, my whole body will combust through desperation.

"Do you want an honest answer?"

He carefully peels my jeans off before tossing them behind him. "I want your honesty, always."

Emmett sucks two thick fingers into his mouth, pulling them out and running them over my thong.

I cry into a palm when he circles and pinches my already-sensitive clit.

"Tell me the truth, Bill," he presses, nuzzling his face between my thighs. "Has a tongue made you scream before? Or was Tucker as selfish in bed as he is in public?"

He knows the answer before I even share it.

"No one has ever gone down on me before."

I thought that Emmett would be only happy with that knowledge. Instead, sadness flattens his smile.

Hooking his fingers into the straps of my thong, he edges them down my thighs.

It's the most intense experience of my life—gray eyes fixated on my face while he strips my lower half.

He shifts closer, gently passing a finger through my heat, and my hips buck of their own accord. Every muscle is coiled tight by weeks, months of anticipation.

Emmett looks wholly pleased at my body's response, pulling off his glasses and setting them down on the floor beside him.

"This cunt"—he pushes a single finger inside my entrance—"is the prettiest cunt I've ever seen."

Curling his finger, he sucks my clit between his lips and swallows down his first taste.

Smooth strokes of his tongue toy with my entrance, lapping at me like he'll never get enough of the way I feel in his mouth.

My legs shake, full-body shudders overtaking every nerve ending.

Christ, he's good.

I might be new to this, but I can tell he's on the opposite end of the spectrum when it comes to the depth of my own sexual experience.

Maybe that thought should make me feel inferior, although nothing about the way this man devours my body could elicit anything other than confidence.

My back arches, and I dig my fingernails into his shoulders when he adds a second finger and curls them toward my front wall like he originally promised he would.

"I'm going to come, Em."

He just grins at me, working my pussy like it's his favorite toy. "You're beautiful like this, Billie. Sprawled out on your couch, pussy dripping with need." His voice is alluring, his touch the perfect balance of firm and gentle when he pumps his fingers harder and draws sounds from me I never knew were possible.

"More," I plead, my orgasm reaching a toe-curling high. "I want more."

Withdrawing, Emmett rises to his feet and licks me from his fingers.

"I really want to fuck you, Bill. Are you ready for my cock?"

Anticipation heightens every sense as I whisper, "I'm ready for you."

Smiling wide, he reaches into the back pocket of his jeans and fetches out his wallet before working on his belt and zipper, his jeans dropping to the floor.

Feral eyes fixate on mine when he pulls a condom from his

wallet and tears the packet open with his teeth. He dips a hand beneath the waistband of his boxer briefs, sheathing himself with ease. I wonder how many women Emmett has slept with.

"Spread those gorgeous thighs for my cock," he instructs, pulling my mind away from thoughts of his past until all I can think about is the next few seconds and how he'll be inside me.

I do as he asked, and he kneels in front of me, bracing a hand on the back of the couch behind my head. With his other hand, he pumps himself slowly, capturing my mouth with his.

"I promise to take it slow with you, Mama. To show you more of how a man should treat a woman." His lustful words tickle my lips, kicking up a heightened sensory bliss. "Tonight, your body deserves to be worshipped, but when the time is right and you're ready, I'll treat it with the disrespect I've been fantasizing about for way too fucking long."

As he notches himself at my entrance, I smirk up at him. "You have a filthy mouth to match that big dick of yours, Mr. Richards."

He pushes halfway inside, coaxing my tight pussy to accommodate him.

As he guides himself deeper, his thick cock invades my body until I've taken every inch he has to give.

I'm having sex with Emmett fucking Richards.

"You might have swallowed my whole dick, but you have no idea how much I'm holding back, Billie," he grinds out, rolling his hips into me for the very first time. "I wanted to eat you out for longer, and I will once I've blown inside this perfect pussy and claimed what's rightfully mine."

Open-mouthed, I stare up at him, my expression pulling a chuckle from his chest.

He kisses my shock away, whispering more dirty words that bring me right to the edge. "I can't wait to discover how we'll both taste as we trickle down your thighs."

I'm tempted to demand that we go without a condom right now. I want to feel him, bask in his warmth as he fills me up.

But after one unplanned pregnancy, we can't risk being irresponsible, even if I have the hottest hockey player hovering over my body.

"Can you feel that, Billie?"

He slips his hands beneath my ass and spins us around until he's sitting on the couch and I'm riding him slowly, the weight of my body pressing his cock deliciously deep inside me.

He feels glorious.

"So good," I whimper, leaning back so my hands are braced on his knees. The change in angle rubs his cock against my front wall, and it's the best sensation of my life.

Emmett's lips find my pulse point, hands tugging at the cami top I'm wearing. "Can I take this off?"

I don't hesitate, lifting my arms overhead.

He tosses it by my jeans and then unclips my bra like a pro, dragging the straps down my arms.

When all my clothes are piled into a heap, his eyes settle on my breasts. As a teenager, there was very little I liked about my body, and following a baby, I like the way I look without clothes even less.

I can't help but flinch at what he must be thinking now that he's seen me fully naked. Most twenty-one-year-old women typically have toned muscles and unblemished skin, free from stretch marks. I'm sure that's what Emmett was expecting each time we undressed each other with our eyes.

But as he cups the back of my head and pulls my mouth down to his, Emmett's next words unleash a swarm of butterflies throughout my body. "It's a goddamn privilege to see you like this, Billie." Hands gently explore my tits, fingertips caressing my stomach. "Your body is the perfect canvas, a testament to the kind of strength I, one day, aspire to have. Don't you dare shy away from what makes you so fucking beautiful, Mama. Show me the confident Billie that has me hooked around your little finger, addicted to what you'll do or say next."

I grin, and he winks, pulling his shirt overhead.

Sitting back into the couch, he braces his thick forearms behind his head. "Now, ride my cock like a good fucking girl. Use me like your plaything."

Wearing the filthiest smirk, he keeps one hand behind his head and the other on my left hip, holding me steady until I come all over his dick.

"Give me another," he commands, my hips losing their rhythm.

I shake my head at him, too sensitive, body trembling from its awesome high.

Licking his lips like he's only just getting started, he sits up straight and grips my chin between his thumb and forefinger. "I really need you to get used to coming multiple times whenever we fuck."

He thrusts his hips up, and I groan deeply.

"And just in case you think this is a onetime thing, it isn't. I'm going to fuck you a lot, Billie." He moves beneath me again; delicious sounds of his body sliding in and out of mine punctuate the silence between his words. "On this couch." Thrust. "In your kitchen." Thrust. "On every surface at my place." Thrust.

His face turns devilish when I release all over him, mouth falling open with another orgasm. I loop my hands around the nape of his neck, surrendering to the control he has over my body. Hungry for his delicious dominance.

"Maybe I'll bend you over next to Freya's new coffee machine one night while everyone's seated at the dinner table, distracted with their conversations."

When I feel his dick pulse, I know he's filling the condom.

Just like I did a few minutes earlier, he shakes and shudders beneath me, although he doesn't miss a beat in his pursuit to pull another orgasm from my body.

He succeeds before wrapping my satiated frame around him as he carries us into the shower and turns on the water.

The bathroom fills with steam, and he sets me down on my

feet. "I'm going to go and grab Blake's monitor so we can hear if she needs us."

There's no way this man can be real.

A minute later, he reemerges with the monitor, setting it down next to the sink.

He joins me under the stream, turning me around so my back is to his chest.

"What are you doing?" I ask.

He snaps the condom off and tosses it in the trash can.

"I already told you, Bill—showing you exactly how you deserve to be treated."

And that's precisely what he does until the warm water runs cold, washing and cleaning me before he drops to his knees and eats me out, like he promised.

CHAPTER THIRTY-TWO

EMMETT

Because I like taking risks with my life, I stayed over at Billie's place.

In her bed.

It's not even light outside, but my mind couldn't be any more awake as I lie on my back, staring up at a ceiling that I'll be calling Billie's landlord about as soon as a semi-reasonable hour rolls around.

If the mold festering in my girl's bedroom is dangerous, then Billie's lazy-ass landlord can join Tucker at the top of my shit list.

Morning skate looms in the back of my mind. I don't even have a toothbrush here, let alone training gear, which means I'll need to swing by my place before I head to the rink. Still, my delinquency—and potential fine—couldn't be more worth it.

Yesterday was ... indescribable.

When I finished making Billie scream in the shower, we curled up on the couch with snacks and watched *The Little Mermaid* with Blake.

It was around eleven p.m. when I finally carried Billie's

crashed-out body to bed and decided right there that I couldn't get up and leave. Not after the day she'd had and definitely not after we'd slept together for the first time.

Small whimpers filter from Blake's bassinet, and I gently pull my arm from under Billie's body. Floorboards creak beneath my feet as I round the bed and lift her onto my chest.

"What's the matter, B?" I whisper quietly.

Like I've seen so many times before with Billie, Blake nuzzles into my bare chest, mouth searching for milk I obviously can't provide.

I look back at Billie, peacefully resting and getting a first night of unbroken sleep in weeks. One hand rests on my pillow, the bracelet I got still fastened around her wrist.

"Let's see what we can do, yeah?" I say to Blake, quietly stepping into the kitchen to find the formula and sterilized bottles I know Billie keeps somewhere in the kitchen.

Big eyes watch me carefully prepare Blake's bottle, no doubt way slower than her mommy can do.

"Measuring out formula and water and screwing a lid on, all with one hand—it's way harder than it looks," I quietly whisper to a feeding Blake as I lean against the counter and cross my ankles, in awe of how quickly such a small baby can nail a relatively large serving.

Five or so minutes later, I've got a full but uncomfortable Blake squirming around on my chest and not a fucking clue how to burp her, which is what I'm pretty sure she needs.

Relieved I left my cell on the kitchen island last night and not on the nightstand, I pull up a new browser and start researching the best burping techniques when a text from Archer grabs my attention.

ARCHER

For reasons I'm not willing to discuss, I will be driving past your place on the way to morning skate. Do you want a ride?

ME

It's not even light outside. Why are you up?

ARCHER

I said that I didn't want to discuss it.

ME

How about you share with me the best way to burp a baby, and I'll stop asking you why you're going to be passing by my place later?

ARCHER

You're banging Billie, aren't you?

ME

For reasons I'm not willing to discuss ... yes. Yes, I am. Keep your lips firmly sealed.

ARCHER

I am nothing if not a vault.

ME

Remember the time I temporarily split with Maria a couple of seasons back and you tried to set me up with Jenna?

ARCHER

Fair point. I got carried away and ran my mouth.

ME

Precisely. Don't do it again.

ARCHER

I'll send you a screenshot of the page in the baby book I used when Emily was born. It really helped me perfect feeding and burping techniques.

screenshot attached

ME

Thank you.

ARCHER

I'll assume you don't need a ride since you'll be banging Billie one final time before racing back to your place to get changed.

ME

Got it in one.

ARCHER

And then you'll be heading straight from the rink to Scott's place to confess before he finds out?

Setting my phone down, I manage to raise a couple of burps from Blake, and a few short minutes later, she's resting peacefully against my chest.

ME

I need to talk to Billie first. Everything kind of came to a head yesterday, and she crashed out in bed.

ARCHER

Jesus, you're in way over your head.

ME

...

ARCHER

Let's look at the evidence, shall we? Sleeping with the off-limits girl after you vowed to stay away, and now you're feeding her baby in the dead of night while she sleeps peacefully. No doubt recovering from the initial months of motherhood, along with the effects of your dick. Tell me that you used protection because with the way you've been pining, she's now likely expecting triplets.

ME

I'm rescinding on our earlier deal. Tell me why you're in my part of town.

ARCHER

Don't deflect.

ME

Likewise.

ARCHER

I needed to run an errand.

ME

Not good enough. And now I'm suspicious.

ARCHER

I'm on my way back from Jon and Felicity's place. I had some paperwork to sign.

ME

Archer, you're starting to freak me out.

ARCHER

Darcy doesn't know yet, and I need you to keep it that way.

ME

Looks like we both have secrets we need to guard.

ARCHER

I just signed the deed to Jon's old apartment in Seattle.

Brows pinched together in confusion, I stare down at Archer's last message.

ME

Why?

ARCHER

I bought it for us as a second home. Darcy gets sentimental over things, and Jon mentioned that they were putting it on the market. They're planning to buy a bigger place in Seattle, one with a backyard for the grandkids.

ME

So, you bought a whole property in an entirely different state, just in case Darcy wanted to keep her stepdad's apartment in the family?

ARCHER

I'm the perfect husband, I know.

ME

Simp.

ARCHER

I think we both know that you're winning in that department.

"Is everything okay?"

Dressed in the training top she wore the first night she stayed in my bed, Billie appears in the bedroom doorway.

As I set my phone down and move toward her, her eyes scan the kitchen, landing on Blake's empty bottle and then her comatose little girl.

"Did you feed Blake?"

I've no idea why I flush—probably because Archer's right. I am a simp.

"She woke and was restless. When I picked her up, she was searching for food so I …"

The warmth of Billie's lips causes me to trail off.

"I didn't want to wake you," I breathe into her mouth as she backs us into the bedroom, and I set Blake back down in her bassinet.

When our eyes next connect, the training top I gave her is on the floor, and she's sitting up on the bed, sliding her feet along the edge of the mattress.

"You promised me a ton of sex," she whispers. "And I want to cash in."

I'm out of my boxer briefs and crawling over her body in seconds, braced on my elbows so I can appreciate her beauty.

"If there's one thing about me, I always keep my promises." I grin against her lips.

She slides her body down the bed beneath me until her face is level with my pelvis, and her mouth swallows the head of my cock.

I reach down between us and tip her chin up to look at me. "Are you sure?"

She wets her lips, hunger burning in her eyes. "Why wouldn't I be?"

Kneeling over her face, I pump my hard cock a couple of times and groan quietly so my desperation doesn't wake Blake. "I'm going to blow down your throat. There's no way I won't."

That seems to spur her on, lips forming the perfect O.

Holy shit. She's waiting for me to slide inside her warm mouth.

I wrap her bedhead in my fist and slowly guide my cock to the back of her throat.

Holy fucking shit. She doesn't gag once, eyes locked on mine when I pull out and push back inside.

It's been a long-ass time since a girl's given me head, but now I know why the blow-jobs before tonight were never particularly memorable—Billie Quinn's mouth was made for my dick, just like her pussy.

"Look at you," I purr, bringing a single finger to my lips. "Sucking my cock in silence."

Her eyes fill with lust, tongue looping around my shaft on the next pump.

"Fuck, Mama," I moan low. "Daddy's little angel is a dirty fucking devil."

I pull completely out of her mouth, her tongue chasing the tip of my cock. I move down her body and lean down for a kiss, the taste of us both is the perfect combination.

Billie's lips tip into a wicked smile, and I adjust myself until I'm kneeling between her thighs.

"Did I do a good job disarming you with my innocence?" She spreads herself wide.

Heaven help me, I'm going straight to fucking hell without passing Go.

"Billie," I rasp, squeezing my eyes tight so I don't come at the thought of fucking her raw, "I need a condom, baby. There's too much risk for you right now."

When I open my eyes, she's studying me intently. "I'm on birth control, but you're right. Even if all I want is to feel you."

I kiss her gently, head spinning out at the thought of one day having zero barriers between us. Both in and out of the bedroom. "If I get you pregnant, I will never forgive myself."

Pulling back, she analyzes me carefully. "Are you saying that because of our situation or because you never want children?"

My heart is hammering in my chest. I intended to wait before we had this conversation. But just like Archer told me earlier, I'm in over my head with this girl, and it's useless to try and pull back.

Fuck distance and fuck the rules.

"I want children, Billie. Even if I don't have any by blood, that doesn't mean I can't picture being a dad one day."

Her eyes glaze over, and I seal my words with a kiss.

"And what about biological kids?" she presses.

I swallow thickly, emotions clogging up my throat. "With the right girl and at the right time, yes."

Lying down beneath me, she pulls my mouth to hers. "Am I the right girl for you, Em?"

While there are so many doubts over how we're going to get there, I have no question about my desire to make Billie Quinn mine to keep.

Forever.

"If I didn't think you were, then I wouldn't be here, risking everything, just so I could descend a little deeper under your spell."

Eyes still glassy, she silently points to her nightstand, and I reach into the drawer, eyes trained on hers while I ready myself for the girl I'm falling in love with.

With a condom in place and her legs around my waist, I spend the next hour making secret love to my best friend's only daughter.

CHAPTER THIRTY-THREE

BILLIE

Coach Morgan's face set above a stone fireplace was not what I expected to see when I pushed through the door of the Italian restaurant that Darcy had booked for lunch.

As soon as she sets eyes on me, she's out of her seat and racing to help me through the door with Blake's stroller.

After a quick hug, I tip my chin at the photograph. "Is that your stepdad?"

She rolls her eyes, hands propped on her hips. "Ridiculous, isn't it?"

Reaching into Blake's stroller, I pull back her blanket so that she doesn't overheat now that we're in the warm. "But why is it there?"

"He owns the joint," Kate confirms, approaching me from behind. "He and Zach Evans—his former Seattle teammate—decided to go into business, owning a chain of Italian restaurants. They're about to close on a second restaurant in Seattle, which will take their total to three."

I cast my eyes around the place. With a wine-red finish and brass accents, it's luxurious, but it still embodies a homey feeling that you would find in your grandmother's living room. "Why the name Luigi's?"

"Long story ..." Kate exhales, bending down to greet Blake. For the most part, this woman is your classic stony-faced lawyer, but give her a cute kid, and she melts into a pile of goo. "When we used to live in Seattle and JJ still played for the Scorpions, the guys used to hit up this Italian place called Luigi's." She stands up straight and turns to me. "Anyway, when the owner, Luigi, finally retired and was looking to sell, Jon couldn't let the place go. That's where his restaurant journey began. After years of relentless persuasion, Jon managed to get Zach to invest, and that's when they bought this place."

"Oh," I simply say, trying to take in my surroundings.

"And now my husband thinks he's Chef Ramsay and is making the business duo a trio," Kate adds.

Darcy flicks her long blonde hair, eyeing Kate carefully. "So, the other day, after he returned from morning skate, Archer dropped a bomb on me—it was a pleasant one, but a bomb nonetheless."

Kate looks intrigued, and while I'm still trying to wrap my head around this wild new world, where people have stacks of cash to chase whatever dreams they want, Darcy continues with her story.

"Archer bought Jon's old apartment in Seattle."

"The one he lived in when he played for the Scorpions?" Kate questions.

Darcy nods, twisting her lips in thought. "It was a really sweet thing to do because he knew how sentimental I get over things. I hated Seattle when I lived there as a teenager, but that was only because I missed my shitty ex and wanted to head back to the UK. Jon meeting Mum was the start of everything changing in our lives when you think about it." She wraps her arms around her middle, eyes flicking to Jon's ridiculous photograph. "He might be a cocky bastard, but he's the glue that sticks everyone together, and I don't think I could ever imagine my life without him—or a part of Seattle—in it."

Kate taps Darcy on the shoulder. "You're thinking that Archer is going to go in on the business too, aren't you?"

After the sentimental speech she just gave, laughter bubbles from Darcy's chest. "If I know my hubby, then yes. He's going through a midlife crisis early, and he keeps rattling on about how he'll be bereft when his pro career is over."

As we move through to another room, Kendra and Esme, Collins, Jenna, Felicity, and two other women with children a similar age to Kate and Jensen's kids, June and Will, who are also here, are all sitting around a huge table.

Darcy clears her throat, and the room falls silent. "Now, I know that most of you have already met our amazing new friend and her beautiful baby girl." Her eyes fix on the redhead first. "Billie, this is Luna Evans, Zach Evans' wife." Luna waves a hand at me and smiles warmly. "And this is Mia Callaghan, Jessie Callaghan's wife." Mia offers a similar smile to Luna as Darcy claps her hands excitedly. "Guys, meet Billie and Blake."

"Can we see the baby?" The little girl sitting next to Mia points at Blake's stroller.

Mia sets a kiss atop her head, smiling into her hair long dark hair. "Perhaps Blake is sleeping, Drew."

Jumping up from his seat at the head of the table, Will wastes no time as he sticks his head inside Blake's stroller. "She's awake, Drew." He scrunches up his nose as he looks at me. "Although I think she might've pooped."

"Nah, that's me. I just farted." Another boy I'd pin as a similar age to Will and June appears from behind me. He's the spitting image of Luna with a mass of red hair to match.

Will looks disgusted at him. I thought all kids found bowel movements hilarious.

"You have zero class, Aster," he scolds.

Kate watches her son rejoin his sister at the table, picking up his soda and taking a pull. "Excuse my son," she breathes. "The older he gets, the more he's turning into my husband. Who knew a seven-year-old could be the snob of the century?"

I snort a laugh and lift Blake out of her stroller, briefly checking to make sure she hasn't, in fact, pooped.

"Okay." Darcy claps her hands, bouncing excitedly on her feet. "Now that we're all here, I guess we can eat." She motions to an empty chair between Kate and her mom. "I put you between the two fearsome lawyers, if that's okay?"

Being invited to spend time with this great group of women was both nerve-racking and delightful, although it's only sadness I feel as I nod my head and take a seat with Blake.

I haven't had any interactions with Felicity Morgan before now, but she looks at me and then Blake like she can read minds.

"Darcy tells me that you were in your third year of college before you came back to Brooklyn." Her wide smile and British accent have my daughter enraptured.

At the mention of college, thoughts of Clara pop into my head. It's been weeks since we last spoke, and while I've always considered her to be my closest friend, it's clear that our wildly different lives are pulling us apart. It feels like every friendship I've ever made doesn't last, and I'm tired of making temporary connections.

I gaze around the room and pray that the women in here will end that disheartening cycle.

"I was," I reply quietly, separate conversations going on around us. "Until I dropped out of college when Blake's dad decided he couldn't cope with the responsibility of being a father."

There's nothing but understanding in Felicity's emerald eyes. "I had Darcy and Jack when I was still in college. My dream was to be a lawyer at the time."

Joining the conversation, Kate reaches around me, squeezing her friend's shoulder in a comforting gesture. "And here we both are—in our forties and about to start up our own law practice."

My head darts between them both. "Seriously? That's incredible."

Felicity smiles warmly at her new business partner. "I never thought that I'd make it as a lawyer, never mind own a practice with my best friend. One more week, and we'll be opening our doors to clients."

Kate couldn't look any prouder. "We're about to show our husbands what running a business really looks like." Leaning forward, she snags a breadstick from a pot in the center of the table. "Give it a few years, and we'll be opening offices all over the country."

When Blake starts mouthing, I quickly reach into her diaper bag set by my feet, pulling out a bottle and popping the cap.

She immediately begins feeding, and all I can think about is Emmett—half naked in my kitchen with my milk-drunk daughter in his arms.

"Which area of law were you hoping to specialize in, Billie?" Kate asks, loving eyes dropping to my daughter.

My sadness remerges, but it's quickly strangled by a growing sense of mom guilt for feeling anything other than grateful to have Blake. "Being a defense attorney was the dream."

"*Is* the dream." Felicity nudges my shoulder with hers. "Dreams never disappear, not unless you decide that you want something else." She picks up a bottle of Pinot and offers to fill my glass.

"Sure," I reply, more memories of Emmett and my twenty-first birthday resurfacing, along with lavender bath salts and fluffy socks.

"Maybe, one day, the dream will happen," I ruminate, taking a small sip and setting the glass back down on the table. "Right now, my priorities lie in getting back on my feet financially and raising Blake."

Kate dips her head down, lowered voice to go with her secretive persona. "What's the latest with the boy?"

It's like whenever anyone mentions him, an automatic grin

spreads across my face, no matter what mood I'm in. "He's ... doing well," I reply, wondering how Kate knows about Emmett.

She lifts a single brow. "If you thought I hadn't noticed the way he was looking at you after the Scorpions game, then you can't think that I'm a very good lawyer. Boy has it *bad*."

Like we're a trio of witches, Felicity ducks her head too. "And who is this boy you speak of?"

Kate's eyes flick to Felicity, and I give her a small nod to go ahead and tell her who he is. Half of the people around this table know what's going on anyway, and I don't think there's a woman sitting here who wouldn't take it to her grave.

It feels like that kind of friendship group.

Kate's expression is full of excitement. "Billie and Emmett Richards have a little something between them."

Felicity's jaw hangs open. "He just got a divorce from Maria, right?"

Switching Blake from one arm to the next, I speak through my teeth. "And Maria is also my mom's best friend." I look between them both. "And my dad is Emmett's."

Kate sits back in her seat, and Felicity gasps.

"That's ... quite the secret to keep," she declares, offering me a reassuring smile that it's exactly what she'll do. "Is it serious?"

After last week and the best night of my life, I'd definitely be more inclined to say yes. But we've hardly had a chance to speak or see each other between my busy life with Blake and the hockey season reaching a crescendo. The playoffs are now only days away.

"I'm not sure how to answer that," I tell her quietly. "To say that it's complicated doesn't really do the whole thing justice." I drop my eyes to a feeding Blake.

"Oh, trust me"—Kate bites off another piece of breadstick—"Emmett is serious about Billie." She smiles victoriously. "*Really* serious."

"A boy obsessed."

I turn over my shoulder to find Collins standing behind us.

Reaching down, she runs a light finger over Blake's cheek.

"Darcy just told me that Archer said Emmett was feeding Blake in the dead of night. No man cares for another guy's child if his world doesn't revolve around their mama."

The use of that name has my thighs pinching in the best way possible.

All three of them notice, and Kate's dirty giggle causes me to snort right before Darcy stands from her chair, clinking a fork against a glass.

"I want to make a little announcement before we all eat and drink way too many cocktails."

"Alcohol is bad for you," Will pipes up. "It's important to treat your body like a temple."

"And now he's quoting his father too," Kate mumbles behind a hand. "Lord save me. My daughter might also go by the name JJ, but my son is basically his dad."

Darcy deadpans at Will before continuing, "I know some of you have traveled all the way from other states to be here today ..." She looks at Mia and Luna. "And I'm so happy to have the whole Scorpions-Blades family here together to celebrate a milestone in two amazing women's lives." Her eyes land on Felicity and then Kate. "Morgan Jones LLP is going to take over the world!"

She thrusts her fist into the air right as the kitchen doors swing open, and two servers wheel out the biggest cake I have ever seen. It's five tiers of buttercream deliciousness.

"Umm ..." Luna looks confused. "Don't we eat cake after lunch?"

"We shouldn't eat cake, period."

Kate tosses what remains of her breadstick at her son. "Give it a rest, William."

Darcy waves a hand in front of her. "Eh, it's a small detail. Some rules are there to be broken."

Will's upper lip tips up at that, and he raises his water glass in the air. "Eat well. Play hard."

Against my foot, I feel a vibration coming from my bag.

Kate must've felt it, too, as she reaches down and hands me my purse. "Let me guess. It's the boy."

I don't need to say anything since my giddy grin provides the answer.

EMMETT

We're flying back from Dallas earlier than originally scheduled. The boys all want to go out and celebrate making the playoffs, but I want to celebrate in a different way.

I type out a quick response as Darcy begins cutting the cake.

ME

Is this where you turn all coy and suggest we watch another soccer game in your bed?

EMMETT

Nah, being coy was so last season. I'm entering my candid era.

I want to fuck you in my bed. Hard.

I tingle everywhere.

ME

I'm sitting around a table full of your teammates' wives. You're so inappropriate.

EMMETT

Inappropriate is the perfect way to describe what I'm going to do to you later.

ME

And as much as I'd love to do all of those things, you should definitely head out and celebrate with the boys. You deserve to.

A couple of minutes pass before my cell vibrates on the table with another text from Emmett.

EMMETT

Do you know how fucking perfect you are, Billie? You're everything I want.

"*Down baaaaad*," Collins sings, shimmying past me with a couple of cocktails.

ME

You could always come over to my place afterward?

EMMETT

I've got a better idea. When you've finished up with the girls, head home and pack for three nights for you and Blake. I'll swing by and pick you up after I spend a couple of hours with the team.

ME

Three nights? And where are we going?

EMMETT

Initially? Back to my place, followed by two nights in the Catskill Mountains. I just booked us a secluded cabin.

My heart actually flutters. Two nights of uninterrupted time together.

ME

But what about hockey?

EMMETT

Coach has given me two days off ahead of our first playoff game.

ME

Has he granted that to the whole team?

EMMETT

Only me. Giving my body some extra rest time.

Just to clarify, when I say "rest time," I'm talking about hockey-related activities and not sleep. I'm going to keep you awake for forty-eight hours solid.

ME

Sounds perfect. If sleep wasn't necessary to care for Blake.

EMMETT

Well, rest easy, Mama. I have B and all her needs covered.

With Blake nuzzled into my chest, her gentle inhales and exhales keep my racing brain centered. Each time I speak to or see Emmett, I can't help but wonder if it will be the last. So much of what we have feels borrowed, even stolen, from the hands of fate. It's only a matter of time before everything goes up in flames.

ME

I can't wait.

CHAPTER THIRTY-FOUR

EMMETT

Clipping Blake into the back of my G-Wagon, I slide into the driver's seat and wait for Billie to finish up stressing over whether she has everything packed for the next couple of days.

"Do you think fifty diapers will be enough?" she asks, dropping into the passenger seat beside me.

Allowing myself to touch this girl is equivalent to a river breaking its banks, and as I take her chin between my fingers and smile against her lips, I realize that the rush of adrenaline every time we kiss is only getting stronger.

"Fifty diapers will be enough."

We fall into a deep kiss, one I never want to end.

Two nights away is not nearly enough.

"How long will the drive take us?"

Leaning across the center section, I wrap my hand under her perfect ass, so damn tempted to lift her into my lap and reenact all the things we did last night in my bed.

There's a baby on board, Emmett.

"We'll be there before lunch," I say, setting a soft kiss against her forehead.

When I pull back and crank the engine, there are more questions in her eyes.

My lips are back against hers. "What's eating at you?"

She sighs quietly, soft pieces of hair framing her face. She isn't wearing an inch of makeup today—mainly because I kept her busy until we were rushing to hit the road.

Her hands are twisting in her lap, and I break them apart and kiss across her knuckles.

"Where's that anxious brain taking you this time?"

Almost like she's searching for answers elsewhere, she turns her head to stare out of the windshield. "As soon as I ask you the question, it's going to sound about as juvenile as it does in my head." She focuses back on me. "And given that there's already a huge age gap between us, I'm thinking that I should probably keep my mouth firmly shut."

I study her for a beat, wondering where the hell this is going.

"Does it honestly feel like we're fourteen years apart to you? Because other than my aching knee and graying hair"—I narrow my eyes at her—"along with the wooden money in my wallet ... it doesn't feel like we were born in different decades at all."

She tips her head to one side, and I wait patiently for her response, heart beating a way faster rhythm than before.

"Yeah, that's true actually. You can be quite immature."

My fingers tickle her ribs, and she throws her head into the rest, attempting to grab any part of my black henley, desperate for me to grant her a reprieve.

"Okay, okay!" she pleads. "You're a silver fox and mature gentleman." She bites down on her bottom lip, mischief twinkling in those pretty green eyes. "Both in and out of the bedroom."

My jeans tent because I'm a horny fucker for Billie Quinn and her bratty mouth.

"What were you going to ask me before you got in your head about our age difference?"

Her flushed cheeks are a similar crimson to how they were last night when I pulled a third orgasm from her body. We're the perfect combination in bed since Billie likes to ride me and I can't take my eyes off her beautiful figure.

My plan is for her to ride my face as soon as Blake goes down for the night.

She hesitates for a moment, and I unclip her belt and pull her into my lap.

Fingers tangling through my hair, Billie peers down at me. "I thought we were supposed to be at the cabin by lunch?"

"This is more important," I volley back, hitting the button to warm her seat for the journey. "Ask what you were going to, or I'll never order pineapple pizza again."

She drops her forehead to mine. "That's fighting talk, Mr. Richards."

My cock twitches. "Ask your question, or we're going back upstairs."

Billie breathes out slowly. "What are we, Em?"

Pressing my head back into the rest so I can get a better look at her, I cup Billie's face in my hands.

So much goddamn beauty.

Deep down, I knew this moment would come, whether it was me asking or her. At some point, everyone wants to know where they stand with each other.

When that time came with Maria, our conversations centered more around hockey and the pressure it would put on us. The dangers to my relationship with Maria had nothing on the land mines Billie and I will face. Like the hurt and betrayal that my best friend is going to feel when we ultimately step out into the open together. The rage my ex-wife will likely embody when she discovers that I fell in love with her best friend's daughter.

Regardless of all the odds, Billie and her baby girl aren't just what I want for my future; they're the only route forward I can see.

Another kiss against her swollen lips pulls a whispered confession from my own. "We're so fucking good together. That's what we are."

"But ..." She massages her fingers into my scalp. "When you say *together*, do you actually mean that we're dating, or are we stuck in a—"

"You're my girlfriend, Mama," I cut off her anxious rambling. "If that's what you want, too, then I'm yours."

She presses her mouth against mine, and it feels like the Fourth of July just came early.

Her voice is buoyant, almost giddy when she bursts out, "I can't believe we're doing this. You, me, and Blake. We're actually going to give us a shot."

I'm burning to tell her that this isn't "a shot" to me even though I totally get why she's viewing our relationship like that.

"Can I update my social media with a profile picture of us together and tell the world that I'm officially dating the NHL's hottest hockey player?"

I pull off my glasses and set them on her face. Jesus, she looks fucking cute in them. Especially when she wears my favorite smile.

"When we get home, I want to talk with Scott and Freya."

Billie worries her lip at the thought, and I hold her face again in my palms.

"This is my mess to clean up, Bill. And the fallout is my responsibility to bear."

She shakes her head at me. "I want this as much as you do, and that means I need to be there when you talk to my parents."

My girlfriend is even cuter when she's determined, even if she's also wrong. There isn't a chance that she could want us as much as I do. I'm a fucking *boy obsessed,* and I'll happily wear that badge with honor.

"I get that—honestly, I do. But trust me when I tell you that your parents will want to murder me for this, and it's going to take some time for them to wrap their heads around the fact that I'm in ..."

The sentence dies on my tongue, burning to be voiced.

"And then there's Maria," I eventually tag on.

Billie stiffens at the mention of my ex-wife.

When she tips her chin up to look at me, I don't fucking like where this is heading.

"What's going on, Billie?"

Like she wants out of the conversation and car, she moves to climb off my lap.

I drop my hands to her thighs, holding her place against me. "Talk to me. Please."

"I don't want to cause trouble. It's probably nothing."

My hand is back under her chin. "That's not going to be good enough for me, I'm afraid. I want to know all that's happening in here." I tap the side of her temple. "Every. Single. Thought."

Delicate fingers pluck at my henley. "I don't think Maria likes me all that much, and that's been particularly apparent since I returned from Austin." She looks up into my eyes, an ocean of thoughts swirling in them. "I've always had the impression that Maria thought there was something going on between us. I felt it that time you came for Christmas before I left for college, and that was only confirmed when you told me that she accused you of flirting with me." She chews on her lip. "I'm not a home-wrecker, Emmett. Sure, I thought you were hot when I was younger, but we were only ever friends."

Taking her hand in mine, I kiss her palm and then place it over my tattoo.

"We've always been friends, Bill, and we always will be. Let me handle Maria. Whatever personal thoughts or conclusions she wants to draw about us have nothing to do with the truth. You know that, and so do I, and that's all that really matters."

"Apart from when she shoots death stares across the dining table."

Billie's words cut me because the thought of anyone—even Maria—being mean to her makes me want to tear the world apart. They also hurt because I know the chances of us all sitting around a table again after I tell Scott that I supported his family through a financial crisis and then took his daughter to bed are slim to fucking zero.

"Promise me that it's going to be okay?" Billie asks me to make an impossible statement. Not because I have doubts over us, but because of all of the above.

Capturing her mouth with mine, I let her lips soothe away my anxieties for us both.

"I promise that I will always be here for you and Blake. That I will care for you and be right by your side when you need me the most. I promise you that I'm nothing like Tucker Price and that my ex-wife will never get a chance to pin any of this on you or tell lies about what we were in the past. And I promise"—I heave in a heavy breath and fill my lungs—"tonight, when our baby girl has gone to sleep and the stars are the only thing lighting up a clear night sky, I will make you feel every vow that just left my lips."

CHAPTER THIRTY-FIVE

EMMETT

Before Mom passed away, I remember her explaining that it wasn't until she had me and Beau that she truly understood what my grandma had meant when she said that having a baby was equivalent to being ripped from a warm bed in the dead of night and dunked into an ice-cold bath.

No one and nothing can prepare you for the biggest shock you'll ever experience, both mentally and physically. Never has a baby been born with a bespoke instruction manual on the best way to keep them happy and safe. Every parent or guardian is flying without a net, trying to figure shit out on next to no sleep and, for a lot of women, with a healing body that has been through a traumatic birth.

These past two days have been my own personal ice bath and a brief insight into Billie's daily life.

Earlier today, I strapped Blake to my chest, and we went hiking around the Catskills. Being alone with nature and my girls for hours were some of the best ones of my life so far, but also some of the most revealing.

No one warns you that just because you're up the side of a mountain, a baby won't poop or need to feed and that finding a flat boulder to lay a changing mat on could take way longer than you first anticipated.

Changing Blake's diaper was a two-person job, but Billie made it look like she was pulling off a saucer pass in her sleep.

When she sat in my lap and we agreed to be together, I was in awe of my girlfriend. Now, I have no doubt that she's the strongest woman I've ever met.

If my mom were still here, she'd tell me to "put a ring on that girl's finger before some other man snaps her up." Over and over, she would repeat her warning until I finally got down on one knee and asked Billie to be my wife. Mom never had the chance to meet Billie or Blake, but when she did meet Maria, her plea was very different. My parents wanted me to *take my time* to make sure that she was the one. With the benefit of hindsight and life experience, I think that's the reason why we eloped in Vegas. Maria had kept telling me that she didn't want a fuss, and I couldn't see any logical reason why we had to wait. It felt like true love, but the truth is, I've only started to appreciate what that looks like over the past couple of months.

Now, I understand why my parents urged me not to rush. While they never explicitly said that Maria wasn't right for me, I think they hoped that I would heed their advice and figure that out for myself.

It took me well over a decade to gather the metaphorical pieces together. There was something always holding me back from walking out of the door for good each time we argued. We'd tell friends that we were over and then fall right back into the same cycle, each round only getting worse for us both.

Billie and Blake are the final piece in my jigsaw—the reason why I would take a freezing bath straight from my bed and scale every mountain until I found the perfect place to change Blake's diaper. Everything I do for them, I don't question it, and I don't hear my mom's familiar voice asking me to think it over before I dive right in.

"Is she sleeping?" Billie's question filters from over my shoulder as I stand over Blake's bassinet, her baby monitor in one hand and her metaphorical heart in my other.

Dressed in black sleep shorts and a matching top, Billie glides toward me like an angel would approach you in a dream.

Who knows? Maybe she isn't from this world, but a figment of my imagination. All I know is, when I set my hands on her hips and pull her body into mine, she sure as shit feels real to me.

We feel real. Indestructible.

Rising onto her tiptoes, she hooks her arms around my neck, brushing our noses together before we kiss.

"I think we wore her out," I muse, breaking my lips from hers.

Billie rocks back on her heels, suppressing a yawn with the back of her hand. "I feel her on that. I can't remember the last time I went hiking in the mountains." She chuckles. "Or exercising in general."

When I lift her into my arms, she squeals and circles her legs around my waist, and I walk us both into the bathroom.

Her eyes flare wide when she takes in the candles and huge tub, lavender floating over the top, steaming water turned lilac from the bath salts I secretly brought with me.

"W-when did you do all this?"

Setting her down on her feet, I drop to my knees in front of her, fingertips teasing her waistband.

Best fucking view of the day.

She rests her hands on my shoulders, and I edge down her shorts and then remove her top when she lifts her arms overhead.

"Right before I put Blake to bed."

When she steps out of her bottoms and I toss them to one side, her right hand finds my hair, anticipation tightening her fingers around the roots.

Placing one palm at the small of her back, I lift her left leg over my shoulder, the sweet scent of her warm pussy shooting straight to my dick.

Parting her with my fingers, I breathe in what's mine.

"I thought I was taking a bath?" She gasps when I circle her clit with the pad of my thumb.

"And we will, but right now ..." I rasp, passing my tongue through her cunt in one slow, long lick. "It's time for Daddy's princess to be crowned."

A bigger cry leaves her lungs as my tongue spears her pussy, driving deep to savor her unique taste.

She shakes her head when I suck and bite gently on her clit. "I'm so close, already."

Good.

Lapping at her entrance, I let Billie's arousal flow down my throat, passing my tongue over her clit like a needy boy begging for more.

The steam in the bathroom fogs my glasses, but I can still see Billie better with them on, and I appreciate the way her jaw hangs open when I grip her upper thigh, encouraging her hips to grind against my face.

"Mama tastes so fucking good," I praise, pushing my middle finger into her pussy.

I pump her a few times, and her delicious release slides down my hand when I add another finger and curl them toward her front wall.

Billie tries to speak, but her voice fails under the weight of pleasure, and pride swamps my chest. "I'm c-coming ..."

"All over me," I croon, mesmerized by how wet my girlfriend gets.

When lustful eyes gaze down at me, I tip my chin at the skylight. "Watch the stars while I play with your perfect body."

Breathless laughter leaves her chest. "You always keep your promises."

"Always," I repeat, lifting her into my arms before lowering her satiated body into the bath.

Peaked nipples disappear beneath the water as she lies down in front of me, lavender and bubbles scattered around her face.

She lifts a hand out of the water, crooking her finger at me.

I waste zero time getting naked and climbing into the bath before I'm kneeling between her thighs like I'm praying at an altar.

Asking for forgiveness like the sinful friend I am.

"Straddle me," I whisper, taking both her hands in mine and pulling her into position.

Long hair sticks to her shoulders, and I kiss my way across them.

"How long have you been on birth control for?"

Trustful eyes drink me in. "Long enough to be protected."

Billie watches me swallow down her response. I've been desperate to fuck without any barriers between us.

"Are you ready to take me bare, or do you need more time?"

With our bodies pressed together like this, I can't be sure whose heart is racing faster.

"I'm not scared to feel everything. I want you to come inside me."

"Okay," I exhale. "I want you to know though that if anything ever happened and you got pregnant with my baby, I—"

"I know you would be there for us, Em," Billie whispers. "Which is why I trust you so much."

Wrapping my hands under her ass, I carefully lower her petite frame onto my dick, and both our jaws fall open at the feel of me entering her.

Fingernails dig into my shoulders, and the biting pain is a welcome distraction from my overwhelming urge to shoot straight inside my girlfriend.

Not yet.

Billie's hips rock over me for the first time, and water splashes over the edge of the oversize tub.

"Attagirl. You're milking me so well."

Her skin pebbles, and my balls coil tighter.

"This is the first time I've had sex without a condom." Her confession hangs in the steamy air between us.

I kiss the underside of her jaw. "Not with Tucker?"

Dropping her face into the crook of my neck, she licks a sexy trail along my collarbone. "Never. He always insisted on wearing one. I guess no form of contraception is a hundred percent effective."

Memories of our conversation in her bed that night come roaring back, specifically when she asked me about having children of my own one day.

Pushing my hips into her, I let Billie feel what she does to me. How much I want this with her.

"Just because now isn't the right time, that doesn't mean I haven't thought about getting you pregnant one day."

I swear to God, her walls tighten around me.

"If you wanted them, I'd give you a hundred of my babies. Just like you've given me one of yours."

My cock grows even harder, both of us dangling on the edge of falling apart.

"Is that what you want one day, Mama? To take my cum and make another baby?"

Even with warm water surrounding us, there's no mistaking Billie's orgasm as her pussy spasms around me, a sweet release coating my dick.

"That's it." I grin, hands looping around her thighs so I can lift and fuck her suspended body into another high. "Give yourself to me, Bill, and I promise to keep you safe."

It takes only a few more pumps of my hips before I hold her against my thighs, and our eyes are locked on each other while I shoot inside her for the first time.

Voice barely audible, her soft whispers admit to another orgasm.

A confession of my own rises up my throat, too significant for me to swallow down, like I've successfully done in the past.

Tonight, it feels right, even if I know how big our next mountain will be.

Taking a big gulp of air, I revel in the way the words trickle from my tongue. "I'm in love with you, Billie Quinn. And when we get back, I'm going to drive to your family home, walk up the driveway, and let Scott know that you're my girl."

CHAPTER THIRTY-SIX

BILLIE

The day after we got back from the Catskills, my world came crashing down to reality with a thud when Mom invited Blake and me to join her and Maria for breakfast at Rise Up, the café where I first met Collins.

Trying to take inspiration from my pink-haired friend's couldn't-give-a-fuck attitude, I add another sweetener to my coffee and act like I haven't noticed the frequent looks Maria keeps shooting at me when she thinks my mom isn't watching.

Except I do give a fuck what she thinks, and with every side-eye from Maria, the knot in my stomach coils a little tighter.

There's no way that she can know about Emmett and me. Every move we've made was carefully planned.

"How is motherhood treating you, Billie?" Maria asks with a faux smile designed for Mom.

I attempt a similar expression, picking my coffee up to buy myself a few seconds.

"Up and down," I casually answer, tipping my head from side to side as I set the mug back down on the table.

She flicks her hair to one side, shoulders bunched around her ears. Nothing about this breakfast is relaxed. A need to jump up from my seat and wheel Blake out the door burns inside me.

From across the table, Mom's brows draw together, almost like she can sense my discomfort. "Is everything okay, sweetheart?"

It's the worst question she could've asked as I take a huge gulp of coffee to rinse away emotions I definitely shouldn't allow on display.

"She's just tired." Maria fixes her dark eyes on me. "Aren't you, Billie?"

Her tone is anything but concerned, although I nod in agreement anyway.

Shoulders still tight, she bites into a croissant and sets it on the plate in front of her. "I imagine that taking a newborn away must really be hard work."

Mom's head darts to me, brows furrowed even deeper. "But Billie hasn't been away with Blake yet?" Her statement comes off as more of a question, and both women wait on clarification.

Glancing at the exit, I wonder how many seconds it would take me to grab Blake's stroller and be out of the door and whether either of them would chase after me for answers.

Of course they would.

I clear my throat and look between them. "We haven't been away yet." Adding a light chuckle to sell the lie I hate telling, I double down and confirm, "I'm barely able to cope at home, let alone somewhere else."

Reaching across the table, Mom takes my hand, circling her thumb over the top.

I force down another swallow, knowing this could be the last time in a while that I'll benefit from her comforting touch.

After practice, Emmett plans to make good on another promise when he sits my parents down in their living room and confesses everything that's been happening between us.

"Oh." Maria looks doubtful, sarcasm lacing her voice. "Silly me. I must have mistaken you for somebody else carrying a baby and a suitcase."

Instantly, my mind races, cycling through potential moments when Maria could've seen us.

Mom just chuckles, like this whole atmosphere isn't the most awkward situation to have ever existed. Surely, she can sense the tension. It's written right across her best friend's face.

After a few unbearable seconds, Mom claps her hands. "How about a coffee? I could sure go for another caffeine hit after this week at work."

I motion to my half-full mug and then to an untouched plate of eggs. "I'm good, thanks."

Snapping out of a trance, Maria clicks her tongue as Mom stands and grabs her purse. "I'll take one of their scones with jelly and clotted cream. It's been too long since I had a layover in London, and I'm craving British baking."

With a nod, Mom sets off to join an ever-growing line at the counter.

Great, even more alone time with Maria.

"So, how was Thailand?" I ask, knowing she recently returned from a vacation out there with a couple of friends. It was splashed across her social media for days on end.

Do I particularly care about her vacation to Bangkok? No. But I'll take any conversation if it avoids the previous subject.

As she stares straight down at her half-eaten croissant, I watch lines crease into Maria's forehead, full lips coated in peach gloss pulling into a frown.

"You can deny it all you want, Billie." Her expression is menacing as she looks at me. "But I know that was you getting into my ex-husband's car the other day. I was walking past the entrance to his parking lot on the way to visit him when I caught sight of you. And before you ask." She pins me with a glare. "I was visiting him because I wanted to clear the air after the divorce. Emmett still means a lot to me."

I'm tempted to call her bluff. Maria is smart enough to try and accuse someone of something she didn't witness in the hopes that they'll unwittingly admit to their crimes. And while it's really bad luck that she was passing by at that precise moment, it's quite possible that she did see me climbing into Emmett's car the other day, the gates to the parking lot were open and ready for us to leave.

I work to keep my body language casual and open, resisting the urge to fidget with my hands.

"I'll take your silence as confirmation," she presses, sitting back in her chair, eyes never leaving mine.

I quickly glance over at Mom, who hasn't moved forward in the line.

Shit.

"Perhaps this is a conversation you should be having with your former husband," I respond, choosing my words carefully so I don't accidentally confirm anything. "Although, given that you are divorced, I don't really see how Emmett's private life concerns you anymore."

She bolts up, pushing away her plate before pointing a red-manicured finger straight at me. "Don't get smart with me, Billie. You know as well as I do that if you're involved with my ex-husband, then it has *everything* to do with me." She scoffs, and I know what's coming before she's even opened her mouth. "You've always had a thing for Emmett, and you couldn't wait to get your claws into him the second you returned from Austin." She drops her disgusted gaze down my body. "If you even waited until we separated, that is."

I've never been an angry person, always choosing to avoid confrontation above my own needs. But as my blood boils and burning rage shows no sign of calming, I reach into Blake's stroller and pull my baby girl into my arms. In the absence of Emmett, she's the only one who can prevent me from going nuclear on this woman's ass.

Who the fuck does she think she is? And why do middle-aged people with fancy jobs and money think that they've got me all figured out?

Fuck them.

"That isn't true, Maria," is all I say. Truthfully, it's all I can manage while remaining respectful, even if she doesn't show an ounce of it to me.

Leaning forward, she plants her elbows on the table, voice deep when she asks, "Have you been screwing my ex-husband?"

Courage I didn't know I possessed pins my eyes on hers. I'm determined not to lie, even if she has zero right to know the truth.

"This conversation is ridiculous."

She just grins, and it isn't a friendly one. "Let me guess," she muses. "You think he's serious about you."

Well, he told me he's in love with me, so, yeah, I do.

I say nothing, attention diverted to my daughter.

"You're a rebound, Billie. We were married for way too long and were much too in love to simply click our fingers"—she mimics the action with her hand, a loud snap turning a few heads —"and fall in love with someone else."

"You're making a fool of yourself, Maria," I warn.

That doesn't deter her. "He's thirty-five and worried about being left on the shelf. I know he is because I've felt the same way at times. Along comes a younger woman who shows even a modicum of interest, and, poof ... the famous NHL star is between her parted thighs in no time."

When her eyes focus on Blake, I know that even the slightest mention of my daughter will change the course of this conversation entirely. There's no chance that I'll be able to hold my temper.

"Let's be really real here, Billie."

I close my eyes and wait for her to overstep.

"Emmett didn't want children when he was married to me. I doubt very much that he'd want to take on another man's baby. As cute as Blake is, that's not the kind of shit my husband would sign up for."

"Ex," I grind out, arms trembling as they hold Blake.

"Excuse me?"

"Ex," I repeat. "Emmett is your *ex*-husband."

Again, that doesn't deter her. If anything, she's bolstered by her own judgmental words. "Ex or not, I think I know Emmett better than anyone else on this planet."

"I highly doubt that." The words are out before I can stop them.

"Oh, really?" She braces herself on her elbows again, dropping her voice to a low rumble. "Well, riddle me this then, Billie. If he's so damn serious about you, why hasn't he come forward to your parents before now?"

If I tell her that Emmett plans to do exactly that in a matter of hours, I'll blow this whole thing out of the water.

"I think it's best if you stop talking, Maria," I politely reply.

She waves a hand in front of her as a satisfied grin overtakes her face. "Ah, you don't need to worry about that anyway. I already had a good talk with your father just before we arrived here." Maria winces, like she's pained on our behalf. "After I saw you both, I sat in my feelings for a while, convinced that my *ex*-husband couldn't be stupid enough to go there with our best friends' daughter." When she sucks a breath through her teeth, her victorious smile only grows wider as she pushes back her chair and unhooks her purse from the back of it. "But then I got to thinking about how I'd want to know if that was my daughter who was being made a fool of." She looks at me like she genuinely cares about my feelings. "It's a terrible thing to take advantage of an impressionable young woman who just got out of a bad relationship and is left holding the baby." Pressing a palm to her sternum, she delivers a final line. "In the end, I concluded that, as a longtime family friend, it was my duty to raise the alarm."

With that, she turns on her heel and makes for the restroom.

A shaky hand rummages through Blake's diaper bag, and I pull out my phone and hit Call on Emmett's number, praying that his practice is over.

My heart sinks when I'm connected with his voicemail.

"Hey, it's me." My voice is as shaky as my hands. "Listen, I think we have a problem. I'm out for breakfast with Maria and Mom and ..." I force back tears. "Maria saw us that day in your parking lot before we headed to the Catskills. Sh-she told Dad about us—or at least what she saw. So, I just need you to be aware that Maria has already put a lot of ideas in his head this morning." Despite my best efforts, the first tear hits Blake's onesie. "She made it out like you'd been taking advantage of me, Em. I think this could be really bad, and I'm so fucking sorry."

CHAPTER THIRTY-SEVEN

EMMETT

Coach Morgan granting me an extended rest period has worked wonders for my knee, although you wouldn't have believed it with the way I played in practice.

I've never been this nervous in my life, which is understandable, given the conversation I plan to have with Scott and Freya later today.

The inner coward in me wanted to suggest to Billie that we hit the road from the Catskills and never return to Brooklyn, even if disappearing wouldn't make our lives any easier—or happier—without Scott and Freya being a part of it.

"What's going on, man?" Archer pauses halfway out the exit of the training rink as Jack and Tommy keep walking toward their trucks on the far side of the parking lot.

I choose to keep my eyes on them rather than my goalie. "You were right with what you said; I am in love with Billie."

Initial excitement turns to concern, and my teammate bites his lip. "So, there's only one route forward."

Fate sealed, I nod my head once. "Let's be honest, buddy. There was only ever going to be one outcome."

Scratching the back of his neck, Archer doesn't argue. "What's your next move?"

Eyes still on Jack and Tommy as they laugh and joke around beside their parked trucks, I swallow thickly. "Get in my car and drive to her parents' place. They should both be home since Freya doesn't usually work today and Scott is still off from work."

An ominous silence falls between us until Archer breaks it. "What's the worst-case scenario?"

I shrug and go to answer right before the sound of screeching tires cuts me off.

Arms up in the air, Jack motions for the driver to slow down, but I know there's zero chance of this car hitting the brakes. Not before it collides with me.

"I think we're about to find out," I quietly reply, pointing at Shelby and knowing that there can only be one person behind the wheel, even if he shouldn't be driving yet.

As the car skids to a halt around twenty feet in front of me, I know that Scott found out before I got the chance to tell him. And as he swings his car door open and stalks toward me, a profound limp slowing him to an average pace, I brace myself for the panic to set in.

"Hey! Whoa there, Scott. Let's ..." Archer lowers his hands in tandem, asking my best friend to take a moment. "Let's just calm down, shall we?"

Scott pulls up around five feet from me, fists tightening, white knuckles forming as his dark eyes burn black. I've never seen him like this before, but he's everything I expected when he ultimately found out about me and his daughter.

The details of who told him should be important to me in this moment. After all, whoever let their mouth run just dug my metaphorical grave. Instead, all I can think about is Billie and Blake and how quickly I can get to them.

"Shut it, Archer," Scott grinds out, eyes fixed firmly on me. "I'm willing to bet that you knew all about this too. Hell, you were probably in on it."

Making the correct choice, Archer takes a single step back, physically leaving the conversation.

"The fuck is going on?" Tommy announces with Jack hot on his heels until they pull up alongside Scott.

Hands sliding into my pockets, I force my shoulders to relax. I want my best friend to know that I have no intention of turning aggressive, even if the same can't be said for him.

"Nothing that you need to be worried about," I reply to my teammate.

While Tommy and Jack have both had suspicions about me seeing someone, neither of them knows about Billie. With Jack, I made the decision not to complicate my captain's already-difficult job. Just because my relationship with Billie might not affect the team directly, that doesn't mean he wouldn't stress over the potential war that might ensue over a player's personal life.

And Tommy, that guy has always kept to himself. Gossip has never been his thing, even if the well-being of his teammates absolutely is.

"Could've fooled me," Tommy volleys back, positioning himself to intervene in a physical altercation.

I shake my head at Tommy, asking him to stand down.

"Have you been fucking my daughter?"

A shiver follows the question I've been dreading for weeks. Scott's choice of words is an echo of the ones that would wake me in the dead of night, cold sweats coating my body.

There's no way I'm going to lie to him. He deserved the truth from the outset, even if the time was never right to unearth it.

Attempting to keep my tone calm, I inch closer to the rabid bull standing in front of me. "Fucking Billie? No. Sleeping with my girlfriend? Yes."

A brief puff of air leaves his nostrils before he casts his gaze to the open parking lot.

When he shows me his eyes again, I see the hurt in them. Hurt I knew would be there but was powerless to prevent because Billie and Blake were all I wanted in my life, and now that I have them, I won't walk away.

Hurting my best friend is equivalent to taking a knife and stabbing me straight through the chest, especially after everything he's helped me through with Maria. However, hurting his daughter and her baby girl? The Devil might as well rip every organ from my body and cast it into the flames of hell, destined to burn long after my heart has stopped beating.

And that's precisely where Scott's first punch lands. Most people might predict the face or jaw, but my best friend plans to inflict maximum pain.

I don't move, hands still planted firmly in my pockets.

"Hey!" My captain steps in front of Scott, one hand raised in his face. "Whatever has gone down between you, punching my defenseman is not how we're going to resolve it."

"It's okay, Jack," I say, gaze still locked on Scott. "He needs this, and I deserve it."

Jack spins on his heel, his eyes blown wide when he looks at me. "Have you lost your mind?"

With a slow headshake, I ask my teammate to step aside, and a punch lands on my lower jaw and then another to my right cheek.

I already knew that he'd split the skin before I notice the red staining Scott's knuckles.

When he rears back again, Tommy catches Scott's fist in his palm. "One more hit, and I'll show you a side to me that I buried last season."

"Leave it, Tommy." Archer's warning is deathly serious. "Let Scott and Emmett figure this out between them."

"Not by having a fight in the players' parking lot," Jack adds. "And how did you get access?" He points his question at Scott, who doesn't bother to respond. I'm not even sure he can hear anything above his murderous thoughts.

"I trusted you," he grits out, pulling his fist from Tommy's grasp. "God, Jesus." He swipes a hand through his hair. "With baby scans, trips to the park ..." Fearsome eyes narrow. "I took money from you to help feed and clothe my granddaughter."

Archer's gasp slices through the air. "Is that true, Emmett?"

Bile rises up my throat. "Yes."

"Were you fucking her when you wired money to my account?!"

Shaking my head, I wish I could tell Scott that he's wrong. But when I gifted money for a second time, I knew when this moment inevitably arrived that I wouldn't have the truth to fall back on. While I might not have slept with Billie, our bodies and minds were way past involved. Trying to fool myself into justifying the thigh ride was as ill-advised back then as it is now.

"When Billie returned from Austin, nothing had ever happened between the two of us. And that's the way it stayed for a good while." Like my body is willing him to listen as much as my mind, I edge closer to Scott. "I knew how it would look when I gave you more money, and I wanted to tell you right then what was happening."

He scoffs loudly. "Fuck off, Emmett. The only thing you wanted was to keep buying your way into my daughter's life." He gets into my face. "Having her move out and across town was the perfect fucking solution, wasn't it? Maybe you'd even planted the idea of getting her own place into Billie's mind."

"No," I deny.

"Yes," Scott tosses back. "Maria was right."

At the mention of my ex-wife's name, I catch a glimpse of Archer shaking his head.

"Fucking witch," he whispers.

"What did she say to you, Scott?" I ask.

He just shrugs like the detail doesn't matter when it absolutely does.

"What did she say?" I repeat, rain starting to pound the asphalt beneath our feet.

Still, no one makes a move, every one of my teammates now standing by my side.

My throat grows thick when Archer's hand lands on my shoulder, fingers squeezing gently.

"Emmett asked you a question." Jack speaks up, voice devoid of aggression. "How can he defend himself if he doesn't have all the facts?"

Something in my captain's logic resonates with my friend, and his hardened expression twitches with the faintest hint of empathy.

Resetting his hard demeanor, Scott delivers the news I was dreading. Not because my ex-wife discovering my relationship with Billie is a problem, but because she was the first one to speak with Scott. Hell knows what kinds of twisted bullshit she planted in his head.

Fingernails bite into my palms as I form fists at my sides, thinking about the hurtful things she likely said about my girl. Finding out your ex-spouse has a new lover is a hard pill to swallow, but that's exactly what you should do—swallow it and move on with your own life since you are no longer an active part of theirs, especially when you don't share children.

As Scott clears his throat, sadness enters his eyes. "Maria showed up at our place first thing this morning when Freya was taking a shower."

"And?" I bite through clenched teeth.

"And she told me the truth that should've come from your mouth, Emmett."

"For what it's worth, I was headed to your place straight after practice." Heart racing in my chest, I know that Jack is right; I need to hear the accusations that Maria has landed at my door. "Whatever Maria has alleged, I guarantee it isn't true."

He snorts a doubtful laugh. "Well, she said she thinks you're fucking my daughter, and you just confirmed it." His fingers twitch by his sides as his jaw tics before he speaks again. "She expressed concerns that you're taking advantage of an impressionable young woman who just got screwed over by her ex-boyfriend."

Hot breath hits my cheeks. "But Maria's main concern revolved around you and the way you have clearly gone off the rails since the divorce was finalized, searching for affection wherever you can find it." His lips twist wickedly. "And what better place to stick your dick in than in my beautiful baby girl? I'm sure it was a real power flex—your millions keeping her dad's head above financial water while you secretly lured his daughter into your bed. She'd trust you after all; you've been like an uncle to her."

How I don't empty the contents of my stomach, I'll never know.

There's only one person and her daughter on my mind, forcing me to swallow down every bit of pride that I possess. "Have you spoken to Billie?"

When Scott shakes his head, I heave a sigh of relief.

"Nope, but when Maria suggested that she and Freya head out for breakfast and invite Billie, I'd hazard a guess that your former wife wanted to talk."

"Why *the fuck* didn't you stop her?" I yell, all sense of calm fully out of the window.

I guess Scott and Freya have never seen the side of my ex-wife she reserved especially for me. Not that I even thought for one fucking minute that Maria was capable of this level of manipulation. Billie was right to express concerns over her, and I should've taken them more seriously.

My racing heart splits at thoughts of how upset my girlfriend will be right now. How Maria will have cornered her away from Freya so she could have her say.

"I need to get to Billie," I whisper out loud, not waiting for Scott to address my previous question.

Seething eyes bore into mine. "Over my dead body. You'll never breathe the same air as my Billie and Blake, never mind get a chance in the same room."

"Whoa!" Jack lurches forward, but it's in vain as another blow lands into the pit of my stomach.

Stepping back, I'm sure Scott expects me to double over in pain. Little does he know, he already delivered his best shot, wrapped inside the last words he uttered.

"Never a-fucking-gain!" he spits, already backing toward his car.

When he yanks open the driver's door, he pauses. "And don't bother swinging by her apartment. I'm using the last of your money to move her out as we speak."

CHAPTER THIRTY-EIGHT

EMMETT

What's left of my heart urges me to take a left out of the parking lot and head straight to Billie and Blake. Even if Scott wouldn't allow me on the premises, I know my girl wouldn't let her dad call the shots and prohibit his only daughter from seeing me.

She's twenty-one, for fuck's sake.

With my Aston Martin idling and my brain spinning out, a sharp knock on my passenger window jumps me back to reality.

Sawyer motions for me to lower my window.

"That's the second time I've scared the shit out of you." He chuckles, face immediately turning serious when he takes me in.

"What are you doing here?" I ask, absentmindedly staring out of the windshield.

Sawyer hesitates before confirming, "Felt like a skate and knew the practice rink had a free slot."

"Maria outed me and Billie to Scott."

When I turn to look at him fully, he practically falls backward as he takes in my face, blood still seeping from the cut on my cheek.

He tries the door handle, but I don't bother to unlock it. Other than Billie, there's only one person I want to talk to right now.

"Talk to me, Emmett," he pleads, trying the handle once more.

I shake my head, back to staring out of the windshield. "I love you, man, and I always come to you when I need advice. But on this occasion, even your wisdom can't repair the fucked-up situation."

Dropping his head between his shoulders, Sawyer exhales a slow breath into the morning air. "Have you tried to call Billie?"

"Yeah," I reply, the taste of acid still burning my mouth. "Picked up a voicemail she sent a half hour ago and tried to call her back. I'm not getting an answer right now."

Sawyer's brows knit together. "Why isn't she picking up?"

I slam my hand into the steering wheel. "How the fuck should I know?!"

He doesn't deserve my wrath. Truthfully, I should be pointing all the blame internally. If I hadn't taken so long to tell Scott and Freya, then Maria never would've gotten the chance to fuck everything up. Billie and I were already battling the odds.

Offering my friend an apologetic glance, I shrug my shoulders, hopelessness settling over me. "The last thing Scott told me before he sped off was that he was moving her and Blake out of the apartment and, I assume, back home. My best guess is, he's confiscated her phone, thinking that he's doing her a favor and protecting her from me."

My former captain only looks more confused. "Listen, I get why Scott is mad over all of this, but ..." He swipes a thoughtful hand across his jaw. "Why would he see you as a danger to Billie and Blake? You've been close friends for years."

The rain begins to fall again, and I open the passenger door, allowing Sawyer to climb in.

Squeezing his huge frame and training bag into the seat, he

makes an appreciative face at the classic car he's never ridden in before. Over the past few weeks, I've driven this car way more than I normally would; each time I sit in it, the smell of nutmeg and the image of Billie's happy face as we drove the country roads fill my senses. I haven't had the chance to see her and Blake nearly as much as I want, and if Scott has his way, I'll never set eyes on them again.

My stomach roils at the thought, but Sawyer's calm voice helps it to settle.

"Talk to me, Emmett. There's got to be a way to make the guy see reason. He's clearly overreact—"

"I gifted him money to help settle Billie's student finances and then to get her and Blake set up in their own place."

Sawyer's head whips to me, jaw agape. "Y-you w-what?"

My forehead finds the steering wheel as we sit in the entrance to the practice rink parking lot. No one has tried to enter or leave so far, which is just as well because I don't think I'm capable of driving right now.

"It's not how it looks," I grind out. "You need to trust me on that."

Sawyer doesn't initially respond, and I turn my face to look at him.

Like he's connecting the dots, he slowly nods his head. "Scott thinks that you basically bought his daughter or at least took advantage of a situation." He winces. "It's like the perfect storm —your divorce from Maria, leaving you single and out looking for someone else to boost your ego, Tucker and his family pulling financial support, Scott's accident resulting in Freya needing to work all hours. I can see how this looks bad to him. Manipulated even."

"I haven't manipulated shit," I declare, voice commanding, frustration threatening to bubble over.

Sawyer exhales into my car. "Yeah, I know you haven't. I guess the question is, what are you going to do about it?"

"That's what I was deciding when you showed up. If I take a

left, then I can be at Scott and Freya's place in ten minutes, which is likely where Billie and Blake are."

"And right?"

I crush the steering wheel in my grip as anger over Maria's audacity ripples through every muscle. "A right turn will take me to the house I haven't set foot inside since I moved out last year."

Deep in thought, Sawyer chews on the inside of his cheek. "Hear me out with this."

I'm already sighing, knowing I won't like whatever he's going to suggest.

He holds up a hand in surrender. "Go to Maria's and get all of the facts before you fly off the deep end."

Jack's statement to Scott about facts rings true, and once again, I'm resenting my perceptive teammates.

"And then?" I press.

Sawyer's smile is the perfect blend of determined and alpha. "And then it's simple ... go get your girl and don't walk away until you have her safely back in your arms."

MARIA'S white BMW sits in the driveway of where we spent night after night arguing.

Most of our fights are a blur to me, each one feeling as trivial and inaccurate as the next. As I ring the smart doorbell and take a step back, I wish I could say the same about today and the conversation we're about to have. Maria overstepped and let her jealousy and need to control get the better of her, and I'm not about to leave my former home without setting the record straight.

For years, I let my ex-wife get her own way, whether it was to do with my hockey career, heading out after games, or general shit like how we would redecorate the living room.

Not anymore.

Everyone has their limits, and I reached mine the second she decided to interfere in my dating life, pretending like she cared about my girlfriend's well-being when all she really wanted was to drive a wedge between us, convinced that I'd never be able to move on from our marriage.

News flash, Maria: I moved on years ago and then—after our divorce—fell in love with the woman of my goddamn dreams.

"Emmett." Maria's face is rosy and all smiles when she swings the door open, acting like she was expecting to see me.

Taking in her perfect makeup, hair, and outfit, I thumb over my shoulder. "Are you headed out?"

She tips her head to the side, broad fake-ass smile still plastered to her face.

Yes, I'm bitter and really *fucking angry right now.*

"Why would you think that?" She shimmies in the doorway. "Or did you forget that this is how I look on the daily?"

I swear to God, when I married this woman, she didn't resemble any part of who she is today.

"I came to talk." My voice is cold and cutting, and it wipes the smile clean from her face, a stony expression materializing in its place.

"Jesus, Emmett." She blows out a breath. "You are, aren't you?"

"I'm what?"

"Sleeping with Scott and Freya's daughter."

Molars grinding, I'd be in awe of her acting skills if she wasn't so transparent.

"You mean Billie?" I clarify, determined that she'll refer to my girlfriend by name and not infantilize a fully grown woman who acts more maturely than my thirty-five-year-old ex-wife. "Cut the crap, Maria," I scold. "I'm here to find out why you think that you still have some kind of control over my life, including who I do and don't date."

When she steps to one side, I go to enter the house that I always hated from the day she insisted that we buy it when a manicured hand lands on my upper arm.

"Have you had sex with her?"

I stare straight down the hallway, freaked out to see portraits of our wedding day lining the walls.

"Did you fuck her?" Maria bites at me again.

Shrugging off her grasp, I step farther inside, and she closes the front door behind her before drawing a deep breath into her lungs.

With her back still to me, Maria punctuates each word of her next statement, not waiting for me to answer her previous question. "You slept with a twenty-one-year-old right after we dissolved our marriage."

"Turn around, Maria," I demand, done with the way she's making this all about her.

Spinning on her heel, she pauses for a second before she dives right for me, slapping her palm across my injured cheek. "YOU FUCKED BILLIE QUINN!"

"I'm *dating* Billie Quinn," I correct her, rocking forward onto the balls of my feet, cheek stinging like a motherfucker. "She's my girlfriend, and I'm her boyfriend."

Holy hell, that felt good.

Maria scoffs, rearing back to slap me once again. I catch her forearm before she connects with my face.

"Stop hitting me, or this conversation will go a whole lot further than these four walls."

Dropping her hand, she knows I'm deadly serious in my threat to report her for assault. Maria's late father was an absolute bastard to her mother, and too many times have I seen the same traits in my former wife. Although this is the first—and final—time she's hit me.

"I can't believe you did this to me," she whispers, slumping against the wall, a photo of us standing outside a Vegas chapel hung next to her head. "I thought that, in time, you would see reason and come back to me."

"Why, Maria?" I ask. "It sure as shit isn't because you want me. We were through a very long time ago."

I can tell she agrees, even if her body language denies it.

"How can you choose someone so young and immature over me?"

"That's where you're wrong," I counter, taking the opportunity to put some distance between us. "Billie is ..." I struggle to find the words to describe my incredible girl. "She's fucking amazing and everything I want."

Tears fill Maria's eyes. Before today, I'd have felt genuine empathy for her. But not after what she did this morning.

"Are you in love with her?"

I nod once, and my broken heart from the exchange with Scott finds a steady rhythm. "Yes, I am. And you just went and destroyed what we had."

Truthfully, I don't know if she did. All I know is that Billie still hasn't returned my calls, and I've got multiple bruises and lacerations, courtesy of my former best friend.

"What you told Scott—about me being a predator and trying to take advantage—that isn't right." I push a hand through my hair and take another step back. "You can believe or convince yourself of whatever you want, but the honest truth is that I started to fall for Billie when she returned from Austin. And after Blake was born, I spent even more time with her. I'm in awe of so much more than you give her credit for. Her strength, brains, courage. The way she cares for people unconditionally."

Maria remains silent.

"How did you find out about us?" I ask, already knowing the truth from Billie but wanting to hear the full story from Maria. We were always so careful not to be caught.

She just shrugs. "I saw her getting into your G-Wagon in your parking lot. Billie had a suitcase, and you were clipping Blake into the back seat. It looked suspicious at best, although I didn't hang around to see anything more. What I saw made me sick to my stomach. When I questioned Billie this morning at breakfast, I knew I'd made the right call to express my concerns to Scott. Her mortified face told the whole story of what's been going on between you both."

I decide not to ask why Maria was outside my apartment building. If she planned to visit me, I'm glad she never got the chance.

"What did you say to my girl?" My voice is dark, so low that it's almost nonexistent.

"I confronted her about you and then pointed out that she was, in fact, a rebound."

"It's a good thing you're a woman, Maria. Because if you were a guy, you'd be through the fucking wall by now."

She squares up to me, loving the toxicity brewing between us.

This is where my ex-wife flourishes—playing psychological games, engaging in verbal wars. I'm so fucking done with her bullshit.

"Stay away from me. Stay away from Billie." I bite the inside of my cheek. "And definitely stay away from Blake."

I'm halfway out the door when the mask completely falls, Maria's true narcissism rearing its ugly head. I've never heard an insidious tone like it, and I hope I'll never hear it again.

"I fucked my way through a whole roster of male flight attendants while we were still married." She chuckles as she moves toward me. "Sometimes two at a time."

If she was hoping to land the final punch with her admission, she should know that the slap stung more.

"But I guess there's nothing you can do about that now, you know"—she glides her fingernails down my sweatshirt—"since the divorce has already been finalized."

I'd laugh if this woman wasn't so evil.

Dropping my face down to hers, I let her see the kind of smile I only ever wear when I think about my girl. "Incorrect. There's nothing I can do about it because I simply don't give a fuck anymore. I guess that's what happens when you fall in love for real."

Reaching up, I pluck a framed wedding photo from the wall, open the back, and pull out the print. I tear it straight down the center as Maria watches on in horror. Not that this photograph carries any sentiment for her. It was only ever an image in its truest form.

I hand the empty frame to her, and she looks down at it and then back up at me.

A smug grin plays on my lips. “Now you have the space to hang your next victim.”

CHAPTER THIRTY-NINE

BILLIE

"I can't even look at you right now, Scott."

As I sit at the top of the stairs, it feels like I'm ten years old all over again, listening to my parents argue over money.

When I was a kid, my mom and dad rarely fought, but whenever they did, it was nearly always about bills and how they were going to scrape enough together to make it through the month.

Today isn't any different. Mom is pissed at Dad for exaggerating the value of his shares so he could hide the money he took from Emmett to help repay my student loans and fund the apartment he is determined that I'll move out of immediately.

I can't believe that, all along, Emmett was paying for everything.

And truthfully, I don't know how I feel about that, other than being mad over the fact that he didn't tell me himself.

After I finally escaped from Rise Up and an oblivious Mom dropped me back home, it took around an hour for the moving trucks to arrive, closely followed by Dad with bloody knuckles and a face like absolute thunder.

He insisted that I allow the moving guys to take my stuff.

When I refused, his rage boiled over, and he spouted off about how Emmett had gifted the family money to basically care for me and Blake.

That brings me to where I am right now—ignoring calls from my boyfriend because I don't know what to say to him while listening to Dad beg for my mother's forgiveness.

"I had no choice, Freya! It was either that or remortgage the house, and that was before my accident at work." Dad tries once more to make my mom see reason.

A slamming sound filters from the kitchen right before Mom volleys back, "What about Shelby? You could've sold her! Or is she so damn precious that you chose to deceive your wife?"

Silence.

"No," Mom bites out. "I don't want your hugs right now. I'm mad as hell. Who gave you the right to make financial decisions without consulting me?"

Mom makes a very good point, and Dad knows it. I don't need to be a fly on the wall to picture his face—one of regret and anguish. Dad worships the ground Mom walks on, although I've never heard either of them as distressed as they are in this moment.

Dropping my head between my shoulders, I exhale a deep breath, praying Blake will stay napping a while longer and grant me some time to gather my thoughts.

Emmett always predicted that a war would ensue when news of our involvement eventually broke. I just wish that he'd been up front about the money.

"The only person to blame is Emmett. He basically paid for access to our daughter."

I shake my head to no one. Dad's got it all wrong if that's what he thinks about his best friend. Emmett gave that money with all the right intentions.

Mom clears her throat. "I don't think that Maria gets a free pass in this. Billie tells me that she confronted her at breakfast while I was in line, right after she decided to tell only you about what she'd witnessed between Emmett and Billie."

"Freya—"

"No, Scott!" Mom interjects. "You should've spoken to me, and so should Maria. She capitalized on my absence because she knew that you would lose your shit and hunt down Emmett. Maria manipulated everyone for her own ends, and I've seen a side to my friend that I never knew existed. Maybe that's why her marriage failed—because if she was as calculating in the past as I've witnessed today, then I don't think that I'd want to remain married to her either."

More silence falls between the two of them, eventually broken by the sound of the doorbell.

Moments later, the kitchen door opens, and Dad half stalks, half hobbles into the hallway, unable to see me since the top of the staircase sits directly behind him.

I draw a deep breath into my lungs, convinced that this day cannot get any worse, regardless of whoever is standing on our porch.

Enraged, Dad practically rips the door from its hinges, ready to slam it back in the jamb when a familiar hand and sparkling Rolex comes into view.

"I need you to hear me out, Scott." Emmett's soft and calm voice washes over me in waves of emotion that pool in my eyes.

I can't see Emmett, and he can't see me, but I can see Dad clearly as he points a finger straight at my boyfriend, venom in his voice and body language.

"What part of my last warning did you fail to understand? Stay away from my family."

A single tear runs to the edge of my chin before it cascades to the carpet. I shouldn't have agreed to stay here tonight instead of at my apartment. Emmett and I need to talk, and there's no way Dad will allow him within a hundred feet of me. After all, he can call the shots on who enters his property.

"Scott ..." Emmett begins speaking but trails off into silence.

Dad's fingers curl around the door, knuckles white, grip poised to slam it straight in Emmett's face.

"If you don't get off my property in the next thirty seconds, I'll have Freya call the police to remove you from it." Dad grinds out a promise that I know he'll keep.

"You need to leave, Emmett," Mom reiterates, walking down the hallway toward the door.

When she wraps her arms around her middle, Dad attempts to loop his free arm around her shoulders, but his efforts are immediately shrugged off.

"Freya, I—"

Mom raises a hand, cutting Emmett off in his tracks. "I'm not ready to talk to you. Today has been a revelation and not a good one. I thought that we could trust you, and you violated that by going behind our backs with Billie."

For a second, I think Emmett has walked away until he speaks again.

"I understand why you both feel like you do, but I need you to know that if things hadn't gone the way that they did and if Maria had kept her nose out, then I would be sitting in your living room right about now, explaining that I'm in love with your daughter."

Heart lurching, I jump to my feet, the movements attracting Mom's attention, and she turns her head to look at me.

"Billie, I thought you were taking a nap with Blake."

Dad keeps his eyes plastered on Emmett, no doubt guarding his family from a predator.

"With the way you've been fighting?" I say, taking a couple of steps down. "I'm surprised Blake hasn't already woken."

"Billie." Emmett's hand appears in the doorjamb. "Billie, I need to talk to you."

His voice is a plea that rips my soul in two. He thinks he's lost me, but he should know that I'm not the type of person to quit on someone I love, even if they could've handled a situation better.

"Let me talk to him," I whisper to Dad as I continue to descend the stairs.

"Get back to your room, Bill," he warns, never taking his eyes off Emmett.

I ignore him and his patriarchal bullshit. I'm twenty-one, not twelve.

"You need to hear him out, Dad," I urge, taking the last step until I'm standing behind my parents, jaw almost hitting the floor when I see the state of my boyfriend's face.

Like there's an invisible thread between us, I jerk forward, searching for Emmett's arms.

"Don't you even fucking dare." Dad thrusts the heel of his hand into Emmett's sternum. "You've got some fucking gall," he continues, rearing his hand back to hit him square in the face.

I figured the blood painting Dad's knuckles a few hours ago was Emmett's, although nothing could've prepared me for the mess he's made of Emmett's face.

"Stop!" I cry right before Dad's fist connects with Emmett's jaw. "Please, stop!"

Mom spins on her heel, wrapping her arms around me in a bear hug.

"He needs to stop hitting him," I sob into her sweater, body going limp in her embrace.

"Scott, you're going to get yourself arrested for assault," Mom quietly breathes into my hair.

I peek beneath her arm, only to catch another swipe of Dad's fist across Emmett's jaw.

My hockey player boyfriend just stands there, hands in his pockets as he takes beating after beating from his best friend.

As he spits blood onto the ground, I can see the physical and emotional pain in his eyes.

"I'm not going to retaliate, Scott. You can take swings at me all day, but I refuse to hit the man I've idolized for over a decade. The father of the woman I'm fucking crazy about."

Growing weary, Dad takes the weight of his bad leg on his

good one. "Idolized?" He laughs. "You must be fucking joking! You've betrayed me in the worst way possible. Hopping into bed with my already-vulnerable daughter."

Emmett swipes blood from his bottom lip.

Yearnful eyes lock with mine as he delivers an admission that melts my bones. "When Billie returned from Austin, I walked back into her life as a friend and a person that she and her baby girl could count on. Did I mean to fall in love with the woman who stole the air from my lungs on her twenty-first birthday?" He shakes his head slowly, eyes moving to my dad. "I tried not to. For you and for Freya, for the respect we've built between us and our families over the years." Emmett's gaze tracks back to me, a warm smile tracing his split lips. "But the best things in life often come along when you least expect them, and that's what Billie and Blake are to me. I can't live without them, and I refuse to walk away until I have what I came for."

Dad steels his shoulders. "I thought you showed up to apologize?"

Emmett's gaze drops to the ground, brows pinched together in thought. "I guess it's understandable for you to think that way. Maria really managed to twist your mind up good, right before she admitted to multiple counts of infidelity during our marriage."

Mom gasps, but Emmett's face doesn't change as he reaches out one hand for me to take.

"If you're asking me to make a choice between our friendship and your daughter, Mr. Quinn, then I gotta tell you that there can only ever be one winner. Maybe, one day, you'll give me the grace to prove why I have my priorities the right way around."

Neither Mom nor Dad prevents me from taking my boyfriend's hand.

Stepping across the threshold, I turn back to my parents. "I need to talk with Emmett for a while." My gaze lands on Mom. "Can you watch Blake for me?"

She gives me a tight nod as I center my attention on Dad. The pieces of my shattered heart crumble into dust when I realize that none of Emmett's words have resonated with him. His expression is stony as his fingers flex at his sides.

"Say something," I plead.

Pained eyes drop to our joined hands. "This is all going to end in tears. This is all a rebound for him, and you and Blake will wind up as collateral damage."

"I already am in tears," I point out, Emmett squeezing my hand tighter.

Dad just shakes his head at me. "Then I don't know what to say to you, Bill. There's only so much a father can do to protect his daughter from making the biggest mistake of her life."

CHAPTER FORTY

BILLIE

With my hand still in his, Emmett leads me down the driveway and then across the road to where his Aston is parked by the curb.

He opens the passenger door for me, and I climb in before he rounds the hood and slides into the driver's seat. Neither of us says a word when he cranks the engine and pulls into the road.

For a few minutes, we drive in silence, me occasionally glancing over to observe Emmett's bruised face.

Despite his injuries and current circumstances, I can't help but appreciate how handsome he is. Even when his mind is drowning in turmoil, there's an air of composure to this man, which is unique, classy, self-assured yet humble in just the right balance. He wasn't driving away without me sitting next to him, and goddamn if that wasn't the sexiest thing ever.

Pulling up along another curb a few streets away from my parents' place, Emmett slides his chair back. He adjusts his glasses and massages the bridge of his nose, one of the only places Dad didn't land a punch.

There's so much to say, but absolutely nothing to say, all at the same time, and the longer we both remain silent, the harder it feels to be the one to speak first.

Emmett just told his closest friend that, if pressed, he'd choose his daughter above him. I haven't had many close friends in my life or at least friendships that have stood the test of time, but that doesn't mean I can't understand how deep that must have cut him, even if I'm the one he's choosing.

Hands back on the steering wheel, Emmett turns to look at me, eyes full of apology, fingers twitching, like he's desperate to pull me into his arms.

"You should've told me about the money and where it was coming from." I finally find my voice. "I had a right to know about that."

He nods, never taking his eyes off me. "Yeah, I should've. I guess I didn't because you'd never have accepted it if you had known the truth. Just like Scott wouldn't have either if he had known about everything going on between us."

I want to argue back even though I know that he's right. There's no way I would've knowingly spent Emmett's cash. I'd have lived in my childhood bedroom and found any type of job before I entertained the idea.

"And the longer things went on," he adds, "the harder it got to tell you or Scott and Freya. If you'd have asked me outright how your dad was affording all this, then I wouldn't have lied to you, but looking like the hero sweeping in to save you and Blake was not why I offered to help. I did it because I'd always cared about you, even if romantic feelings were never involved until much later down the line."

White blossoms fall from the trees that line the road, swirling around Emmett's car. With the way it cascades gently to the ground, you could easily mistake it for snow. Winter feels like the more appropriate season right now, a better reflection of our relationship.

Closing his eyes slowly, Emmett scrubs a hand across his jaw.

"You need an antiseptic wipe for the cut on your cheek. The

packet I have in my purse would be really handy if it wasn't sitting on top of my duvet."

A small chuckle vibrates in his chest as Emmett's hand creeps across the center section, his little finger brushing slowly against mine.

Delicious shimmers break out in response to his touch.

"I need to know that you don't believe the crap Maria fed you and Scott."

We haven't had a chance to talk about what went down in Rise Up, partly because I haven't answered his calls.

Lips rolling together, I edge my hand closer to his. "I know you well enough to be sure that you aren't the type of person to use me because you're lonely and you need to get over your cheating ex-wife."

He looks pained and relieved.

"What exactly did she say to you at breakfast, Billie?"

My brain struggles to recall a conversation that took place only hours ago. Mainly because I want to forget that it ever happened. "I don't want to talk about it because it doesn't mean anything."

He shakes his head, hand moving to rest on my cheek, and his thumb strokes small circles beneath my left eye. "Whenever someone tries to hurt my girl, every small detail matters to me. Protecting you and Blake is my number one priority."

As I nuzzle into the warmth of his palm, Emmett leans across and sets a gentle kiss against my chin.

When he pulls back, our noses are touching, his eyes darting between mine.

"Maria insinuated what my dad warned a few minutes ago—that I'm a rebound and an easy target for an older guy who's earned my trust over time."

"You aren't a rebound," he breathes slowly. "You're the real deal for me."

When he goes to kiss my lips, I let him take it deeper, tongues gently massaging together.

Emmett releases a small whimper, fingertips dipping beneath my red sweater and skating across the waistband of my leggings.

"I'm in love with you, with Blake, with a future I know we can have together."

"But what if having that future means that others can't be a part of it?" My statement breaks our kiss, and Emmett studies me intently.

A few months ago, those words wouldn't have entered my brain, never mind left my mouth. But today, I'm not the same person I was when I sat in the library with Clara and stressed over grades, which would prove to be insignificant when I ultimately dropped out of college.

Blake's arrival has changed so much about me, and while I'm still Billie Quinn, the thought of my daughter living a life without her grandparents in it doesn't feel like a happy future I can consciously choose. It's possible that my parents might come around to the idea of Emmett being my man, but I'm not being asked to make the same choice as him. I'm not choosing the person I love over a close friend. In this moment, I'd be choosing my romantic heart over family, and something about that notion doesn't make a whole lot of sense. If Emmett were Blake's daddy, then maybe this would be different. All I know is that I vowed never to put myself above my daughter's needs when it came to Tucker, and I can't, in good conscience, do it now. Just because the man sitting in front of me is everything I could ever want and more.

"What are you trying to say to me, Bill?"

The heartbreak in Emmett's voice sends tears rolling down my cheeks.

Frantically, he kisses each one away, holding my face in his palms, like he so often does when he knows that I need the comfort of his embrace.

I wish that his callused palms were all I needed right now.

I wish that the path to our love were simple and not a replica of our hike in the Catskills.

I wish that Emmett Richards were the exact same man, but not associated with my family.

I wish that my dad could see what this was doing to us both.

I shake my head, a blizzard of conflicting thoughts and desires making it impossible to find the right response.

A low sob leaves Emmett's chest. "Are you breaking up with me, Mama?"

Through blurry vision, I analyze the face of pure love. The kind every girl dreams about seeing when she looks at her man. One I mistakenly saw in Tucker's.

"I'm not ending it, Em," I whisper, and he kisses me softly, resting his forehead against mine.

"Then what do you need from me? Anything, everything, the whole fucking universe. Tell me, and it's yours and Blake's."

I heave a shuddering breath. "Distance."

A word we've repeatedly fought against resurfaces between us, and I hate that it does. I detest myself for saying it even if I know that it's the only feasible way forward. Breaking up with Emmett is too painful to consider, but we both need time to let the dust of today settle into tomorrow.

He hates the idea as much as me—I can see it in the lines etched into his forehead.

"How much and for how long?"

That's something I can't fully quantify.

"I don't know. A week maybe? I don't know at this point."

"Okay," he replies, voice gravelly. "But here's the deal. After a week, I get to take you out somewhere. You and Blake. We'll have some fun, and if you want to talk more, then we can."

I can't help a cocky smile from forming. "Has anyone ever called you bossy?"

When he gives me a hopeful grin, it somehow feels like my world might not implode.

Not today anyway.

"Rarely. Maybe because I've never wanted to fight so hard for something I know is right."

Breaking eye contact, I gaze through the windshield, blossoms now building on the hood of Emmett's Aston.

"Dad wanted me to move out of my apartment, and I think I might need to. The chances of me finding a job before overdue bills start piling up are slim to zero."

Emmett shakes his head in my peripheral vision. "No. I gifted that money, and I don't want it back."

"Dad said that he spent the last of it hiring an emergency moving company."

Emmett's jaw tics. "He told me the same thing, but I don't believe him. How much did he transfer into your checking account?"

I fucking *hate* this conversation. "Pretty much all of it. But I don't want to use what's left of it to live on. I want to stand on my own."

Emmett's drawn-out exhale fills the car with his scent. "I know that this means nothing to you, but I've got more money than I can spend. Even if you accept it as a gift from a friend, I want you to take it and use it to fund the next however long you need with Blake before you find a job. The money is yours, and I'm not willing to bend on that, Bill."

With one finger under my chin, he tilts my head to look at him. A playful expression I wasn't expecting flushes Emmett's prominent cheeks with color.

"And one day, when you're a kick-ass lawyer and earning stacks of cash on the daily, you can take me out for steak and buy your retired hockey boyfriend a priceless bottle of Italian Pinot."

CHAPTER FORTY-ONE

EMMETT

Game three was ... not my finest hour.

Still, it was enough to maintain a shutout and keep Jessie Callaghan at bay.

"Nice game, Richards."

It's rare for opposing players to shake hands and even less so for them to acknowledge their rivals after a loss, but I take the hand Callaghan has offered as we glide out of the rink.

"Thanks, man," I reply, eager to get a shower, finish up press duties, and head home, where I'll wallow a little longer over not having contact with Billie in days.

Reaching the tunnel, I set my stick back in its holder, finding Callaghan again when I turn on my skates and make for the locker room.

"The Blades have come a long way since Coach Morgan took over," he comments, still showing no signs of moving.

Other than when he reamed out Freeman earlier this season, I've only interacted with Jessie a few times over the years. One of my clearest memories was when he was going through a deep battle with alcohol addiction, successfully hiding its effects beneath incredible talent. This guy is one of those players that comes along every few generations, and his legacy is bound to hang around long after photographs of action shots have faded.

"He's worked wonders with the team," I agree, memories of when we lifted the Cup last season lining the tunnel walls around us.

Pulling off his helmet, Jessie runs a hand through his dirty-blond hair as teammates waltz past us. Jack gives me a big smile on his way to the locker room.

"This is obviously none of my business, but I have to ask ..." He motions to his face. "I haven't seen you get into it on the ice with anyone over the past few days, so what's the score with the bruising and cuts?"

At first, everyone thought that Jessie's past was a bunch of rumors, fueled by press reports looking for headlines to sell news stories. I don't think anyone involved with the league or in the wider general public could comprehend or even want to acknowledge the level of abuse the news outlets were purporting about his father. That was, until Callaghan came forward and set up a charity, specifically centered around supporting victims of domestic abuse. He and his wife, Mia, work tirelessly throughout the year, organizing fundraisers across the US.

I guess I shouldn't be surprised that when this guy sets his sights on unexplained bruising, he wants to know the answers. Even when his team has just suffered a humiliating three to zero loss.

Pulling off my gloves, I rest a bare palm on his shoulder, appreciating the kind of person he is. "I'm fine, buddy. It was a family feud that I'm trying to keep ..."

My eyes travel down the tunnel as Coach's ominous figure stands at the end. He motions for me to join him as soon as possible right before he steps inside his office.

I set my attention back on Jessie. "It's just something I'd rather not talk about."

He cocks his head to one side. "I'm sorry to hear about your marriage. I don't know the circumstances surrounding your divorce, but it has got to suck."

I puff out a breath.

If only he knew the truth.

"I think if my eldest daughter, Drew, found out that Mia and I were planning to split, she'd lock us in a room until we renewed our wedding vows," he muses.

I just smile at him because, honestly, there isn't anything else for me to say. I'm stoked that he's happily married and has been for years.

Approaching Jessie from behind, Tommy reaches out and ruffles a hand through his hair. "Callaghan, my man." Walking backward down the tunnel, he throws the Scorpions forward a wink. "Can we play you every week? Because that game was FUN."

Not biting, Jessie shakes his head.

"He'll never change." I chuckle.

Shooting me a salute, Jessie spins around and walks away, leaving an unexpected warmth in his wake. It's good to know that there are people—even the most unlikely ones—out there to check that you're doing okay.

TEN MINUTES and a quick shower later, I'm sitting in front of an inquisitive coach as he finishes up typing something on his iPad.

From his demeanor and considering that we just rolled over one of the league's best in the playoffs, you would have a hard time believing that this is the same guy who was coordinating porcelain swans and peacock feathers back in February.

"What did Callaghan have to say?" he questions, voice monotone, eyes still centered on his iPad.

I clear my throat, wondering where the hell this is going. The last thing I need is to be reamed out over a less than decent performance tonight. I know my head was all over the place, and that was plain to see when I found myself puck-watching deep in the third, handing the Scorpions a turnover.

I haven't slept on the ice in years, but then I haven't been head over heels in love with a girl like this in forever. Billie is all I can think about, and not seeing Blake's smile—whether on video call or in person—is practically killing me.

"He was asking about the bruises on my face." I decide to be candid with a guy who can smell lies from a mile away.

He glances up at me, confirming that's the exact reason why I'm in here.

"I was going to let it slide since in all the seasons I've coached and played against you, I've never known you to fight outside of hockey." He folds his arms across his chest, leaning back in his black leather chair so he can take me in better. "But the GM has been asking questions, and clearly, from your conversation with my former teammate, so is the opposition."

I take in his office, which is more like a shrine to his family. Pictures of Jack and Kendra's daughter, Esme, line one wall while Emily, Darcy and Archer's daughter, fills the other.

"What do you want to know, Coach?"

Leaning forward, he locks the screen on his iPad and sets his focus straight on me. "Remember when I told you that you could always come to me if you needed anything?"

I nod once. "Yeah."

Coach adjusts his Blades tie, loosening it around the collar. "Well, that time has come, Emmett. Tell me how you got those bruises and whether the PR team needs to be concerned over a personal issue bleeding into team matters."

Scott might be fantasizing over burying me ten feet deep, but he's not a vindictive character. Out in the open is where he does business, not by going to the press and dragging my reputation.

Maria, on the other hand, is different. But pulling my name through the dirt would mean risking a potential retaliation from me, where I could out the multiple affairs she had during our marriage.

"It won't," I confidently confirm.

Something shifts in Coach then as he shows me the guy I saw back at Tommy and Jenna's wedding. The next phase of this conversation is off the record, I can tell.

"Does it have to do with the divorce?" he asks, chewing on his bottom lip. "I'm being really careful here not to overstep, Emmett, but it was no secret that Maria didn't always treat you ..." He blows out a long breath, taking a second to find the right words. "She didn't always treat you well. You never talked directly to me, but I know a couple of the guys were aware of the troubles you both faced."

It's hard for me to maintain eye contact as he continues ruminating.

"If those wounds and bruises are from a domestic altercation involving your ex-wife, then you should know that the Blades will be there if you decide to take this further and press charges. Domestic abuse of any kind is unacceptable, no matter who inflicts the—"

"I don't need to press charges," I quietly interject, being careful to ensure that I'm not downplaying the seriousness in this moment or the subject Coach has brought up.

Emotions I never anticipated to feel flood my senses, and I swallow thickly.

Fuck, life has been a goddamn roller coaster lately.

He raises a single brow at me. "Are you sure?"

I bite the inside of my cheek, twisting my hands together on the table in front of me.

Just like Billie does.

"Listen, I'm not saying that Maria didn't do some questionable stuff in our marriage, but I'm out of that situation now and looking ahead to the future." More emotions threaten to emerge, which I physically shake off. "And that's where the bruises actually came from—my future, not my past."

Coach looks on, waiting for me to elaborate. I knew that none of my teammates would breathe a word about Billie, and that same loyalty is why we're one of the strongest teams in the league —both on and off the ice.

"This can go no further," I warn. "The team doesn't need to be concerned about it, so I'm talking to you as a friend rather than as your player."

Coach gives me a tight nod.

"The bruises came from Scott Quinn."

He takes a second before his eyes grow wide. "Wait. The guy who came to the game earlier this season?" His eyes dart about as he racks his memory. "Billie? This is over the pretty redhead, isn't it?"

My stoicism gives him all the answers he needs.

"Oh jeez, Emmett. How old is she?"

"Twenty-one, and we're dating. The bruises are from when Scott found out, courtesy of Maria, who happens to be best friends with Billie's mom."

Coach can only grimace.

"Scott caught up with me when we were leaving practice the other day. Jack, Archer, and Tommy were witnesses at the time, although no one laid a finger on Scott. I let him take his rage out and maintained my calm."

More emotions stick in my throat when I mentally replay all the messages from the boys that night. Jack showed up at my penthouse at one point with arnica cream that Kendra had once used on his face after an ex-Blades player, Tyler Bennett, bruised up his jaw pretty badly.

"That was a wise move, Emmett. Getting into it with a member of the public never ends well."

"I'm in love with her." The declaration falls from me like it's the most natural sentence I've ever said. "Yes, I have my reputation as a pro athlete to consider, but more than that, Scott is the father of the woman I love." I drop my head between my shoulders, picking it back up slowly to look at Coach. "Understandably and after everything, Billie has asked me for some space. That's why I played like trash tonight—I'm losing my mind over this girl and her beautiful baby daughter. To be honest … I've been losing my mind ever since I laid eyes on her when she got back from college in Texas."

Coach smiles at me knowingly. "Felicity was out with Billie the other week; they met at my restaurant, and when she came home, she couldn't stop talking about a stunning redhead that was going places in law. She didn't tell me that Billie had captured your heart too. Wild horses couldn't drag girl secrets from those women."

Pride overtakes my features. It makes me so damn happy that Billie is making friends with an amazing group that will have her back like their husbands do my own.

"Is there any chance of a reconciliation with Billie's dad?" Coach tentatively inquires.

I shrug. "We've been close friends for years, and he's helped me through a lot of shit—from injuries to a divorce. He feels betrayed in the worst way possible, not least because I was actually helping his family out financially."

"Oh fuck."

"Yep."

There isn't much more Coach can say or do, and that's evident as he pushes back his chair and stands opposite me.

He holds out his hand for me to take, and at first, I think he's just going to shake it. Although as we lock grips, he smooths his other hand over the top.

"I've said this to pretty much every one of your close teammates, and I'm going to say it to you now, Emmett." He lifts his hand and points toward the door. "Go after the one because when you hang your skates for the final time, you'll wish that you'd quit fucking around and made her yours."

He presses his lips together, deep in thought.

"When Jack got the captaincy, I could see how difficult that was for you to take, even though you never really let it show. You are and have always been a true professional, a beacon for the Blades well before I stepped foot through the coach's door. I want to see you happy, man, and I know that the rest of the guys do too."

"I think it will take Scott as many years to forgive me as there is an age difference between me and Billie," I quietly muse.

He lifts a single shoulder, releasing my hand as he moves toward his door. "You don't seem like the kind of guy to let that deter you."

As he twists the handle and I step over the threshold, I turn back to him, never more determined to make Billie and Blake my future.

"By this time next season, when we're sitting inside this office and discussing the announcement of my imminent retirement, Billie Quinn will be my wife."

CHAPTER FORTY-TWO

One Week Later

BILLIE

I don't think I'll ever be over the sight of Emmett with Blake strapped to his chest in a baby sling. Or the way she gazes up at him like he holds the moon and stars in his addictive gray eyes.

Approaching Luna Park in Coney Island on a bright spring day, Emmett reaches out for my hand as we walk along Riegelmann Boardwalk and into the main park itself.

He wiggles his fingers when I hesitate for a second.

"We don't have to hide anymore, Mama. Not now that the news is out."

He stops alongside me when I grind to an abrupt halt, eyes still focused on his outstretched hand.

"Aren't you worried about people taking photos and posting them to social media? Those close to us might know, but we haven't gone public yet."

He fixes the pink band around Blake's head, making sure the bow is at the exact angle I like. True to form, the second our week of "distance" was up, Emmett was sliding into my text messages, asking when he could see me and Blake. The playoffs schedule is insane, and the Blades are going deep into the finals, which only allowed for us to do something this afternoon.

When I told Emmett that I needed time, I didn't know where I would find answers about what to do next. Whether they came from a conversation with Mom or Dad, I wasn't sure, but since neither of them is ready to talk yet, I spent a lot of the week taking local walks with Blake and going over everything with Collins, Darcy, Kendra, and the rest of the girls.

Felicity advised me to *sit in my feelings* a while longer, and the others agreed.

Initially, I thought that was crazy thinking because how can doing nothing lead you forward? Turned out, it was the best advice I could ever receive. As the murky waters from last week's storm settled, the way I missed Emmett confirmed that regardless of what other people might think, I'm falling in love with the man standing in front of me, and so is my daughter.

Blake needs him as much as I want him, and walking away to keep my parents happy would only break their daughter in return.

I'm still waiting for a chance to speak with Mom since I think she will come around before Dad, although the painful truth is, they might never be able to accept our relationship.

Turning to face me fully, Emmett takes both of my hands in his. I know we're being watched by onlookers—my boyfriend's face is famous in Brooklyn.

"How much longer do I need to go without claiming you as mine in front of everyone?"

His brows knit together, and I rise onto my tiptoes, still not close enough to his lips.

"Not much longer," I softly whisper.

With a grin, Emmett leans down a little further, Blake sandwiched between the both of us. His attention drops to my mouth, and I smooth my tongue across my bottom lip, memories of how good he tastes urging me to kiss him for the first time in days.

He closes his eyes, savoring our close proximity as the wind whips my hair around us.

“I know there’s still so much we need to talk about,” he breathes. “But for now, I’ll take you and Blake being here with me as the win I desperately needed.” He casts his eyes around the park, glasses rising slightly on his nose when he grins. “I hope you didn’t mind me bringing you here. I thought we could spend a couple of hours on the rides and then eat on the beach. I have a blanket and picnic basket in my trunk.”

He casts his gaze down my body. The black ankle boots, skinny blue jeans, and green sweater I’m wearing were a practical and safe choice when Emmett only gave me a single clue that we’d be outdoors today. Although the heat burning in his eyes tells me he appreciates the simple outfit way more than I predicted.

I reach up and smooth a hand down his black jacket. “You don’t look so bad yourself, Mr. Richards. And, no, I don’t mind at all; a fun afternoon sounds perfect.”

His grin grows even bigger, morphing into something more childlike. “I think Blake wants to try out the carousel first. Right, B?” He directs his question straight at my daughter, and I struggle to stay upright at the loving way she glows in response.

Leading us toward the carousel, Emmett brings my knuckles to his mouth as we walk, kissing across each one in turn. “Can I ask you for a favor?”

“Of course.”

We pull up by the ride, and he releases my hand, sliding his into the pocket of his black jeans.

“Can you take some photos and videos for me?” He hands me his cell and drops his attention to Blake. “I realized when I was scrolling through my phone this morning that I don’t have any good photos with her, and I need to change that, stat.”

An answer sticks in my throat, so instead, I just nod.

He thumbs over his shoulder, animated in a way I haven’t seen Emmett before. He looks genuinely happy in this moment, despite the shitshow we’ve both endured. He’s contagious in all the best ways, pulling my daughter’s first giggle from her tiny body.

He's already halfway to the carousel when he turns on his heel. "Are you going to ride with us?"

I consider it for a second before shaking my head. "No. I'll be able to get better shots from here."

And as Emmett straddles a horse way too small for his huge frame, holding the leather reins between Blake's tiny fingers, I snap away on his phone, trying hard to capture the best images I can through blurry eyes.

It's the picnic of dreams, all laid out on a huge plaid blanket.

"Wait," I say, picking up a container and pulling off the lid. "You packed pineapple pizza slices?"

Emmett grins at me like he has done all day. Blake is buried beneath a fluffy brown onesie and nestled between his parted thighs. She hasn't taken her eyes off the ocean since we arrived on the beach.

"I woke early and made it. Figured you'd never forgive me if I showed up with a picnic basket, minus the pizza."

Dipping my hand into the basket, I pull out a final container. "Cheese?"

Emmett points to a box on the opposite side of the blanket. "No picnic is complete without cheese and crackers."

I bite down on my bottom lip to prevent it from shaking. "I think you just aged another decade."

He deadpans at me, reaching across and taking the cheese from my grasp. Popping the lid, he talks me through every kind he's wrapped individually before I switch off completely and just go ahead without him, loading up my plate with sandwiches, chips, and dessert.

He quirks a brow at me.

"What?"

"Nothing," he replies, shaking his head at my lunch. "Did you think Blake would steal your brownie if you didn't claim it right away?"

"Hey, I'm really sorry to ask, but could I get a photo with you?" A middle-aged guy wearing a Blades cap approaches Emmett from behind, pulling out his phone and handing it to a friend. "It's just ... I'm a really big fan, and I'd have kicked myself all year if I didn't ask."

When Emmett looks across at me, his eyes are seeking permission, but I'm already holding my arms out to take Blake.

"Are you sure it's okay if I do this?" he asks, standing and lowering her into my arms.

I know that I look confused. Surely, photos with fans are an everyday occurrence. "Why wouldn't it be?"

He hesitates for a beat, looking like he wants to say something, but then he leans down and sets a kiss on my cheek. "I'll be right back."

A few minutes and a sandwich later, Emmett takes a seat beside me and Blake on the blanket, all of us now facing the ocean.

Forearms balanced on drawn-up knees, he wears a thoughtful look.

"I think it's time for me to reach out to Beau again."

Emmett hasn't mentioned his estranged younger brother to me since before I left for college. Sometimes, he came up in conversation around the dinner table when Mom asked after him during the holidays, although I never actually met a single member of Emmett's biological family.

Holding Blake in one arm, I balance the plate in my lap and take a bite of his delicious homemade pizza. One of the best I've ever had.

"What happened with Beau? If you don't mind me asking."

Fingers sifting through the loose sand by his feet, he finds a smooth pebble and tosses it out into the ocean. It lands a good distance away with a *plop*.

"Honestly? I'm not sure. He started a family, and I let hockey and life get in the way. Florida is only a plane ride away, but we've never found the time to see each other." He tosses another pebble. "We were never that close or really saw eye to eye as adults. When our parents died, we drifted even further apart."

Sometimes, I wonder how different my life would look if I had siblings. Less lonely, that's for sure. Being an only child is the last thing I want for Blake.

His deep exhale is blown away by the wind.

"Losing Scott has reminded me of how fragile relationships can be." His shrugs, the smile I witnessed earlier completely gone. I can definitely relate to what he's saying. If it wasn't for her social media posts, it would be easy to believe that Clara never existed in my life. "No one ever told me that when I signed the divorce papers, I wouldn't know the meaning of pain until my best friend turned his back on me," Emmett concludes.

I stay silent because none of this is really about me, and I know it. If Emmett didn't want to be here, then he wouldn't. What he needs right now is for someone to listen and understand the shit situation he was largely powerless to prevent. We both were.

Reaching up, I pull off his glasses and set them on my face.

He flicks a finger under my chin, smiling at me sweetly. "Have they blurred out my wrinkles?"

I run a hand through his messy brown hair. "I was actually checking something."

He drops his forehead to mine, circling the pad of his thumb over Blake's cheek. "And what did Mama conclude?"

Resting my head on his shoulder, I look up at him. "That you're still the same amazing person whichever lens you look through. Reach out to Beau, but only because you want to, not because you're chasing the relationship you think you should have."

Deep in thought, he rests his pointer finger in Blake's palm, and she wraps her tiny fingers around it.

"Do you think Scott will ever forgive me or accept the fact that I'm in love with his daughter?"

Delicious tingles fizz into each nerve ending. I'll never grow tired of hearing those words.

"That one is more difficult to answer. My dad is a proud man, and he feels betrayed."

"I was thinking of stopping by in a few days to see if he's—"

"Don't," I quickly interject, hating that I have to burst his hopeful bubble. "Scott Quinn might be your long-term friend, but I know my father almost as well as his wife. If he's going to move on, then it has to be when he's good and ready."

Crashing waves punctuate several beats of silence as a few teenagers tear past us down the beach.

"Mom will be the key to Dad. If anyone can bring him around, then it'll be the woman he loves."

Emmett chuckles low, planting a chaste kiss across my lips. "That sounds really fucking familiar," he whispers so Blake doesn't hear his profanity. Not that she's even close to saying her first word.

I lift a playful shoulder, no doubt looking ridiculous in glasses way too big for my face. "What can I say? Us Quinn girls wield that kind of power."

Emmett's heavy breath fans my cheeks as he studies me for longer than usual. "With respect, I don't think that your last name has anything to do with my obsession." Another kiss lands on my lips. "Since I'm certain that you would call the same shots over me with *Richards* stamped across your back."

CHAPTER FORTY-THREE

EMMETT

"Impromptu get-togethers are my favorite thing in the world."

Darcy's declaration from her place on the opposite end of the table pulls a few agreeable noises from my teammates as we all dig into our food.

"Hell yes, Darcy Doll." Raising his fork loaded with salmon pasta, Archer takes a huge bite and sets a kiss against his wife's cheek.

"Fishy breath!" she guffaws, pink staining the apple of her cheeks.

Sitting at the head of the table, Jack gazes around at his teammates and their girls, a sense of pride filling his expression.

"I know we generally get together after, but I felt like a meal the night before a big game was the right way to go this time."

Picking up his pint of beer, Sawyer tips his glass at the rest of the table. "I'll be the first to admit how much I like this idea—more beer for me while you all hit the water and energy drinks."

From beside Tommy, Jenna shifts uncomfortably in her chair. "And here I was, thinking the sickness bouts had stopped ..." She frowns at the huge bowl of pasta set in the center of the table. "Turns out, the smell of salmon can still turn my stomach."

"You were like that, weren't you, Princess?" Jensen rubs Kate's belly. "The smell of meat had you wanting to puke around the clock."

Collins holds up a hand. "As much as I care for a pregnant friend in need, can we hold all talk around vomit until after we've finished eating?"

"I can't believe you're still struggling, babe." Kendra's soft voice floats toward Jenna. "I thought you'd be well past that by now."

Jenna huffs out a doubtful breath. "Apparently, this baby is destined to make me sick for the whole nine months."

Lowering down so only his wife can hear, Tommy whispers something in Jenna's ear, pulling a dirty giggle from her throat.

"And no filthy talk at the dinner table." Jack points his knife straight at Tommy. "This is a respectful meal, not an opportunity to get down to it with your woman."

"Yeah, Tommy." Archer smirks at his captain. "The time to bang comes after the main course."

Jack's knife moves from Tommy to his goalie. "Are you deliberately trying to raise my blood pressure, Moore? Or are you naturally that antagonistic?"

"He's an opportunist," I muse, smiling around a mouthful of pasta. "He lives for chances to remind you about how he married your sister."

Jack just rolls his eyes. "At least nothing ever happened under my own roof."

Unable to control herself, Darcy bursts out laughing. "That's what you think, oh brother almighty."

Jack's head darts to Kendra, eyes wide in disbelief. "What are they talking about, Kitten?"

"I believe Archer is referring to the first time he hooked up with your little sister." She points toward the hallway.

Jack jumps to his feet. "Kend, call a realtor. We're putting the apartment on the market. First thing tomorrow."

"Don't be so melodramatic," Sawyer replies. "You've cleaned the sheets, right?"

"Annnd ... all of a sudden, I'm not the only one fighting the urge to puke." Jenna chuckles, dipping her chin at a pale-faced Jack.

"*I know what I'll do, Kend,*" Jack mumbles sarcastically to himself, loud enough so the whole table can hear what he must've said earlier to his wife. "*I'll drop all my players a last-minute text and cook up a nice meal ahead of tomorrow's game.* No one appreciates me around here."

"Well, I appreciate you," Billie confirms, fork circling her dinner, "and this gorgeous meal."

Kate shakes her head. "Don't encourage him, Billie. The Morgans are needy enough as it is. I, for one, am just glad we only have to cope with one tonight."

Sliding my hand under the table, I squeeze Billie's thigh in my palm, leaning down to whisper into the shell of her ear, "All this talk of hooking up is making me so fucking horny."

She whips her head around to look at me, eyes wide with shock. "Emmett!"

Her coy response turns me on further. We haven't had sex since our getaway, and I blame that entirely on our playoffs schedule, plus my hesitancy to push Billie any further than a few dates over the past two weeks.

But there's only so long I can hold off on putting my hands on this girl, as I've come to realize all too well since February.

My hand ascends toward her apex, and instead of stopping me, she opens her legs wider.

"Bad girl," I softly croon.

Clearing her throat, Billie centers her attention on Kendra. "Your apartment is beautiful. Really homey."

Jack motions to his wife. "Everything you see is at the hands of my girl. When I moved in, the place had stark white walls and not much else."

The temptation to let Billie know that she can style my penthouse however she wants when we move in together threatens to spill from my tongue as she finishes up her last mouthful of pasta, a shaky hand replacing her fork on the plate when I dance my fingers higher.

Standing from her chair, Kendra begins collecting dishes from one end of the table, Jack starting on the other.

The table falls into separate conversations, and I take full advantage of the distraction. "Meet me outside the guest room in a couple of minutes."

Billie shakes her head, although the heat behind her eyes doesn't match her body language.

I rise from my chair before the tent forming in my pants becomes impossible to hide.

She tracks my movements, tongue sweeping across her bottom lip when her gaze falls to my crotch. "You're serious, aren't you?"

Nodding once, I thank Jack and Kendra for a delicious meal before throwing my girl a wink that leaves her in no doubt over what I want for dessert.

Several earth-shatteringly frustrated minutes later, Billie finally emerges at the end of the hallway.

I waste zero time pulling her into a darkened room and softly close the door behind us.

Her eyes sparkle from the moonlight as she gazes up at me, back pressed against the door.

"You're a bad boy—you know that? Jack will be mad if he discovers what we're doing while everyone else is in the other room."

Taking both of her wrists in one hand, I pin them above her head.

I drop a kiss to her collarbone, licking across sensitive flesh. "Is this the point where I'm supposed to pretend like I care what my captain thinks?"

A whimper leaves her throat, and I pop the button on her pants, fingers finding her drenched thong.

"Baby," I praise, pushing her jeans down so I can gain better access to what I want, "just because I'm a good boy in public doesn't mean I don't get the urge to bang my girl on the regular."

Our mouths meet, tongues tangling in a frenzied kiss that's been way too long in the making.

Just having Billie here tonight and spending time with a group of people I adore dares me to fall in deeper love with my girlfriend.

"Stay at my place tonight," I beg like the needy boy I am.

She shakes her head. "Mom is dropping Blake off early in the morning before her shift, and I can't risk not being back home in time."

Under any other circumstance, I'd suggest that I drive us both back to Billie's. But we both know I'd be staying the night, only for the morning to bring an awkward exchange with a woman who can't stand to even look at me.

I can't do that to Billie. Things are hard enough right now with her parents.

Like she can read my mind and hates the anguish I'm feeling over what to do next, Billie gazes up at me.

"Fuck me, Emmett. Right here, right now. Fuck me until I'm screaming your name."

After I release her wrists, my finger presses against her closed lips, the other hand stroking her thong-covered clit.

"As much as I love to hear what I do to you, I really need you to come on my dick in silence." I tip my head in the direction of the living room, muted voices and laughter filtering through the walls. "We can hear them; they can hear us."

Interlacing our fingers, I guide my girl to the four-poster bed and lay her down on the duvet, slowly stripping her bare.

When I flick on a side lamp, Billie's green eyes are almost black as she watches me unloop my belt, unbutton my shirt, and push down my boxer briefs until our clothes are left in random piles around the bed.

"How long do we have?" she whispers as I drop to my knees in front of her, hands wrapped around her upper thighs so I can pull her to the edge of the mattress.

Legs parted, she rests her feet on my shoulders, tiny moans of pleasure filling the room as I push a single finger inside her pussy.

Stealing a taste from my finger, I drag the fist of my other hand from the base to the tip of my cock.

"As long as we want. They've likely worked out what we're doing anyway."

She sits up on her elbows, watching me eat her cunt and pump my dick in rhythmic motions. "But I thought you wanted me to stay quiet so they wouldn't hear?"

Ninety percent of the time, Billie acts well beyond her years. But every now and again, her naivete shows, and I'd be a liar to claim that I didn't eat that shit right up. It's cute as fuck.

Lifting her into my arms, I walk us across to the wall that adjoins the living room, pressing her back against it as I notch myself at her entrance.

"Hiding the fact that I'm banging the woman of my dreams is not the reason why I asked you to stay quiet," I confirm, sliding all the way home.

She gasps into my shoulder, and I hold her tiny frame in one arm, freeing up a hand to play with her clit while I take deep strokes inside her pussy.

"Your pleasure is for my ears only, Billie. Every whimper and moan I pull from you belongs to me. Every time you cry my name and beg me to stop because you're too sensitive to go on—they're words only I get to witness."

A second later, she's coming all over my cock, muted joy tumbling from her lips.

I'm not even close to blowing inside her because I know that the second I do, our alone time will be over. I'm not ready to let her go yet. Basking in Billie is my favorite thing.

"You're dripping down me, Mama."

She presses her forehead into mine. "That's because I'm coming again."

I know she is. Her tight pussy clamping my cock in a death grip makes it hard to bang her how I want.

"You're so fucking beautiful. So fucking perfect for me."

She reaches down between us, cupping my balls in her palm. "Tell me I'm a good girl."

That praise kink of hers will be the undoing of me. Maybe of us both.

Sliding my finger from her clit to her ass, I pause over her tight hole. "Has my good girl ever been touched here?"

Lust-filled pupils gaze back at me before she whispers, "No."

This girl is the perfect combination—a level of innocence that drives my inner alpha while her devilish tendencies keep me right on my toes.

Peppering kisses across her jaw, I move us back across to the bed. "Soon, baby. When we don't have dinner to rejoin and I have you to myself all night"—I crawl on top of her, and we fuck in missionary—"I'll claim your ass and make it all mine."

"I'd like that," she breathes.

Sitting back on my heels, I spread my thighs and pull her into my body.

"I'm never letting you go. Not even when other people tell me to or because they judge us when, really, they don't understand how much you and Blake light up my goddamn world."

Lifting up, she lowers herself back over my dick, taking what she wants from my body before a gentle confession makes me the happiest man alive.

"I love you, Emmett. Even if it's just you, me, and Blake against the rest of the world. I want you to know that I'm here, and I love you."

The first jets of cum squirt from my dick, filling my girl with warmth.

I'm a trembling mess, shaking beneath the weight of Billie's last words, when there's a sharp knock against the bedroom door.

Billie squirms in my arms, her embarrassed groans pulling a deep chuckle from my chest.

"Jack here with a dinner update." A hesitant, almost-pained British voice echoes from the hallway. "Your dessert is now ruined, and if the same is true about my bedsheets, then I'll never step foot inside that spare bedroom again."

CHAPTER FORTY-FOUR

BILLIE

It's wild how, in only a matter of weeks, a relationship you once had with someone very close can flip right on its head.

I never expected that to happen with my parents, least of all my mom, but as she stands in the center of my living space with Blake in her arms, it's almost like she's reacquainting herself with my life or perhaps viewing it through a different lens now that she knows about Emmett.

I know that this is hard for her. Hell, if Blake dropped the kind of news on me that I have with Mom, I'd be fully reeling for weeks.

But now that I'm a mom myself, I'd also be eager to ensure that Blake knew I'd never turn my back on her, no matter what decisions she made or who she fell in love with.

"Did you change the color in here?" Mom asks, squinting at the walls as she bounces Blake against her chest.

It's typical that the first question she asks has an answer involving my boyfriend.

"Emmett spent a whole day refreshing the walls before the playoffs started," I reply without any hesitation. I point toward my bedroom and cringe at what she must think I'm about to say next. "There was mold on the ceiling above my bed. It wasn't dangerous, but Emmett wanted to make sure it was removed."

Yeah, that didn't land the way you'd planned, Bill. Why don't you go ahead and mention your bed and Emmett again?

Nodding once, Mom pushes past the conversation, moving into my kitchen and transferring Blake into a cradle hold so she can start emptying bottles from Blake's overnight bag into the sterilizer.

The awkward atmosphere is bordering unbearable right now.

"How's work?" I ask as brightly as I can.

Closing the lid on the machine, Mom spins on her heel and leans back against the counter.

She looks tired, and so does her work uniform. The wrinkles in her white blouse are a rare occurrence and a sure sign that she's struggling with even the simplest tasks in everyday life.

"No change. Although your dad is now starting to pick up some hours, which is taking the pressure off a little."

It's not lost on me that in my parents discovering the truth about Emmett, their marriage has also been under immense strain.

Stepping toward her, I take Blake from Mom, although I don't put any space between us, choosing to lean into the building tension. We need to talk, and even if it's the most uncomfortable exchange we've ever had, I'll be damned if I let her drive to work when we have the perfect opportunity to voice our thoughts now that some time has passed for us to gather them.

"How are things between you both?" I tentatively ask.

Her eyes fall to the floor. "Quiet. There's a huge elephant in the room whenever we're sitting down for dinner or watching TV, and neither of us knows how to address it. I know he's sorry about the shares, but he's also closed off like I've never seen him before."

"A bit like how things are between us," I muse, the correlation painfully obvious.

Mom's eyes snap to mine. "Yeah, I guess so."

Teeth press into her bottom lip. "While I was shocked by everything that came out, I want you to know that Scott's lies about money hasn't been the only topic we've argued over."

"No?"

"No," she repeats. "I don't agree with some of the comments and accusations Scott pointed at Emmett; neither do I think that he deserved to be punched."

Blake wraps her hand around my finger, and I close my eyes to block the tears from falling.

When I reopen them, Mom is standing even closer.

"Are you in love with him, Billie?"

I croak out a, "Yes."

It's obvious that she already knew the answer; I can see it in the warm smile Mom offers.

"You know that you are always welcome to come over for dinner whenever you want. We have both missed you and Blake terribly."

I nod an acknowledgment. "Does the invitation extend to Emmett?"

She winces. "If it were left up to me, then yes. I personally believe that we should rip the Band-Aid off and talk everything through." Mom pauses. "Scott ... he isn't ready for that."

"Do you think he will ever be ready?" I hate asking the question, but I force out the words because I know there's a real chance that he won't.

Reaching out, Mom smooths a hand down my shoulder. "I don't know, honey."

Tears prick in the corners of my eyes. I hate that—even though it was never my intention—I have effectively driven a wedge between a long-term friendship. Both men are hurting deeply.

"As for Maria ..." Mom's voice takes on a harsher edge, almost cutting. "Our friendship is definitely dead and buried."

My eyes practically bust from their sockets.

Mom waves a hand in front of her, metaphorically dismissing my boyfriend's ex-wife. "Do you know how many hours I spent comforting that woman? In person, over the phone. Hell, I even got on a flight to Kansas once because she was inconsolable over their temporary split a couple of years ago. Vacations to Florida, where she cried nonstop over their divorce, and meanwhile, I was trying to get home to my pregnant daughter and injured husband, both of them heading for the hospital." Her eyes narrow at the memories. "And all along, she was screwing half of the cabin crew behind his back while simultaneously slinging accusations about how he was cheating."

I lower my eyes to Blake and cover my baby girl's ears.

Mom flashes me a grimace and then continues her rambling. "When I confronted her about everything, she broke down, spouting more trash about you trying to steal her husband away from her." She scoffs. "Maria only has herself to blame for the demise of her marriage, and petty jealousy makes her look even more of a fool. Going behind *my* back to speak to *my* husband about *my* daughter ..."

Without another word, I pull her into my body, one arm wrapping around her slender shoulders. It feels like she's dropped weight since she was last in my arms, and that breaks my heart.

She gazes down at Blake and then at me.

"There was nothing going on between me and Emmett before I returned from Austin. I promise."

Mom shakes her head. "I know, and you don't need to go there. Even Scott knows that too. Maria is all kinds of paranoid, and I've seen a side to her that I just cannot hang in with. I'll always choose my daughter. Over anyone or anything."

Our embrace with Blake nestled between us is all that's left to be said, and we stay like that for the longest time until Mom eventually pulls away, checking her watch on a sigh.

"I have to get to work."

I'm not ready for her to leave, even though I need to jump in the shower and get ready myself.

"Do you have plans today?" she asks, strolling into my living area and collecting her purse from the couch.

"I'm meeting some friends for coffee at that bakery, Rise Up."

She looks intrigued. "Which friends are these, and do I know them?"

I shake my head, a slow smile creeping onto my lips when I think about the amazing women I've met over the past three months. "Remember that biker girl with pink hair and a banging body?"

Mom twists her lips to one side, snapping her fingers when she recalls Collins. "Ah, yes! The queen."

I chuckle. "Well, it turned out that she is the wife of one of Emmett's former teammates." I gaze around my apartment. "And this is actually the place she rented before she met him."

Mom's mouth pops open. "No kidding! Small world."

"Well, through Collins, I met a few other incredible women, and two of them have invited me and Blake for coffee this morning."

Beaming on my behalf, Mom hangs her purse over one shoulder and heads for the front door. "Well, in that case, I'd best not keep you." She pauses halfway out the apartment. "Tell Emmett that Freya says hi."

"Billie!" Kate pushes back her chair and moves another one out of the way so I can wheel Blake's stroller directly up to the table she and Felicity reserved.

Kate plants a single kiss on each of my cheeks, and Felicity does the same before I take a seat between them. Then Kate slides a warm cappuccino toward me.

"I have one question." I begin talking, attention shifting from Kate to Felicity.

"Shoot," Felicity replies, stirring sweetener into a cup of Yorkshire Tea.

"How is it that y'all can both smell and look so insanely good this early in the morning?"

Felicity blows out a harsh laugh, flicking her chocolate waves over one shoulder. "I'll let my business partner answer that one. Jon kept me up all night."

Kate holds up a hand. "All right, babe. Enough with the overshare."

Felicity snickers, and Kate turns to me.

"You're probably wondering why we invited you here for breakfast and preordered your coffee?"

I shrug and suppress a yawn.

Kate wiggles her brows. "Or was your evening similar to Felicity's?" Leaning forward, she smirks at me. "Don't pretend like we didn't all know what you and your boy were up to in that spare room last night."

I flush, still feeling the aftereffects between my thighs. "Unfortunately, after we left Jack and Kendra's, Emmett dropped me back at my place, and then we spent the night apart. It was the memories that kept me awake."

Kate makes a face akin to pride. "Good for you, girl."

Clearing her throat, Felicity gets the conversation back on track. "Anyway, the reason—other than three friends having a coffee—we invited you here today was because we have a proposition for you, and we didn't want to wait too long to let you know our plans." She flicks her eyes to Kate.

Rolling her lips together, Kate takes over speaking. "As you know, we recently established our own law firm with offices here in Brooklyn, and if all goes to plan, we'll expand our offices into other states."

Throat running dry, I try not to get ahead of myself, anticipation and excitement swirling in my stomach.

"It's truly amazing," I say, picking up my coffee and taking a sip.

Felicity and Kate share a silent moment between them.

"We would like to take you on as a legal intern," Kate begins.

"We made some inquiries with local colleges, and you would be able to transfer the credits you already accumulated in Austin and finish out your bachelor's degree with Morgan Jones LLP footing the remaining study costs. Once you graduate, we would then pay to put you through law school and eventually the bar exam."

"Furthermore ..."

Eyes wide, I dart my head to Felicity as she picks up Kate's thread.

"We understand and appreciate that Blake has to come first. So, if you accept an internship with us, we would like to put you on the payroll with immediate effect. That way, we can pay you a salary while you spend time with Blake, without having to worry about money or finding another job, only to quit a couple of months later."

I'm speechless, genuinely unable to form words.

Kate pulls me into her side when she notices the tears forming in my eyes, resting her beautiful-smelling head on mine. "In terms of child care for Blake, we can also help with that. Darcy has recommended a great nanny who would be able to care for Blake whenever you need, and we can build the cost into a remuneration package for you."

I cast my eyes to Blake's stroller, where my baby girl is sleeping peacefully beneath her favorite pink blanket.

"I know things are difficult with your parents, and so we're not sure how involved they are with Blake's care ..." Kate trails off, and I take advantage of her pause.

"Mom and Dad will always step up for Blake, no matter what's going down between us."

Smiling, Kate nods once. "Well then, the nanny can work days to suit them."

Struggling to find words over their generosity, I pull a deep breath into my lungs. "Why are you doing all of this for me?"

Felicity reaches across the table, dropping her hand over mine. It's warm and soft and just like an angel's.

"Remember our conversation that time in Luigi's? Well, I had to wait way too long to finally realize my dreams and all because of a rotten ex and a lack of funding. Kate had Will and June when she least expected it, but with the most amazing man by her side, just like you do with Emmett. Years of hustling have given us the financial capabilities to set up a law firm where women and family are at the heart of everything we do. We're tired of a male-dominated industry that doesn't give priority to talented female lawyers." Her eyes soften as she looks at me. "We don't need to see your college grades to know that you will make a fine lawyer one day; we can tell simply from the courage and determination you possess." She pauses for a second. "If becoming a lawyer is still what you want?"

I half speak, half laugh out a response. "It's what I want. Being a lawyer, making a difference for people, is what I want."

Kate's hand lands on top of Felicity's. "Then that's finalized then. Billie Quinn will be the first legal intern at Morgan Jones LLP, and together, we'll all chase after our dreams."

CHAPTER FORTY-FIVE

BILLIE

Lloyd's during the daytime carries a very different vibe to how I've seen it at night. The place feels more like a luxury restaurant, only with live sports on the screens above the bar.

Taking a bite of Caesar salad, I tip my head at Blake as she sits in her stroller, mesmerized by the soccer game in front of her.

"Kendra has a hundred dollars on Blake playing for the New York Storm by the time she's eighteen. She and Jenna want me to sign her up for their soccer program as soon as she turns five."

Taking a sip of water, Emmett sets his glass back down on the table. The second I told him that I'd accepted an internship with Morgan Jones, he has been desperate to take me out and celebrate. Easier said than done when trying to fit in a few hours around playoff games, endless team briefings, and practices at every hour of the day.

"I can personally see her following in her mommy's footsteps and ruling the world, one court case at a time."

I snort out a laugh, still high from meeting Felicity and Kate at Rise Up a week ago.

Reaching across, I go to steal a cherry tomato from his plate when Emmett catches my hand in his, bringing my knuckles to his mouth.

He kisses them gently, never taking his eyes away from mine. "I'm seriously so damn proud of you, Bill. You deserve all the good things that are coming your way."

"I honestly can't wait to have my own money," I say when he releases my fingers.

Emmett clasps his hands under his chin, expression pensive. I kept the money he gifted to Dad, but he knows I've only ever wanted to pay my own bills and not lean on others.

"I wanted to talk to you about finances and get your opinion on something. But maybe we can put a pin in that conversation until we get back to my place."

Intrigue and excitement buzz through my body. Tonight will be the first night I've stayed over at Emmett's penthouse in way too long. *Finally*, a night where we can put Blake to bed, and neither one of us has anything early scheduled the following morning. God bless Coach Morgan for giving the boys a rest day tomorrow.

I quirk a playful brow at my boyfriend. "Sounds ominous."

He just chuckles, laughter fading when he notices that I'm no longer looking at him, but over his shoulder.

Emmett turns in his chair, fixated on my dad as he takes a seat at the bar and orders a drink, eyes glued to the soccer game.

I know that other than a mutual interest in classic cars, Emmett and Dad would frequently catch live sports, and so seeing him show up alone must feel a painful kind of weird.

"Do you think he's noticed us?" Emmett asks.

I shrug and take another bite of salad. I've seen and spoken to Dad when they've cared for Blake, but we haven't uttered a word about Emmett. Mom was right when she said that he would need more time.

When Dad briefly glances in our direction, his eyes burn into the back of Emmett's head. I don't need to be a mind reader to figure out that he's still as mad as he was weeks ago. Not that

Emmett needs to know that. I guarantee he's sitting here, thinking over ways he can break the ice and make everything right again.

Pushing his plate of food away, Emmett runs a stressed hand through his hair. "Maybe now that Freya has calmed down, she has had an influence on Scott?" He inconspicuously thumbs over his shoulder. "Is he still sitting there, or has he left?"

"He's still sitting there," I reply.

Dad's eyes remain lasered on Emmett's back. The tendons in his jaw flex as he accepts a beer from the bartender and takes a large pull.

Emmett shakes his head slowly. "I didn't think it through, bringing us here, or even register that Scott could show up, unannounced. Lloyd's was a place where we'd frequently catch the games."

The way he refers to their friendship in the past tense breaks my heart.

This time, I take Emmett's hand in mine, fingers stroking his palm. "And maybe, one day, you will watch a game together again or hit up a classic car show."

I flick my eyes back to Dad. Bumping into him in here was a total coincidence, but maybe it was also a sign from the universe. Emmett thinks that this is all his fault, but honestly, I'm fifty percent of this relationship, too, and maybe the time has arrived for me to tackle things head-on.

After all, at the sight of us having lunch together, Dad hasn't stormed straight out of the bar, and that can only be a good omen …

Right?

"Is Blake due for a diaper change?" Emmett pulls my attention to him.

I nod once and push back my chair, unhooking Blake's change bag from her stroller.

Emmett rounds the table, lifting Blake into his arms. "Let me take this one, Mama. The male restrooms have a change table, and

B doesn't mind her daddy taking charge in the diaper department."

He sets a soft kiss against her forehead, and my heart detonates.

Dad watches Emmett's every move as he heads for the restroom, and I pick up my purse and approach the bar, rehearsing what I'm going to say right up until the point where I take the seat next to him.

In the end, it's a long moment before either of us speaks. Dad is watching but not really absorbing the soccer game as it heads into halftime.

"Daddy Emmett sure is taking to the role like a duck to water." His tone drips with sarcasm, and all I can do is respond with facts.

"He's incredible with Blake, and she loves him too."

At the use of the L-word, Dad's eyes meet mine before they're back on the TV.

Sarcasm is replaced with disdain when he asks, "Is he still giving you money?"

"You make it sound like he's buying access to me and my daughter when you couldn't be further from the truth," I challenge, done with the passive-aggressive way this conversation has started.

"That's precisely what he's doing, Bill," Dad volleys back.

I huff out a despondent breath and ask the bartender for a Diet Coke.

"With the way you're carrying on right now, it's almost like you never knew Emmett before you found out about us dating."

He winces as I finish up my sentence, taking another mouthful of beer, likely to wash away reality.

"I didn't know him before," he argues. "Sometimes, it takes years for people to show you their true colors, no matter how well you thought you knew them. Look at Maria."

Anger swells in my gut. "Emmett is nothing like Maria, and

you know it. That's a really unfair comparison to make. And a really hurtful one too," I tag on.

He just scoffs at that, finally turning to look at me. Maybe it's the bar lighting, but Dad's face is way more drawn than the last time I saw him a week ago. Just like Mom in my apartment, he looks like he's merely going through the motions of life, no longer thriving in the close relationships he once had. Including with me and Emmett. I'm desperate to wrap my arms around his large frame, like he has done so many times with me, and whisper a promise that everything will be okay. And I would, if I thought he would listen.

"You want to know what's hurtful? Finding out that your friend has betrayed you in the worst way possible and pulled your only daughter and her baby into his post-divorce midlife crisis."

I shake my head at him, and he nods back.

"Mark my words, sweetheart. In six months, this will all end in disaster. Freya and I will be the ones picking up the pieces of your life."

"My life is going great," I clarify. "I just got offered a position as a legal intern at a friend's law firm."

Swallowing another mouthful, he sets his glass back down. "Freya told me all about it. I'm happy for you."

Everything, even landing my dream job, is overshadowed by this goddamn mess that no one seems able to fix.

I gaze over at my dad as he watches the halftime commercials.

Nothing is ever going to be the same again, is it? The devastating damage Emmett feared is being perpetuated by my stubborn dad, who won't even hold a reasonable conversation with me, let alone his former best friend.

"Have you heard from Tucker?"

"Why would it matter if I had?" I snap, right on the edge of losing my cool.

He lifts a single shoulder. "He's Blake's real father, and I wanted to check that he was at least keeping his end of the bargain."

My parents don't have a clue about Tucker's visit to Brooklyn, and right now, that's the way I intend to keep it. If Dad caught wind that Tucker had asked me to get back with him—even if it was for all the wrong reasons—Dad would likely try to set me back up with my ex, his deluded mind convinced that Tucker and his dreadful family would be a better match for me and Blake than the man I'm actually in love with.

"He pays the bare minimum, and that's where his efforts end. Emmett is way more of a real father than Tucker will ever be."

My words bounce off Dad's impenetrable armor.

"Bill?"

We both spin around at the sound of Emmett's voice.

With Blake in his arms, he points toward the exit, eyes briefly flashing to Dad's. "I'm going to take Blake back to the car and wait for you there."

"Sure," I confirm, my voice barely able to form a single word without it wobbling.

Emmett rolls his lips together as Dad smiles at his granddaughter. This whole situation is heart-wrenchingly fucked up.

"Hey, Scott."

Dad doesn't even look at Emmett, let alone return his greeting.

It's the final straw—or maybe nail in the coffin—as I jump down from the stool and hook my purse over my shoulder.

Turning back to Dad, I set a single kiss against his cheek.

"I love you with every piece of my heart, so please, don't let pride and bitterness stand in the way of the truth. When you're ready to talk, I'll always be here, and when you want to see Blake, I'll always bring her over to see you. But for now, I need to step away from our relationship because, clearly, this level of anger isn't doing either of us any good."

CHAPTER FORTY-SIX

EMMETT

Stepping into the elevator, we ascend to my penthouse in silence, Billie wearing a fake smile as she tries to hide her pain from the exchange with Scott.

She doesn't want to give me the details, for fear of making me feel worse when nothing could hurt me more than knowing that my girl is upset.

As Blake happily snores away in her stroller, I reach behind Billie and hit Stop on the elevator.

Her eyes grow wide. "What are you doing?"

Moving into her space, I plant my hands on her hips and brush my nose across hers.

"Even if it's just you, me, and Blake against the world and for the rest of time, I love you." I whisper a similar sentiment to the one she gave me in Jack and Kendra's spare bedroom.

I'm tempted to ask her all about what Scott said, but truthfully, I don't think she wants to revisit it, and I don't see how hearing his words of rejection will help to heal the invisible wounds of our friendship. My face might be fully healed, but it's going to take a whole lot more than arnica cream and Steri-Strips to mend the internal traumas we're all still living with.

Billie's shoulders drop an inch, and I cover her mouth with mine, taking the kiss deeper in a bid to drive home my love for her.

When we come up for air, we're both breathless, and I'm desperate to get her in my bed.

"You wanted to talk about financial stuff."

I kiss her once more. "I do. But I have a surprise for you first."

Her eyes narrow, as she's wary about surprises. "Wait. Are we talking a good surprise?"

Nodding my head from side to side, I hit the Stop button again to set the elevator going. "I guess that all depends on whether or not you like what I've done with the place."

Her confused expression doesn't last long as the doors open to reveal a completely different living and kitchen space from the one Billie saw last time she visited my penthouse.

Hands in front of her mouth, she takes a few steps out of the elevator and slowly turns around in my new living area.

"Oh my God, Emmett!" she squeals. "The contrasting blues and golden accents are just ..."

Racing over to the kitchen, she smooths a palm over deep blue cabinets, and happy tears fill her eyes as I release the brake on Blake's stroller and wheel her into the penthouse.

"I ... I don't even know what to say."

Wetness glides down her cheeks as she heads into my living room and takes in the pictures of me and Blake on the carousel at Luna Park. There's three in total, all in huge frames and hanging above a new powder-blue corner couch—something the interior designer said was "so on point right now."

Coming to stand behind Billie, I wrap my arms around her waist and rest my chin over her shoulder, gazing up at Blake's delighted beam.

"She was in fits of giggles in that one," I say, pointing to the middle image. "You caught her just right."

"They're truly stunning." My girlfriend's voice is full of wonder.

I turn her in my hold, looping my hands under her ass. She wraps her legs around my waist, hands secured tightly at the nape of my neck.

"Did you have the whole place renovated?"

I nod. "Even the bath towels match."

Throwing her head back, she laughs out loud, and, fuck, could I play that sound on repeat for the rest of my life.

Even better, I pray that I get to hear it live until the day I leave this earth.

"Want to see my favorite room?" I ask.

Billie casts a hand around the open-plan space. "I'm not sure you could top this, to be honest."

Walking us down the hallway, which has been finished in a similar style to the living area, I depress a door handle with my elbow and ask Billie to flick the light switch directly in front of her.

"Holy ... moly." Both hands cover her face, and I pull her closer to my body when she forgets that she needs to hold on to my neck.

"What do you think?"

Billie presses her lips together, more tears emerging. "I think this is every little girl's dream."

Cotton-candy pink, lacy ruffles. A huge dollhouse, complete with all the furniture Blake could ever want when she's old enough to play with it. Books and sensory games are scattered across a soft pink rug, ready for her to explore, and in the center of the room sits a crib, which is small enough for Blake now, but big enough for her to grow into.

"Emmett ..." Billie casts her eyes up to the golden stars painted on the bedroom ceiling. "They're beautiful."

I tuck a piece of hair behind her ear. All I want is to be around my favorite girls twenty-four/seven.

"They illuminate in the dark. So, when Blake's falling asleep, they're the last thing she'll see and the first image she'll wake up to."

Memories of the first time I woke to Billie's face were the reason behind that idea. Everyone should open their eyes to something beautiful each morning.

"I want our baby girl to shoot for all of her dreams. Whether that's as a pro soccer player, like Kendra and Jenna, or a lawyer, like her mommy, or whatever she chooses to be. I made you a promise, Bill. A promise that I will always be here, and I wanted to show you how serious I am about that by transforming my stark penthouse into our home."

It takes her a second to catch up to what I just said. "*Our* home?"

"Our home," I repeat.

I walk us back through to the living area, where I sit down on the couch with Billie straddling me.

"When the playoffs are over and I've got the time to help you pack up your things and we have late-night pineapple pizza on speed dial, I want you both to move in with me."

I'm met with silence, although it doesn't make me anxious. Billie's overwhelmed—I can see it in her eyes.

Moving my mouth up her neck, I pause my lips over the shell of her ear. "While others speculate over us being a rebound, I'm over here, knowing that you're my soulmate." I rest her palm over the sunrise tattoo on my chest. "I know that Scott doubts my love for you, and I'm going to make it my life's mission to prove him wrong by loving his daughter harder than any man has ever loved a woman before. If you want my heart, then it's already yours. If you want my life, then it already revolves around you and Blake. And if you want more babies with me"—I smirk, my dick growing hard at the thought—"then I'll be too happy to put some inside you."

"You want us to move in with you now?" Voice dazed, Billie wriggles in my lap, and, Christ, I'm desperate to be inside her.

"As soon as practically possible," I reaffirm. "If you're ready, then I'm ready to build the rest of our lives together."

Blake's tiny whimper lets us know that she's stirring from her nap, and Billie turns toward the stroller before centering her attention back on me.

"You don't have to answer right away. You can always think about it."

"I don't need to think anything over, Em."

Anxiety hits me right between the eyes as I wait on her decision.

When she cups my face in her palms, I get a hunch that I'm going to like her answer.

"There isn't a second in the day that I don't miss you whenever you aren't around. Yes. Yes, we want to move in with you ..." Her previously animated tone turns more sultry, big green eyes burning with need. "And when Blake goes to bed tonight, I want you to make good on what you promised the last time we were sitting in this position."

I cast my eyes down between us, wishing my girl were bare and sprawled out for me right now.

"Tell me what you want, Mama."

Leaning down, she licks across my bottom lip. "I want you to bend me over our bed and slowly take my ass."

"BILLIE ... BABY ..."

I bite down on my knuckles when I take a step back and absorb the stunning view—my girlfriend, dressed in my jersey and a tiny black thong, waiting on all fours for me to play with her body all night.

Fuuuuck. There's no chance that I'll survive the next hour.

"Do you like what you see?" she teases, spreading her knees wider on the bed.

I'm fucking speechless. The dark blue of my jersey sits perfectly against her fair complexion, and her deep red hair is pulled over one shoulder so I can read my last name on her back.

"How hard do you want me to go with you tonight?" I ask, swiping a hand across my mouth.

Reaching behind her, she pulls her thong to one side, revealing a perfect glistening pussy. "I want to be sore for days."

I take a single pace forward and crack my palm across her ass, red immediately rising on her skin.

She bites on her bottom lip, hungry for more.

Dropping to my knees, I take her thong with me, tossing it to one side. "Are you my little whore, Bill?"

She whimpers when I part her ass cheeks and then her pussy, passing my tongue from one hole to the next.

"If it means that you'll fuck my ass tonight, then I'll be whatever you want."

If I wasn't already naked, I'd have ruined my bottoms by now, needy pre-cum leaking from the tip of my rock-hard cock.

Swiping a palm over the head, I use my arousal to lubricate the first pump, bottom lip pinned between my teeth as I think over all the ways I'm going to make this girl chant my name.

Since that night at Jack and Kendra's, all I've thought about is tonight, determined to take precious care of the trust that she's placing in me.

Rising to my feet, I open a drawer on the nightstand and retrieve a bottle of lube and blue anal beads.

"I bought these one night after practice," I tell her, gently passing them through her wet pussy.

She moans at the sensation, coating the beads in her glorious release.

"How would you feel if I fed your ass while I slid my cock inside your cunt?"

More moans confirm what I already knew—Billie wants to be full of me, and I'm desperate to bring those fantasies to life.

Wiggling her ass, she grips the bedsheets tighter. "I want to feel them. Now."

"So impatient." I tut, flicking the lid on the lube bottle and squirting some onto the beads.

She's trembling with anticipation when I notch them at her entrance.

"You trust me, right?"

"I trust you, baby," she responds, holding her weight on one hand while using the other to spread herself wider.

"Good girl," I praise, pushing the first bead into her ass.

"Oh my God," she gasps, so I slide another slightly larger bead inside right away.

Cheeks flushed, my girl looks like she's a second away from coming.

"Do you like that, Billie?"

She gives me a nod. "So, so good."

Her ass accepts the next bead, arousal leaking down her thighs. I bend down and capture it with my tongue.

"I'm going to come."

I press a finger inside her pussy, applying pressure to her walls. "So soon?"

When my girlfriend squirts, we both stare at each other, open-mouthed.

Crimson creeps across her cheeks. "I-I didn't know that I could do that."

I hang my head, knowing that she just sealed my fate. I've never been with a woman who could squirt, and Billie has just unlocked a brand-new kink for me.

Pushing a second finger inside her tight cunt, I add another bead to her ass.

She's fighting to stay upright, and I'm battling not to shoot my load before I've taken a single stroke inside my dream girl.

Inserting the final bead into her ass, I immediately pull the string out, relishing the way she flows all over my hand.

“Oh fuck,” she cries, dropping her face into the duvet. “Do that again.”

I don’t even hesitate, feeding her gorgeous ass exactly what she craves while my fingers massage her front wall, milking my favorite pussy for everything it has.

When I retract my hand, she whimpers at the loss before I notch myself at her pussy.

“Tell me you want the beads and my cock at the same time.”

She nods.

“Words. Tell me you want both.”

Shuddering, she whispers a confirmation, and I set one foot on the edge of the mattress, guiding my dick inside Billie.

“You’re so good at this, Mama.”

Pushing back into my cock, she takes me deeper. “Fuck me hard.”

Beads firmly in place, I do as she demanded, gripping her hips as I plow into my girl on repeat.

We’re both moaning, joint gasps filling our bedroom with long-overdue desires. This is the perfect night, and I’m the luckiest man in the world.

“I can feel so much pressure,” she grinds out.

Reaching behind me, I’ve never been more grateful that the interior designer talked me into buying a vanity mirror for the dresser.

I snatch it off the side and snap my hips into her once more.

“I want you to witness what I get to see,” I tell her, positioning the mirror so she has a great view of her ass and pussy, double-stuffed and so fucking beautiful.

“Pull the beads out, Em,” she begs after a few more strokes of my dick.

I go one better, pulling out the beads and my dick at the same time.

Her squirt is insane, and I drop to my knees, clamping my mouth over her pussy before any more of her orgasm goes to waste.

Desperate to eat her like this for hours, I go to pull off my glasses, but Billie shakes her head at me.

"No, keep those slutty little glasses on while you tongue-fuck my cunt."

And that's exactly what I do for the next half hour before I climb to my feet and take her ass with my cock in the way I promised—slow, deep, and all damn night.

CHAPTER FORTY-SEVEN

BILLIE

"That has to be a five-minute penalty!" Will throws his arms up in the air, pointing at the Jumbotron. "It was a premeditated hit on Jack!"

"Why don't you head down to the ice and set him straight?" Kate suggests, eyes rolling into the back of her head.

Will crosses his arms over his chest, seriously considering his mom's sarcastic response. "This ref is biased. It's like he wants Colorado to lift the Cup because the Blades had their time last season."

Continuing his rambling, Will takes a seat a few chairs down from where I'm nestled between Collins and Kendra in the family box.

Turning to me, Collins goes to speak, but Will is back on his feet and out onto the balcony, yelling something at the Colorado coaching staff this time.

Kate's out of her seat and tapping furiously on the glass that separates them both. The rest of our girl group is amused at the back-and-forth between mother and son.

"William, will you calm the f—fudge down? Some people

around here are trying to enjoy a live hockey game and not a running commentary of your thoughts."

Rounding the glass partition, Will shoves his hands into his pockets and flops back down in his chair, legs outstretched in front of him.

June nudges her brother in the ribs. "You do talk a lot, Will."

He screws his face up at her. Kate and Jensen's kids are like mirrors of each other in terms of their mannerisms and looks. I guess that's hardly surprising, given they're twins. Although something tells me that June rules the roost between them and Will would do anything for his sister.

"I need an update on how things are going with number seventy-seven." Winking, Collins plucks at my top. "You know, since you're now at the jersey-wearing stage."

Suddenly, I'm surrounded at all angles. Darcy is standing in front of me, and Jenna is to her left while Collins and Kendra lean in closer.

Darcy squeals with glee, "They're so in love!"

"They really are." Kendra rubs her hands together when my face says it all.

Jenna cups her ear. Her beautiful baby bump is now really obvious beneath Tommy's jersey. "I hear wedding bells!"

I scoff despite the flutters that break out low in my belly. "Let's not get ahead of ourselves."

"How are things now with your dad?" Kendra asks cautiously, earning a glancing side-eye from Kate.

When I dropped Blake off this morning, Dad wasn't home. Mom explained that he was taking extra shifts at work to earn back some of the money they'd missed out on due to the accident and the cost of repairs to his van.

"No real change," I quietly reply. "I know Emmett is desperate to talk things through with him, but that would be the worst move right now. I guess all we can do is get on with our lives and hope that, one day, he'll work out that Emmett is serious about me and Blake."

Collins narrows her eyes. "I could make the man see reason."

Darcy shudders at a thought. "You genuinely scare me, Collins. Like, every day, I spend a second thinking over what it would be like to get on the wrong side of you."

"It's not pretty, trust me." Ezra, her teenage stepson, randomly dips his head into the conversation, tossing a red jelly bean into the air and catching it in his mouth.

Turning one-eighty in her seat, Collins reaches up and ruffles a hand through Ezra's messy brown hair. "Are you planning to share those, or have I lost my in-game candy stash forever?"

He just smirks, tossing a couple more beans in the air.

Collins intercepts one. "Snooze, you lose, my friend."

"Nope, nope, nope, nope, nope!" Will declares, motioning toward the rink. "Their forward just put a hit on Emmett."

He winces as I leap to my feet and stand next to him, and the both of us watch as Emmett heads off the ice, stick tucked under one arm, a hand covering his brow.

"We can't afford to lose Richards this deep into the second period," he groans.

"You think that he's out for the rest of the game?" I ask.

This kid acts like he's already in his mid-thirties as he pulls an uncertain expression. "Depends. It's all about concussions these days and whether he passes the trainer's checks."

"You're big into hockey like your dad then?"

Will thumbs over his shoulder, grinning. "Like my dad and my sister. Although I kick my sister's ass on the regular."

June's foot flies out, catching Will's leg.

He reaches down, rubbing at the back of his calf. "Ow! That really freakin' hurt. Now I'll have a bruise there for Saturday's game."

When I glance at June, she wears a victorious smile that reminds me of her mother. "Then don't tell lies, and you won't get bruises."

CHEWING on what's left of the French manicure I had done last week, I will away the final three minutes of the game.

"I swear to God, if they throw away the Cup tonight, I'm going to lose my ever-loving mind." Jenna drops her head into her hands as all the girls stand alongside each other on the balcony. "Or go into early labor."

"Yeah, no, we don't want that at this stage in the pregnancy," I say, gently rubbing her back to try and ease the nerves for us both.

Although at least Emmett was cleared to rejoin play by the trainer, a few strips above his left brow doing the job.

"He *has* to win tonight," I murmur to myself.

Jenna lifts her face from her hands so she can look at me. "Why do you say that?"

With ninety seconds left on the clock and only one goal separating the teams, I grip the railing in front of us. So much more is riding on this for Emmett than a lot of the other guys on the team. Even if my boyfriend won't talk about it much, I know his knee is way worse than he would ever admit. Even to himself.

"I assume you know all about Emmett's knee injury?"

Jenna nods once. "I do."

"Let's just say that Emmett's talents don't just stop at hockey, but in his ability to hide pain too."

The New York Storm goalie blows out a long breath, and the countdown enters the final thirty seconds, Blades fans starting to sing out each second.

Jenna slides her hand along the railing and rests it on top of mine. "That may be true, Billie. But something tells me that what Emmett's gained in the past few months more than makes up for all the struggles he's faced throughout his life so far, both on and off the ice."

When Emmett clears the puck toward Jack for a breakaway, there's only ten seconds left on the timer.

They're certain to win now.

"Come on, come on, come on ..." I chant under my breath,

one eye on the clock, the other on Jack as he takes it into the corner to run down the dying seconds.

I don't hear the buzzer because the entire arena erupts like a freaking volcano. Kate and Felicity are already on their way out of the family box with Kendra, Jenna, and Collins hot on their heels.

Darcy taps me on the shoulder, eyes wide with excitement. "Come on! We need to leave now if we want to celebrate on the ice."

I shake my head at her, glancing back at the rink, where the boys are already gathering into a huddle, Coach Morgan punching the air with both fists. Then Jensen loops an arm around his shoulders, and both guys take a second to exchange a few words.

"I feel like I'll be imposing if I go down there."

Chewing on my bottom lip, I watch Emmett embrace each one of his teammates, although he isn't centering his full attention on them as he looks in the direction of the tunnel—where wives and partners will shortly emerge.

Darcy wraps a palm around my upper arm. "Trust me, babe, there isn't a chance in hell that you'll be imposing."

She pauses, and I study her carefully. She never looks nervous; in the final period, she was the only one smiling throughout the entire twenty minutes.

"What if I slip in my sneakers and fall straight on my ass?"

She bursts into giggles, dropping her eyes to the floor. "And you think that my Converse are any more practical?"

"Probably not," I muse.

Interlacing our fingers, she part guides, part drags me back into the main family box and out of the door.

I thumb over my shoulder. "What about my purse?"

She waves away that small detail, picking up speed until we're breaking into a light jog. There's no way I could successfully navigate this arena alone, hallways twisting and turning, random doors seemingly leading nowhere, until we eventually wind up standing in front of two security guards, dressed in dark blue suits and Blades baseball caps.

Since Emmett and I haven't officially gone public with our relationship yet, I cast my eyes to Darcy, hoping she can explain away why this random woman, dressed in a Richards jersey, is trying to gain access to the rink.

"Mrs. Moore." One security guard tips his chin at Darcy before his eyes shift to me. "Miss Quinn."

As they both step to one side like an ocean parting for Jesus Christ himself, I practically choke on my own tongue.

"Come on!" Darcy retakes my hand.

I pull back. "How do they know about me already?"

She just shrugs, a sassy glint shining in her eyes. "Beats me. Perhaps Emmett let them know about his girl in advance?"

As we approach the edge of the tunnel and the sheer size of the arena hits me, I stop dead in my tracks.

Kate, Felicity, Kendra, Collins, and Jenna are already celebrating. Sawyer strides past us and onto the ice.

My mouth runs dry, and my palms are sweating. "Holy ..." I trail off. "I'm going to fall on my ass, live on TV."

Darcy just ignores my anxious rambling, pulling me into the rink.

"Small, slow steps, Bill! Just watch me," she yells over the deafening noise, streamers now falling from the ceiling and filling the ice.

Will may as well be wearing skates as he glides around the ice, fist-bumping his dad and a few of the other guys on the team. June does the same.

"Hey there," a deep voice rumbles in my ear, arms looping around my waist to steady me. "Don't worry, Mama. I got you."

I could be buried two hundred feet deep beneath the ocean bed, and I'd still hear Emmett's voice.

He rests his chin on my shoulder. "Relax your knees for me."

"I'm going to fall on my ass, Em."

"Never. Not when you have me holding you."

Reluctantly, I do as he previously instructed.

"Attagirl," he praises, and I'm not ashamed to admit that in front of twenty thousand people, I grow a little wet.

"What are you doing?" I whisper, almost sure that he won't hear me.

"Taking my girlfriend for a spin. It's standard practice when she wears her man's jersey for the first time."

Circling me, Emmett takes my hands in his and then glides backward, pulling me along with him.

At first, my eyes are everywhere, and I wonder what the hell people must be thinking or even saying about a girl they've never seen before, holding hands with their golden-boy defenseman.

But as we approach center ice and the players and their partners move to one side for us, all the noise fades to nothing but a low hum, Emmett's bright smile capturing all of my attention.

"Are we doing a lap of honor?" I tease.

"Do you want to?"

I shake my head quickly. "Absolutely not. There are way better—and safer—ways to announce our relationship to the world."

Reaching the center of the rink, Emmett brings us both to a stop.

Thank God.

In his skates, he towers over me, tipping my chin up to look at him.

"What if I just kissed you right here? Would that be a better way to reveal the woman I love?"

My knees grow weak. "I've had worse introductions."

Hands loop around my ass, and I just about wrap my legs around his hockey padding, crossing my feet over at the ankles.

"Want to know something?" I ask.

He brushes his lips over mine, the low murmur of our surroundings rising a few decibels louder. Still, it isn't enough to drown out this moment.

"Tell me," he replies, closing his eyes at the feeling of my fingers sifting through his damp hair.

I bring my lips closer to his ear. "Hockey gear smells so unbelievably bad."

He pulls me into his body. "Are you trying to say that I smell bad, Bill? You already think that I'm old as shit."

Smirking like a brat, I bury my face into the crook of his neck. "That's exactly what I'm saying."

He releases a long sigh. "Well, that's a crying fucking shame. Here I was, thinking that you loved every part of me until the end of time."

When I lift my head to take in the arena, all of Emmett's teammates are arranged in a perfect circle around us, along with their family members.

I pull back, hands wrapped around his neck. "Em, what's going on?"

Sliding me down his body, Emmett's hands grip my hips tighter, keeping me steady while I find my footing back on the ice.

Like a freaking swan, Darcy slides up alongside Emmett, a face full of delight when she passes something to him.

"Em," I repeat, "what are you doing?"

He clears his throat, whatever Darcy just handed to him hidden inside a tight fist. "Adding some more bricks as we build our lives together."

When my eyes fall to his hand, Emmett opens his fingers. A small powder-blue box rests in his palm.

My breath catches in my throat, heart racing a million beats per minute.

"If someone had told me back in February that I'd be standing at center ice and celebrating a second Cup win, I'd have probably believed them. My teammates are that good." He casts his eyes around the group of players I know he considers to be family.

"But if they had told me that I'd be standing in front of my best friend's daughter, planning to offer her my ring, I'd have called out that lie in an instant."

Over Emmett's shoulder, I can see Jack excitedly fist-bump his stepdad.

Pulling a deep breath into his lungs, Emmett slowly drops to one knee, one hand still wrapped around my hip.

The hum of the arena falls completely silent, anticipation fizzing in the air as I pull deep gulps into my lungs.

"You're probably going to think that I'm an idiot for choosing this moment to ask you." He chuckles, gorgeous gray eyes staring up at me as he flips the lid on the box, and a blue oval diamond ring, set on a thin white band, glistens under the lights. "Maybe even delusional to think that the most beautiful woman I've ever laid eyes on could want to spend the rest of her life with an old man like me."

When I drop to my knees in front of him, dampness soaks through my jeans and trickles down my cheeks.

"Emmett," I breathe, reaching out to touch the ring of my dreams, nestled in the palm of the greatest person ever.

Emmett tucks his other knee beneath him so we're almost face-to-face.

It's like we're washing and drying dishes in my parents' kitchen or lying awake, talking in bed until the early hours of the morning.

There's just us and no one else.

"I promised you that I'd always be honest, Bill." He rubs his thumb under my eye. "And I'd be a liar if I said that I wanted to or even could wait another day to make you my wife. We may have our doubters, and to them, I say, *Watch me love this girl and our baby until I breathe my last goddamn breath.*"

I blow out a wet sob, not caring that my mascara isn't waterproof.

"I want to wake up to your face each morning and kiss your lips every night. I know that there are so many years between us and that we've only been dating a short while. But what I've recently learned about the metric of time is that it doesn't actually matter at all. Not when you realize that love doesn't play by the rules. All it cares about is how two souls fit together, never to be torn apart." He rolls his lips, mouth no doubt as dry as my own. "So, what I want is for you to say yes as I pluck this ring from its box and lower it to your finger, asking for permission to make you mine forever."

As Emmett does as he just described, he hands the box off to Sawyer.

With our foreheads pressed together, his trembling hand hovers the ring over my finger.

"Billie Freya Quinn, will you marry me?"

Emmett could've asked me this question today, next year, or a whole decade from now. There was only ever going to be one answer.

"With every piece of me, Em, yes."

EPILOGUE

Eleven Years Later—June

Seattle

EMMETT

"How many goddamn floors does this building have?" I grumble to myself when I hit the twelfth floor and pause, gazing up at the seemingly endless stairwell.

Reaching into the back pocket of my jeans, I pull out the map the security guard gave me down in the lobby and study it quickly. This floor is circled as the location of the new Seattle offices for Morgan Jones & Richards LLP, even if the new plaque hasn't been fixed above the door.

As soon as I key in the security code and enter, the smell of fresh paint hits me, quickly followed by the scent of a thousand different flowers, all set in vases that line a wooden reception desk, which is located in the center of a vast white space. I have no doubt that every single arrangement has been sent by clients and friends to celebrate Billie's recent appointment as managing partner, one of them from my little brother, Beau, and his family.

For the past eleven years, my wife has been gradually conquering the world, with me riding along to enjoy the show.

After I won the Cup and we had a very public marriage proposal, my knee decided it was time to call it quits. I spent the entire offseason convincing the trainers and my body that I had another season left in me, questioning and fearing what it would be like to live life without pro hockey in it.

The answer? Fucking spectacular. It wasn't that I didn't miss the buzz of the crowd each time my skates hit the ice—because I did. I still do. But what I found in place of my career was a side to life I had been missing and trying to compensate for through hockey. There are only so many seasons a pro athlete can last before it's time to take a step back and enjoy what really counts. Family. And, man, do I have it in spades.

"Can I help you?"

I spin around to find a small middle-aged woman dressed in a smart black suit. She must be a new member of staff since I've never seen her before.

She definitely recognizes me though, a warm smile spreading across her face.

Lifting the bouquet of blue roses I picked up a few blocks from here, I chuckle at my own foolish thoughts. Of course Billie doesn't need another two dozen roses to go with the endless bouquets she already has.

"I'm looking for Billie. This morning, before she left home, she explained where her new office was located ..." I trail off, gazing around at various wooden doors. "But since there aren't any door plaques in here either, I'm a bit lost."

Holding out a confident hand, she strides toward me. "Caroline Peach. Recently appointed senior partner. I've heard so much about you, Emmett."

I take her hand and try not to wince when she squeezes my fingers in a vise grip.

Jesus, lawyers are scary people.

When she drops my hand and points toward a door on the right, I flex my fingers, checking all extremities are still attached.

"The workman who was supposed to be fitting the plaques

this morning called ahead of time to say that he'd be running a little behind schedule. He got caught in traffic while dropping his granddaughter off at school or something." She rolls her eyes, doubtful that it's a genuine excuse for his tardiness, and I just smile at her.

"The traffic around Belltown is insane today, and my daughter, Blake, just started at a new school across the other side of town."

Her eyes flare wide as she goes to apologize for her cynicism.

I hold up a hand. "Don't worry about it. Scott has never been the best timekeeper, and I'll make sure to kick his ass for the both of us when he finally shows up." I shake my head and tut, pretending like I'm mad about it. "No door plaques on office opening day. You just can't get the staff these days, can you?"

"Are you going to stand there all day with those roses or come say hi before my nine o'clock meeting?"

Wearing a fitted blue suit dress and matching heels, Billie stands in the doorway to a panoramic office I've seen the plans for more times than I can count, looking even more beautiful than when I first opened my eyes at five a.m.

With a parting smile for Caroline, I head toward my wife, arm outstretched so she can take the roses.

She pulls them into her chest and steps to one side so I can enter before she closes the door behind us.

Her office—if you can even describe it as that since it probably has its own point of gravity, as it's that large—is even more spectacular than I expected. Pretty much every place of interest Seattle has to offer can be seen from here, Billie's desk and meeting area in a prime position to take in the sights.

"What do you think, Em? Do you like it?"

I watch my wife arrange the flowers in the center of her meeting table, and it's like I'm transported to when I caught her dancing around the kitchen in her new Brooklyn apartment, baby Blake clutched to her chest.

Billie's smile is as broad now as it was back then, a blush of pride accentuating the freckles across her cheekbones. Her rose gold bracelet catches the sunlight and love floods my insides. She's worn it each day. Even on our wedding day.

"Come here," I say, flipping my hands as I prop myself against her desk.

She saunters toward me, and my mouth runs dry.

Christ. When the fuck did I get so damn lucky? Married for over a decade, and I'm still insatiable for more of everything with —and from—this woman.

My hands land on her hips, and she steps between my parted thighs.

"How does it feel to rule the world, Mama?"

Luscious waves of red frame her stunning face, and I reach up and run my fingers through her hair, eventually resting my palm at the back of her head so I can pull her in for a kiss.

"Pretty damn good," she whispers against my lips, more pink staining her cheeks.

I'd like to think that her coy response is down to the way my hand travels up the inside of her right thigh, fingers brushing against my favorite lacy thong. And while that may be partially responsible, there's no denying that my girl hasn't changed an inch since the day I set eyes on her in Scott and Freya's living room.

I think, deep down, that she's aware of the enormity of her achievements—making managing partner at thirty-two years old is fucking extraordinary, even if she'd never let it go to her head.

When I slide my fingers through her wet pussy, her body goes limp in my grasp, small breaths leaving through parted lips that I immediately want to cover again with my own.

"Shouldn't you be meeting up with Jessie Callaghan right about now? I thought you had coaching things to discuss."

I push a finger inside her tight cunt, slowly stroking her front wall. "We're meeting tomorrow now. He had a couple of errands to run, so I thought I'd take advantage and pay two of my favorite girls a visit." Massaging her clit, I leave my wife in no doubt about who those two girls are.

A small gush of fluid coats my hand, and her head falls into the crook of my neck. "I'm going to be soaking all day, and I didn't bring any spare panties with me."

"Crying fucking shame," I coo, absolutely delighted with myself, thinking of how she'll be sitting at her meeting table in around a half hour, the legacy from my impromptu visit coating the inside of her legs.

When I insert another finger, Billie releases a low moan against my sensitive flesh. "I'm going to come, Em."

"Such a bad boss," I croon. "Setting naughty examples for your staff. It's only your first day in charge, and you're already dripping all over your fancy new office."

"Your first day on the job and my last day on planet Earth now that I've seen this."

Billie's head darts up, and we stare at each other, neither of us daring to look at him. I don't know when Scott opened Billie's door or how much he's seen, but I'm pretty sure that our friendship is back on the rocks.

"Dad," Billie whispers, "I thought you said that you'd be stopping by with the door plaques after lunch so the traffic could subside."

Slowly, my eyes connect with my best friend's, hand still nestled between his daughter's thighs.

"Hi."

He scowls at me. "Remind me again why I decided to forgive you. I should've made you wait at least another six months."

I smile sweetly at him, dying inside with each passing second he stands in the doorway. "Because you knew that I'd make the best son-in-law."

He narrows his eyes at me, briefly flicking them to Billie. "I'm selling Shelby to fund your divorce."

When he pulls the door closed, there's a beat of silence before we both fall into fits of hysterical laughter, Billie resting her forehead against my chest as she giggles through the pain of being caught.

Hooking my finger under her chin, I'm eager to have her eyes back on mine so I can finish what I started.

Catching me with my hand between his daughter's thighs or not, Scott Quinn knows—and has for several years now—that I'm the only man capable of loving his little princess how she deserves. It took a long time to prove it to him, but in the end, he knew I wasn't going anywhere, and now I get to kick his ass on golfing vacations and get away with it as family.

"What time will you be done today?"

Spinning us around, I plant her ass on the desk and roll her dress up for better access.

"Why?" She parts her thighs wider, tongue swiping across her bottom lip.

I stroke her again, thinking how inappropriate it would be to fuck her with Scott standing outside the room, fixing a plaque to her door.

I'm a bad fucking friend.

Popping the button on my pants, I free my cock and slide it all the way home, and our mouths meet so we can swallow down each other's moans.

"You'll need to leave your new DB5 in the office parking lot. Because once I've given you my cum and your workday is finished, I'll need you in my Jaguar by five p.m."

BILLIE PAUSES at the entrance to Luigi's restaurant and bar in downtown Seattle.

"Weren't we only here the other night to celebrate Archer buying into the restaurant chain?"

"Yes," I reply, reaching over her shoulder so I can open the door for us both. "But tonight, we're celebrating something else."

Immediate cheers fill the restaurant, and Billie swats me in the chest, shrugging off her coat as Darcy, Kendra, Jenna, Collins, Kate, and Felicity all race toward her.

"Happy first day, boss lady!" Darcy throws her arms around Billie's neck, greeting her like they didn't just see each other a few days ago.

Billie moves between each of her friends, asking Kate, Felicity, and Collins when they flew in from New York.

"You know how it is." Felicity waves a hand in front of her. "The New York office is well established and can pretty much run itself these days."

Collins shrugs. "This morning. Ezra sends his apologies that he couldn't be here. Motocross championships just started back up, and he needs to be in Michigan."

Taking Billie's coat, I hang it on the stand by the door, pausing to absorb everyone who has shown up tonight to celebrate my wife's promotion. Literally all of our friends.

"Dad, can you tell Hunter to stop being an idiot?"

With dark brown hair in a messy bun, Blake stands in front of me, hands propped on her hips in a petulant teenager pose.

"What's he done this time?"

She steps to one side, and my eight-year-old son, Hunter, comes into view, balancing on his tiptoes at the high bar as he drops a scoop of vanilla ice cream into a glass of Coke.

It fizzes everywhere, and Blake rolls her eyes in his direction. "Why did you have to have another child?"

Wrapping my arm around her shoulders, I pull my daughter into me, setting a soft kiss on top of her head. "Because you were so damn perfect, we thought that we'd try our luck again."

My heart melts when she takes my pointer finger in her palm and squeezes it—her little way of expressing love. The truth is, I love her more than words could ever do justice and definitely enough to make up for the absence of her biological dad who signed his parental rights away before he dropped off the face of the planet. Tucker Price never changed his selfish ways, and his career in law didn't work out either. Legally adopting Blake nine years ago was the single easiest decision I ever made, alongside marrying her mom the following year.

"How did the meeting with my boy Jessie go?" Jensen taps me on the shoulder.

I release Blake, watching her stalk straight toward Hunter, arms out in front of her as she points at the mess he's making.

"Postponed until tomorrow. He had something he needed to sort out for one of his girls."

Jensen nods in understanding, swiping a hand across his mouth. "Probably to do with Drew. I heard that she's switching her college degree to public relations at the final minute."

I nod once and watch on as Billie hugs Tommy and Jenna and their ten-year-old son, Milo.

A hand cups my ear from behind. "You know you shouldn't be exchanging niceties with the opposition, right?" Archer whispers as he sidles up next to me, Jack and Sawyer quickly following behind.

Arms folded across his chest, Jensen rolls his eyes. "What opposition? Everyone knows that expansion teams take years to get a foothold in the league." He chuckles under his breath as he looks at me. "And we both know that Jessie and our boy Emmett here are going to have their work cut out for them."

Jack sucks in a sharp breath. "You're a brave guy, Emmett. That first season for the Seattle Rogues was ... let's just say, I could see Jessie growing grayer by the minute."

He's not wrong. I must be fucking crazy, but I couldn't turn down the opportunity to further my coaching career, even if it's as an assistant coach for the NHL's newest and most brutal team.

I look around at all the guys as Jon starts leaving the kitchen with dishes of food, and Billie motions for us to come and join them around the table.

Throwing her a quick wink, I turn back to the guys standing around me, a mischievous smile pulling at my lips as I center my attention back on the Blades' goalie coach.

"I guess there's only one benefit to finishing last in the league ..." I trail off.

Jensen shakes his head at me, well aware of what's coming, even if he's repeatedly refused to acknowledge the real possibility of where his insanely talented son could wind up playing pro hockey. Speculation has been bouncing around in the press ahead of the draft tomorrow night, and everyone's convinced of our first choice. I guess there's no harm in me revealing our selection a little early between close friends.

"Don't you even dare," Jensen warns, dark eyes ablaze as he cracks his neck to one side.

I shrug, and Jack leans in closer as Archer rubs his hands together with glee.

"William Jones," I breathe quietly, a hint of victory permeating my voice, "on behalf of the Seattle Rogues, we want to extend a very warm—and early—welcome to this year's first-round draft pick."

ALSO BY RUTH STILLING

Seattle Scorpions

Boarded Hearts

Frozen Over

Dead Rinker

Ruled Out

The Blade Kings

Perfect Deke

Total Shutdown

Shots Fired

Full Tilt

Within Range

ACKNOWLEDGMENTS

My husband: I'm sorry for talking about Emmett nonstop, but you know how much this book means to me. Thank you for sitting and listening to every idea I have during drafting. You are my ultimate book boyfriend and—just like Jon and Jack—the glue that sticks me together.

My dad: Thank you for every phone call, text message, and general check-in while I have been writing this story, but mainly, thank you for being the inspiration behind Emmett and the amazing dad he is. From the bottom of my heart, I love you.

My little boy: A little like how Billie and Emmett scale the Catskills, we climb that mountain a little more each day. I'm so proud of you and everything you are. Keep shining, H.

My beta team: What a team you are! I have had the MOST fun, working on *Within Range* with you all. Thank you for helping me shape and fine-tune one of my favorite stories to date. You are an incredibly talented group of women, and I am so lucky to have you by my side.

My ARC and street teams: When I say that I have the best group of people in my corner, I really do mean it. Seriously, there isn't a day that goes by where I don't take a second and think about how lucky I am to have you all. Kendra, Collins, Darcy, Jenna, and Billie have nothing on my luck. I love and appreciate you all so much, and I hope you love Billie and Emmett's story.

Nay: My rock, my cleanse (IYKYK), and a person I genuinely could not live without. You are a special person, and I am so honored and fortunate to have you in my life. Thank you for working on another book with me. You are truly so gifted as an alpha reader.

Erica: My girl, my wonderful PA, and an absolute badass boss bitch. Enough said. Thank you for guiding me through another release.

Alyssa at Plot Twist: Our first release together, and what an amazing journey it's been so far. I count my blessings every day to be working with you, and I am so truly honored to have you by my side.

KP: Echoing everything I said to you back at Thanksgiving. You are a dream to work with, and I don't know where I would be without your support and guidance. Thank you for everything.

Kayla: By the time you read this, I'll probably be sitting next to you on your couch, giving you the biggest squeeze ever. Love you squillions, my queen.

Jenny: You should know that I have framed the list of all the things you loved about *Within Range* and hung it on my office wall. Seriously, you are the most incredible friend, such an intelligent and awesome woman, and I thank the universe daily for bringing us together.

To the Bookstagram community: Are you ready for Emmett and Billie?! This story has knocked me off my feet, and I am an absolute puddle for Emmett Richards. The *yearning* this man does for his girl is nothing short of panty-melting, and I am so excited to share him with you. Thank you from the bottom of my heart for all the continued love and support you show me. I'm forever in awe of the edits, reviews, and talent on display within this community. You are amazing! P.S. Bring on William!

To all my readers: Every time I sit down to thank my readers for another release, I pause for a second to think about each one of you who takes the time out of your life to sit down and read my words. I know that every single one of my characters is truly honored to be a part of your life, whether that's for a few hours or if one of their stories sticks with you for years. It blows my mind to know that people out there are picking up my books and spending time in a world I've created. Thank you for being a part of it and for helping make my dreams come true. I cannot wait to share what's coming next in the universe!

ABOUT THE AUTHOR

Ruth Stilling is an avid romance reader turned writer. Having spent many years reading about and dreaming of her ideal book boyfriend, she finally decided to create her own and to share them with the rest of the world.

Living in a small town in Derbyshire, England, Ruth is an introvert by nature and spends much of her time talking with her book-crazy friends from across the globe.

When she isn't writing your next book boyfriend, Ruth enjoys watching all kinds of sports and is an Aston Villa and Derby County fan. The outdoors is a real favorite, and if the British weather were kinder, she would spend all her time writing outside.

Ruth is a wife to her best friend and number one cheerleader, whom she married in 2015, and a mom to her beautiful son, who has shown her a new perspective on life—enjoy and celebrate who you are as a person and cherish those who are there for you through rain and shine.

Ruth is incredibly excited to share *Within Range*, the fifth and final installment in her second-generation series The Blade Kings!

You can follow Ruth and keep up to date with what's coming next via Instagram and TikTok by searching @authorruthstilling.

www.ingramcontent.com/pod-product-compliance
Ingram Content Group UK Ltd.
Pitfield, Milton Keynes, MK11 3LW, UK
UKHW040826100326
11169UKWH00016B/744

9 781068 600081